D1260266

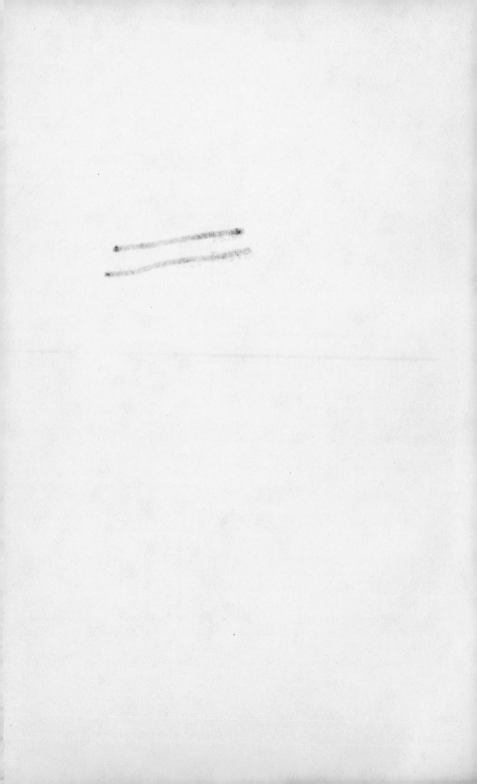

# LÉLIA

George Sand, 1830
Portrait by Eugene Delacroix
Paris, Musée Carnavalet

# GEORGE SAND

# Lélia

TRANSLATED WITH AN INTRODUCTION BY
## Maria Espinosa

INDIANA UNIVERSITY PRESS
BLOOMINGTON AND LONDON

Manufactured in the United States of America

Library of Congress Cataloging in Publication Data
Sand, George, pseud. of Mme. Dudevant, 1804-1876.
Lélia.
Bibliography: p.
I.   Title.
PZ3.S21Le   1978      [PQ2406]      843'.8      77-23639
ISBN  0-253-33318-0      1  2  3  4  5  82  81  80  79  78

# CONTENTS

# ACKNOWLEDGMENTS

I am very grateful for the time and help that Heléna Knox has given me in preparation of this work. I would also like to thank Max Knight, without whose encouragement the translation might never have been completed. Ernest Callenbach's comments proved invaluable, André Gabriel and Gilbert Chaitin painstakingly helped me with parts of the translation that were obscure. Ellen Moers gave valuable encouragement and help. Barbara Atchison, Amrita Forest, Alan Friedman, Penny Michaels, Walter Selig, and many other friends, as well as my parents, gave me moral support. Finally, I would like to thank my daughter, Carmen, for her patience and understanding while I was completing the translation.

# FOREWORD

*Lélia* is an historical curiosity—but what a curiosity! for here George Sand created the Romantic hero as a woman. *Lélia* takes her place beside Werther, René, Obermann, Childe Harold, Adolphe, Alastor, Raphaël de Valentin and the rest of the swollen masculine egos of the age. *Lélia* feels the guilts, the aspirations, the alienation, the boredom, the sterility, the pride, the rebelliousness of the Romantic hero; she plays the cold dandy, the demon lover, the inspired prophet, the doomed soul—and remains all Woman. Though it is a palimpsest of romanticisms, what we find in *Lélia* is not so much borrowings and imitations as glosses by a very intelligent (and at the time very unhappy) woman on a masculine literature.

The right way to read *Lélia* is of course in Sand's French. Ideally it should be read in Pierre Reboul's superb edition (Garnier, 1960), which thoroughly documents Sand's reworkings of her predecessors and effect on her followers, such as Baudelaire. But for those who do not read French with ease, Maria Espinosa supplies the first translation into English since the work was published in 1833. Anglophonic readers can now see for themselves what made Elizabeth Barrett "blush in my solitude to the ends of my fingers"; and what prompted George Henry Lewes to "earnestly forbid" the reading of *Lélia* except by those "whose minds are strong enough to witness its desolating skepticism"; and how Thackeray could damn its "topsyturvification of morality" yet praise it as "a wonderful book indeed, gorgeous in eloquence, and rich in magnificent poetry"; and why Matthew Arnold regretted his "days of *Lélia*, days never to return!" Even, perhaps, why Kate Chopin named her daughter Lélia, and Willa Cather had her Thea Kronborg retreat to the desert.

In 1974 a letter came from a university press asking my opinion about the mad project on which a young Californian was engaged, that of translating *Lélia*. I replied with a whoop of enthusiasm and relief: at last someone was doing the work on Sand that "feminist scholarship" required: someone was reading her books and making it possible for others to do so as well. What I read then of the Espinosa translation-in-progress convinced me that she had set about her task with energy and conviction, and with a fresh, contemporary response to Sand's passionate prose. I have never met Maria Espinosa, nor indeed read her translation through, but I believe George Sand herself would have been pleased with what she wrote of her reasons for undertaking the translation: not for its historical interest, not solely for its feminism, "but also because *Lélia* is a book haunted with religious doubt, torment, searching. And at this time our own culture is experiencing this, perhaps more on the West Coast than in the East...."

As 1974 turned to 1975 and 1976, a British television series made George Sand, or at least her costumes and coiffures, live again. Georges Lubin came to America, and word began at last to spread here about his editions of Sand's correspondence and autobiographical works, which are the basis of all serious work on Sand today. Curtis Cate reached a wide public with his biography based on the new scholarship. And specialized studies began to appear, the most recent and best of which, Patricia Thomson's *George Sand and the Victorians*, discusses at length the impact of *Lélia* on Matthew Arnold. The time for *Lélia* in English had at last arrived, and to many readers a lost voice of the Romantic age will now speak for the first time.

George Sand, it is worth remembering, was not a follower of the Romantics, but one of them. She went to Paris to become a writer in 1831, one year after the stormy debut of Victor Hugo's *Hernani* began high Romanticism in France. In the narrow sense she was an *enfant du siècle*, that is, about the same age as the century itself and thus substantially older than the women writers in English—Brontë, Fuller, George Eliot, Dickinson—to whom we often try, with difficulty, to relate her. Elizabeth Barrett Browning was closest to Sand in age, and she moved, like Sand, from Romanticism to Victorianism in her literary development (a transformation marked in Sand's case by the 1839 revision of *Lélia*).

While English Romanticism, unlike the European movements, was essentially a poetic literature, the German and French Romantics moved more easily from poetry to fiction to drama and back to poetry again; or, as in the case of Chateaubriand, Senancour, and George Sand, wrote only prose. Alfred de Musset, for example, the brilliant poet and playwright who became Sand's lover after the publication of *Lélia*, wrote in prose (and with *Lélia* in mind) his *Confession d'un enfant du siècle* in 1836, a work of the Romantic movement, which in England had come to a close in the 1820s.

Had *Lélia* been written in verse it would have appeared less strange and perhaps less shocking to English and American readers of the nineteenth century. But prose it is, and prose fashioned in a way still strange to our eyes and ears. What are these chapter-long dithyrambs addressed from Lélia to Trenmor or from Magnus to Sténio? Rousseau provided Sand with one formal source in *La Nouvelle Héloise*—but these are not letters, not even such extraordinary letters as Julie wrote to Saint-Preux. Madame de Staël provided a closer model, and a feminist one, in her *Corinne* of 1807: the long prose improvisations, on such subjects as Genius, Fame, and Italian destiny, that her heroine addresses to a large, adoring public, out of doors. The outpourings in *Lélia* are simultaneously monologues and exchanges between characters; they are both private rhapsodies and public utterances. Thus they seem to me, especially when Sand's style is at its most musical, to be essentially arias in prose. *Lélia* seems a work highly operatic in character—and opera, as readers of *Consuelo* and the *Lettres d'un voyageur* are well aware, was a form dear to George Sand.

The bravado climax of the work, Sténio's night of love with the false Lélia (played in mask by her sister, Pulchérie) comes to a close with an orchestral fanfare, a flotilla of gondolas, and the singing voice of a black-haired woman which reaches Sténio's heart from the sunlit wave. " 'Oui, c'est vous, c'est ma Lélia; c'est elle dont la voix est si puissante et si belle. . . . ' Quand la chaloupe qui la portait fut au pied du pavillon, le jour était pur et brillant sur les flots. Lélia se tourna tout à coup vers Sténio et lui montra son visage en lui faisant un signe d'amicale moquerie" [see pp. 145–46 of text]. One can almost hear the barcarole and see the spotlight rising on a prima donna before a Venetian backdrop: opera in prose, with all the vulgarity, the pomposity, the artificiality, and the magic of the form. It is as if Sand predicted (and perhaps indeed she prompted) Offenbach's musical setting for the third act of *Les Contes d'Hoffmann*. And E.T.A. Hoffmann's tales, as much as Balzac's and Senancour's and Byron's, were certainly in George Sand's mind as she wrote her prose fantasy of Romantic heroinism.

Ellen Moers

# INTRODUCTION

## I

George Sand, perhaps the most renowned and controversial French woman writer of the nineteenth century, published *Lélia* in 1833. Sand's reputation had become established in Europe and Russia the preceding year with the publication of *Indiana*. In his biography of Sand, André Maurois considered *Lélia*, along with *Indiana* and *Consuelo*, one of her three finest novels.[1]

Historically, *Lélia* is an important document in the evolution of woman's consciousness. The singular fact that it has been overlooked by the English-speaking world for more than a century does not lessen its importance. In her biography of George Sand, Marie Jenney Howe stated:

> No other book George Sand ever wrote created such a stir or added so greatly to her fame. Many little Lélias sprang up in France and Germany. She had created a new vogue. . . .
>
> [Sand] was a precocious feminist. The slow, conservative woman movement would some day pave the way for feminism. But the woman movement had not begun. Her ideas were therefore not chronological. They antedated history. She confused the thinkers, angered the critics, and threw the times out of joint.[2]

More recently, Ellen Moers has devoted a long section of her *Literary Women* to a discussion of Sand. Of *Lélia* she suggests:

> . . . George Sand was claiming all of Romanticism for women, its guilty frenzy, its warped sexuality, its despair. . . .

*Lélia* was the only one of her works that Sand substantially revised, and through her long struggle to produce a second *Lélia* (1839) can be traced the development in her literary ethos from romantic egotism, to mystical humanitarianism, to radical activism.[3]

What of the woman who at twenty-nine wrote this book which created such a scandal?

George Sand was born Amandine Aurore Lucie Dupin on July 1, 1804. Her father was a French army officer of noble birth. Her mother was "of the people" and had lived as a courtesan of sorts until she met Sand's father, whom she dearly loved. When Sand was five years old her father died in a riding accident on his country estate in Berry. She remained there with her paternal grandmother for eight years.

Sand's grandmother, herself an illegitimate though recognized descendant of the Maréchal de Saxe and of King Augustus II of Poland, was imbued with an eighteenth-century view of life. Schooled in the tradition of Voltaire, she had also been profoundly moved by the pre-Romantic ideas of Rousseau. A highly cultivated woman, she imparted her ideas on life and literature to her granddaughter, to whom she grew very close. As a young girl, Aurore (as George Sand was called) was given her father's former tutor, who encouraged her independence of thought. She was allowed to mingle freely with the peasant children of the countryside. In addition to her academic studies, she received a thorough musical education on the piano and harp.

At the age of thirteen Aurore was sent by her grandmother to the convent of the English Augustinians in Paris. Over the years her own mother had gradually become estranged from her. "Oh, my dear, dear mother, why is it that you do not love me while I love you so truly?"[4] Aurore wrote in one letter from the convent. There, deeply attracted by religious life, she acquired a sense of mysticism, and would have become a nun had it not been for the wisdom of her confessor–priest and the wishes of her grandmother. Although she later questioned this religious faith, it never entirely left her. While in the convent, she read *The Lives of the Saints*,[5] which evidently had a profound influence on her. She refers to it repeatedly, not only in *Lélia*, but in other works.

Returning to her grandmother's estate at Nohant three years later, she enjoyed over a year of unrestricted freedom, going hunting with her tutor, riding in man's clothes, talking with the peasants, reading widely in both French and English.

When Aurore was seventeen her grandmother died. Aurore inherited her grandmother's entire fortune and estate, but as a minor she was under the control of her mother, who, due to the difficult conditions of her own working-class life in Paris, had grown increasingly hostile and was "within measurable distance of going completely mad."[6] Seeking protection from her mother, in 1822 Aurore married Baron Casimir Dudevant. He moved to Sand's estate, where two children were born, Maurice and Solange. However, the union was not a happy one. Sand indirectly alludes to the physical and emotional frustrations of the marriage in *Lélia*.

In 1831 Aurore left Casimir to live openly in Paris with her lover, Jules Sandeau. Her first novel, *Rose et Blanche*, was a collaboration with Sandeau. Her pen name—Sand—was adapted from his. After this came *Indiana* and *Valentine*, and in 1833 *Lélia*.

Sand scandalized society by the openness of her romantic liaisons—with Sandeau, Musset, Chopin, and others. However, she lived out her "free love" with the highest moral principles.

As she grew older, her novels became less subjective, more conservative in moral values. An eight-year liaison with Chopin (for the most part platonic, despite the notoriety surrounding the affair) gave stability to her life and probably prolonged his. In the 1840s her interests expanded into politics; she felt a natural sympathy for the working classes and supported the socialist proletariat in the Revolution of 1848. Today she is best known for her pastoral tales written in the 1840s, such as *Little Fadette* and *The Devil's Whirlpool*, which express her feelings of compassion for the country peasants whom she knew so well. While these pastoral novels possess great charm, they do not contain the ideas that catapulted her to fame and to the status of a social rebel. The bold young woman who had expressed her yearnings with unparalleled freedom gradually gave way to the public-minded "grande dame" of literature. She spent most of her later years on her beloved country estate, devoted to her grandchildren, continuing to write prolifically but with a more objective passion. She supported her large entourage with her earnings and was, in effect, one of the great literary "hacks" of history. In 1876, at the age of seventy-two, she died, a venerated and beloved public figure.

Although she wrote more than eighty novels, a four-volume *Histoire de ma vie*, plays, political tracts, and numerous volumes of correspondence, until recently her only books widely available in English were translations of *La Petite Fadette* and *La Mare au diable* and an edition of her correspondence with Flaubert, translated by Aimée McKensie. However, with the resurgence of interest in George Sand, more of her work in translation is being reprinted and more, I am hopeful, will be translated.

## II

When I first looked for an English translation of *Lélia*, I found only French editions. Further, I was struck by the fact that only a small proportion of her work was available in English translation. George Sand was in vogue during the 1830s and 1840s, though her reputation declined in the late Victorian era. At one time more than thirty of her novels, with the notable exception of *Lélia*, had been translated. Most of them have long since gone out of print.

While *Lélia* is technically less accomplished than her later novels, it appealed strongly to me because it seemed to be her most subjective and self-revealing work. Her lover Alfred de Musset laughingly used to address her as "Lélia." In a letter to Sainte-Beuve she wrote, "I am utterly and completely Lélia . . . I had wanted to convince myself this was not so."[7] And Maurois chose to title his biography of Sand with the title of this novel, which he considered central to her personality.

*Lélia* concerns the spiritual quest of its heroine who, while passionate, questioning, and a personage of noble dimensions, is "emotionally impotent," that is, unable to love fully. Sténio, a poet, is destroyed by his longing for her, as is Magnus, a fanatic priest. But Trenmor, a renunciate who observes their conflicts with compassion, and Pulchérie, Lélia's courtesan sister, survive.

In her *Journal Intime* Sand wrote:

I have lived so many lives . . . Magnus is my childhood; Sténio my youth; Lélia my maturity; Trenmor will be my old age perhaps . . . all these types have been within me.[8]

She lists their qualities: "Lélia—doubt; Trenmor—stoicism; Sténio—credulity; Magnus—superstition, repressed desire; Pulchérie—the senses, opposed to *Psyche*" (italic Sand's).

That *Lélia* was connected so closely to her own youthful feelings is substantiated by the fact that in 1839 she published a revised, expurgated version which expressed more optimism and religious faith and in which the plot was considerably changed. However, this new edition never took hold with the public, despite the fact that for over a century it remained the standard edition. It had been deprived of its essential strengths.

*Lélia* is symbolic, poetic, philosophic, full of outrage against society and God. It is an excursion into Sand's doubts, fears, ideals, and sensual and mystical longings. Sand asks: Why do we exist? Why are we placed here on earth with so many conflicting elements within us—the senses; the doubting, analytical intellect; a desire for the Absolute; and physical desire, which by its very nature can never be appeased. It was Sand's "immense ethical quest," as Dostoevsky called it, that enabled her to describe her heroine's sexual longings.

The heroine asks: How can I make sense of the universe? Is there a God, and if so, what is His nature? Why must I be a slave to the artificially defined role of a woman? What is the nature of sensuality, and is it compatible with spiritual love? Are love relationships between the sexes designed to be transitory? Lélia craves sexual variety in her fantasies—despite or because of her inability to achieve satisfaction through physical love. She asks how to deal with this. Should she live as a nun or as a courtesan? (She never considers the role of wife!) These are the queries of an intense, passionate, and singularly courageous woman.

*Lélia* is a melodramatic tale of improbable encounters. Lélia, loved by Sténio, introduces him to Trenmor, who has expiated his crime of stealing to support his gambling habit by five years of hard labor in prison. Lélia nearly dies of cholera. Magnus, a priest who has previously saved her life, is brought to her bedside. He denounces her as demon-possessed. Magnus himself is obsessed with a desire for her that ultimately drives him insane. Trenmor, Sténio, and Lélia attend a ball at

which Lélia appears in a man's costume. There Trenmor tells Sténio
that she embodies all the heroic ideals of history and literature—the
genius of the poets—she is Hamlet, Juliet, Dante combined. She possesses all the noble attributes, even the light, feminine qualities. "All,"
says Sténio, "except love. If Lélia cannot love, she is not complete.
Where there is no love, there is no woman." Sténio grows increasingly
desperate for Lélia's physical love, as well as for her emotional support
and her spiritual guidance. In effect, he asks her to take the dominant
masculine role and says, "I ask only to obey and follow you."

They attend another ball, given by the Prince of Bambuccj. There
Lélia meets her long-lost sister, Pulchérie, and their ensuing dialogue
takes up the following seventy pages or so. Lélia makes striking observations on the nature of prostitution:

> To be lover, courtesan, and mother. . . . These are three conditions
> of a woman's fate which no woman escapes whether she sells herself in
> a market of prostitution or by a marriage contract.

Lélia laments her own coldness of the senses. It may be that Lélia is
frigid because she does not want to submit to the mastery of a man. If
she remains unmoved by a man's embraces, her spirit is allowed to remain untroubled and her soul free. She describes the torment that
physical arousal without orgasmic release had created within her:

> Oh, I remember the burning nights I passed pressed against a man's
> flanks in close embrace with him . . . I sensed one could simulta-
> neously love a man to the point of submitting to him and love oneself
> to the point of hating him because he subjugates us. . . . When he had
> broken me in ferocious embraces, he slept brusque and uncaring at
> my side, while I devoured my tears so as not to awaken him. . . . How-
> ever . . . the more he made me feel his domination, the more I cher-
> ished it. But I also began to curse my slavery. . . . One day I felt so
> worn-out with loving that I stopped suddenly. When I saw how easily
> this bond was broken, I was astonished at having believed in its eternal
> duration for so long.

Lélia goes on to describe her failure to find peace in a self-imposed
monastic retreat. "If you cannot be a nun, be a courtesan," says Pulchérie. "With what?" asks Lélia. "I have no senses." "They will come

to you," replies Pulchérie. "The body is less rebellious than the spirit."
Pulchérie suggests that she seek happiness by giving physical love, even
if she remains unmoved.

And so Lélia determines to let Sténio make love to her that night.
But at the last moment, fearful and repulsed, she flees the darkened
chamber, leaving Pulchérie in her place. When Sténio learns that Lélia
has deliberately tricked him, he sets off on a course of bitter, vengeful
debauchery.

In self-justification, Lélia writes to him:

> I would have been humiliated and debased if I had served like Pul-
> chérie as a torch to light your descent into the abysses of nothingness
> and solitude . . . it was not necessary to worship me like a divinity and
> then ask me to be your slave . . . I should have shone before you like
> the star which led the Magi . . . Pulchérie [on the other hand] gave
> herself to you without degradation and without money . . . Her pas-
> sions are not feigned . . . She worships only one God—Pleasure. . . .
> You have confused two very distinct things: sensual and spiritual love.
> One I can inspire and share. But the other isn't made for me, or rather
> I'm not made to feel it. . . .

A year later Trenmor comes to retrieve Sténio from Pulchérie's
"palace of love." Sténio has greatly degenerated. Trenmor attempts
to save him by taking him to the monastery of the Camaldules. In the
best nineteenth-century moralistic tradition Trenmor says, "Suffering . . . should make one compassionate and good. Feeble souls are
corrupted by adversity; strong souls are purified by it."

Sténio replies:

> The strong man fears neither God nor men nor himself . . . skepticism
> preserves him from everything . . . He knows that all his hopes are
> registered in a book whose leaves are turned by the wind, and that all
> projects are written in sand . . . There is only one virtue—to wait for
> the wave and to remain firm when it inundates you, to swim when it
> carries you along . . . [to] die heedlessly when it submerges you . . .
> [The strong man] is martyr to his faith. He lives, suffers, and dies for
> it . . . denying . . . that other absurd, evil God you worship.

Trenmor is forced to leave Sténio at the monastery while he goes on
a journey. By chance, Magnus also happens to be there. In a last at-

tempt to save his religious faith, Sténio questions Magnus. He succeeds only in unearthing the fear that underlies Magnus's religious beliefs; and Magnus admits that his religion has not purified him of lust. Sténio commits suicide. Lélia rushes from afar to weep over his bier. Completely mad with grief and guilt, Magnus strangles her.

The work far transcends its plot by virtue of its philosophic content and the very human conflicts it embodies. *Lélia* is imbued with the ideas prevalent in early nineteenth-century Romanticism: a belief in the glory of suffering, individualism, a fondness for nature and exotic cultures, a strong attraction for the Middle Ages, revolt against social conventions, the cultivation of emotion and sensation for their own sake, a preoccupation with the supernatural, longing for the Absolute and the Unattainable, despair, skepticism, and introspection.

Pierre Reboul noted that at the time Sand wrote *Lélia* she was strongly influenced by certain writers, notably Balzac and the Romantic writers Sénancour and Nodier. Reboul speculated that Sand drew material for her heroine and for Trenmor's tale of gambling from Balzac's *Peau de Chagrin* (*The Wild Ass's Skin*), published in 1839. Reboul speculated too that Sand was also inspired by Sénancour's novel *Obermann* (1804), written in the form of letters that describe the author's wandering in forests and his restlessness and disillusionment. Reboul believed that Nodier, poet and short-story writer whose major work appeared in the 1820s, influenced Sand with his cynicism, pessimism, and introspection.[9]

For many people *Lélia* is difficult reading. Structurally, it is hardly a novel at all—it reads more like a group of essays. There is little action, and there are long abstract monologues. All the characters' thoughts are expressed in the most elevated nineteenth-century language.

Although this is not the first French novel in which a writer dared to deal explicitly with problems of female sexuality, *Lélia* was probably neglected by Victorian translators precisely because of Sand's frankness regarding sex and her very emancipated ideas about the relations between men and women. I suspect that the violent reaction the book aroused among its contemporary audience was due not only to the sexual content (the examination of a woman's sexual inadequacy, an allusion to a youthful, homosexually-tinged incident) but also to the woman's examination of her *emotional* incapacity to love. Sand, as

writer, had invaded a terrain previously held by men—the terrain of
the spiritual *and* carnal being who reflects and questions. A woman
whose physicality and intelligence were complete and whose capacity
for love was incomplete was a threatening subject. Woman as nun,
woman as whore—both sustained woman's position within society.
Neither of these alternatives was, perhaps, so frightening to the consciousness of Sand's time as woman a complete human being.

Dostoevsky wrote of his impression of Sand in *Diary of a Writer*:

> As for her heroines, I was astonished from the very start—ever since
> the age of sixteen—by the strangeness of the contradiction between
> what people had been writing and saying about her and what in reality
> I personally perceived. In fact, many—at least several—of her heroines
> represented a type of such elevated moral purity that it could not have
> been conceived without an immense ethical quest in the soul of the
> poetess herself. . . .
>
> These heroines of hers thirsted for sacrifices and heroic deeds—
> "Why did everybody say such things about her?" But right here at
> this point warning voices began to sound: "Precisely in this pride of
> woman's quest, in this irreconcilability of chastity with vice; in this
> rejection of any compromises with evil; in this fearlessness with which
> innocence rises to the struggle and looks brightly into the eyes of the
> offense—therein precisely is the venom, the future poison of woman's
> protest, of woman's emancipation."[10]

*Lélia* is primarily a spiritual novel, a brooding and tormented work,
especially fascinating because Sand's questionings and conflicts, her
painfully honest introspective search for meaning in life, for religious
certainty, and for sexual fulfillment seem as relevant today as ever.
Critics and biographers, with the exception of Dostoevsky, have gener-
ally overlooked the mystical quality of the novel. Yet, this is at the core
of *Lélia* and is perhaps more essential than the heroine's frigidity or
even the man–woman question.

### III

The basis of this translation has been the André Maurois edition. I
have also made use of Pierre Reboul's edition and commentary. Both
editions contain the original 1833 text.

As far as possible I have tried to keep the tone consistent with nine-teenth-century English, because this seemed inseparably linked to content. For example, I tended to avoid contractions except when it would have been jarring *not* to use them.

Although some writers and scholars urged drastic condensation, I decided against it. *Lélia* is a historically important document as it stands, and I felt it essential to translate the work in full. However, in the interest of readability I have made minor omissions of repetitious adjectives, adverbs, and phrases. I have tried at all times not to violate the spirit and style of the original. And, as much as possible, I have attempted to retain the poetic, musical qualities of the French.

Certain untitled chapters consist of monologues. For clarification I have added chapter headings in brackets.

Inconsistencies have been left as they were. For example, Sténio's hair changes inexplicably from black to blond. (Here Sand seems to have been merely careless.) In only one place did I actually alter the text: at the climax, when Lélia makes a dying speech after she has been "strangled" by Magnus, who believes she is demonically possessed. I changed "He strangled her" to "He choked her until there was only a faint breath of life left within her."

Technically, *Lélia* "fails" as a novel: the characters are allegorical rather than real, the momentum of a well-constructed novel is lacking, Sand will set up scenes only to forget them, and the story is anything but concisely written. On the positive side, there are some beautiful narrative passages describing nature, and there are several deftly written ironic scenes approached from the point of view of comedy. Perhaps the novel should not be judged as a "novel" in modern terms but read rather as a treatise or an account of a spiritual odyssey, an interplay of different psychic aspects of the woman George Sand.

Maria Espinosa

## NOTES

1. *Lélia, the Life of George Sand.* Tr. by Gerard Hopkins (New York: Harper, 1953).

2. *George Sand: The Search for Love* (New York: John Day, 1927), p. 129.

3. New York: Doubleday, 1976, p. 132 and p. 33.

4. Maurois, p. 39.

5. Alban Butler, *The Lives of the Fathers, Martyrs, and Other Principal Saints*. First published in London between 1756 and 1759 in four volumes, it has been translated into many languages and Sand may have read it either in English or in French.

6. Maurois, p. 61.

7. Maurois, p. 155.

8. George Sand, *Journal Intime* (Posthume), published by Aurore Sand (Paris: Calmann-Lévy, 1927), pp. 143–46. Also available in an English translation as *The Intimate Journal of George Sand* (New York: Haskell, 1974; New York: Gordon Press, 1976).

9. George Sand, *Lélia*, text edited, introduced, and annotated by Pierre Reboul (Paris: Garnier, 1960).

10. *The Diary of a Writer*, tr. by Boris Brasol (New York: Scribner's, 1949), vol. 2, pp. 343–49.

# LÉLIA

When credulous hope risks a confident glance amidst the doubts of an isolated and desolate soul to fathom and heal them, its foot totters at the edge of the abyss, its eye is troubled, it is stricken with dizziness and death.

*Unpublished Thoughts*
*of a Solitary Man**

---

*Unnumbered page before p. 1, source unknown. Reboul suggests Sénancour or Latouche as possible authors. (Sand dedicated the first edition of *Lélia* to Latouche, a colleague.)

# PART ONE

## I  [STÉNIO TO LÉLIA]

Who are you? And why does your love cause so much evil? There must be some terrible mystery in you, something unknown to men. You are certainly not formed from dust and animated with the same life we are! You are an angel or a demon, but you are not human. Why do you hide your nature and origin from us? Why do you live among us when we aren't enough for you and we can't understand you? If you come from God, speak, and we will adore you. If you come from hell . . . you come from hell! You are so beautiful and so pure. Would an evil spirit have your divine gaze, your harmonious voice, and your words which inspire the soul and transport it to God's throne?

But, Lélia, there is something infernal about you. Your bitter smile belies the promises of heaven in your glance. Some of your words are as desolate as atheism: there are moments when you make me doubt God and yourself. Lélia, why are you this way? What do you make of your faith and your soul when you deny love? Oh, God, you blaspheme! But who are you then if you actually think what you sometimes say?

## II [STÉNIO TO LÉLIA]

Lélia, I am afraid of you. The more I see you, the less I understand you. You toss me into a sea of anxiety and doubts. You seem to make a game of my anguish. You raise me to heaven, only to crush me beneath your feet. You carry me with you into radiant clouds, and then you plunge me into black chaos! My reason succumbs to such trials. Lélia, spare me.

Yesterday when we were walking on the mountain you were so sublime I wanted to kneel and kiss your perfumed footprints. When Christ was transfigured into a golden cloud and seemed to swim in a fiery fluid before the apostles' eyes, they fell to their knees crying, "Lord, you are truly the son of God!" And then when the cloud had vanished and the prophet descended the mountain with his companions, they asked themselves doubtless with anxiety, "Is this man who walks with us, who talks as we do, and who is about to share our food the same man we just saw enveloped in veils of holy fire, radiating the spirit of the Lord?" I feel this way about you, Lélia! Each moment you change, and then you strip away your divinity to become my equal again. I ask myself fearfully if you aren't some celestial power, some new prophet, the Word incarnate once more in human form, and if you act as you do to test our faith and to seek out the true believers among us.

As for Christ, that grand personified thought, that sublime embodiment of immaterial soul, He was always above the human nature into which He had been incarnated. Despite the human form He had assumed, He could not hide the fact that He was first among men. But, Lélia, you frighten me. When you descend from your glory, you aren't even at our level. You fall beneath us, and you try to dominate us only by the perversity of your heart. What is this profound, bitter hate you have for the human race? Can one love God as you do and detest His works so cruelly? What mission of salvation or vengeance are you fulfilling on earth?

Yesterday when the sun set behind the glacier, drowned in vapors of a bluish rose, the warm winter evening glided through your hair, and the church bell threw its melancholy echoes into the valley. Lélia,

I tell you that then you were truly the daughter of heaven. The soft light of the setting sun caressed you. Your eyes burned with a sacred fire as you looked up at the first timid stars. As for me, poet of woods and valleys, I listened to the mysterious murmur of the water, and I watched the slight undulations of the pines. I breathed the sweet perfume of wild violets which open beneath dried moss on the first warm, sunlit day. But you scarcely noticed all this—neither the flowers, the trees, the rushing stream, nor any object on earth aroused your attention. You belonged entirely to the sky. And when I showed you this enchanted spectacle at your feet, you raised your hand toward the heavens and cried, *"Look at that!"* Oh, Lélia, you long for your native land, don't you? Do you ask God why He has left you so long among us, and why He doesn't give you back your wings to ascend to Him?

Alas, when the cold began to blow on the heath, we were forced to seek shelter in the village. Drawn by the pealing bell, I begged you to enter that church and attend the evening service with me. Lélia, why didn't you leave me at that moment? Why, since you can accomplish much more difficult things, did you not bring down a cloud to veil your face from me? Why did you stand there frowning haughtily, heartlessly? Why didn't you kneel on the paving stones, which were less cold than you? Why didn't you make the sign of the cross, like the others? The presence of God should have filled you with emotion or reverence. Why this arrogant calm and apparent scorn for the rites of our worship? Lélia, do you come from burning regions where they sacrifice to Brahma, or the banks of nameless rivers where men worship the spirit of evil? I know neither your family nor your place of birth. No one knows, and the mystery surrounding you makes us superstitious in spite of ourselves.

I cannot believe you are insensitive or impious! But tell me, what happens to you during those terrible hours? Of whom were you dreaming last night, and what had you done with yourself when you stood in that church like a Pharisee, mute and glacial, measuring God without trembling, deaf to the hymns, indifferent to the flowers, the incense, and the sounds of the organ? How beautiful the church was, permeated with moist aromas, as it pulsated with sacred harmonies! Flames from silver lamps burned a dull white amid opal clouds of resin, while the incense holders gave off spirals of odorous fumes. How the gold gleamed beneath the light of the wax tapers! And that tall, austere, black-haired Irish priest. When he slowly descended the altar steps, his velvet cloak trailed on the carpet. He raised his voice, as sad and penetrating as the winds that blow in his country, while he presented to us the glittering vessel containing the host; and he pronounced: *Adoremus*. Lélia, I felt myself penetrated then by a sacred fear. I threw myself to my knees, beat my chest, and lowered my eyes.

But the thought of you is so intimately linked with all my nobler thoughts that almost immediately I turned around to share this delicious feeling, or perhaps, may God forgive me, to address half of these humble adorations to you.

You were standing! You did not kneel or lower your eyes! You looked coldly and scrutinizingly at the priest, the host, and the prostrate crowd. None of all this meant anything to you. Alone among us, you refused to pray. Would you prefer to be a power above God?

Lélia, may God once more forgive me. For a moment I believed this, and I nearly withdrew my homage to offer it to you. I let myself be dazzled and subjugated by your power! Alas, I must confess this. I never saw you so beautiful. Pale as one of those marble statues which guard tombs, you no longer had anything terrestrial about you. Your eyes burned with a somber fire and your high forehead, from which you had brushed aside your black hair, rose sublime with pride and genius above the crowd, above the priest, even above God. This depth of impiety was frightening, and to see you measuring the space between us and heaven made everything there seem small. Did Milton visualize you when he made his rebellious angel whose expression is so noble and beautiful?

Must I tell you all my terrors? When the priest saw you standing alone in front of him as he raised the symbol of the faith over our bowed heads, he seemed to lower his eyes, with their profound, severe expression, and to pale before your impassive gaze. His trembling hands could no longer hold up the chalice, and his voice broke. Is this a dream of my troubled imagination; or did it really happen? Did anger suffocate the priest when he saw you resist his orders? Or else, tormented as I was by a strange hallucination, did he believe he saw something of the supernatural in you, either a power evoked from the abyss or a revelation sent from heaven?

## III [LÉLIA TO STÉNIO]

Young poet, what does that matter to you? Why do you want to know who I am and where I come from? . . . Like you, I was born in this vale of tears; and all the unfortunate ones who creep the earth are my brothers. Is this earth so large? A thought embraces it, and a swallow can fly around it in several days. What is so strange and mysterious about a human existence? What influence do you think a beam of sunlight falling more or less vertically over our heads can have? This entire world is so very remote from the sun: the world is cold, pale, and restricted. Ask the wind how many hours it takes to toss from one pole to the other.

Even if I had been born at the other end of the earth, there would be little difference between us. You and I are both condemned to suffer. We are both feeble, incomplete, wounded by all our joys, anxious, and greedy for a nameless happiness. We are always seeking something outside ourselves. This is our common fate. This makes us brothers and companions in this land of exile.

You ask if my nature is different from yours. Don't you think I suffer? I have seen people who were less fortunate than I but whose characters made them much less unhappy. Not everyone has the ability to suffer to the same degree. In the eyes of the great artisan of our miseries, no doubt these differences are minute. But we, with our limited vision, pass half our lives examining each other and noting our slight dissimilarities. Before God these are like the distinctions between blades of grass.

This is why I don't pray to God. What would I ask? That He change my fate? He would laugh. That He give me the strength to struggle against my suffering? He has put this strength within me, and it is for me to use.

You ask if I worship the spirit of evil. The spirit of evil and the spirit of good are one. They are both God. God is the mysterious and unknown will above our own. Good and evil are only distinctions we have created. The Holy Spirit knows only good and ill fortune. So ask neither heaven nor hell the secret of my fate. Rather, I reproach you for continually placing me above and below myself. Poet, my soul is the sister of yours. You only sadden and frighten me when you probe me in this way. Take me for what I am, a soul that suffers and waits. If you interrogate me so severely, my soul will fold in on itself and no longer dare open up to you.

## IV  [STÉNIO TO LÉLIA]

Lélia, I have expressed the strength of my concern for you too frankly. I have wounded your modesty. Lélia, I too am very unhappy! You believe I cast detached eyes over you, but you are wrong. If I didn't feel that I belonged to you, that from now on my existence is inextricably linked to yours, if, in a word, I didn't love you passionately, I wouldn't have the boldness to question you, even if you were the most remarkable *subject* offered to the observations of a physiologist.

These anxieties I have dared to express are shared by all who have seen you. Astounded, they ask themselves if you are a cursed or privileged being, if they should love or fear you, welcome or repulse you. Even the unthinking common people turn their attention to you. They don't understand your look or the sound of your voice, and when I hear absurd tales about you, I realize that people are equally ready to fall at your feet or ward you off like a plague. The most intelligent observe you attentively, some with curiosity, others with sympathy. But no one else makes the solution of this problem a question of life or death. I alone have the right to be bold and ask who you are, for I sense, and this sensation is linked to my existence, that from now on I am a part of you. You have taken hold of me, perhaps unknowingly; but I am enslaved. I no longer belong to myself. My soul can no longer live alone. God and poetry are no longer enough. Without you there is no poetry, there is no God, there is no longer anything.

Tell me then, Lélia, since you want me to take you for a woman and talk to you as an equal, tell me if you have the power to love, if your soul is fire or ice, and if giving myself to you as I have done is my loss or my salvation. Because I don't know, and I don't think of the life ahead without fear. My future is enveloped in clouds, sometimes brilliantly pink like those on the horizon at sunrise, sometimes as dark and somber as those which precede a storm and conceal thunder.

Have I begun life with you or have I left it only to follow you into death? Will you blight or rejuvenate those years of calm and innocence behind me? Have I known happiness only to lose it or will I now taste it for the first time? Those years were beautiful, fresh, sweet. But they were also calm, obscure, sterile. What have I done but dream, wait, and hope since I came into the world? Perhaps I am finally going to create. Will you make something great or something abject of me? Will I leave this void of repose to climb or fall?

This is what I anxiously ask myself each day, but you don't answer. Lélia, you don't seem to realize that a life hangs in the balance, a fate is linked to yours. And from now on you are accountable to God for this life as well as your own. In a careless, distracted way you grip my chain, only to forget and let it fall!

At each moment, frightened at seeing myself alone and abandoned, I must call and force you to descend from those unknown regions where you wander without me. Lélia, you are cruel! How happy you are to have your soul free and the power to dream alone, to love alone, to live alone! I can no longer do this. I love you, and I love only you. All those graceful beauties, all those angels dressed as women who used to appear in my dreams, tossing me kisses and flowers, have gone. They no longer come, neither when I am awake nor when I am asleep. It is you, always you, whom I see pale, calm, sad, and silent beside me.

I am miserable. My situation is not ordinary. Not only is it that I want to know if I am worthy of your love. I want to know if you are capable of loving a man and—I write this with effort, it is so horrible— I think *no*!

Oh, Lélia, this time will you answer me? Now I tremble, having asked. Tomorrow I would still have been able to live with my doubts and illusions, but now I may have nothing left either to hope or to fear.

## V  [LÉLIA TO STÉNIO]

You're a child. You've scarcely been born, but you're in such a hurry to live. Because, Sténio, I must tell you, you haven't lived yet. I can define what living is in two words for you, but later.

Why are you in such a hurry? Do you fear you won't get to that cursed destination where we all run aground? Sténio, you'll be smashed against it like the others. So take your time, play truant, and cross the threshold of life's school as late as you can.

Naive child, to ask where happiness is, how it's made, if you've tasted it yet, or whether you will taste it one day! Oh precious ignorance. Sténio, I won't answer you.

Don't be afraid. I won't crush you by telling you any of the things you want to know. Whether I can love, whether I'll make you happy, whether I am good or perverse, whether you will become great through my love or destroyed through my indifference: this is all dangerous knowledge. God refuses it to a person your age, and He forbids me to enlighten you. Wait.

Young poet, I bless you. Sleep peacefully. Tomorrow will be as beautiful as the other days of your youth. And it will be adorned with Fate's greatest blessing: the veil that hides the future.

## VI  [STÉNIO TO LÉLIA]

You always answer me with the same evasiveness. Your silence gives me a presentiment of such suffering that I am reduced to thanking you for it. However, Lélia, this state of ignorance you believe so blissful is painful to me. You treat it with such contemptuous lightness only because you are not familiar with it. Perhaps your childhood passed like mine, but I don't imagine that the first passion aroused in you was the anguish I am experiencing now. Surely you were loved, before you yourself loved. You did not know torments of jealousy and fear. Love and happiness awaited you. It was enough for you to consent to receive them. You cannot know how I suffer or you would pity me because you are good. Your actions prove it despite your words, which deny it. I have seen you practice Christian charity with an ironic smile on your lips. I have seen you feed and clothe those who were naked and hungry, all the while displaying an odious skepticism. You are innately good, and your cold reflectiveness cannot change this.

If you knew how unhappy you make me, you would have compassion. You would tell me whether to live or die. You would give me immediately either the happiness that intoxicates or intelligence that consoles.

## VII [STÉNIO TO LÉLIA]

Who is this pale man that I see like a sinister vision wherever you are? What does he want of you? How did he meet you? The first day he appeared here publicly, why did he make his way through the crowd to gaze at you, and why did the two of you immediately exchange sad smiles?

This man frightens me. When he approaches, I feel cold. If his clothing brushes against me, I feel almost an electric shock. You say he is a great poet who doesn't devote himself to the world but who is superior to Byron. Indeed, his high forehead reveals genius; but I don't find there that ethereal purity, that enthusiasm which characterizes the poet. This man is as gloomy and disheartening as the Giaour,* or Lara,† or you, Lélia, when you are suffering. I don't like to see him always beside you, absorbing all your attention, taking possession, as it were, of all the benevolence you reserve for society, and all your interest in human affairs.

I am aware that I have no right to be jealous. I won't tell you what I sometimes suffer. But it grieves me (this is permitted) to see you under this despondent influence. You are already so sad and discouraged that you need to be uplifted by hope and sweet promises. Instead, I see you in contact with a withered, desolate soul. Because this man has been exhausted by passion. Every trace of youthful freshness has left his petrified features. He no longer knows how to smile; his face is never animated. He acts mechanically, as if from habit or memory. But the principle of life has long since been extinguished in his breast. Madame, I am sure of that. I've observed this man intently, and I have pierced the mystery in which he surrounds himself. If he tells you he loves you, he is lying! He can no longer love.

But can he who feels nothing still inspire love? I've debated this question for a long time, ever since I've known you. I cannot bring myself

---

*Heroine of the narrative poem *Lara* by Byron (1814).

†Hero of the narrative poem *The Giaour* by Byron (1813). He was a secret Christian who lived among Mohammedans.

to believe that so much love and poetry radiates from you without feeling that you too conceal love within your soul. This man emits coldness through all his pores! People feel repulsed by him, and this consoles me. If your heart were as dead as his, I would not love you. I'd have a horror of you, as I have a horror of him.

My reason struggles in such a labyrinth! You don't share the horror that he inspires in me. On the contrary, you seem drawn toward him by an invincible sympathy. At times I see you with him in the midst of our festivities, and you two are so pale and distracted among the swirling dancers, the laughter, the strewn flowers. Then I feel that you two alone among all of us can understand each other. A mournful resemblance seems to be established between your sensations and even your features. Is it the scourge of misfortune that has imprinted that air of being related on your somber faces? Or, Lélia, is he truly your brother? Your life is so mysterious that I am ready to suppose anything.

Yes, there are days when I convince myself that you are his sister. I say this so that you will understand my jealousy is neither narrow nor childish. I don't suffer less with this thought, nor am I less wounded by your intimacy with him. Sometimes you're so cold, so distrustful, and so reserved with me. Lélia, if he is your brother, what superior rights does he have? Do you think I would be able to love you with more tenderness, care, and respect if you were my sister? Truly this isn't so. You should trust me, and you should recognize the chaste, deep feeling that you arouse in me. Doesn't one love one's sister passionately when one has a passionate soul and a sister like you, Lélia? The bonds of blood carry great weight with vulgar natures, but what are they in comparison with those mysterious sympathies of the spirit that we forge?

If he is your brother, he cannot love you more than I do, and you don't owe him more confidence. He is happy, cursed man, that you take pleasure in talking to him about your suffering and that he has the power to lessen it. Alas! You don't give me this right. I am then worth little! You must see me as a very feeble, useless child if you're afraid to confide in me at all. Oh, Lélia, I'm unhappy because you are, and yet you've never shed a tear on my breast. Sometimes you force yourself to be gay with me, as if you were afraid of burdening me by showing your true feelings. How insulting this delicacy is, Lélia. It hurts me. You're never gay with *him*. You see, I have reason to be jealous.

## VIII  [LÉLIA TO STÉNIO]

I have shown your letter to the man who goes here by the name of Trenmor and whose true name only I know. He has taken such an interest in your suffering, and he is so compassionate (this man whose heart you believe dead!) that he has authorized me to confide his secret to you. You see, you are not going to be treated like a child, because this secret is the greatest that one man can confide to another.

First, know that I feel great interest in Trenmor because he is the unhappiest man I have ever met. He has had to drain the cup of sorrow down to its very dregs. Over you he has the immense superiority of having suffered.

Young man, do you know what unhappiness is? You have scarcely entered life; you're enduring its first agitations; your passions rise up, they quicken the movement of your blood, trouble your sleep, arouse new sensations in you, convulsive anxieties, nervous torments, and you call that suffering! You believe you have received the solemn and terrible baptism of unhappiness! It is true that you suffer, but what precious suffering it is to love. Isn't it the source of a great deal of poetry? How warm, how productive this suffering is, which can be expressed and for which one can be pitied.

But Trenmor has experienced suffering that must be kept hidden at the bottom of the entrails. It always waits there, cold, pale, and paralytic. On Judgment Day he can boast of this to God, because he must hide it from men.

Listen to Trenmor's story. He is more complex than the rest of you. For him, an ordinary life was not enough. For men like him the universe does not offer enough substance. However, like you, he was once young, naive, and amorous. Like you, he was once twenty years old. Only, because he lived more rapidly, he was as mature as you are now when he was sixteen.

After he had exhausted love, he was devoured by the energy of a very different passion, more imaginatively fertile, more intense, intoxicating, and heroic in the acts it incites. I mean gambling! Because, alas, this must be said. If in appearance its goal is vile, the passion it inspires is powerful. Women never inspire such sacrifices. Gold has a power far superior to women's. In courage and devotion the lover is only a weak child whose efforts are pitiable when compared to the gambler's. How many men have you ever seen sacrifice honor to their mistress? Honor is the only condition that makes human existence bearable. Yet every day the gambler immolates his honor and continues to endure life. The gambler is keen-edged and stoic. He triumphs or loses with equal coldness. In a few hours he may pass from the bottom rank of society to the highest. In several more hours he descends again, and all this without a change of expression. In a few hours, without leaving the place to which his demon chains him, he passes through all the vicissitudes of life. In turn beggar and king, in a single bound he climbs the ladder, always calm, always master of himself, upheld by his ambition, excited by a devouring thirst. In a few minutes will he be prince or slave? Will he emerge from the cave naked or weighted down by gold? What does it matter? He will return tomorrow to lose or triple his fortune again. What is impossible for him is rest. He's like a bird of the tempest that can't live without waves and furious winds. People accuse him of loving gold! He loves it so little that he throws it away by the handful. These gifts of hell can neither profit nor appease him. He has scarcely grown rich when he is eager to be ruined so that he can again taste that nervous and terrible emotion which saves his life from being insipid. Gold in his eyes is less by itself than grains of sand to you. But gold for him is a symbol of the happiness or suffering he risks. Gold is his plaything, his dream, his god, his demon, his mistress. He pursues this shadow, attacks and grasps it, then lets it escape in order to have the pleasure of beginning the battle again and confronting his destiny once more face to face. All this is beautiful but absurd! One must condemn him because the energy he uses this way is profitless to society, because he who directs his strength toward such a goal robs his fellow men of all the good he would have been able to do with less egotism. But, in condemning, don't despise him, you petty natures who are capable of neither good nor evil. Only measure his colossal will that struggles for the sole pleasure of exercising its strength. His egotism pushes him into fatigue and danger, as yours chains the rest of you to tedious professions. How many men can you count who work for their fatherland without dreaming of themselves? He frankly isolates himself; he exhausts his future, his present, his peace of mind, and his honor. He condemns himself to suffering and tremendous pressure. Deplore his error, but don't secretly compare yourself to him to glorify yourself at his expense. Let his fatal example serve only to console you for your inoffensive nothingness.

Today I will stop here. At your age a person is intolerant, and you would be overwhelmed if, in a single day, I were to divulge Trenmor's entire secret. I wish to let this part of my tale make an impression, and tomorrow I will tell you the rest.

## IX [STÉNIO TO LÉLIA]

You are right to spare me, because what you have said is very upsetting. But you must credit me with far more concern than I feel if you think that I am so affected by Trenmor's secret. It is your judgment of his actions that troubles me. Are you so far above society that you can treat the crimes committed against it lightly? Perhaps this question insults you. Society may be so contemptible that I myself am worth more than it is. But forgive the confusion of a child who still knows nothing of real life.

Everything you say produces the effect of a sun too intense on eyes accustomed to darkness. But, Lélia, I sense that you are sparing me a great deal through friendship or compassion . . . oh, God! What is there for me to learn still? What illusions have cradled my youth? You say a gambler isn't contemptible. Or if he is contemptible to superior natures, he cannot be contemptible to me. I have no right to judge him and say: "I am greater than that man who harms himself and helps no one." It is true that I am young. I don't know what will become of me. I haven't overcome the obstacles of life. But Trenmor was also once twenty years old and had noble passions! Lélia, you are greater in your soul and genius than anyone on earth. You have a right to condemn and hate Trenmor. And you don't want to! Either your indulgent compassion or your imprudent admiration (I don't know how to say it) follows him in the midst of his guilty triumphs, applauds his successes, and respects his reverses.

If this man has such energy, why doesn't he use it to curb his morbid inclinations? Why does he make such bad use of his strength? If he is noble, then pirates and bandits must be too! Anyone who distinguishes himself by bold crimes or unusual vices is consequently a hero before whom the emotion-struck crowd should open with respect! Lélia, a man must be a hero or a monster to please you. . . ! Perhaps. When I imagine the full, troubled life you must have led, and I see how many of your illusions have died, I tell myself that a dull, obscure existence like mine can only be a useless burden to you. Only violent impressions can awaken the sympathies of your satiated spirit.

Please, Lélia, say something encouraging. Tell me what you want me to be, and I will be it. You think the love of a woman can't give the same energy as the love of gold. . . .

Is it my dishonor or my shame that you ask? All right, Lélia, all right. But tell me, if I offer you these sacrifices, will you despise me afterward? You don't despise Trenmor, and you say he has sacrificed his honor. To what? To the passion for gambling. Continue this story. It interests me terribly, because above all it is a revelation of your soul, that profound, moving, shifting, evanescent soul I am always seeking and can never penetrate.

## X [LÉLIA TO STÉNIO]

Young man, without a doubt you are worth much more than we. Be reassured in your pride. But in ten years, even in five years, will you be equal to Trenmor or Lélia? That is an essential point.

I love you exactly as you are, young poet. Don't let this either frighten or intoxicate you. I'm not claiming to give you a solution for your problems. I love you for your ingenuousness, for your ignorance of all the things I know, for that naiveté you are so impatient to be rid of. I love you differently than I do Trenmor. In spite of his strong passions and his superior character, I find less charm in his conversation than in yours. In a little while I will explain why I am not sacrificing myself to the point of abandoning you for him.

However, before I continue with my story, I will answer one of your questions.

You ask why a man with such a powerful will hasn't used his strength to restrain himself. Why not? . . . Happy Sténio! What do you conceive man's nature to be? What would you foresee for his strength? —Alas, what do you expect of yourself?

Sténio, you are very imprudent to throw yourself into our whirlpool! See, this is what you are forcing me to tell you!

I have never yet met a man who represses his passions in the interest of others. I have seen heroes of ambition, of love, of egotism, and especially of vanity. —Philanthropy?— Many have boasted of this, but the hypocrites were lying through their teeth. Sadly I observed the depths of their souls and found only vanity. Because, after love, vanity is man's most beautiful passion; and you should know, my poor child, that even vanity is rare. Greediness, snobbishness, debauchery, all these vile impulses,—even laziness, which for some people is a sterile but stubborn passion—these ambitions, you see, move most men. At least vanity is noble in its effects. It forces men to be good through the desire they have to appear so. It pushes a man into heroism because it is so sweet to imagine oneself carried in triumph. Popularity has powerful and adroit seductions! And vanity is something that will never admit its own existence. The other passions can't dupe people, but vanity can hide behind another word which fools will accept—philanthropy! My God, what a childish lie! Where is a man who prefers the happiness of others to his own glory?

Christianity has produced what is most heroic on earth. And what is its basis? The hope of reward, a throne in the sky. Those who made this great code, which is the finest and most poetic monument of the human spirit, knew man's heart so well, with its vanity and its pettiness. Consequently, they organized a system of Divine promises. Read the writings of the Apostles, and you see that there are distinctions in heaven, hierarchies among the blessed. Adroit commentary on these words of Christ: "The first shall be last, and the last shall be first! Verily, I say unto thee, he who is least on earth shall be greatest among the royalty of heaven!"

Now, why didn't Trenmor use his moral strength to control himself in the interest of his fellow men? —Because he had a mistaken conception of life. Egotism guided him wrongly. Instead of climbing onto the boards of a sumptuous theater, he performed in a traveling circus. Instead of spending his time declaiming specious moralities and playing heroic roles, he amused himself by exercising his muscles, performing tours de force, and risking his life on a brass wire. Even this comparison is worth nothing! The saltimbanque has his vanity, as does the tragedian and the philanthropic orator. The gambler does not have this; he is neither admired, applauded, nor envied. His triumphs are so brief and won at such risk that they are hardly worth talking about. On the contrary, society condemns him, the masses despise him, especially when he loses. His charlatanism consists simply in maintaining a front, failing decently before a group of players who don't even glance at him because they're so absorbed in their own efforts. If, in his hours of rapidly passing fortune, he finds pleasure in satisfying the vulgar vanities of luxury, this is a very small tribute to human frailty. Soon he will pitilessly sacrifice these joys to the devouring activity of his soul which doesn't permit him to live for even a day as other men do. Is he vain? He doesn't have time to be! He has so much else to do! Doesn't he have to torment his heart, overwhelm his brain, lose his gold, put his life on the line, reconstruct, undo, twist, tear into bits, risk, reconquer bit by bit, put gold into his purse, throw it on the table continually? Ask the sailor if he can live on land, the bird if it can be happy without its wings, the human heart if it can abstain from emotion.

The gambler is not necessarily a criminal, but his social position nearly always makes him one. It is his own family he ruins or dishonors. But suppose, like Trenmor, he is isolated in the world, without affections, without relatives who are close enough to be taken into consideration, and he has been either satiated or betrayed in his love. Then you will pity his transgression; you will regret for his sake that he wasn't born with a cheerful, vain temperament rather than a bilious, intense one.

Where do you get the idea that the gambler is in the same category as pirates and brigands? Ask governments why they draw a portion of their wealth from such shameful sources. They alone are guilty of offering these terrible temptations to the anxious, these morbid resources to the hopeless.

But you still don't understand why I excuse this man. You should know I met him one day in the midst of his most brilliant success, and I turned away from him contemptuously. I would still despise him if he hadn't expiated his offence; but perhaps you will forgive him when you know everything.

If the love of gambling isn't in itself more shameful than most other propensities, it's the most dangerous, the most irresistible, and it has the most miserable consequences. After a few years it is nearly impossible for a gambler not to dishonor himself.

For a long time Trenmor endured this life of anguish and upheaval, with the heroism that is at his core, but finally he let himself be corrupted. That is, bit by bit his spirit wore down in this perpetual struggle. He lost the stoic strength with which he had been able to accept losses, endure miserable privations, and rebuild his fortune, sometimes with only a sou, sometimes to sacrifice an entire month repairing a day's losses. For a long time his life was like this. But finally he grew weary of suffering; and in spite of his strong will and his virtue (for the gambler has his virtue, too), he began to seek ways of regaining more quickly the money he had lost. He borrowed. And from then on he was lost.

At first a man suffers cruelly when he finds himself in an indelicate situation. Then he makes himself at home with it; he becomes numbed and blunted. Trenmor did exactly as other gamblers and prodigals have done. He became harmful and dangerous to his friends. He accumulated on their heads the evils he had courageously borne for so long. He was guilty. He risked his own honor, then the existence, the property, and the honor of his closest friends. Gambling has something horrible about it, because no matter how harsh its lessons, they never seem irrevocable. The gold never exhausts itself, and it is always before your eyes. It follows you, invites you, tells you: "Hope!" And sometimes it keeps its promises. It makes you bold, reestablishes your credit, and seems to delay dishonor. But dishonor has already been consummated the very first day that honor is voluntarily jeopardized.

It was at this time that I met Trenmor, and I despised him. My contempt hurt him, and he stopped borrowing from his friends. But he needed to get over his passion, and perhaps that was beyond his strength.

He resorted to those deplorable methods which, for a limited time, sustain lost lives. He delivered himself up to usurers, and for several weeks he managed to bridge his enormous deficits. But then again his debts grew, his fortune diminished, and the hydra with a hundred heads became more and more menacing. One day Trenmor found himself without even a sou to throw on the gaming table, not a sou to show as security for the millions he owed.

He told me a thought came to him that day from heaven, but his bad angel snuffed it out. He thought of me. I was not his friend, and I had no right to refuse him help. I had wounded him in the depths of his soul, and yet he felt more sympathy for me, in that moment of despair, than for any of his dangerous companions. But shame spoke louder; he did not come.

On that unhappy day he was inspired with the idea of committing a degrading act. The opportunity tempted him, embellishing itself with hideous charms, and reached his misguided soul in its desperation. This man, who had always refused to profit from a game of either chance or skill against friends, this great gambler, intrepid but scrupulous in his own way, now felt himself too proud to borrow a modest sum. He decided to swindle one hundred francs from an old millionaire, a crook and libertine who had never helped him in any way at all and who hardly counted the banknotes he threw to his prostitutes. Sténio, in reality this was much less a crime than all those he had committed without breaking written laws. He had made honest men suffer through his unlimited borrowing, and now he was taking an imperceptible sum from an evil, wealthy crook. This cost him more than anything else he had ever done. The fraud was discovered. And Trenmor was sentenced to five years of forced labor.


## XI [STÉNIO TO LÉLIA]

This is indeed a terrible secret, and in my heart I feel a great respect for the man who is not afraid to entrust it to me. You must esteem me, Lélia, and he certainly esteems you. How else could this secret have come to me in such a short time? A sacred bond has been established between the three of us. However, I'm afraid of this bond, and this I won't hide from you. But I no longer have the right to break it.

Lélia, in spite of all your oratorical precautions, I am crushed. An hour before I read your letter I saw him pressing your hand, which I have never dared touch. I have never seen you offer your hand to anyone else. An icy coldness fell over my heart. To think of you forming an alliance with that decayed man! You are angelic. I worship you on my knees. You are the sister of the stars, and for a moment I believed you to be the sister of . . . I won't write his name. And now it seems you're more than his sister! A sister would only be carrying out her duty if she forgave him. But you have chosen to make yourself his friend, his consolation, his angel. You have said, "Come to me, afflicted man. I'll give you back the paradise you lost! Come to me. I am undefiled, and I will conceal your blemishes." Lélia, you are even greater than I thought. Your action hurts me, I don't know why, but I admire it, and I adore you. What I can't endure is that Trenmor, whom I hate and pity, dared touch the hand you offered. He was proud enough to accept your friendship, which the greatest men on earth would implore humbly if they knew its worth. Trenmor possesses your sacred friendship, and Trenmor doesn't talk to you with his forehead in the dust. Trenmor stands next to you and walks with you through the astonished crowd. And he has been imprisoned for five years with thieves and murderers. . . . Ah, I hate him! But I no longer despise him.

As for you, Lélia, I pity you, and I pity myself, too, because I am your disciple and your slave. You know life far too well to be happy. I wonder whether unhappiness has soured you and if you exaggerate evil. I reject the overwhelming conclusion to your letter: that the best men are the vainest and that heroism is an illusion.

Poor Lélia, you believe this! Poor woman. You are unhappy, and I love you.


## XII [LÉLIA TO STÉNIO]

Trenmor had only one way to earn my friendship: to accept it. And he has done this. He trusts me. He doesn't believe that my generosity is beyond my strength. Instead of being humble and fearful with me, he is calm, he relies on my delicacy, he doesn't fear that I'm going to humiliate him by making him feel the weight of my protection. Truly, he has a noble soul, and no friendship has flattered me more than his.

You no longer despise his character, but you do despise his condition, don't you, Sténio? You are young and proud! Do you dare raise yourself above this man who has been struck by lightning? Because he has been reckless, because he has gone off course and struck the rocks, you turn away from him, and you watch him make his way, all bloody and broken, out of the abyss! Ah, you are truly of the world! You share its prejudices, its egotistical vengeance. When the sinner is still standing, you tolerate him; but once he is on the ground, you crush him beneath your feet, you gather stones and mud to do as the crowd does, so that as they watch your cruelty the other executioners will believe that you are virtuous. You'd be afraid to show a little pity because they'd interpret it badly and think you're the victim's brother or friend. And if they thought you were capable of the same crimes, if they were to say: "See that man who has stretched out his hand to the criminal. Isn't he his companion in degradation?" Rather than have people say that about me, let's stone him, let's grind his face beneath our heels! When the hideous cart carries the condemned man to the scaffold, the mob hurls itself around this remnant of a man who is about to die, and they heap him with insults. Do as the mob does, Sténio! What would they say here in this town, where you are a stranger like us, if they saw you touch his hand? Perhaps they would think you were with him in prison. Rather than expose yourself to that, young man, flee the ex-convict. His friendship is dangerous. The ineffable pleasure of doing good to an unfortunate is too dearly paid for by the curses of the crowd. Sténio, is that how you feel?

Didn't you weep when you read in the history of England about the young girl who, on seeing the death of King Charles I, forced her way through the curious, indifferent crowd, and not knowing what token of tender feeling to give him, poor and simple child, she offered him a rose that she held in her hand, a rose as pure and sweet as she was, a rose that perhaps her lover had given her. This was the only, the last sign of affection and pity that a king received as he walked to his torture. Weren't you touched, too, in the sublime story about the leper of Aoste, by the narrator's simple, natural action of stretching out his hand? The poor leper, who hadn't touched the hand of another human being in many years, found it terribly painful to refuse that friendly hand. But he did so for fear of infecting him with his illness.

However, why would Trenmor have repulsed my hand? Is misfortune as contagious as leprosy? Then let the reproaches of the vulgar herd envelop us both, and let Trenmor himself be ungrateful! I have God and my own heart to support me. That is worth a great deal more than the esteem of the vulgar and one man's gratitude. Oh, to give a glass of water to someone who is thirsty, to carry a little of Christ's cross, to hide a brow flushed with shame, to throw a blade of grass to a poor drowning ant; these are small deeds. However, public opinion forbids or challenges them. We don't have one good impulse that isn't repressed or hidden. People teach children to be vain and pitiless, and this is called *honor*! A curse on all of us!

What if I were to tell you that, far from considering my conduct an act of mercy, I feel passionate respect for this man who has spent five years in prison? What if I were to tell you that, stigmatized and ruined as he is, I find him morally superior to any of us? Do you know in what way he endured his misfortune? With your pride, you would certainly have killed yourself; you would not have accepted such disgrace. But he found the punishment just, not only because of the fraudulent act to which despair had driven him, but because of the harm he had done that went unpunished for several years. And since he deserved this punishment, he wanted to submit to it. For five years he lived with strength and patience among his abject companions. He slept on stone next to the parricide; he stretched his back silently beneath the guard's whip; he endured the stares of the curious. For five years he lived in filth, among bestial human beings. He submitted to the contempt of the most flagrant scoundrels and to the domination of the most cowardly bullies. This man who had been so wealthy, such a voluptuary, a man of such elegance and poetic feeling, an artist and a dandy, was now a convict. He had once skimmed over the waves in a gondola in Venice, surrounded by women, perfume, and singing. He had won prizes at Newmarket. He had wearied the most beautiful Arabian horses with his wild races. Like Byron, he had slept beneath the skies of Greece. He had exhausted a life of luxury and excitement. And he had come to prison to acquire new strength. Prison, that infected sewer, can pervert even a father who has sold his daughters, even a son who has violated and poisoned his mother. Prison can leave a man disfigured and crawling like an animal. But it left Trenmor standing, calm, purified, a creature of God. His face reflects the Divine light cast on the man who thinks!

.   .   .   .   .   .   .

# XIII

The lake was calm that evening, as calm as it is in the last days of autumn, when the winter wind does not yet dare trouble the mute waves and the pink gladioli along the bank scarcely sleep, rocked by soft undulations. Pale vapors ate imperceptibly at the angular contours of the mountain, and as they descended over the waters, they seemed

to make the horizon recede, and finally they made it disappear entirely. Then the lake's surface seemed to become as vast as the sea. No
object, whether pleasant or strange, any longer stood out in the valley.
There were no possible distractions, no more sensations imposed by
exterior images. Reverie became solemn and profound, as vague as the
misty lake, as immense as the limitless sky. There was no longer anything in nature but the sky and man, the soul and doubt.

Trenmor, standing at the helm of the boat, was delineated in the
blue night air, his large form enveloped in a dark cloak. He raised his
face toward the heavens, which for so long had been angered with him.

"Sténio," he said to the young poet, "can't you row more slowly so
that we can listen, at our leisure, to the harmonious, fresh sound of the
water raised by the oars? In rhythm, poet, in rhythm. This is as beautiful and important as the cadence of the most beautiful poem. *That's
right!* Listen! Do you hear the plaintive sound of the water as the oars
cut through it? Do you hear the frail drops that fall one by one behind
us as they die, like the high-pitched notes of a refrain that is receding
into the distance?"

"I have spent many hours," continued Trenmor, "seated on a peaceful seashore under the beautiful Mediterranean sky. And later I would
listen with pleasure to the wash of small boats at the bottom of our
prison walls. During the night, in that terrible silent insomnia that
follows the noise of work and the infernal curses of the suffering, the
faint, mysterious sound of waves beating at the base of my prison
always calmed me. Later, when I felt myself to be as strong as my fate,
when my soul was no longer forced to demand help from exterior influences, the gentle sound of the water rocked my reveries and plunged
me into a delicious ecstasy."

At that moment a grey gull was flying across the lake. Lost in the
mist, it brushed lightly against Trenmor's damp hair.

"Another friend," said the convict. "Another sweet memory! When
I used to rest on the strand, as motionless as the flagstones, sometimes
these birds, taking me for a statue, would approach and observe me fearlessly. They were the only creatures who felt no aversion or contempt
when they saw me. They did not understand my misery, nor did they
reproach me for it. And when I moved, they flew away. They didn't see
that I had a chain on my leg and couldn't follow them. They didn't

know that I was a convict, and they fled as they would have from a man."

"Poet," said the young man to the convict, "tell me where you, with your rocklike soul, found the strength to endure the first days of such an existence."

"I won't tell you, Sténio, because I no longer know. In those days I didn't feel, I was scarcely alive, and I understood nothing. But when I realized how horrible this life was, I found in myself the strength to endure it. What I had feared was a life of monotonous repose. When I experienced hard labor, fatigue, burning days and freezing nights, blows and cries, the vast sea before me, the motionless stone of the coffin beneath my feet, heard frightful tales, and saw hideous suffering, I understood I could live because I could struggle and suffer."

"You survived because you needed violent sensations," said Lélia. "But, Trenmor, tell us, how did you become accustomed to calm? Because you said a little while ago that calm came to you even amid criminals. And furthermore, all sensations are dulled with repetition."

"Calm," said Trenmor, raising his sublime gaze to heaven, "is God's greatest blessing. Calm is blessedness. It is the goal toward which the immortal soul endlessly strives. Calm is God. And in prison I found this. Otherwise I would never have understood the secret of human life. I had been a gambler, without religious beliefs or goals. I was tired of a life that had no meaning, tormented by a freedom I didn't know how to use. I had never taken the time to dream about life because I was in such a hurry to push time forward and cut short the boredom of existence. I needed to be relieved of my will for a period of time and to fall under the rule of an alien, brutal will, which would teach me the value of my own. The excess energy with which I had desperately clutched at a dangerous but wearying worldly existence at last found an outlet in the anguish of expiation. My new life led to a solitary contentment. For the first time I knew the sweetness of sleep. It was as full and voluptuous in prison as it had been rare and incomplete when I lived in luxury.

In prison I learned what self-esteem is worth, because, far from being humiliated by my contact with these cursed men, when I compared their cowardice and fury to my calm resignation, I was raised in my own eyes, and I dared believe that some faint communication between heaven and a courageous man could exist. In my days of fever and audacity I had never been able to hope for that. Calm gave birth to this regenerative thought, which slowly took root. Finally I raised my spirit entirely toward God, and I prayed with confidence. Oh, then torrents of joy ran through this poor, devastated soul! Divine promises made themselves humble, small, merciful enough to descend and reveal themselves to my weak perceptions! Then I understood the mysterious symbol of the Divine Word made human to console and uplift men. I understood the true meaning of Christian mythology, which is so poetic and tender, the relation between earth and heaven, the magnificent effects of spirituality, which finally opens a path of hope and consolation to the unfortunate man. Oh, Lélia! Oh, Sténio! You believe in God too, don't you?"

"Always!" said Sténio.

"Nearly always," said Lélia.

Trenmor continued. "With faith, another blessing revealed itself— poetry. Amid the storms of my past life, this sentiment had barely touched me. I had a mere intellectual understanding of the great poets I read, and perhaps that was a great deal for a man as greedy and incapable of understanding himself as I was. Now calm gave birth to poetry, as it had given birth to the thought of God as a friend. How many treasures would have been forever denied to me without my five years of penitence and meditation? The agony of prison was for me what a sweeter, more flexible soul would have found in the peace of the monastery.

"In days of anguish and fruitless remorse I had at times tried to flee the presence of man. But wherever I traveled, solitude always fled from me. Man, or his influence, or his despotic power over all creation, had pursued me even into the desert. Now in prison, in the midst of all that vice and crime in tatters howling beside me, I finally found isolation and silence. Although their voices beat on my ears, none reached my soul. These men had no moral connection with me. I was more alone in my relations with them than I could ever have been in the outside world. Within this calm and solitude my heart opened itself to the charms of nature. In the past, the most beautiful regions lit by the sun had not satisfied my blunted imagination. Now a pale beam of light between two clouds, the melodious refrain of the wind on the strand, the sound of waves, the melancholy cry of gulls, the far-off singing of a young girl, and the scent of a flower growing in a wall crack were vivid treasures. Often I looked through a murderer's narrow barred window onto the sea with its convulsive surge and its long waves of foam which moved from one end of the horizon to the other with the speed of lightning. My eyes stuck jealously to that opening. Did not this great sea, which my vision could embrace and over which my thoughts could freely wander, belong entirely to me? What did prison and chains matter? My imagination rode the tempest like the waves called forth by Ossian's harp.

"Since then I have crossed the sea on a small boat. I confess it seemed less beautiful. The winds were too slow and heavy, the waves less sparkling, less undulating. The sun rose and set less splendidly. This was no longer the sea that had rocked my dreams and that I had enjoyed all alone amid chained slaves."

"What is your life like now?" asked Sténio. "And what are your pleasures? Men like you care so little for material things that I see you aren't enjoying the advantages of affluence and freedom, which someone else would be drinking in great gulps after such a long abstinence."

"I would be arrogant," said Trenmor, "and worse, I would be stupid if I told you I'm insensitive to the return of all these long-lost pleasures. I have told you by what strange concurrence of events I managed to acquit myself toward my creditors and assure prosperity for the rest of my days. This came about as a result of travel, work, and certain well-directed activities. But prosperity was less of a necessity to me than to most men. Habituated as I am to the miseries of slavery and later of travel, I would have been able to accept as a blessing a rude hut on the shores of some new settlement, with the simple resources of nature and the fruit of my labor. Indifferent to my social future, I left it to chance, and what chance was given me I have gratefully accepted. Today I am perhaps the happiest of men because I live without plans or desires. My extinguished passions have left me an immense reservoir of memories and reflections. I live languidly, effortlessly, like a convalescent after violent illness. Have you ever felt this delicious numbness of the soul and body after days of nightmarish delirium? During these days, which are at the same time slow and swift, devoured of dreams, weary of incoherent and brusque sensations, one scarcely perceives the passage of time. Then perhaps you've emerged from this fantastic drama into which fever throws you to return to a calm, lazy life with idyllic walks under a warm sun, among plants you left as seeds that are now in flower. Perhaps you've walked slowly, still weak, along a placid stream, and you've listened vaguely to all nature's noises, nearly forgotten on a bed of suffering. Perhaps you've smiled at a bird's song and at the scent of a rose. Perhaps you, too, have taken to life again through all your pores. Then you can understand what repose is after the tempests of my life.

"But I must confess, I sometimes promised myself more happiness in this new life than I have found. This is how man's imagination is. It finds enjoyment beyond the present. As a slave I experienced intense joys through my hopes, my dreams of the future. When I was free I had to seek these promised joys in the memory of slavery, in dreams of the past. Well, all of that is sweet. These vague sufferings of a soul which seeks, waits, desires, and doesn't know itself, which builds marvels of future life and reconstructs the ruins of past life, these tender, sad aspirations toward an unknown happiness which never yields and is never exhausted—all this is the life of the soul. Those who don't know this and who put their ambitions into material wealth are unhappy. Wealth is unstable and capricious. But one never lacks dreams. There are always the treasures of expectation and memory."

Trenmor fell into a deep reverie. His companions imitated his silence. Beautiful Lélia watched the boat's wake, where the reflections of trembling stars made thin, moving threads of gold. Sténio, his eyes fixed on her, saw only Lélia in the universe. When the breeze, beginning to rise in brusque, occasional gusts, threw a tress of Lélia's black hair or a fringe of her shawl against his face, he shuddered like the waters of the lake, like the reeds along its shores. Then the breeze fell suddenly like an exhausted breath. Lélia's hair and the folds of her shawl fell back onto her bosom, and Sténio vainly sought a look from those eyes whose fire could pierce the shadows when Lélia deigned to be a woman. But what was Lélia thinking as she watched the boat's wake? —The breeze had dispersed the fog. Suddenly Trenmor perceived the trees of the shore only a few feet in front of him and, toward the horizon, the reddish lights of the town. He sighed deeply.

"We are here already!" he said. "Sténio, you row too fast. You have torn a very dear illusion from me. This fog deceived me. The noise of the oars, the evening cold, and above all the religious calm within me made me believe I was still in prison."

# XIV

A few hours later they were at a ball at Spuela's, the wealthy musician. Trenmor and Sténio stood beneath the cupola at the rear of a courtyard; and they watched the large rooms full of noise and movement. Dancers turned in capricious circles beneath dim candles. The flowers were dying in the heavy atmosphere. The sounds of the orchestra were muffled by the vaulted marble roof, and pale, sad, beautiful figures passed back and forth in their costumes through the hot, vaporous air. But above this rich tableau, above these tones, softened by the blurred depths of the courtyard and the weight of the atmosphere, above the costume masks, the sparkling apparel, the stylish quadrilles, the groups of young, laughing women, Lélia's tall, isolated figure stood out. She, too, was observing the ball as she leaned against an antique bronze column on the steps of the amphitheater. Dressed in a man's costume, austere but elegant, she had the serious gaze of a long-ago poet. Lélia's black hair, pulled back, left her face uncovered. God seemed to have impressed there the seal of a mysterious misfortune. Young Sténio gave her endless, questioning glances, with the anxiety of a navigator attentive to the least puff of wind and the slightest cloud in a clear sky. Lélia's cloak was less black, less velvety than her large eyes. The flat whiteness of her face and neck merged with her large ruff, and her cold breathing did not even seem to stir the black satin of her doublet and the triple chain of her gold necklace.

"Look at Lélia," said Trenmor with calm admiration, while the young man's heart beat violently. "Look at that tall Greek figure dressed in Italian clothing. Statuary has lost the mold of that antique beauty. Look at her features and at that richness of nature. Only a Homeric sun could create such types, now forgotten. Her physical beauty alone would affirm great strength. And God has endowed her with all the intellectual power of our time...! Can one imagine anything more complete than Lélia dressed, poised and dreaming as she is now? She is Pygmalion's Galatea, the perfect marble. She has Tasso's ethereal expression and Dante's somber smile. She has the easy, cavalier attitude of Shakespeare's young heroes: she is Romeo, the poetic lover; Hamlet, the pale, ascetic visionary; and Juliet, half-dead, hiding the poison and the memory of a broken love in her heart. You can inscribe the greatest names of history, theater, and poetry on such a face whose expression concentrates it all. Young Raphael must have fallen into that ecstatic contemplation when God made a virginal ideal of woman appear before him. Corinne,* dying, must have been plunged into mournful attention when she listened to her last poems being spoken at the Capitol by a young girl. Byron's mute, mysterious Lara is contained in this contemptuous isolation from the crowd. Yes, Lélia embodies all these ideals, because she embodies the genius of the poets, the grandeur of all heroisms. Lélia's luminous, pure brow and expansive heart contain all the exalted thoughts, all the generous feelings: religion, enthusiasm, stoicism, pity, perserverance, suffering, charity, forgiveness, ingenuousness, boldness, contempt for life, intelligence, activity, hope, patience—all the virtues! Even the innocent weaknesses, the sublime lightness characteristic of a woman, even the impulsive thoughtlessness, which is perhaps her sweetest privilege and her most powerful seduction."

"All except love! Alas!" said Sténio. "Then it is true! Trenmor, you haven't mentioned love, and you know Lélia. If Lélia cannot love, you have lied, because she is not complete. She is a dream men can create of her, gracious and sublime, but a dream that always lacks something unknown, something which has no name and which a cloud always veils from us, something beyond these heavens, something we continually reach for without attaining or understanding, something true, perfect, and immovable. Perhaps this is called God! In order to replace this lack in the human spirit, God has given man love, a weak emanation of heavenly fire, the soul of the universe perceptible to man. Without love, the most beautiful creation is without value. Without love, beauty is only a lifeless image. If Lélia cannot love, who is she? A shade, at the most a shadow of an idea. Believe me, where there is no love, there is no woman."

"And do you also believe," asked Trenmor, without answering what Sténio had hoped was a question, "that where there is no love, there is no man?"

---

*Heroine of *Corinne, or Italy*, a novel by Madame de Staël (1807). Corinne's lover marries her younger sister, and Corinne's consequent suffering brings about her death.

"I believe it with all my soul!" cried the young poet.

"In that case I too am dead," said Trenmor, smiling, "because I have no love for Lélia, and if she does not inspire it, who else could? Believe me, child, I hope you're mistaken and that love is like other passions—where they finish, man begins."

At this moment Lélia descended the steps and approached them. The sad majesty that surrounded her like an aura nearly always isolated her in a crowd: this was a woman who never expressed publicly what she left. She hid herself, and in her depths she laughed at life; but she made her way through it with bitter defiance. She appeared rigid so as to withdraw as much as possible from social contact. However, she loved festivities and public gatherings. She had come to enjoy a spectacle, to dream alone amid the crowd. People had to accustom themselves to seeing her hover around them, taking in impressions without ever communicating any. Between Lélia and the crowd there was no communication. If Lélia abandoned herself to mute sympathies, she refused to inspire any. She didn't need sympathy. People failed to understand this, but they were fascinated, and while they sought to disparage this unknown creature whose independence offended them, they made way before her with an instinctive respect tinged with fear.

The poor young poet who loved her began to understand a little better the source of her power, although he didn't yet want to admit this to himself. Sometimes he was so near the sad truth, which he both sought and repulsed, that he felt horrified by Lélia. Then she seemed to be his demon, his evil genius, and his most dangerous enemy. Seeing her come toward him, alone and pensive, he experienced something like hate for this woman who was held by no apparent bond to nature. He didn't realize that he would be suffering much more, the foolish man, if he were seeing her converse and smile.

"You are here," he said to her in a hard, bitter tone, "like a corpse that has opened its coffin to wander amid the living. See, people are moving away from you; they are afraid to touch your shroud; they scarcely dare look you in the face. Silence and fear hover around you like night birds. Your hand is as cold as the marble from which you come."

Lélia responded only by a strange look and a cold smile; then, after a moment of silence, "I had a very different idea just now," she said. "I took you all for dead people, and I myself, alive, examined you. I told myself that there is something strangely funereal in the invention of these masquerades. Isn't it sad to revive centuries that no longer exist and force them to entertain us now? Aren't these costumes of the past, which represent vanished generations, a frightening lesson to make us recall the brevity of human life in the midst of all this drunken festivity? Where are the passionate minds which once burned underneath these cardinal's caps and turbans? Where are the young, vivacious hearts which palpitated beneath the silken doublets and the bodices embroidered in gold and pearls? Where are the proud, beautiful women who draped themselves in heavy fabrics and who covered their elaborately done hair with these Gothic jewels? Alas! Where are these kings for a day who once sparkled like us? They have passed on without dreaming of the generations that preceded them or of the ones to follow, without dreaming that they themselves, who were covered with gold and perfume and who surrounded themselves with luxuries, were awaiting the cold of the shroud and the oblivion of the tomb."

"They are resting from having lived," said Trenmor. "Happy are those who sleep in Divine peace."

"Man's spirit must be very poor," said Lélia. "And his pleasures must be empty. Simple joys must be quickly exhausted, since at the depths of his joyous ceremonies he always meets with such an impression of sadness and terror. Here is a rich, happy man who numbs himself to forget that his days are numbered, and he can imagine nothing better than to dig up the spoils of the past and make his ancestors' ghosts dance in his palace!"

"Your soul is sad, Lélia," said Trenmor. "One would say that you alone fear not to die in your turn."

## XV [TRENMOR TO LÉLIA]

Lélia, this young man deserves more compassion. I believed you had only the graces and the adorable qualities of a woman. Do you also have a woman's ferocious ingratitude and her vanity? I prefer to doubt God's existence rather than the goodness of your heart. Lélia, tell me what you intend to do with that poet's soul, which has been entrusted to you and which you have received, perhaps imprudently. You can no longer repulse him without shattering him. So take care, Lélia, one day

God will demand an account from you. If God lowers His gaze enough to appreciate differences, doubtless young Sténio must be one of His chosen children. Doesn't Sténio reflect the beauty of angels? What is purer and sweeter than that child? Don't his soft eyelids, constantly lowered to veil a modest glance, seem to recall the chaste kisses of those winged virgins we see in our dreams? I have never seen a more angelically calm face, nor eyes of a more limpid and celestial blue. I have never heard a young girl's voice more harmonious than his. His words are like the velvety notes the wind confides to the strings of the harp. I think of his slow step, his dispassionate, sad attitude, his fine, white hands, his frail, supple body, his hair of such silken softness, his complexion that changes like the autumn sky, the blush a glance from you spreads over his cheeks, the bluish pallor your words imprint on his lips. He is a poet, a young man, a virgin. He is a soul God has sent among us to suffer and be tested before he is made an angel. If you surrender that young soul to the gust of corrosive passions, if you devastate him with icy despair and then abandon him, how will he find his way again to heaven? Oh woman, be careful! Don't crush this frail child beneath the weight of your fearful intelligence! Woman, help him walk. Cover him with your cloak. Guide him on the edge of the reefs. Can't you be his friend, or his sister, or his mother?

I know everything you have already told me about yourself, and I understand. But since you are as happy as you can be, I am no longer anxious about you. It is he who suffers and whom I pity. Look here, woman! You know so much more than most people. Can't you lessen his suffering? Can't you give anyone else a little of your God-given knowledge? Are you incapable of doing good?

Lélia, if this is so, you must send Sténio away or flee from him.

## XVI  [LÉLIA TO TRENMOR]

Send Sténio away or flee from him! Oh, not yet! You have such a cold, aged heart, my friend, that you speak of this as if it were merely a matter of leaving one town for another, or as if it were as simple as it would be for you to stay away from me.

I know you have escaped shipwreck, and you have reached your goal. No affection within you rises to passion. You need nothing, and you

depend on no one for your happiness. You are your own artisan and
guardian. Trenmor, I admire you, but I don't understand you. At the
most I suspect who you are. I admire the solid product you have created,
but it is a prison created by your intellect. I am a woman, an artist. Inside your walls of ice and stone I would die within a day. I need a palace.
I won't be happy there, but at least I won't perish. No, I don't feel that
it is God's will that I do as you say yet. If I am meant to attain your
development, it will be when I am ripe for wisdom and sure enough
of myself not to look back with sadness.

I can hear you say, "Weak, miserable woman. You fear obtaining
what you demand. I have seen you aspire to the triumph you repulse. . . ." Well, then, leave me. I am weak and cowardly, but I am
not ungrateful or vain. I don't have those feminine vices. No, my
friend, I can't break a man's heart, destroy a poet's soul. Be assured, I
love Sténio.

## XVII  [TRENMOR TO LÉLIA]

You tell me you love Sténio! Woman, you are lying. Think of whom
each of us is. You tell me you love Sténio. That can't be. Think of the
centuries that separate the two of you. You are a withered flower,
beaten, broken by the winds; you are a skiff tossed about by the seas,
stranded on all the shores, and would you dare attempt a new voyage?
Ah, you can't be serious, Lélia. What you need now is the repose of the
tomb. You have lived. Let others live. Don't throw yourself, a sad, fugitive ghost, in the way of those who haven't finished their work and
haven't lost their hope. Lélia, Lélia, haven't you suffered enough, poor
fated one? Sleep in your winding sheet. Sleep in your silence, weary
soul whom God no longer condemns to toil and suffering!

It's true you're less advanced than I am. You still retain a few memories of the past. You still struggle sometimes against man's enemy,
hope. But believe me, my sister, only a few steps separate you from me.
There is so little of the road to travel before we walk with the same
step toward eternal beatitude. You are certainly nearer to me than to
Sténio. And to join me you must advance; but to go to him you would
have to retreat; and that isn't possible. It is easy to age, but nothing
can make you young again.

Once more, let the child have faith and let him live. Don't suffocate the flower in its seed. Don't throw your icy breath over him. Don't hope to give life, Lélia, because life is no longer within you. There is only regret. Soon, like me, you will retain nothing but memory.

## XVIII [LÉLIA TO STÉNIO]

You promised you would be patient in your love and we would be happy. Sténio, don't try to advance time. Let life carry you along in its flow. Do you fear me? You must fear yourself. You must repress yourself. Because at your age imagination spoils the most delicious fruits and impoverishes all joys. At your age one doesn't know how to profit from anything; one wants to know, possess, and exhaust everything; and then one is astonished at the paucity of man's wealth, when one should be astonished only at man's heart and its needs. Believe me, walk slowly, savor the ineffable joys of a word, a look, or a thought, all the subtleties of a nascent love. Weren't we happy yesterday underneath the alders when we sat beside each other? We felt our clothing touch, and we understood each other with our looks. It was a dark night, but I still saw you, Sténio. I saw you as handsome as you are, and I imagined that you were the sylph of those woods, the spirit of that breeze, the angel of that mysterious and tender hour. Sténio, have you observed that there are hours when we are forced to love, hours when poetry floods through us, when our heart beats faster, when our soul rushes from us, breaking all the bonds of will as it seeks another soul with which to merge? How often at dusk, when the moon rises, at dawn, during the silence of midnight, or during that other silence of noon, so overwhelming, so unquiet, so devouring, I have felt my heart surge toward a formless, nameless happiness which is everywhere like an invisible magnet, or like love! But Sténio, this isn't love. You believe it to be, you who know nothing and who hope for everything. But I who know all, am aware that there lies something beyond this love which is formed out of ineradicable desires, needs, and hopes. Without this, what would man be? He has been given so few days on earth to love!

But at those hours what we feel is so alive and powerful that we diffuse it through our surroundings. At those hours, when God possesses and fills us, we reflect the burst of light that envelops us over all His creation.

Have you ever wept with love for the white stars strewn in the blue veils of night? Have you ever knelt down before them, stretched out your arms, and called them your sisters? As man loves to concentrate his affections, and as he is too weak for vast emotions, did you ever grow passionate over one of them? Did you choose lovingly, among them all, sometimes that red, scintillating star that rises over the black forests of the horizon, sometimes that pale, soft star that veils itself like a chaste virgin behind the reflections of the moon, sometimes the three sisters, equally white, equally beautiful, who sparkle in a mysterious triangle, sometimes those two radiant companions who sleep side by side in the pure sky among myriads of lesser glories. And all those cabalistic signs, all those strange, gigantic, sublime symbols they trace over our heads. Have you ever let yourself enjoy the fantasy of explaining them and discovering there the great mysteries of our fate, the age of the world, the name of God, the future of the soul? Yes, I know you have questioned these stars with ardent sympathy, and you believed you met currents of love in their trembling rays. You believed you felt a voice from on high caress you and say: "Hope. You come from us. Will you return to us? It is I who am your fatherland. It is I who call you. It is I who must belong to you one day!"

Sténio, love isn't what you think it is. It isn't that violent aspiration of our entire being toward another. Rather, it is the aspiration of our most ethereal part for the unknown. As we are limited creatures, we continually try to deceive our burning, insatiable desires. We try to fulfill them in a nearby goal, and, poor prodigals that we are, we array our perishable idols in all the immaterial beauties perceived in our dreams. Sensual emotion is not enough for us. Nature has nothing rare enough within the treasury of its naive joys to appease the thirst for happiness within us. We must have heaven, and we don't have it!

That is why we seek heaven in a creature like ourselves, and we expend on this creature all that high energy we've been given to use more nobly. We refuse God the emotion of adoration, an emotion which was put in us to return to God alone. We transfer it to an incomplete, feeble human being who becomes the god of our idolatrous cult. In the youth of the world, when man hadn't warped his soul and misunderstood his own heart, the love of one sex for the other such as we conceive it today did not exist. Pleasure alone was a bond. Moral passion with its obstacles, its suffering, its intensity, is an evil that those generations did not know. Then there were gods, and today there no longer are gods.

Today, with poetic souls, the feeling of adoration even enters physical love. Strange error of a greedy, impotent generation! When the divine veil falls and the human being reveals himself, puny and imperfect, behind those clouds of incense and that halo of love, we are frightened by our illusion. We blush, overturn the idol, and trample it beneath our feet.

And then we look for someone else! Because we must love; and we continue to be deceived until disillusioned, enlightened, purified, we finally abandon hope of a durable affection on earth. Then we raise to God that enthusiastic, pure homage that we should have directed only to Him.

## XIX [STÉNIO TO LÉLIA]

Lélia, why did you write to me? I was happy, and now you cast me back upon my old anxieties. That hour of silence we spent together had revealed such joys to me! And Lélia, already you repent of this. What do you fear from my greedy impatience? You misunderstand me expressly. You know I'll be happy with very little, because nothing you do for me seems trivial, because I will attach to your least favors their proper worth. I am not presumptuous. I know how far beneath you I am. Lélia, you are cruel! Why do you continually make me conscious of this trembling humility that makes me suffer so much?

I understand, Lélia! Alas, I do. You can only love God. Only in heaven can your soul rest. When, in an hour of reverie, you looked lovingly at me, you were thinking of God; and you mistook a man for an angel. When the moon rose, it lit my features and dissipated that darkness so favorable to your gilded fantasies. Then you smiled with pity as you recognized Sténio's face, on which, however, you had imprinted a kiss!

Lélia, you want me to forget. You're afraid I might cling to that intoxicating sensation. Be reassured, I haven't tasted this happiness blindly. If it has devoured my blood and shattered my heart, it has not unhinged me. Lélia, I am not one of those unscrupulous Don Juans for whom a woman's kiss is a pledge of love. I don't believe myself endowed with the power to animate marble and revive the dead.

However, your breath set my brain on fire. Scarcely had your lips brushed against my hair when I felt an electric spark, so terrible a turmoil that a cry of suffering escaped me. Oh, you are not a woman, Lélia, I see this clearly. I dreamed of heaven in a kiss from you, and at that instant you made me know hell.

But your smile was so sweet and your words so soft and consoling that I gradually let myself be made happy by you. That first terrible impression was blunted, and finally I was able to touch your hand without trembling. You showed me paradise, and I ascended there with your wings.

I was happy that night when I remembered your last glance, your last words. I wasn't flattering myself, Lélia, I swear to you. I knew very well that you didn't love me, but I went to sleep in that soft numbness into which you had plunged me. Now you awaken me to cry out in your mournful voice: "Remember, Sténio, that I cannot love you!" I know this, Madame, I know this only too well.

## XX [STÉNIO TO LÉLIA]

Farewell, Lélia. I am going to kill myself. Today you have made me happy. Tomorrow you'll very quickly tear away the happiness that you gave me this evening through either carelessness or caprice.

The poison is prepared. Now I can speak freely. You won't see me again. You can no longer drive me to despair. Perhaps you'll regret the victim it amused you to torment with your capricious whims. You told me you love me more than Trenmor, although you esteem me less. It's true that you can't torture Trenmor as you please; against him your power fails. Your tigerish woman's nails have no grip on that diamond heart. I was soft wax that received all your impressions. I understand that, as an artist, you found more pleasure in tormenting me. When you were sad, you imprinted that feeling on your work. When you were calm, you gave him the calm atmosphere of angels. When irritated, you communicated the frightening smile that the devil had put on your lips. This is how the sculptor makes a god and then a reptile out of the same clay.

Lélia, forgive these instants of hate that you inspire in me. I love you with passion, with delirium, with despair. I can say this to you without offending or disobeying you, since this is the last time I speak to you. You have hurt me so much! However, it would have been easy to make me happy, a poet with laughing thoughts, with buoyant sensations. With a word each day, a smile each evening, you would have made me great. Instead, you sought only to blight and discourage me. All the while saying you wanted to conserve the sacred fire within me, you quenched it to the last spark. Then you relit it viciously so as to surprise the outbreak and smother the flame. Now I renounce love. I renounce life. Are you content? Goodbye.

It is nearly midnight. I am going . . . where you will not go, Lélia. Because it is impossible for us to have the same future. We don't worship the same god; we don't inhabit the same heavens. . . .

## XXI

Midnight sounded. Trenmor entered Sténio's dwelling. He found him seated pensively near the fire. Outside it was cold and dark. The north wind whistled sharply beneath the empty, resonant paneling. On the table in front of Sténio was a cup filled to the brim, which Trenmor knocked over as he brushed against it with his coat.

"You must come with me to Lélia's," he said with grave calmness. "Lélia wants to see you. I think her hour has come and that she is going to die."

Sténio rose abruptly, then fell onto his chair, pale and without strength. Then he got up again, convulsively took Trenmor's arm, and they ran to Lélia's.

She was lying on a sofa. Her cheeks had a blue reflection. Her eyes seemed sunken beneath her deeply arched brows. A deep line crossed her forehead, ordinarily so white and polished. But her voice was full and assured, and a disdainful smile wandered, as usual, over her mobile lips.

Near her was Doctor Kreyssneifetter, a charming young man, blond and rosy, with a nonchalant smile, white hands, and sweet, protective speech. Doctor Kreyssneifetter had familiarly taken one of Lélia's hands between his own. From time to time he would feel her pulse. Then he would pass his other hand through his beautiful curls, which were artistically raised to a point on the crest of his noble skull.

"It's nothing," he said with an amiable smile, "nothing at all. It's cholera, cholera morbus, the most common thing in the world these days and the best-known illness. Reassure yourself, beautiful angel! You have cholera, a sickness that can kill in two hours those who are weak enough to be frightened of it. But it is not dangerous at all to our firm spirits. Don't be frightened, charming stranger! You and I don't fear the cholera, we defy it! Let's frighten off this villainous specter, this hideous monster which makes people's hair stand on end. Let's jeer at the cholera; it's the only way to deal with it."

"But," said Trenmor, "have you tried Doctor Magendie's medicine?"

"Why not Doctor Magendie's medicine," said Doctor Kreyssneifetter, "if the invalid has no aversion to that concoction."

"I have heard," said Lélia with caustic coldness, "that it is very disagreeable. Let's try the laudanum instead."

"Let's try the laudanum if you believe in its virtue," said Doctor Kreyssneifetter.

"But what would you advise, according to your conscience?" asked Sténio.

At the mention of conscience, Doctor Kreyssneifetter threw a look of mocking compassion at the young poet. Then he regained his composure and said gravely, "My conscience tells me to recommend nothing at all, and not to intervene at all in this illness."

"That's very well, Doctor," said Lélia. "Then since it's late, good night! Don't interrupt your precious sleep any longer."

"Oh, don't bother about that," he replied. "I'm fine here. I enjoy following the progress of the illness. I study, I love my profession with passion, and I willingly sacrifice my pleasures and my rest. If necessary I would sacrifice my life for the good of humanity."

"What is your profession, Doctor Kreyssneifetter?" asked Trenmor.

"I console and I encourage," replied the doctor. "That's my vocation. —Study has revealed to me the importance of the diseases that afflict man. I diagnose, I assist at the denouement, and I profit from my observations."

"To arrange for the hygienic precautions applicable to your amiable person," said Lélia.

"I believe little in the influence of any system whatever," said the doctor. "We are all born with the principle of death in the more or less immediate future. Our efforts to retard death often only hasten it. It's best not to think about it and to wait for it while forgetting that it must come."

"You are very philosophic," said Lélia, taking some tobacco from the doctor's gold snuff box. But she had a convulsion and fell dying into Sténio's arms.

"Come, my beautiful child," said the young, beardless doctor. "A little courage. If you let yourself be affected in the least by your state, you are lost. But you run no more risk than I do if you keep the same sang-froid."

Lélia raised herself on one elbow and, looking at him with eyes dulled by suffering, still found the strength to smile with irony.

"Poor doctor," she said. "I'd like to see you in my place!"

"Thank you," thought the doctor.

"You were saying just now that you didn't believe in the influence of remedies. Don't you believe in medicine then?" she asked.

"Excuse me, the study of anatomy and the knowledge of the human body, with its deteriorations and its infirmities, is a positive science."

"Yes," said Lélia. "You cultivate it as an art of amusement. My friends," she said, turning her back to the doctor, "go find me a priest. I see the doctor has abandoned me."

Trenmor ran to get a priest. Sténio wanted to throw the doctor from the balcony.

"Let him be," Lélia said. "He amuses me. Give him a book and take him into my dressing room so that he can occupy himself in front of a mirror. When I feel courage abandon me, I'll call him so that he can give me stoic counsel, and I can die laughing at the man and at the science."

The priest arrived. He was the tall, handsome Irish priest of the Chapel of Sainte-Laure. He approached austerely and slowly. His manner inspired religious respect. His calm, profound gaze, which seemed to reflect the sky, was enough to give faith. Lélia, broken by suffering, had hidden her face beneath her bent arm, which was entwined with her black hair.

"Sister," said the priest in a full and fervent voice.

Lélia let her arm fall and slowly turned her face to the man of God.

"This woman again!" he cried, drawing back with terror.

He had been thrown into confusion. His eyes grew fixed, he turned ashen, and Sténio remembered the day he had seen him tremble as he met Lélia's skeptical look above the prostrate crowd.

"It's you, Magnus!" she said. "Do you recognize me?"

"Do I recognize you, woman!" cried the priest. "Do I recognize you! Lies, despair, desolation!"

Lélia responded only with a laugh.

"Let's see," she said, drawing him to her with her cold, bluish hand. "Come here, Priest, and speak to me of God. You know why they asked you to come. A soul is about to leave the earth and must be sent to heaven. Don't you have the power?"

The priest remained silent, terrified.

"Come, Magnus," she said with a sad irony, turning up to him her pale face, already covered with the shadow of death. "Fulfill the mission the Church entrusted to you. Save me. Don't waste time. I'm going to die."

"Lélia," said the priest. "I can't save you. You know this very well. Your power is superior to mine."

"What does that mean?" asked Lélia, raising herself up on the couch. "Am I already in the land of dreams? Do I no longer belong to the human species which crawls, begs, and dies? And is this frightened shadow a priest? Magnus, is your mind troubled? You stand here alive, and I am dying. But your thoughts are confused, and your soul grows weak while mine calmly summons the strength to die. Come, man of little faith, invoke God for your dying sister and leave to children these superstitious fears that ought to arouse your pity. Truly, who are you all? Here is Trenmor, astonished. Here is Sténio, the young poet, who looks at my feet and thinks he perceives claws there. And here is a priest who refuses to absolve and bury me! Am I already dead? Is this a dream?"

"No, Lélia," said the priest finally in a solemn voice. "I don't take you for a demon. I don't believe in demons; you know that very well."

"Ah, ah!" she said, turning toward Sténio. "Listen to the priest. There is nothing less poetic than human perfection. So, Father, let us deny Satan, condemn him to nothingness. I don't prize his alliance, although the satanic manner is much in style, and it has inspired Sténio with some very beautiful poems in my honor. If the devil doesn't exist, I'm very much at peace over my future. I can leave life now. I won't go to hell. But tell me, where will I go? Where do you want to send me, Father? To heaven?"

"To heaven!" cried Magnus. "Did your mouth pronounce that word?"

"Is there no longer a heaven?" asked Lélia.

"Woman," said the priest, "there is none for you."

"This is a consoling priest," she said. "Since he can't save my soul, bring in the doctor. Perhaps he will decide to save my life for gold or silver."

"I see nothing to do," said Doctor Kreyssneifetter. "The illness follows a regular, well-known course. Are you thirsty? Let someone bring you water, and be calm, and wait. Medicines will kill you at this point. Let Nature act."

"Ah, Nature," said Lélia. "I would certainly like to call on you. But who are you? Where is your mercy, where is your love, where is your pity? I know that I come from you and I must return to you, but by what right can I implore you to let me stay here another day? Perhaps a corner of arid earth needs my dust to make grass grow. Then I must go to fulfill my destiny. But you, Priest, call on the One who is above Nature and who can command it. Call on the One who can tell the pure air to revive my breath, the sap of plants to strengthen me, the sun to warm my blood. Teach me to pray to God."

"God!" said the priest, letting his head fall despondently onto his breast. "God!"

Burning tears ran over his withered cheeks.

"Oh, God!" he said. "Oh, sweet dream which has fled from me! Where are you? How will I find you again? Hope, why have you abandoned me? . . . Madame, allow me to leave you. When I am with you all my doubts take over. Here in the presence of death my last hope and my last illusion vanish. You want me to help you find God and give you heaven. You are going where you will find out if He does exist. You are happier than I because I don't know."

"Go away," said Lélia. "Arrogant men, leave my bedside. And you, Trenmor, see this doctor who doesn't believe in science. See this priest who doesn't believe in God. However, the doctor is a scientist, the priest a theologian. One supposedly comforts the dying; the other consoles the living; and both lack faith beside a dying woman."

"Madame," said Kreyssneifetter, "if I had tried to play the doctor on you, you would have jeered at me. I know you. You are not an ordinary person. You are a philosopher. . . . "

"Madame," said Magnus, "Don't you remember our walk in the forest of Grimsel? If I had dared to play the priest with you, wouldn't you have ended by rendering me an unbeliever?"

"You see," said Lélia in a bitter tone. "On what is your strength based? The weakness of another is the source of your power. But as soon as someone resists, you draw back, and you laughingly avow that you play a false role among men, charlatans and imposters that you are! Alas, Trenmor, what have we become? What is this century coming to? The scientist denies; the priest doubts. Let us see if the poet still exists. Sténio, take up your harp and sing me verses from Faust, or else open your books and tell me again about the sufferings of Obermann, the transports of Saint-Preux. Let us see, poet, if you still understand suffering. Let us see, young man, if you still believe in love."

"Alas, Lélia," cried Sténio, wringing his white hands. "You're a woman, and you don't believe it! What have we become? What is this century coming to?"


# XXII


"God of heaven and earth, God of strength and love, listen to the pure voice of a virgin soul. Listen to a youth's prayer. Give us back Lélia.

"My God, why do You want to tear away our well-beloved? Listen to Trenmor's strong voice. He has suffered and lived. Listen to the plea of a soul still ignorant of life's evils. Both ask You to save their treasure. If You wish to envelop her in the glory of Your eternal bliss, when she is still so young, take her back, God, she belongs to You. But, in saving Lélia, don't destroy us, oh God! Permit us to follow and kneel on the steps of the throne where she is to sit. . . . "

"That is very beautiful," said Lélia, interrupting him, "but it is nothing more than verses. Let the harp sleep in peace, or put it by the window where the wind will play it better than you. Now come to me. And Trenmor, go away. Your calm saddens and discourages me. Come, Sténio, talk to me about us. God is too far away. I am afraid that He doesn't hear us. But God has put a little of Himself in you. Show me the divinity your soul possesses. I feel that a very ardent aspiration of your soul toward mine, a very fervent prayer addressed to me would give me the strength to live. The strength to live! Yes, it is only a matter of will. Sténio, my illness consists of not being able to find that will in myself.—Trenmor, you are smiling! Go away.—Alas, Sténio, this is true.

I try to resist death, but I try feebly. I fear it less than I desire it. I would like to die through curiosity. I need heaven, alas, but I doubt it exists. ... If there is no heaven above the stars, I would like to continue contemplating it from the earth. Perhaps, oh God, we only need to put our hopes in heaven while we are here below. Perhaps heaven is in the heart of man.... Tell me, you are so young and full of life, is love paradise? See, my mind is growing weak. Forgive this moment of delirium. I would like very much to believe in something, if only in you, if only for an hour before I finish, perhaps forever, with men and God."

"Doubt God, doubt men, doubt me if you wish," said Sténio, kneeling before her. "But don't doubt love. Lélia, don't doubt your heart! If you must die now, and if I must lose you, my torment, my treasure, my hope, let me at least believe in you for an hour, a moment. Alas, will you die before I have seen you live? Will I die along with you without ever having embraced you except as a dream? My God, is love only to be found in a desirous heart, in a suffering imagination, in the dreams which lull us during lonely nights? Is love an impalpable breath? Is love a meteor that burns and dies? Is it a word? My God, what is love? Oh, God, oh, Lélia, won't you teach me?"

"This child demands the secret of life from death," said Lélia. "He kneels at a coffin to obtain love. Poor child. My God, have pity on him and spare my life so that I can save his. If You do this, I vow to live for him. He says I have committed a sacrilege against You in desecrating love. Well, I will be humble, I will believe, I will love. ... Only let me live the life of the body, and I will try to live the life of the soul."

"Listen, oh, my God, do You hear?" cried Sténio deliriously. "Do You hear what she says, what she promises? Save her. Save me. Give me Lélia...!"

Lélia fell stiff and cold on the parquet floor. It was a last, horrible crisis. Sténio pressed her against him, crying with despair. His heart was burning, his hot tears fell on Lélia's brow. His kisses brought the blood back to her lips, and perhaps his prayer reached heaven: Lélia weakly opened her eyes and said to Trenmor, who was helping her sit up, "Sténio has revived my soul. If you want to break it again with your reason, kill me immediately."

"And why would I take your last day from you?" asked Trenmor. "Your last wing feather hasn't yet fallen."

# PART TWO

## XXIII MAGNUS

One morning Sténio descended the wooded slopes of Mount Rosa.
After wandering aimlessly on a path covered with thick vegetation, he
reached a clearing opened by avalanches. It was a wild, grandiose place.
Somber, vigorous verdure crowned the ruins of the crevassed mountain.
Old black, powdery rocks, which lay helpless, scattered in the ravine,
were entwined by the fragrant branches of long clematis. On each side
of the ravine the open flanks of the mountain rose in gigantic walls,
bordered by dark pines and tapestried with Virginia creepers. At the
depths of the gorge a torrent ran its clear, noisy waters on a bed of
richly colored pebbles. If you have never seen such a torrent, purified
by its thousand waterfalls, on the naked entrails of a mountain, you
don't know the beauty of water and its pure harmonies.

Sténio loved to pass the nights wrapped up in his coat beside a waterfall, under the religious shelter of the great, wild cypresses, whose mute,
motionless branches muffle the breeze. The wandering voices of the air
are stopped by their thick leaves, while the profound, mysterious notes
of the water run out of the bosom of the earth and pass into the air like

religious choruses in the depths of funereal caves. As he lay on the fresh, glowing grass that grows on the banks of streams, the poet forgot the hours he could have spent with Lélia while he contemplated the moon and listened to the water: because at that age everything in love, even absence, is joy. The heart of the one who loves is so full that he needs reflection and solitude to savor everything that he believes he sees in the object of his passion, which is in reality only in himself.

Sténio spent many nights in ecstasy. Tufts of purple heather hid his head, agitated with burning dreams. The morning dew strewed his fine hair with tears. The great forest pines wafted over him the perfumes they exhale at dawn, and the sparrow, beautiful, solitary bird of the torrents, came to throw out its melancholy cry amid the blackish stones and the white foam. This was a beautiful life of love and youth. It concentrated the happiness of a hundred lives, but it passed as rapidly as the churning water and the fugitive bird of the waterfalls.

A thousand diverse, melodious voices, a thousand somber or brilliant colors are in the fall and running of water. Sometimes, furtive and discreet, it flows with a nervous trembling against marble fragments which cover it with the reflection of their bluish-black hue. Sometimes, as white as milk, it froths on the rocks with a voice that seems choked by anger. Sometimes, as green as the grass it barely touches in its passage; sometimes, as blue as the peaceful sky it reflects, it hisses amid the reeds like an amorous snake. Or else it sleeps in the sun and awakens with feeble sighs at the least breath of wind. At other times it roars like a lost heifer and falls, monotonous and solemn, into a whirlpool, which swallows it. Then it throws out jetting drops to the sun, colored with all the hues of the rainbow. When this capricious iridescence dances over the gaping chasm of the ravine, there is no sylph transparent enough, no juggler smooth enough for the imagination contemplating it. Reverie can evoke nothing, because in the creations of thought nothing is as beautiful as brute, savage nature. One must look and feel before nature: the greatest poet invents the least.

But Sténio had love, the source of all poetry in his heart. And because of love he crowned the most beautiful scenes with a great thought, a great image: Lélia. How beautiful Lélia was, reflected in the waters of the mountain and in the poet's soul! How grave and sublime she seemed to him in the moonlight! How her voice rose, full and inspired, in the moan of the wind, in the harmonies of the waterfall, in the magnetic respiration of plants that seek each other out, call each other, embrace each other in the darkness of night, at the hour of sacred mysteries and divine revelations! Then Lélia was everywhere, in the air, in the sky, in the waters, in the flowers, in the bosom of God. Sténio saw her mobile, penetrating look in the reflection of the stars. He seized her uncertain words in the sound of the wind. In the murmur of the wave he heard her sacred chants and her prophetic tears. In the pure blue of the firmament he believed he saw her thought hover, sometimes like a disembodied spirit, pale, unsure, and sad, sometimes like an angel bursting with light, sometimes like a mocking demon full of hatred: because there was always something frightening about her in the depths of his reveries. And fear pressed the passionate desires of the young man with its sharp spurs.

In the delirium of wandering nights, in the silence of deserted valleys, he called to her with loud cries. When his voice awoke the sleeping echoes, he seemed to hear Lélia's far-off voice respond sadly from the clouds. When the noise of his steps frightened a deer cowering in the broom, he would hear it brush the thin, dry leaves in its path as it fled, and he imagined he heard Lélia's light steps and her gown brushing against the flowers of the thicket. If some beautiful bird of those regions, a grouse with its silver bosom, a pink and grey sparrow, or a black raven came to sit near him and look at him with a calm, proud air, ready to take flight, Sténio would think that perhaps it was Lélia who was flying off in this form toward freer regions.

"Perhaps," he thought to himself with a credulous, childish terror as he descended again toward the valley, "perhaps I will no longer find Lélia among human beings."

And fearfully he reproached himself for having been able to leave her a few hours, although he had carried her with him everywhere in his wanderings. He had filled the mountains and clouds with her; he had peopled the most inaccessible heights, the most inaccessible regions of his hope with her memory and her apparition.

That day he stopped short at the entrance of the clearing and prepared to turn back because he saw a man in front of him. And the most beautiful place loses its charm when one comes there to dream but finds oneself no longer alone.

However, this man was as beautiful and severe as the site. His eyes glowed like the rising sun. The first fires of day, which were lighting up the glacier, also illumined the priest's imposing countenance. It was Magnus. He seemed to have surrendered to strong impressions. Suffering and joy in turn expressed themselves on his face, tenaciously and powerfully. He seemed renewed by enthusiasm.

As soon as he saw Sténio he ran up to him.

"So it's you, young man," he said triumphantly. "I see that you are alone, you are sad, you are here seeking God! The woman is no longer alive!"

"The woman!" said Sténio. "For me there is only one woman in the world. But who are you speaking of?"

"Of the only woman in the world who existed for you and me, of Lélia. Tell me, young man, is she truly dead? Did she renounce God as she rendered her soul to the devil? Did you see the black army of the spirits of darkness besiege her in her last agony? Did you see her cursed soul go out of the body with its wings of fire and its bloody talons?— Ah, now we can breathe! God has purged the earth. He has plunged Satan back into chaos. We can pray and hope. See how joyously the sun rises. See how the fresh, red roses of the valley are opening. See how the birds shake their moist wings and take flight again. Everything is reborn, everything hopes, everything is going to live. Lélia is dead!"

"Unhappy man!" cried Sténio, seizing the priest by his throat. "What delirious thoughts are tormenting you? Where did you get the information of which you dare speak? How long ago did you leave Lélia?"

"I left Lélia on a cold, grey morning just before dawn. The cock was chanting shrilly. Its voice rose in the silence and knocked like a prophetic malediction against the roofs of the town. The north wind cried through the deserted cathedral patio. I walked along the length of the outer arches to get to the lodging of that woman who was dying. The small, jagged columns hid their spires in the fog, and the great statue of the Archangel, which rises on the eastern side, bathed his pale brow in the morning dew. Then I distinctly saw the Archangel shake his great stone wings like an eagle ready to take flight, but his feet remained chained to the cement of the cornice, and I heard his voice saying: *Lélia is not yet dead!* Then an owl skimmed my brow with its damp wings and repeated in a bitter tone: *Lélia is not dead!* And the white marble Virgin who is enshrined in the eastern niche sighed deeply and said: *Not yet!* in a voice so feeble I believed it was a dream, and I stopped several times along the way to assure myself that I wasn't under the spell of dreams."

"Priest," said Sténio, "your mind is troubled. Of what morning are you speaking? Do you know how long ago the things you speak of happened?"

"Since then," said Magnus, "I have seen the sun rise several times in its glory and hurl its beautiful rays on that sparkling glacier. I cannot tell you how many times. Since Lélia is no longer alive, I no longer count the days, I no longer count the nights, I let my life run pure and carefree like the mountain stream. My soul is saved. . . . "

"You have lost your mind, God be praised!" said the young man. "You are referring to the deadly sickness which nearly took Lélia away from us a month ago. Indeed, I see by your hair and beard that you have been on the mountain a long time. Come with me. I will try to console you as I listen to the tale of your suffering."

"I no longer suffer," said the priest with a smile that one would have taken for a celestial inspiration, it was so sweet and calm. "I am alive: Lélia is dead. Listen to my tale of joy. When I reached that woman's lodging, I felt the earth tremble. When I tried to climb the stairs, the stairs drew back three times before I could put my feet down on them. But when the doors opened, I saw a great many people, and I immediately remembered what expression a priest should wear before the world to make people respect both the priest and God. I totally forgot Lélia. I made my way through the apartments without fear or confusion. When I entered the last room, I no longer remembered who I was coming to see because, I tell you, there were so many people, and I felt their looks entirely on me. Do you know the weight of people looking at you? Have you ever tried to raise it? Oh, it weighs more than this mountain. But to know it exactly one must be a priest and wear the habit you see me wearing now . . . I remember, it was a small room with white wall hangings, all filled with traps and ambushes. At first I believed that I was walking on a soft, fine woolen carpet. I believed I saw white roses in alabaster vases and lights in globes of dull green. I also believed I saw a woman dressed in white, lying stretched out on a bed of white satin. But when she turned her pale face to me, when I met her brazen look, the charm that had been weighing on me vanished. I saw clearly around me, and I recognized where they had led me. The roses changed into snakes and writhed on their stems as they raised their menacing heads to me. The walls were stained with blood, the vases of perfume were filled with tears, and I saw that my feet no longer touched earth. The lamps vomited red flames that mounted toward the ceiling in fiery spirals, suffocating me like remorse. I turned my eyes again to the canopy: she was still Lélia, but she was on a blazing stove, and she was expiring in the midst of atrocious suffering. She begged me to save her, I remember this clearly. But I remembered, too, the vain prayers I had once made, the useless tears I had shed at her feet, and resentment filled my heart. She had damned my soul and taken God from me. I was glad to avenge myself, to let her soul be lost, and to strip away God from her in turn. This is why I cursed her, and I was saved. God rewarded my courage, because a cloud immediately spread over my vision. Lélia disappeared, and the snakes too, and the tongues of fire and the blood and the tears all disappeared. I found myself standing alone at the foot of the cathedral arches. Day was breaking; the fog had dissipated a little. Then the stone Archangel carried to his lips the trumpet he had held motionlessly for several centuries. He blew a blasting fanfare in which I distinguished that redeeming cry: *Lélia is no more!* The owl flew back beneath the cornice which serves as his retreat, repeating, *Lélia is no more!* The white marble Virgin, at whom I had not dared look when I passed by her feet because she resembled Lélia, that Virgin, so pale and so beautiful, who had seven sword wounds in her bosom and all the sufferings of the soul on her brow, fell broken on the church steps. If I lived a hundred years I would never forget that. Tell me, have you seen the debris?"

"I passed by her last night," replied Sténio, "and I assure you she is still very beautiful and in good health."

"Young man, don't be impious," said the priest with frightening seriousness. "God will afflict you with the same curse: He will drive you insane. I am afraid you already are, because you talk like someone deprived of reason. Do you know what man is? Do you know what God is? Do you know the world; do you know heaven?"

"Priest, let me leave you," said Sténio, whom the deranged man was trying to lead to his grotto. "I can no longer listen to you without being terrified. You curse Lélia, you condemn her to nothingness. And still you dare speak of God, and you dare wear the clothes of His ministry!"

"Child," said the priest, "I curse Lélia because I fear God and because I respect the habit I wear. Lélia! My loss, my ruin, my seduction. Lélia, whom I was forbidden to possess, even to desire! Lélia, that atrocious, infamous woman who sought me out in the depths of the sanctuary and who violated the sanctity of the altar to intoxicate me with her satanic caresses...!"

"You are lying!" cried Sténio furiously. "Lelia never pursued you, never loved...!"

"Eh, I know it," said the priest tranquilly. "You don't understand. Listen, sit down with me on the trunk of this larch tree, which serves as a bridge above the chasm. There, come nearer, put your hand in mine, fear nothing. The tree bends, the torrent moans, the whirlpool foams down there in those black depths: all this is beautiful. It is the image of life."

Speaking like this, the insane man clasped Sténio in his feverish arms. He was taller than Sténio by an entire head, and delirium augmented his muscular strength. He looked bleakly into the whirlpool, measuring its depths, while his distracted, convulsive hands seemed entirely ready to throw the young man down into it. In spite of the danger of this situation, Sténio was so eager to hear about the secret between Lélia and the priest, which had long tortured his jealous soul, that he remained seated tranquilly on a single tree trunk trembling above the precipice. This is called the *bridge of hell*. Each gorge, each torrent has its perilous crossing called by the same exaggerated name, and passable only to the chamois,* to hardy hunters, and to slender daughters of the mountain.

"Listen, listen," said the priest. "There were two Lélias. You did not know that because you weren't a priest. You had no revelations, visions, or presentiments. You lived naturally—a coarse, easy, common life. I was a priest. I was acquainted with the things of heaven and earth. I saw Lélia as double and complete, woman and idea, hope and reality, body and soul, gift and promise. I saw Lélia as she had left the bosom of God: she was beauty, that is to say temptation; she was hope, that is to say, a test; and she was a blessing, that is to say a lie. Do you understand me?—Oh this is very clear. And if all men were not insane, they would listen to a wise man's words. She was my enemy! She was my double. She would sit down in the evening in the gallery of the nave, I saw it clearly. I knew the place she habitually appeared only too well. It was in an ornate alcove, all draped in pale blue velvet. I can still see

---

*A goatlike animal, native to the mountains of Europe.

that accursed place! It was between two projecting columns which suspended it between the arch and the ground on frail garlands of stone. There were two sculpted angels, as white as snow, as beautiful as hope, who joined their white hands and crossed their marble wings over the shield of the balustrade. It was just there she would sit, that woman! She would lean over with an impious calm and support her insolent elbow on the bent brows of those two beautiful angels. She would play with the silver fringe of the draperies; she would rearrange her curls; she would look boldly over the church instead of bowing her head and adoring the Eternal. Oh no, she hadn't come to pray. She came for diversion, to exhibit herself, to rest from parties and masquerades while she listened for an hour to the organ and the hymns. And all your fops, all your fine ladies and gentlemen, all your useless people were there, following each one of her movements with their eyes, watching for her slightest glance, trying to seize the thought in the impenetrable depths of her eyes, and stirring themselves up like the damned in their tombs at midnight to draw her envied attention on themselves. But how great and imposing Lélia was! How she hovered over them all with disdain. And I loved her then. I blessed her for her pride. She was so beautiful beneath the dull light of the candles, pale and serious and proud, but with a certain sweetness. Oh, you others never possessed her. You didn't know what was going on in her heart. You were no more fortunate than I! How that thought drew me to her. Tell me, did you ever penetrate her soul? Did you ever divine the ideas fermenting in her great brow? Did you ever hollow out her head and burrow there in the treasures of her thought? No, you have never done that. Lélia never belonged to you either. You don't know who she is. You've seen her smile sadly or dream with a bored air. But you've never seen her bosom swell and her tears flow. You've never seen her anger, her hate, or her love spill out! Tell me, young man, have you been more fortunate with her than I have? If you tell me you have been, understand, this chasm won't be deep enough to receive you."

"And the other Lélia, who is she?" asked the young man, without the slightest fear of Magnus's vehemence.

"The other Lélia!" cried Magnus, striking his forehead as if an atrocious torment had been awakened there. "The other! She was a hideous monster, a harpy, a disembodied spirit, but she was still the same Lélia. Only it was her other half!"

"Where did you find her?" asked Sténio uneasily.

"Oh, everywhere!" said the priest. "At night when my duties were finished, when the tapers had gone out and the crowd spilled through the church doors, pressing close behind the pale woman called Lélia, who walked slowly away, dressed in her black velvet coat, a cortege following in her wake at whom she did not deign to glance . . . I followed her, too, with my eyes, with my soul, and I realized I was a priest. I was chained to the foot of the altar. I couldn't run out beneath the columns, mix with the crowd, gather up her glove, steal a rose petal fallen from her bouquet. I couldn't offer her holy water and touch her slender hands, so soft and so beautiful."

"And so cold!" said Sténio, carried away. "Granite continually washed by water from the glacier is no colder than Lélia's hand."

"Have you touched her hand?" asked the priest, gripping him in rage.

Sténio dominated him with one of those magnetic looks in which a man's will is concentrated to the point of subjugating even ferocious animals.

"Continue!" he said. "I command you to go on with your story, or by my very gaze I will make you fall into the whirlpool."

The madman continued his narrative with a child's foolish fright.

"Well," he said in a trembling voice, with a timid look. "Listen to what happened then. I renounced God, I cursed my destiny. I tore at the lace of my clerical robes. I was losing my soul, but I still struggled. . . . Then, oh God, through what trials You made me pass . . . I would see a shadow at the back of the darkened nave which seemed to split the coffin stones. And this shadow, nearly imperceptible and floating at first, grew larger with my terror and would seize me in its pale arms. I struggled against it. I vainly tried to persuade it to leave me. I threw myself to my knees before it, as I do before God.

" 'Lélia, Lélia!' I said to her. 'What do you want of me? Haven't I offered you a profane worship in my heart? Isn't your name mixed on my lips with the sacred names of the Virgin and the angels? Haven't I burned waves of incense to you? Haven't I put you in heaven beside God Himself, insatiable *demander*? What haven't I done for you? To what terrible, impious thoughts haven't I opened my heart? Oh, leave me, leave me, let me pray to God so that tonight He may pardon me and I can sleep without damnation weighing on me like a nightmare!' —But she was not listening. She would entwine me with her black hair, hypnotize me with her black eyes, with her strange smile, and I would struggle with that pitiless shadow until I fell exhausted on the steps of the sanctuary.

"Sometimes, after humiliating myself before God, after watering the marble with my tears, I would find a little calm. Then I would return consoled to my silent cell, overcome with fatigue and sleep. But do you know what Lélia did? Do you know what that mocking heretic contrived to corrupt me and drive me to despair? She would enter my cell with me, and there she would hide herself malignly in the carpet of my prie-dieu, or in the sand of my hourglass, or else in the jasmines on my window. And scarcely had I begun my last prayer when she would suddenly leap in front of me and put her cold hand on my shoulder, saying, 'Here I am!' Then I would have to open my heavy eyelids and struggle again with my troubled heart, perform the exorcism again, until the phantom was finally repulsed. Sometimes it even lay on my poor, narrow, cold bed. The horrible specter would lie on the pallet, exhibiting the graces of a courtesan and trembling voluptuously. This made me shiver with fear. When I opened the serge curtains of my bed, I would find her there, stretching out her lascivious arms and laughing at my shock. Oh, God, what I have suffered! Oh, woman, oh, dream, oh, desire! How much evil you have done me. How many forms you have taken to approach me. How many lies you have told me. How many traps you have laid for me."

"Magnus," said Sténio bitterly. "Be quiet. You make me blush. This is only a priest's lewd imagination."

"No!" said the priest. "Even in my dreams I did not profane her. God hears me. If I am lying, let Him throw me into this whirlpool! I resisted courageously. I exhausted myself in this struggle, but I never ceded. Lélia's ghost always remained virginal after those terrible, burning nights. Is it my fault if the temptation was terrible? Why did that woman's spirit attach itself to me? Why did it seek me out wherever I went? Sometimes, when I sat in the sacred confession tribunal, I would listen reflectively to the sad avowals of some hideous, wrinkled, ragged woman. If I happened to glance at her, do you know what figure would appear at the bars of the confessional instead of the yellow, withered face of the old woman? Lélia's pale face and her cold, evil look, which petrified me. Then my words would be frozen on my lips;

a painful sweat would flood over me, and a cloud pass over my eyes. I felt as if I were going to die. My tongue vainly sought a formula for exorcism. I even forgot the name of God. I could not invoke any celestial power, and this hallucination would stop only when the raucous, broken voice of the old woman demanded absolution. To think that I absolved souls, I whose soul was bound by an infernal power! But fortunately Lélia is no longer alive. She damned herself. And I am alive; I will be saved—because, I confess, while she lived I was prey to horrible temptations. Thoughts much more destructive than anything I have told you fermented in my brain and were victorious for days. Doubt and atheism penetrated me like venom. There were times I was so weary of struggling, when hope of salvation glimmered so feebly and so far off that I threw myself with all my strength into the present. I said to myself, 'At least let me be happy for a day. Since I cannot be an angel, let me be a man. Why should I let a law of death hang over me? Why do I cut myself off from human life in exchange for an illusion about the future? Others are happy and free. They breathe at ease, they live, while I am a corpse stretched out in a coffin, the remains of a man attached to a fragment of religion! They can put their hope into this life and fulfill it because they can act. And, furthermore, the physical world exists. The woman you can clasp in your arms is not a shadow. I have only the hope of another life, and who will tell me if it exists? God, You cannot exist if You leave me prey to these terrible uncertainties! They say there was a time when You performed miracles to uphold men's tottering faith. You sent an angel to touch Isaiah's mute lips with a glowing coal. You appeared in a burning bush, in a cloud of gold, in the night wind, and now You are deaf and indifferent to our errors. You have abandoned Your people. You no longer stretch out a hand to someone who is lost. You no longer address a word of encouragement to someone who suffers and fights for You. You are only a lie, and You are created by man's vain pride. You are nothing. You do not exist!'

"In this way I blasphemed, and I let myself be carried away by the fire of desires. If I had only dared surrender myself entirely to them . . . If I had dared claim my part of life and possess Lélia, if only in fantasy. But I did not even dare that. There was in my depths a shadowy, stupid fear which froze my blood. Satan wanted neither to take nor to leave me. God consented neither to call nor to repulse me. But all my suffering is finished now, because Lélia is dead, and I return to the faith. She is truly dead, isn't she?"

The priest bent his head over his chest and fell into deep contemplation. Sténio left him, unnoticed.

## XXIV

Spring had returned with its bird songs and the perfumes of flowers. Day was ending. The redness of the setting sun was effaced beneath the violet hues of night. Lélia was dreaming on the terrace of the Villa Viola. This elegant dwelling had been built by an Italian for his mistress at the entrance to these mountains. She had died of grief. And the Italian, not wanting to live any longer in a place which brought back to him such sad memories, had rented out the gardens that enclosed the tomb and the villa that carried the name of his beloved. Some sorrows nourish. Others, like remorse, one fears and flees.

Soft and lazy as the breeze, as waves, as that sweet, somnolent day of May, Lélia leaned over the balustrade and gazed down into the most beautiful valley that civilized human feet have ever trod. The sun had set beneath the horizon, but the lake still retained a tone of burning red, as if the antique god, which according to legend entered the waves each evening, had indeed plunged into its transparent mass.

Lélia was dreaming. She was listening to the confused murmur from the valley, the cries of young light brown lambs who knelt beside their darker mothers, the noise of the water when they began to open the sluice gates, the voices of tall, bronzed shepherds, who had Greek profiles, wore picturesque rags, and sang in gutteral tones as they descended the mountain, their crooks over their shoulders. She heard, too, the high-pitched bells that sounded from the necks of long, brindled cows, and the deep barking of those huge primitive dogs which makes the echoes leap on the edges of ravines.

Lélia was calm and radiant as the sky. Sténio had brought a harp and sang the most beautiful hymns to her. While he was singing, night fell slowly and solemnly, like the music of the harp, like the beautiful notes of the poet's smooth male voice. When he had finished, the sky had vanished beneath the first grey coat in which night sheathes itself, when the trembling stars scarcely dare show themselves, far-off and pale like a feeble hope in the bosom of doubt. The sky was barely a white line lost in the mist that formed at the horizon. This was the last light of day.

Then his arms fell, the music of the harp finished, and the young man, prostrating himself before Lélia, asked for a word of love or pity from her, a sign of life or tenderness. Lélia took the child's hand and lifted it to her eyes. She was weeping.

"Oh!" he cried in an outburst of emotion. "You are crying! So you do feel!"

Lélia passed her fingers through Sténio's perfumed hair, and drawing his head onto her breast, she covered it with kisses. Rarely had his beautiful brow been brushed by her lips. Lélia's caress was a gift from heaven as rare as a flower forgotten by winter blooming beneath the snow. This brusque, burning effusion nearly cost the life of this child who had received his first woman's kiss from Lélia's cold lips. He turned pale, his heart stopped beating; near dying, he repulsed her with all his strength, because he had never feared death so much as at this instant when life was revealing itself to him.

He needed to talk to escape these terrible caresses, this excess of happiness which was as painful as fever.

"Oh, tell me!" he cried, escaping from her arms. "Tell me that you love me!"

"Haven't I already told you?" she replied with a look and a smile that Murillo might have given to the Virgin carried off to heaven by angels.

"No, you never have told me," he said. "When you were dying you told me that you wanted to love. That was saying that at the moment of losing your life you regretted not having enjoyed it."

"Do you believe that, Sténio?" she asked with a tone of mocking coquetry.

"I don't believe anything, but I try to understand you. Oh, Lélia, you promised me you would try to love me, that is what you promised me."

"I didn't promise to succeed," said Lélia coldly.

"But do you hope you will ever be able to love me?" he asked in a sad, sweet voice which moved her entire soul.

She enveloped him in her arms and pressed against him with super-human force. Sténio, who still wanted to resist, felt himself dominated by this power which paralyzed him with fear. His blood boiled and congealed like lava. He was in turn hot and cold. Was this joy or was it anguish? He did not know. It was both. It was more than that: it was heaven and hell, it was love and shame, it was desire and fear.

Finally his courage returned. He remembered how intensely he had hoped for this hour of confusion and rapture. He despised himself for the cowardly timidity that was stopping him, and, abandoning himself to an impulse that had something voracious and savage about it, he in turn gripped her in his arms, he pressed his mouth to that soft, sweet mouth whose contact still astonished him. . . . But Lélia, repulsing him all of a sudden, said in a dry, hard voice:

"Leave me alone. I no longer love you."

Sténio fell, annihilated, onto the paving-stones of the terrace. Then he really did believe he was near death, as he felt the cold of despair and shame suddenly strangle that rage of love and that fever of expectation.

Lélia began to laugh. Anger revived him. He rose to his feet and deliberated for an instant whether to kill her.

But this woman was so indifferent to life that he was no more able to avenge himself on her than to frighten her. Sténio tried to be philosophic and cold; but after three words he began to weep.

Then Lélia embraced him again, and as he no longer dared return her caresses, she deluged him with hers until he was intoxicated. Then she put her hand on his mouth and pushed him away when she felt him tremble with pleasure.

"Viper!" he cried, trying to raise himself up to flee. She would not let him go.

"Come back," she said. "Come back and lie beside me. I loved you so much just now when you received my kisses almost against your will, and you were frightened and naive. When you asked: '*Do you hope you will be able to love me?*' I adored you. You were so humble. This is how I love you. When I see you tremble and draw back from the love you want, I feel younger and more passionate than you. Then I no longer feel discouraged because I imagine that I can give life to you. But I lose hope when you grow bold and ask more of me than I can feel. I am frightened of loving and suffering. I don't want to be deceived as I have been in the past."

"Poor woman!" said Sténio, overcome with pity.

"Oh, can't you stay the way you were when you were afraid of my caresses?" she said, drawing his head onto her lap. "Let me put my hand around your neck. It's as white and polished as marble. Let me feel your soft hair unroll and stick to my fingers. Sténio, how white your chest is. How fast your heart beats. This is good, my child. But does this heart enclose the seed of some male virtue? Will you be able to go through life without being corrupted or drying up? Now the moon is rising over you, and its rays are reflected in your eyes. Breathe in the scent of the grassy, flowering meadow. I recognize the emanation of each plant. I can smell them passing one after the other through the air. Now it's the wild hillside thyme, a little while ago it was the narcissus by the lake, and now the geraniums from the garden. How the air spirits must rejoice as they bathe in these subtle perfumes. You are smiling, my poet, are you falling asleep?"

"Asleep!" cried Sténio in a tone of surprise and reproach.

"Why not? Aren't you calm, aren't you happy now?"

"Happy, yes, but calm?"

"Well then, you're a fool!" she said, pushing him away.

"Lélia, you make me so unhappy. Let me leave you."

"Coward, how afraid of suffering you are! Go! Leave me!"

"I can't," he said, falling to his knees.

"My God," she said, embracing him. "Why suffer? You don't know how much I love you. I take pleasure holding you, looking at you as if you were my child. I hav never been a mother, but I have the same feeling for you that I feel I would have had for a son. I take a maternal, childish pleasure in your beauty. . . . And then, after all, what feeling can I have for you?"

"Can't you love me?" asked Sténio with a trembling voice and a torn heart.

Lélia did not answer. She convulsively ran her hands through the masses of black hair curling over the young man's brow. She leaned closer and looked at him as if she wanted to concentrate the power of several souls in her eyes, concentrate the intensity of a hundred lives into one moment. Then the ambitious, impotent creature, finding her heart less passionate than her brain and her abilities beneath her dreams, again felt discouraged. Her hand fell lifelessly to her side; she looked at the moon with sadness; she inhaled the breeze with a dilation of her nostrils which had something savage about it.

"Alas," she sighed, in an irritated voice and with a sad look, "people who can love are happy."

# XXV

Just below the garden terraces a small river ran beneath thick yews and cedars with hanging branches. Underneath one of these mysterious arches a white marble tomb was reflected in the water, pale amid the dark reflections of greenery. Barely a breath of wind stirred its pure, trembling marble edges mirrored in the water. A large, creeping plant had invaded the tomb, and it had entwined garlands of blue, bell-shaped flowers around the sculptures, already darkened by rain and abandon. Moss grew on the breasts and arms of the kneeling statues. Weeping cypresses, whose branches fell languidly over the pale faces, surrounded the tomb, which had been entrusted to neglect.

"There," said Lélia, moving aside the long grass that hid the inscription, "is the tomb of a woman who died of love and suffering. . . . "

"What spiritual and poetic feeling it contains," said Sténio. "See how proudly nature seems to possess it. How those garlands of flowers softly clasp it, how the trees embrace it, and the water kisses it tenderly. Poor woman. To think she died of love! Poor angel exiled on earth and lost among human ways. You no longer suffer, Viola! You are sleeping. You stretch out your weary arms in your bed of marble. Lélia, take this flower, put it on your breast, and inhale it often. But do so quickly, before it loses this virginal scent which is perhaps Viola's soul. Viola, if there is some emanation of you in this flower, if some of your love has passed into this mysterious calyx, can't you penetrate Lélia's heart? Can't you set fire to the air she breathes so that she no longer lies there dead, like those statues which gaze at each other in the brook with mournful expressions?"

"Child!" said Lélia, throwing the flower into the lazy current and following it with a distracted expression. "Do you think I don't suffer too, as intensely as Viola? What do you know? Perhaps she had a very full life. To live and die of love is beautiful for a woman. Viola, under what fiery sky were you born? What gave you a heart so strong that it broke rather than bend beneath the weight of existence? What god endowed you with that indomitable power which only death could strip from your soul? Oh noble woman, you didn't want to accept your fate. But you didn't hasten your end like those weak people who commit suicide to prevent themselves from being consoled. You were so sure you wouldn't be that you deteriorated slowly, without drawing back toward life, without advancing a step toward the tomb. Death came and took you broken, already dead, but still rooted to your love, saying to nature: 'Goodbye, I despise you and I don't want health. Keep your pleasures, your deceptive poetry, your consoling vanity, your narcotic forgetfulness, and your skepticism. Keep all that for others. As for me, I want to love or die.' Viola, you even repulsed God. You frankly hated the unjust power that had given you suffering and loneliness as your lot. You didn't come here singing melancholy hymns, as Sténio does on the days I afflict him. You didn't prostrate yourself in church, as Magnus does when the demon of despair fills him. Unlike Trenmor, you didn't crush your sensitivity beneath meditation. You didn't cold-bloodedly kill your passions to live proudly and tranquilly beneath their debris. And unlike Lélia, you did not. . . . "

She forgot to articulate her thought. She had leaned her elbows on the mausoleum; her eyes were fixed motionlessly over the water; and she didn't hear Sténio, who begged her to tell him what she was thinking.

"Yes," she said after a long silence. "She is dead. And if any human soul deserves to go to heaven, hers does. She did more than was imposed on her: she drank the cup of bitterness to the dregs, then, repulsing the happiness which was supposed to descend from heaven after this trial, refusing the option of forgetting, she broke the cup and kept the poison in her heart as a bitter treasure. She has died of grief! And we are all alive! Young man, you are able to endure suffering. And yet you talk of suicide, which is more cowardly than undergoing this defiled life God's contempt leaves us."

Sténio, seeing her so sad, began to sing to distract her. While he sang, tears ran from his eyes. But he overcame his grief as he sought to console Lélia.

## XXVI

"Lélia, you have often told me that I was as young and pure as an angel. Sometimes you told me you loved me. Even this morning you smiled as you said: 'My only happiness is in you.' But this evening you have forgotten all this, and you pitilessly overturn the foundations of my happiness.

"Well then, throw me to the ground like that flower you have just inhaled and now abandon. If you find some amusement, some ironic, cruel satisfaction in seeing me tossed about and broken, then crush me beneath your feet. But don't forget that when you want to gather me up and breathe me in again like the flower, you will find me ready to be reborn beneath your caresses.

"Poor woman, you will love me in your own way. I am aware that you no longer can love as I do. Moreover, it is just that you be the more adored and the sovereign of us two. I don't deserve the love you do. I have not suffered and fought as you have. I am only a child without glory, without wounds, facing the beginning of my struggles. You have been struck by lightning, overwhelmed a hundred times, and yet you still stand. You don't understand God, and yet you believe in Him. You insult Him and love Him. You're as withered as an old man and as young as a child. Lélia, my poor soul! Love me as much as you can. I will always go on my knees to thank you, and I will give you all my heart, all my life in exchange for the little that is left in you to give me.

"Only let me love you. Accept the suffering that I bring in a holocaust to your feet. Let me consume my life on the altar I have built for you. Don't pity me. I am still happier than you. Oh, if I could only die for you as Viola died for her love. How much voluptuousness is in these tortures you place in my heart. How much happiness there is in being your plaything and victim, and in expiating the injustices amassed on your head. Ah, if one could only wash away the stains of another soul with the sufferings of one's own. If one could redeem it like a new Christ and renounce one's own part in eternity to spare him the void.

"This is how much I love you, Lélia. You don't know this, because you haven't wanted to. I don't ask you to appreciate or pity me. Come to me when you are suffering and hurt me all you want to distract yourself from your torment."

"I am suffering mortally at this time," said Lélia. "Anger boils up in my heart. Do you want to blaspheme for me? Perhaps that will console me. Do you want to throw stones at heaven, curse God, invoke the void, adore evil, summon destruction over all the works of Providence? Are you capable of killing Abel to avenge me on God? Do you want to howl like a frightened dog who sees the moon strewing phantoms on the walls? Do you want to chew the earth and eat sand like Nebuchadnezzar? Do you want, like Job, to spit our anger into vehement curses?

Pure and pious young man, do you want to plunge yourself in atheism and crawl in the mud where I am dying? I don't have the strength to cry out. Go, cry out for me. But you are weeping . . . can you weep? People who can weep are happy! My eyes are drier than a desert where dew never falls, and my heart is still drier than my eyes. Are you weeping? Well, to distract yourself listen to a canto I translated from a foreign poet."

## XXVII TO GOD

"What have I done to be afflicted as I am? Why have You withdrawn from me? You don't refuse the sun to inert plants or the dew to grass. You give flower stamens the power to love, and You give sensations of well-being to the mindless coral. I am also Your creature, and You have gifted me with an apparently rich nature. But You have taken everything away from me. You have dealt with me worse than Your lost angels, because they still have the power to hate. I don't even have that. You have dealt with me worse than mud or gravel, because these are trampled by people's feet and they don't feel it. I feel what I am. And I cannot bite the foot of my oppressor or lift up the damnation that weighs on me like a mountain.

"Why have You treated me like this, Unknown Power whose steel hand I sense stretched over me? Why did You make me a woman if later You intended to change me into stone, leaving me useless and outside common life? Is this to raise me above others or lower me beneath them? Oh God, if this is a privileged fate, sweeten it for me so that I can bear it without suffering. If this is a life of punishment, why have You afflicted me? Alas! Was I guilty before I was born?

"What is this soul You have given me? Is it called a poet's soul? More changeable than light, more vagabond than the wind, always thirsting, always anxious, always gasping for breath, always seeking elements of nourishment outside itself and exhausting them before they've even been tasted! I aspire to everything and reach nothing. I understand everything but possess nothing. I reach a skepticism of the heart as Faust reached a skepticism of the spirit. My fate is more wretched than Faust's, because in his heart youthful, fiery passions were silently engendered beneath the dust of books while his intelligence aged. When Faust, weary of seeking perfection and not finding it, was ready to deny God, the Lord sent him the angel of dark, morbid passions to punish him. This angel gave him new life, set him on fire, led him astray, and old Faust began to live, full of vitality, guilty, accursed, but powerful. He no longer loved God, but he loved Marguerite. My God, will You give me Faust's affliction?

"Because, God, You are not enough for me, and You know this. You don't want to be everything for me. You don't reveal Yourself so that I can grasp You and attach myself to You exclusively. You attract me. You flatter me with the perfumed breath of Your celestial breezes. You smile on me between two clouds of gold. You appear in my dreams. You call me. You endlessly incite me to soar to You, but You have forgotten to give me wings. What good is it to have given me a soul that desires You? You endlessly escape. You envelop nature with heavy, dark fumes. You make a hot, devouring wind blight the flowers, or You blow a north wind on me that freezes me and saddens me to the marrow of my bones. You give us days of fog, starless nights, and You overwhelm our poor universe with tempests. All this makes us bold and skeptical in spite of ourselves. But if we succumb to doubt during these sad hours, you awaken the goads of remorse within us, and all the voices of the earth and sky reproach us.

"Why, why have You made us like this? What profit do You draw from our sufferings? What glory does our abjectness give You? Does man need these torments to make him desire heaven? Is hope a pale, weak flower which only grows amid rocks, beneath the gusts of storms? Precious flower, sweet perfume, fill this arid, devastated heart. . . . Ah, for a long time You have vainly been trying to rejuvenate this heart. Your roots can no longer attach themselves to its stone walls. Its glacial atmosphere freezes you; its winds uproot you and throw you broken, destroyed to the ground . . . Oh, hope, can't you flower again for me?"

"These songs are sad, this poetry is cruel," said Sténio, as he pulled the harp away from her. "You find pleasure in these morbid musings. You pitilessly tear me apart. No, this is not the translation of a foreign poet. Lélia, the text of this poem is in the depths of your soul. Oh cruel, incurable woman, listen to that bird. It sings better than you. It sings of the sun, springtime, and love. That tiny creature is better constituted than you, because you can sing only of suffering and doubt."

## XXVIII

"I have led you into this deserted valley, untrampled by herds, unsullied by hunters' feet. I have led you, Lélia, across precipices. You fearlessly confronted all the dangers. With a tranquil expression you measured the crevasses that furrow the deep slopes of the glacier. You crossed them with a plank thrown out by our guides, which trembled above the bottomless chasms. You have crossed the waterfalls, as light and agile as the white stork that alights from stone to stone and sleeps with a bent neck, its body balanced on one of its frail legs, amid fuming, swirling water. Lélia, you didn't tremble once. But I shivered. How many times my blood froze and my heart stopped beating as I watched you pass over the chasm, heedless, looking up at the sky and disdaining to know where you put your narrow feet. Lélia, you are very brave and strong. When you say your soul is enervated, you are lying. No man possesses more confidence and courage than you."

"What is courage?" asked Lélia. "And who doesn't possess it? Who loves life in these times? This heedlessness is called courage when it produces any good. But when it limits itself to exposing a worthless destiny, isn't it simply inertia?"

"Sténio, inertia is the great scourge of our age. There are no longer any virtues except negative ones. We are brave because we are no longer capable of fear. Alas, all is spent, even weaknesses, even human vices. We no longer have the strength which creates a stubborn, frightened love of life. When there was still energy in the world, people fought with guile and caution. Life was a perpetual combat in which the bravest continually drew back before danger, because the bravest survived the longest in the midst of perils. Since civilization has made life too easy, people find it monotonous. People will expose their lives for a word, for a glance because it has so little value. This indifference about life has established the duel as one of our customs. The spectacle of the duel affirms the apathy of our century: two men, calmly, politely draw lots as to who will kill the other, without hate, anger, or profit. Alas, Sténio, we are no longer either good or evil. We are no longer even cowards. We are inert."

"Lélia, you are right, and when I look upon society, I too am sad. But

I have brought you here to make you forget this society, at least for a few days. Look where we are. Isn't the place sublime, and can you think of anything but God? Sit down on this moss, virgin to human feet, and see the wild land unroll its depths at your feet. Have you ever seen anything wilder and more full of life? Do you see the movement of the trees bent by the wind? Do you see the bands of eagles hovering around the misty peaks and flying in circles, like large black rings on the white surface of the glacier? Listen to the noises around you, rising and receding. The torrents weep like unhappy souls, the stags bellow with plaintive voices, the breeze sings and laughs in the heather, the vultures cry like frightened women. And these other sounds, mysterious, *untold*, moan in the mountains, these colossal glaciers crack in the heart of their blocks, these snows crumble and carry along sand, these great tree roots struggle incessantly with the entrails of the earth and work to split the shale. Listen to these unknown voices, these vague sighs which the earth, always prey to the sufferings of giving birth, exhales through its open flanks. Don't you find all this more splendid and harmonious than the church or the theater?"

"It is true all this is beautiful, and it is here one must come to see that the earth still has youth and vigor. Poor earth! She too is dying."

"Lélia, what are you saying? Do you think that the earth and sky are guilty of our moral decay? Do you accuse them too?"

"Yes, I do accuse them," she said, "or rather I accuse the great law of time that exhausts and makes an end to everything. Don't you see that the wave of centuries is carrying us all off together, men and worlds, to engulf us in eternity like dry leaves swept along by the torrent toward the precipice? Alas, we won't even survive like that withered grass which floats suspended, like the hair of a drowned woman. Dissolution will pass over the corpses of empires. The debris of humanity will be no more than grains of sand in the sea. God will destroy the universe like a piece of worn-out clothing that one throws to the wind, like a coat shed because one no longer wants it. Then God alone *will exist*. Then perhaps His glory and power will shine without veils. But who will contemplate this? Will new races be born in our dust to see or divine what was once created and destroyed?"

"The world will vanish, I know it," said Sténio, "but this will take so many centuries that the number is incalculable in man's brain. No, no, we have not yet reached this agony. Such a thought has flowered in a soul like yours irritated by skepticism. But I sense the world is young. My heart and reason tell me that it hasn't even reached its peak of strength. The world is still evolving. So much remains for men to learn."

"Doubtless," she said with irony. "We haven't yet found out how to revive the dead and make ourselves immortal. But we will make these great discoveries. And then the world won't end. Man will be stronger than God and will exist with no aid except his intelligence."

"Lélia, you are always jeering. But listen to me, don't you think that men are better today than they used to be and that consequently. . . . "

"No, I don't think so, but what does it matter? We simply don't agree about the age of the world."

"And if we knew it exactly we would be no more advanced. We don't know the secrets of its structure. We don't know how long a world made like ours is meant to exist. But in my heart I feel that we are moving toward light and life. Hope shines in our sky. Do you see how beautiful the sun is as it smiles, crimson, generous, over the mountains, which are purpled with its caresses and redden with love like timid virgins! One can't establish the existence of God through logic. One believes in Him because a celestial instinct reveals Him. Likewise, one can't measure eternity with the compass of exact sciences, but one feels in one's soul that the moral world possesses sap and freshness, just as one feels physically that the air embodies vivifying, tonic forces. Can you breathe this aromatic mountain air without feeling it penetrate your pores and strengthen your fibers? Can you drink that limpid, glacial water which tastes of mint and wild thyme without feeling the healthy taste? Don't you feel reinvigorated in this vital, subtle air, among these beautiful flowers that seem so proud to owe nothing to men's care? Turn around and look at those thick rhododendron bushes. How fresh and pure those clumps of lilacs are! They turn up to the sky to gaze at the azure and gather in the dew. Lélia, these flowers are as uncultivated, wild, and beautiful as you. Don't you understand the passion I have for them?"

Lélia smiled reflectively for a long time with her eyes fixed on the wild valley.

Finally she said, "We would need to live here to conserve what little remains in our hearts. But we wouldn't live here for three days without blighting the vegetation and sullying the air. Man is always disemboweling his nurse and exhausting the soil that produced him. He always wants to rearrange nature and redo the work of God. You wouldn't be here three days, I tell you, without wanting to carry the rocks from the mountain to the bottom of the valley and wanting to cultivate the reeds growing at the humid depths on the arid mountain peaks. You would call that creating a garden. If you had come here fifty years ago you would have put up a statue and an arbor with trimmed vines."

"Lélia, you are always jeering! You can laugh derisively even here. Without you, I would have fallen to my knees before the creator of such a sublime scene. But you, my demon, don't want that. I must hear you deny everything, even the beauty of nature."

"I don't deny it!" she cried. "What have you ever heard me deny? I have never been insensitive to what was noble or poetic about a belief. But who will give me the power to delude myself? Alas, why has God created such a gap between man's illusions and reality? Why must one continually suffer from a desire for happiness which reveals itself under the form of the beautiful and hovers in all our dreams without ever descending to earth? Not only our soul suffers from God's absence, but our entire being, our vision, our flesh suffers from His indifference or harshness. Tell me: in what climate does man not know excessive heat and cold? What valley is not wet in winter? On what mountain is the grass not withered and uprooted by the wind? In the Orient the enervated species vegetates and languishes, always inert, stretched out on divans. Women wilt in the darkness of harems because they would be burned by the sun. But when a dry, corrosive wind blows in from the sea, it gives that indolent race a sort of giddiness that causes crimes and heroic feats unknown to us. Then these people work themselves into a fever of activity. They exhale their concentrated strength, which has been dormant, in chaotic noise, bloody pleasures, unbridled orgies, until, worn out by suffering and fatigue, they fall back onto their divans, the stupidest of men.

"However, they are the best balanced and most energetic of the species. They are the happiest in repose and the most violent in action. Look at the natives of torrid zones. There the sun is indeed generous. Plants are gigantic, the earth is prodigal with fruits and perfumes, and there is a luxury of color and form. Birds and insects sparkle like jewels. The flowers emit inebriating odors. Even the trees conceal exquisite scents in the woody tissue of their barks. Nights are as clear as our

autumn days. The stars show themselves four times as large as they do
here. Everything is beautiful and rich. Man, still coarse and naive, does
not know even a fraction of the evils we have invented. Do you think
he is happy? No. He has to battle hideous, savage animals. The tiger
roars outside his hut. The cold, sticky serpent, which horrifies man
more than any other enemy, glides up to his infant's cradle. Then the
storm, that giant convulsion of a robust nature, approaches leaping
like an enraged bull, tearing like a wounded lion. Man must either flee
or perish. Wind, lightning, and flooding torrents carry off his hut, his
field, and his herds. Each night he doesn't know if he will have a native
land the next day. His land was too beautiful. God doesn't want to let
him keep it; and each year he must seek out a new one. The spectacle
of a happy man is not agreeable to the Lord. Oh, God, perhaps You
suffer too. Perhaps You are bored with your glory, since You do us so
much harm!

"These children of the sun, whom we envy, doubtless sometimes
wonder if there exists a region, cherished by heaven, which is neither
furrowed by burning lava nor swept by destructive winds; a region
which awakens in the morning as unchanged, calm, and warm as the
night before. They ask themselves if God in His anger has put panthers
starved for blood and hideous reptiles everywhere. Perhaps these simple
men dream of a paradise under our temperate latitudes. Perhaps in
their dreams they see cold and mist descend over their bronzed brows
and darken their burning atmosphere. When we dream we see the sun
red and hot, the plain sparkling, the sea glowing, and the sand burning
beneath our feet. We summon the meridional sun over our frozen
shoulders, while the people of the South would go on their knees to
receive drops of our rain. Everywhere man suffers and moans. Delicate,
nervous creature that he is, he has vainly made himself the king of
creation because he is its most unfortunate victim. He is the only animal whose intellectual and physical strengths are disproportionate.
With rude animals physical force dominates; instinct merely preserves
life. With man this instinct has developed inordinately and burns and
tortures a frail nature. He has the impotence of the mollusk but the
appetites of the tiger. Misery and necessity imprison him in a tortoise
shell. Ambition and anxiety spread their eagle wings within his brain.
He would like to possess the abilities of all the species, but he has only
the ability of desiring in vain. He surrounds himself with debris. The

entrails of the earth abandon gold and marble to him. Flowers let themselves be pulverized into perfumes for his use. The birds of the air let
their most beautiful feathers fall for him. The loon and the duck surrender their down armor to heat his apathetic, cold limbs. Wool, fur,
scales, silk, the entrails of this, the teeth of that, the skin of the other,
the blood and the life of all creatures belong to him. Human life is
nourished only by destruction, and how grievous and short it is.

"The most hideous things poets and painters have invented in their
grotesque fantasies also appear most often, it must be said, in our night-
mares. We dream of witches' sabbaths of living corpses, animal skele-
tons, emaciated, bloody, with monstrous deformities and bizarre super-
positions—bird heads on horse trunks, crocodile faces on camel bodies,
heaps of bones. One feels this carnage and the cries of suffering, the
threats proffered by mutilated animals with a profusion of fear. Do
you think that dreams are a pure combination of chance? Don't you
think that, outside of the laws of association and the habits that man
endows with right and power, there can exist in him secret, vague, instinctive remorse which he has not wanted to admit rationally and
which reveals itself through the terrors of superstition or the hallucina-
tions of sleep? Although customs and belief have destroyed certain
realities of our moral life, the imprint remains in a corner of the brain
and awakens when the other intelligent faculties sleep.

"There are many other intimate sensations of that kind. Certain
memories seem to be those of another life. Some children are born with
suffering that one would say was contracted in the tomb, for perhaps
man leaves the cold of the coffin to reenter the eiderdown of the cradle.
Who knows? Haven't we traversed death and chaos? These terrible
images follow us in all our dreams. Why do we feel an intense sympathy
for effaced existences; why these regrets and this love for human beings
who have left only a name in history? Is memory perhaps unaware of
itself? Sometimes I feel I have known Shakespeare, wept with Tasso,
and journeyed through heaven and hell with Dante. A name from ancient times awakens emotions in me that resemble memories, as certain
perfumes from exotic plants recall the land that produced them. Then
our imagination wanders in that unknown native land as if our feet had
trampled it, as if we had been born and died there, although we believe
we have never seen it. Poor man. What do we know?"

"We know only that we cannot know," said Sténio.

"And that is what devours us, Sténio," she said. "Beneath its glitter of vain trophies, this impotence cannot be concealed by an enslaved, mutilated universe. The arts, industry, sciences, the entire scaffolding of civilization, what is it all if not the continual effort of human weakness to hide its evils and cover its misery? See if, despite its profusions and its voluptuousness, luxury can create new senses in us or perfect the human organism. See if human reason, with its exaggerated development, has carried its theories into practice. Has study been able to push science beyond certain impassable limits? Has the monstrous excitation of emotion managed to produce complete enjoyments? It is doubtful that the progress achieved through sixty centuries of research has made man's existence endurable. Suicide is still necessary for a great number."

"Lélia, I haven't tried to prove to you that man has reached his apogee of power and greatness. On the contrary, I said that I felt the human race would still bury many more generations before it reached that point. And perhaps the race will maintain itself there for many centuries before it descends again to the decrepit state in which you believe it to be now."

"Young man, how can you think we are progressing when you see around us that all convictions are lost, societies are in turmoil because of their relaxed bonds, and human faculties are exhausted by abuse? All the principles that were formerly sacred fall into the domain of discussion and serve as playthings for children, just as royalty and clergy serve to perform a masquerade for the people, who are king and priest in their own right."

"But you know that thrones have always tottered on fragile bases. This so-called spirit of liberty that is seizing our contemporaries isn't so new that we haven't had the time to read how ancient republics were organized. Everything about our revolutions has a quality of puerile imitation and miserable plagiarism. Didn't the struggle between the rich and poor begin as soon as it had ceased between the strong and weak? Isn't the right of inheritance almost as old as the right of conquest? Did disputes over possession of the earth that sustains us begin only yesterday?"

"Yes," said Lélia. "But after these wars between men, after these social upheavals, when the world was still young and vigorous it would pull itself up and rebuild its structures for a period of centuries. This will no longer happen. We are not only, as you believe, at one of those eves of crisis when the fatigued human spirit sleeps on the battlefield before taking up the arms of deliverance once more. Because of falling and rising so many times, remaining stretched out on its flank and taking on hope again, seeing its wounds open and close over and over again, because of thrashing about in its chains and getting hoarse while it cries out to heaven, the colossus is growing old and sinking. It trembles now like a ruin that is about to crumble forever. A few more hours of convulsive agony and the wind of eternity will pass indifferently over a chaos of unbridled nations reduced to disputing the debris of an exhausted world."

"Do you believe in the approach of the Last Judgment? Oh, my sad Lélia, your gloomy soul creates these immense terrors because your soul is too vast for lesser superstitions. But man's spirit has always been preoccupied with these ideas of death. Ascetic souls have always found pleasure in these images of cataclysm and universal desolation. Lélia, you are no new prophet. Jeremiah came before you. And your angry, Dantesque poetry has created nothing as dark as the Apocalypse, sung during a delirious madman's nights to the rocks of Patmos."

"I know this. But the voice of John the dreamer was heard and gathered in. Unintelligible as it seemed, through terror it rallied to the Christian faith a great number of mediocre intelligences which the sublimity of the evangelic precepts had not been able to touch. Jesus had opened heaven to the spiritualists. John opened hell and made death emerge mounted on his pale horse. War and famine galloped on a charger's skeleton to terrify the masses, who had been submitting tranquilly to the scourges of humanity but who became frightened as soon as they saw them personified in a pagan form. But today prophets cry in the desert, and no human voice responds, because the world is indifferent and deaf. It has gone to bed and blocked its ears to die in peace. A few sparse groups of impotent sectarians vainly try to rekindle a spark of virtue. They are the last remains of human moral power, and they float a moment above the abyss before they join the rest of the debris at the bottom of that shoreless sea to which the world must return."

"Oh, Lélia, why despair like this over these men who aspire to bring virtue back into our age of iron? If I doubted their success as you do, I would not want to admit this. I would fear committing an impious crime."

"I admire these men," said Lélia, "and I would like to be the least among them. But what will these shepherds who bear a star on their brow be able to do in the face of the great monster of the Apocalypse, that immense, terrible figure which is outlined in the foreground of all pictures of the prophet? This pale woman, as beautiful as vice, this great prostitute of nations covered with the riches of the Orient and astride a hydra that vomits rivers of poison on all human paths, is civilization, is humanity depraved by luxury and science, is the torrent of venom that will engulf all talk of virtue and all hope of regeneration."

"Oh, Lélia!" cried the poet, struck with superstition. "Aren't you this unhappy, terrible phantom? How many times this fear has seized me in my dreams. How many times you have appeared to me as a symbol of the unspeakable suffering into which the spirit of research has thrown man. With your beauty, sadness, ennui, and skepticism, don't you personify this suffering produced by the abuse of thought? Great moral strength has been developed through art, poetry, and science. And haven't you surrendered this moral strength—prostituted it to all the newest ideas and errors? Instead of attaching yourself faithfully and prudently to the simple faith of your ancestors and to the instinctive freedom from care with which God imbued man for his repose and preservation, you have abandoned yourself to the seductions of an ambitious philosophy. You have thrown yourself into the torrent of a civilization which is intent on destruction and which, having run too fast, has destroyed the just-built foundations of the future. Because you have retarded the work of centuries by a few days, do you think the hourglass of eternity is broken? Lélia, there is a great deal of pride in your sadness. But God will let this wave of stormy centuries pass. For Him it is only a drop of water in the ocean. The devouring hydra will die for lack of nourishment. And from its corpse, which will cover the world, will rise a new race, stronger and more patient than the former one."

"Sténio, you have great vision. For me, you personify nature, whose virgin child you still are. You haven't yet blunted your faculties. You believe yourself immortal because you feel young, like this wild, beautiful valley that does not dream that in a single day the ploughshare and the hundred-armed monster called industry can blight its heart to ravish its treasures. You grow tall, confident, and presumptuous. You don't foresee that life, as it advances, is going to swallow you up in the weight of its errors and disfigure you beneath the rouge of its promises. Wait.

Wait a few years and you will say as we do: 'Everything vanishes.' "

"No, everything does not vanish," said Sténio. "Do you see this sun, this earth, this beautiful sky, and these green hills. Even that ice has resisted the summer heat for centuries. In this way man's frail strength will prevail. What does the fall of a few generations matter? Lélia, do you weep for so little? Do you think that a single idea in the universe dies? Won't this heritage be rediscovered intact in the dust of our extinguished races? Each day artistic masterpieces and scientific discoveries emerge from the ashes of Pompeii or the tombs of Memphis. What a striking proof of intellectual immortality! Profound mysteries had been lost in the night of time; the world had forgotten its age, and, believing itself still young, it was alarmed to feel itself already so old. Lélia, like you, it said: 'I am near death because I grow weak, but I was born such a short time ago! How soon will I die, since so few days have sufficed to make up my life?' But one day human corpses are exhumed in Egypt. The living image of its mummies, Egypt has slept through the dust of centuries to awaken and reveal itself in all its antiquity to this great scientific age. In the depths of the dried entrails of a human corpse our curious century discovers papyrus. Our greedy hands unroll the embalmed wrappings, those frail shrouds which arrest destruction. Beneath these shrouds are manuscripts lying beside a man's emaciated corpse. In the place of these manuscripts was once a soul, that is human thought, and it has been expressed through writing and transmitted to us through the aid of a lost art. In these Oriental sepulchers is found the art of keeping the remains of the dead from corruption—which is perhaps the greatest power in the universe. Oh, Lélia, when you see the world, which has lived on the forgotten ruins of an unknown civilization, pause ignorantly and naively before the lessons of the past, don't you realize that the world is not young?"

"*To know* is not *to have power*," said Lélia. "Retrieving what was is not advancing; seeing is not living. Who will give us back the power of action and the art of enjoyment? We have gone too far to turn back. What was rest for former civilizations will be death for ours. The rejuvenated Oriental nations will inebriate themselves with the poison we have spread throughout the world. Hardy drinkers, these barbarians will perhaps prolong the orgy of luxury a few hours in the night of time, but our venom will be mortal for them too, and everything will once more fall into darkness. . . . Sténio, don't you realize that the sun is drawing away from us? The earth is drifting perceptibly toward darkness and chaos. Is your blood so young and burning that it doesn't feel the attacks of cold that extend like a blanket of mourning on this planet abandoned to Destiny, the most powerful of all the gods? Oh, the cold! This penetrating evil buries its sharp-pointed needles into all our pores! It blights the flowers and burns them like fire. This evil, which is both physical and moral, invades the soul and body, penetrates the depths of thought, and paralyzes the blood. The cold, a sinister demon, brushes the universe with its wet wings and breathes plague over the frightened nations! This cold dims everything as it unrolls its grey, nebulous veil over the rich colors of the sky, over the reflections of water, over the flowers, and over the cheeks of virgins. The cold throws its white shroud over the meadows, the woods, the lakes, the fur and feathers of animals, and even the coats of wild beasts on Archangel's Arctic shores. The cold discolors everything in the material as well as in the intellectual world. Man's pleasures and the quality of his customs are destroyed wherever this cold approaches. You see clearly that everything is becoming civilized, that is to say everything is growing cold. The bronzed nations of the torrid zones begin to open their fearful, wary hands to our industrial traps. Tigers and lions are tamed and come up from the deserts to amuse people of the North. Animals that have never been able to acclimatize themselves among us have left their habitats, without dying, to live in domesticity. Their sun grows tepid, and they have forgotten the harsh, bitter sorrow that used to kill them in servitude. Everywhere blood becomes impoverished and congeals as instinct enlarges. The soul exalts itself and leaves earth, which is insufficient for its needs, to steal the fire of Prometheus from heaven. But the soul is stopped in its flight and falls, lost in darkness; because God, seeing its boldness, stretches out His hand and removes the sun."

## XXIX SOLITUDE
## [LÉLIA TO TRENMOR]

Trenmor, the child has obeyed me: he has left me alone here in this deserted valley. I am happy here. The weather is mild. An abandoned chalet serves as my retreat, and each morning shepherds from the neighboring valley bring me goat's milk and unleavened bread cooked in the open air over the wood of dead trees. A copious bed of dry heather, a thick cloak for the night, and a few everyday clothes are enough to sustain me a week or two without suffering too much materially.

The first hours that I spent here seemed the most beautiful of my life. To you I can say everything, can't I, Trenmor?

As Sténio moved away from me, I felt the weight of life grow lighter on my shoulders. At first his sorrow at parting, his reluctance to leave me alone in such a deserted place, his fear, his submission, his tears, and his caresses, which held no bitterness or reproach, made me repent of my resolution. When he reached the bottom of the first slope of Monteverdor, I tried to call him back because his defeated walk tormented me. You know that I love him from the bottom of my heart. Pure affection is not dead in me, you know that very well, Trenmor. I love you too, but I don't love you the same way. I don't have that fearful, tender, almost childlike concern for you that I have for him, because he suffers. You never do. You don't need to be loved like this.

I signaled him to come back. But he had already gone too far. He thought I was waving him a last goodbye. He responded and continued on his way. Then I wept because I realized how much I had hurt him by making him leave me, and I prayed God to sweeten his suffering and send him, as always, the sacred poetry that makes sadness precious.

I watched him for a long time as a point, not yet lost in the depths of the valley, sometimes hidden by a knoll or a clump of trees, then reappearing above a waterfall or on the side of a ravine. Seeing him walk so slowly and sadly, I stopped regretting our separation. I thought, he is already admiring the foam of the torrents and the mountain greenery. He is already invoking God, already placing me in the clouds. He is tuning the lyre of his genius and giving his sadness a form that releases it while it diminishes its intensity.

Why would you want me to fear for Sténio's fate? It is unjustly harsh to make me responsible and to predict tragedy. Sténio is much less miserable than he says and believes he is. Oh, I would eagerly exchange my existence for his. How many riches are within him which I no longer possess! How young and noble he is, and how much he believes in life!

When he complains most about me he is happiest, because then he looks at me as a monstrous exception. The more he repulses and struggles against my opinions, the more he believes in his own, and the more faith he has in himself.

Oh, to believe in oneself! Sublime, imbecilic stupidity of youth. To arrange one's future and dream of the fate one desires, to glance contemptuously over the weary, lazy travelers who congest the road and to believe that one is going to bound toward the goal as strongly and rapidly as thought, without ever losing breath or falling by the wayside. To know so little that one takes desire for will. What happiness and naiveté. We were happy, weren't we, Trenmor, when we were like that?

When he was no longer visible in the distance, I felt relieved of remorse. I stretched out on the grass and slept like a prisoner whose irons had been removed.

Then I again descended Monteverdor toward the wilderness, and I put the mountain peak between Sténio and me, between man and solitude, passion and dreams.

Everything that you have ever told me about the enchanting calm revealed to you after the storms in your life I felt as I found myself finally and absolutely alone between the earth and the sky. Not a human figure in this immensity, not a living creature in the air or on the mountains. The solitude seemed to make itself austere and beautiful to welcome me. There was not a breath of wind. Then I felt frightened of my own movements. Each blade of grass that I trampled seemed to suffer. I was destroying the calm; I was insulting the silence. I stopped, crossed my arms over my chest, and held my breath.

Oh, Trenmor, if death were like this. If it were only rest, contemplation, and silence. If all our capacities for enjoyment and suffering became paralyzed and only a feeble consciousness remained, an imperceptible intuition of our nothingness. If one could sit like this in the motionless air of a bleak, empty countryside, knowing that one will no longer suffer and that one rests there beneath the protection of the Lord. But what will the other life be? I haven't yet found a form in which I could desire it. So far, under whatever aspect it appeared, it made me feel fear or pity. But why have I never stopped wanting this other life, even for a day? What is this unknown, burning desire which has no imagined object and which devours the heart like a passion? Man's heart is an abyss of suffering whose depth has never been sounded and never will be.

I remained there as long as the sun was above the horizon, and all this time I felt happy. But when there was only reflected light in the sky, a growing inquietude spread throughout nature. The wind rose.

The stars seemed to struggle against agitated clouds. Birds of prey raised their loud cries and soared into the sky with their powerful wings, seeking a shelter for the night. They were as tormented by need, fear, and habit as if they had been men.

This emotion at the approach of night revealed itself in the smallest things. The azure butterflies, which sleep under the sun in the tall grass, rose in whirlwinds to flee into those mysterious retreats where they can never be found. The green frog of the marshes and the cricket with its metallic wings began to fill the air with their sad, incomplete notes. These produced a sort of painful irritation on my nerves. Even the plants seemed to tremble. Some closed their leaves, contracted their stamens, and withdrew their petals to the bottom of their calyxes. Others, amorous at this hour, undertook communications and embraces, opened themselves coquettishly, palpitating, hot to the touch like human breasts. Everything prepared to sleep or love.

Again I felt myself alone. When everything seemed inanimate, I could identify myself with the wilderness and feel part of it, like one more stone or bush. When I saw everything take on life again, everything filled with care for the next day and manifesting desire or anxiety, I was angry with myself in not having a will, a need, or a fear. The moon rose, and it was beautiful, The grass gave off transparent reflections like emerald. But what did the moon and its nocturnal magic matter? I awaited nothing but an hour more or less in its flow. No regret, no hope attached me to the flight of those hours that interested all creation. Nothing mattered. I withdrew into my hut and tried to sleep, through tedium rather than need.

Sleep is sweet and beautiful for small children who dream only of fairies or paradise, for little birds who press themselves frail and hot against their mother's down. But for those whose faculties have developed excessively, sleep has lost its chaste voluptuousness and its deep languor. Our life, arranged as it is, has taken away what is most precious about the night—forgetfulness of the day. I am not speaking of you, Trenmor. According to your sacred oath, you live in the world as if you weren't there. But in my unbridled life I have acted like the others. I have abandoned the necessities of the body to the contempt of the soul. I have failed to recognize the blessings of nature. I have deceived hunger by savory, exciting foods. I have deceived sleep by aimless excitation or profitless work. Sometimes, beneath the lamplight, I sought the key to the great enigmas of human life in books. Sometimes, thrown into the whirlwind of society, making my way through the crowd with a dejected heart, I sought to seize a sound, a breath that could give me an exalted emotion. At other times, wandering through the silent, cold countryside, I would question the stars bathed in fog and measure, with a sad ecstasy, the impassable distance between earth and sky.

How often day has surprised me in a palace resounding with harmony, in meadows wet with dew, or in the silence of an austere cell. I had forgotten the law of rest which darkness imposes on all living creatures but which has become powerless over civilized beings. A superhuman exaltation would sustain my spirit in its pursuit of some phantom, while my weakened, broken body demanded sleep. I have told you: spirituality taught to the world, first as a religious faith, then as an ecclesiastical law, has passed into people's customs, habits, and tastes. Spirituality has dominated people's physical needs and has tried to poeticize appetites as if they were feelings. Pleasure has fled its bed of grass and the cradles of the vineyard to sit on velvet at tables laden with gold. Elegant life, enervating the body and over-stimulating the spirit, has closed the abode of pleasure to the light of day. How can one live this way without exhausting oneself before one attains half one's allotted days? You see me aging too, as if I were a thousand years old. My beauty, which people praise, is only a deceptive mask hiding exhaustion and agony. At an age when people used to have energetic passions, we no longer have them. We no longer even have desires unless it is to end our weariness and rest in a coffin.

Alas, I no longer know what sleep is. Truly, I don't know what to call the heavy, painful numbness that weighs on my brain and fills it with dreams and sufferings for a few hours at night. But that sleep of my childhood, that good, sweet sleep which an angel seemed to protect with its wings and a mother rocked with her singing, that repairing calm of man's double existence, that soft heat spread over the members, that peaceful, regular respiration, that veil of gold and azure lowered over the eyes, and that ethereal breath running into the hair and around the neck, that sleep I have lost and will never again find. A sort of bitter, dark delirium hovers over my soul deprived of a guide. My burning, oppressed lungs rise with effort, unable to breathe the subtle perfumes of the night, which now has an avaricious, withering atmosphere. My dreams no longer have that charming disorder which condenses an entire life of enchantment into a few hours of illusion. Instead, my dreams have a frightful character of truth. The ghosts of all my disappointments pass continually back and forth. Each phantom evoked by nightmare is a clear, gripping allegory that responds to some deep, secret suffering in my soul. I see the fleeing shadows of friends I no longer love. I hear cries of alarm from those who are dead and whose souls wander in the dark shadows of another life. And then I, too, descend, pale, grief-stricken, into the abysses of that bottomless pit called Eternity, whose mouth always seems to gape at the foot of my bed like an open grave. I dream that I descend slowly, eagerly seeking a ray of hope in those limitless depths which are lit along my way only by blasts of red, sinister light from hell. This light burns my eyes to the bottom of my skull and leads me farther and farther astray.

These are my dreams. They are always about human reason struggling against suffering and impotence.

A sleep like this shortens life instead of prolonging it. It expends enormous energy. The work of thought, more disordered, more fantastic in dreams, is also more violent. There the sensations are awakened through surprise, as bitter, terrible, and tearing as they would be in reality. Trenmor, you judge of this by the impression that the dramatic representation of some strongly expressed passion leaves you with. In dreams the soul is a spectator at the most terrible scenes and cannot distinguish illusion from truth. The body springs up, twists, and trembles beneath the emotions of terror and suffering. And the spirit isn't conscious of its mistake so as to give itself, as at the theater, the strength of going on to the end. One wakes up bathed in sweat and tears. One's spirit is struck with a dumb anxiety and wearied for an entire day by the useless exercise that has just been imposed on it.

There are still more painful dreams. One is to believe you are condemned to accomplish some impossible task, like counting the leaves in a forest, or running as rapidly and lightly as air, or crossing valleys, seas, and mountains as fast as thought, in order to reach a fugitive, uncertain image which always outstrips you but continually draws you on as it changes its form. Haven't you had that dream, Trenmor, when there were still desires and illusions in your life? Oh, how often that phantom returns to me. Sometimes it is in the delicate, pale guise of a virgin who used to be my companion and who was like a sister to me. Happier than I, she died in the flower of her youth and illusions. She invites me to follow her to the dwelling of calm and repose. I try to walk after her. But, as an ethereal substance the wind carries, she outdistances me and disappears in the clouds. But I keep on running because I have seen another apparition surge up from the misty banks of an imaginary ocean. I mistake this for the first, and I pursue it with the same passion. But when it turns around, I see it is an ironic demon, a bloody corpse, a temptation, or a remorse. Still I keep on running. A fatal charm draws me after that Proteus. Sometimes it seems to be swallowed up in the red swell of the horizon. Then it suddenly comes up out of the earth just beneath my feet to send me off in a new direction.

Alas! I have journeyed through so much of the universe in these voyages of the soul. I have traveled over white, frozen steppes. I have looked over perfumed savannahs lit by the moon. On the wings of sleep I have outstripped the finest sailing ships and the large birds of prey. In the space of an hour I have seen the sun rise on the shores of Greece and set behind the blue mountains of the New World. I have seen people and empires beneath my feet. I have contemplated close up the red surfaces of stars that wander in the solitudes of space and in the plains of the sky. I have confronted the frightened faces of shadows dispersed by a breath of night. But what use have these voyages been to me? Have I ever seen anything which resembled my fantasies? Oh, how poor nature seemed to me, the sky leaden and the sea narrow, in contrast to the lands, skies, and oceans that I crossed in my immaterial flight! What beauty is left to charm us in real life, what strengths are left to enjoy and admire in the human soul when the imagination has spent everything in advance by an abuse of its powers?

However, these dreams were the image of life: they showed me life as though darkened in contrast with the too vivid burst of a supernatural light, just as future actions as well as the world's history are written, somber and terrible, in the sacred poetry of the prophets. Drawn after a shadow, across the reefs, deserts, enchantments, and chasms of life, I have seen everything without being able to stop myself. I have admired everything in passing without being able to enjoy anything. I have confronted all dangers without succumbing to any, always protected by that fatal power which carries me in its whirlwind and isolates me from the universe passing under my feet.

This is the sleep we have created for ourselves.

Our days are spent resting from the nights. Plunged into a sort of annihilation, we are made listless by the hours of activity for all creation; we are occupied in waiting for the night to awaken us and expend the little strength amassed during the day in useless dreams. This is the way my life has progressed for many years. All the energy of my soul is devoured, and the exterior effect is to weaken and destroy the body.

I slept no more tranquilly on my bed of heather than on my bed of satin, except that I did not hear the hours sound from the churches, and I could imagine that I had lost only a long hour instead of an entire night to that insomnia mixed with bad sleep. I feel that a great affliction is attached to inhabited places—the necessity always to know what hour of one's life it is. It is useless to try to escape this. One is made aware of it during the day by the use of everything surrounding us makes of time. And at night, in the silence, when everything sleeps and when forgetfulness seems to hover over all lives, the melancholy timbre of clocks pitilessly counts your steps toward eternity as well as the number of moments your past has irremediably devoured. How grave and solemn are those voices of time, which sound like a death cry, breaking indifferently on the resonant walls of dwellings or on echoless tombs. They seize you and make you tremble with rage and fear on your burning bed. "Once again," I have often told myself, "once again part of my existence has detached itself from me. One more ray of hope is extinguished. Again the hours! All the lost hours fall into the abyss of the past without bringing me to a point at which I feel myself alive."

Yesterday I was deeply depressed. I thought about nothing. I believe I rested an entire day, but I didn't feel rested.

In the evening I resolved not to sleep but to use the strength my soul finds for dreams to pursue an idea, as I formerly had. For a long time I have struggled neither against waking nor against sleeping. Last night I wanted to resume the struggle again, and since matter cannot extinguish spirit in me, I at least wanted to make spirit dominate matter. I didn't succeed! Crushed first by one and then the other, I spent the night seated on a rock. At my feet lay the glacier sparkling beneath the moon like a diamond palace out of the *Arabian Nights*. Over my head in the pure, cold sky, the stars shone as large and white as silver tears on a shroud.

This wilderness is truly beautiful, and Sténio the poet would have passed a night of ecstasy here. As for me, alas, I felt only indignation and resentment, because the deathlike silence weighed on my soul. I asked myself to what purpose this curious, greedy, anxious soul knocked continually against a brass heaven that never half-opened to its gaze and never responded with a word of hope. Yes, I detested radiant nature because she rose up before me like a stupid beauty who holds herself proud and mute beneath men's looks and believes she has done enough by merely showing herself. Then I fell back into this discouraging thought: "Even if I *knew*, I would only be the more to be pitied, being *powerless*." And instead of falling into philosophic calm, I fell into the tedium of this nothingness to which my existence is riveted.

## XXX [LÉLIA TO TRENMOR]

Trenmor, I am leaving the wilderness. I am going among people. I don't know where I will go. Sténio has resigned himself to live for a month without me. Whether I pass this time here or somewhere else doesn't matter to him. As for me, I want to be clear about one thing: whether it is worse for me live on earth with or without an affection. When I began to love Sténio I believed affection would carry me further than it has. I was so proud to believe that a trace of youth and love remained inside me . . . but that has become doubtful. I no longer know what I feel or who I am. I wanted solitude to reflect, because to abandon one's life without a rudder or oars on a flat, dull sea is to fail in the saddest way. Better the tempest and thunder; at least one can feel oneself perish.

But solitude is everywhere for me, and it is madness to seek it in the wilderness rather than anywhere else. Except that in the wilderness it is calmer and more silent, and I find that unbearable! I have discovered, I think, that suffering still sustains me. Suffering excites, revives, and irritates the nerves. It makes the heart bleed and shortens the agony. Suffering is the violent convulsion that lifts us off the earth and gives us the strength to rise toward heaven in order to curse and cry out. To die in lethargy is neither to live nor to die; it is to lose all the advantages and not to know all the voluptuousness of death.

Here in the wilderness all the faculties sleep. For an infirm body whose soul were still youthful and vigorous this vital air, this rural life, this absence of violent sensations, these long hours for rest, and these frugal habits would be blessings. But it is my soul which makes my body weak, and as long as my soul suffers, my body will waste away, whatever the salutary influence of the air and the primitive regime. Now this solitude is weighing on me. How strange! I used to love it so much, but I no longer do. Oh, Trenmor, that frightens me.

When all the earth failed me, I used to take refuge in God's bosom. I would invoke Him in the silence of the fields. I took pleasure staying there for days, entire months, absorbed in the thought of a better future. Today I am so worn out that even hope no longer sustains me. I still believe because I still desire, but this future is so far away, and this life does not end. Is it impossible to attach myself and find pleasure in this life? Is everything irredeemably lost? There are days I believe this, and those days are not the cruelest because then I am annihilated. Despair has no goads. The void is without terrors. But days when, with a warm breath of air, a pure morning sunbeam, a slight desire for existence awakens within me, I am the most unfortunate of beings. Fear, anxiety, and doubt gnaw at me. Where can I flee? Where can I take refuge? How can I come out of this marble, which, according to the beautiful poetic expression, *ascends to my knees** and keeps me imprisoned just as the tomb retains its dead?

So let us suffer. This is better than sleep. Suffering grows blunted and the heart impoverished in this peaceful, silent wilderness. Nothing but God is too much or too little. Within the turmoil of society the idea of God does not console our understanding. And in isolation God is too immense a thought: it crushes and frightens. Doubt insinuates itself into a soul that dreams; faith descends into a soul that suffers.

I have grown used to my suffering. It has been my sister, my companion, cruel, pitiless, but persistent, always accompanied by stoic resolution and austere advice.

Oh, suffering, come back. Why have you left me? If only you can be my friend, at least I don't want to lose you. It is through you alone that man is noble. If he could be happy in today's world and tranquilly observe the ugliness of the human species, he would no longer be any better than that stupid, cowardly mob which inebriates itself with crime and sleeps in filth. It is you, oh, sublime suffering, which makes us realize our own worth, as you make us weep over men's confusion.

---

*Reboul notes that the source is unknown to him.

Suffering sets us apart and places us, sheep of the wilderness, in the hands of the celestial pastor who watches us, pities us, and perhaps waits to console us.

The man who has not suffered is nothing. He is incomplete, useless, brute and worthless matter. The craftsman's chisel may break him. For this reason I esteem Sténio less than you, Trenmor, although Sténio has no vice and you have had them all. But you are like tempered steel. God has melted you in the burning furnace; and, after having twisted you in a hundred ways, he has made you into a solid, precious metal.

As for me, what will become of me? If I could only raise myself to your level and become more powerful than all life's evils and blessings.

## XXXI

Lélia descended the mountains and, with a little gold dispensed en route, she rapidly crossed the valley borders. A few days after having slept on the heath of Monteverdor, she was living in queenlike luxury in one of those beautiful towns of the lower plateau which compete in opulence, where the arts originated and still flourish.

Like Trenmor, who had restored and strengthened himself in prison, Lélia hoped to be reborn through her courage in the midst of this world she detested and these joys that horrified her. She resolved to overcome herself, to dominate the revolts of her wild spirit, to throw herself into the current of life, to shrink within herself for a time, to numb herself so as to see at close range the cesspool of society and to become reconciled with herself in comparison.

Lélia had no sympathy for the human race, although she suffered from the same weaknesses. But this blind, deaf race did not want to be aware of its unhappiness and degradation. Some people hid the wounds of their hearts and the exhaustion of their blood beneath a burst of useless poetry. They blushed to see themselves so old, so poor, in the midst of a generation they did not realize was pierced everywhere by old age and poverty. To make themselves look as young as they believed others to be, they lied, they hid the nakedness of their ideas beneath layers of rouge, and they denied their feelings. They were innocent, simple-minded braggarts who had been dotards ever since they left their mothers' breasts! Others, less brazen than their forebears, let themselves be carried by the current of the century. Slowly and weakly they went the way of the world without knowing why. By nature they were too mediocre to be very upset about their disquietude. Petty and feeble, they drooped in resignation. They didn't ask themselves if they could find help either through virtue or through vice. They were equally beneath both. Faithless, without atheism, enlightened just enough to lose the benefits of ignorance, ignorant enough to want to submit everything to narrowly rigorous systems, they could establish what occurrences had composed the material history of the world, but they never wanted to study the moral world or read history in man's heart. They had been stopped by the imbecilic inflexibility of their prejudices. These were the men of the day who reasoned about past and future centuries without perceiving that their genius had all issued from the same mold and that, assembled all together, they would still have been able to seat themselves on the benches of the same school and follow the law of the same pedant.

A few, who represented a social force, however, had survived the poisoned atmosphere of the times without losing the primitive vigor of the species. These were exceptional men. But among themselves they all resembled one another. Ambition, the last remaining impetus of an epoch without belief, annihilated their distinctive, male nobility to merge them all into a type of beauty that was coarse and without prestige. They were still steel men of the Middle Ages. They had the same fierce gaze, the strong thoughts, the robust muscles, the thirst for glory, and the taste for blood, as if each had been named Armagnac or Bourgogne. But the sap of heroism was lacking in these strong personalities. All that gives birth to heroism and nourishes it was lacking: love, fraternity in arms, hate, pride of family, fanaticism, all the personal passions that give intensity to character. There was no longer anything to motivate these courageous men except illusions of youth, which are destroyed in two mornings, and virile, stubborn, filthy ambition, the daughter of civilization.

Blighted by the consciousness of her degradation, Lélia alone was aware enough to ascertain it, sincere enough to avow it to herself. Lélia, weeping for her burnt-out passions and her lost powers, made her way through the world without seeking pity or finding affection. She knew very well that these people, in spite of their frantic, wretched agitation, were no more alive than she. But she knew too that they had the effrontery to deny this or the stupidity not to know it. She watched the agony of these people just as the prophet, seated on the mountain, wept over Jerusalem, that opulent, aged debauchee stretched out at his feet.

# XXXII

The richest of the small princes of the State was giving a ball. Lélia appeared there dazzlingly arrayed, but sad beneath the sparkle of her diamonds and less happy than the least of the wealthy bourgeoisie who strutted so proudly in all their finery. Naive womanly pleasures did not exist for her. She wore velvet, ropes of jewels, and long, light, soft feathers. She didn't even glance at herself in the mirrors with that look of childish vanity which sums up all the glories of a sex still childish in its old age. She didn't play with her diamond ornaments in order to show off her white, tapering hands. She didn't lovingly pass her fingers through her curls. She scarcely knew with what colors she was adorned, with what materials she had been dressed. With her impassive air, her pale, cold brow, and her rich clothing, she resembled one of those alabaster madonnas that Italian women devotedly cover with silken robes and brilliant chiffon. Like the marble Virgin, Lélia was insensitive to her beauty and charm. She was indifferent to the eyes fixed upon her. She despised all the men too much to take pride in their praise. What then had she come to do at the ball?

She came there seeking entertainment. These vast moving tableaux, arranged more or less with taste and skill within the frame of a ball were for her objects of art to examine. She did not understand that in a poor, cold climate where narrow, ungracious dwellings cram men together like bundles of merchandise in a warehouse one boasts of knowing luxury and elegance. She simply thought that in such nations a feeling for the arts was alien. She had pity for what are called balls in those sad, crowded rooms where the ceiling crushes women's coiffures and where, to spare their naked shoulders from the night cold, they replace fresh air with a feverish, suffocating, corrosive atmosphere. At those balls one makes a show of moving and dancing in a narrow space marked off by double rows of seated spectators who, with great difficulty, save their feet from the attacks of the waltz and their clothing from the candles.

She was one of those difficult people who love luxury only on a grand scale and who desire no middle ground between the well-being of private life and the lavishness of aristocratic social existence. Moreover, she granted only to Southern people the understanding of a life of pomp and display. She said that commercial and industrial nations have no taste, no instinct of the beautiful, and that the use of color and form must be sought among those ancient people who, lacking the energy of the present, have kept the religion of the past in their style of life.

Indeed, nothing is further from realizing the pretension of the beautiful than an ill-arranged ball. So many things difficult to assemble are necessary that during an entire century perhaps only two are given that can satisfy the artist. There must be the right climate, locale, decoration, food, and costumes. It must be a Spanish or Italian night, dark and moonless, because the moon, when it reigns in the sky, throws an influence of languor and melancholy over men that is reflected in all their sensations. It must be a fresh, airy night with stars shining feebly through the clouds. There must be large gardens whose intoxicating perfume penetrates the rooms in waves. The fragrance of orange trees and of the Constantinople rose are especially apt to develop exaltation of heart and mind. There must be light food, delicate wines, fruit of all climates, and flowers of all seasons. There must be a profusion of things rare and difficult to possess, because a ball should be a realization of the most voracious imaginations and the most capricious desires. One must understand one thing before giving a ball: rich, civilized human beings find pleasure only in the hope of the impossible. So one must approach the impossible as closely as one can.

The Prince of Bambuccj was a man of taste, which is the rarest and most superior quality for a rich man to possess. The only virtue one demands of such people is that they know how to spend their money suitably. On this condition one relieves them from the necessity of any other merit. But usually they are beneath their vocation, and they live in a bourgeois fashion without giving up the pride of their class.

Bambuccj was the first man in the world to pay for a horse, a woman, or a painting without bargaining and without letting himself be cheated. He knew the price of things almost to a *scudo*. His eye was as sharp as an official auctioneer's or a slave merchant's. His olfactory sense was so developed that he could tell simply from the bouquet of a wine not only the degree of latitude and the name of the vineyard, but

how the slope of the hill which had produced it faced the sun. No arti-
fice, no miracle of sentiment or coquetry was able to make him mistake
the age of an actress by six months—from seeing her walk across a stage
he was ready to establish her time of birth. From simply seeing a horse
run at a distance of a hundred feet he could perceive in one of its legs
the existence of a softness imperceptible to the veterinarian's fingers.
From merely touching the fur of a hunting dog he could tell in what
generation the purity of its race had been altered. And in a painting of
the Florentine or Flemish school he could tell how many brush strokes
had been given by the master. In a word, he was a superior man, and he
was so known for his abilities that he could no longer doubt himself.

The last ball that he gave contributed not a little to his reputation.
Large alabaster vases placed in the rooms, the stairways, and the corri-
dors of his palace were filled with exotic flowers whose name, form, and
perfume were unknown to most who saw them. He had carefully dis-
tributed twenty savants throughout the ball. These men were charged
with serving as ciceroni to the ignorant and explaining to them, without affectation, the use and the price of the things they were admiring.
The front of the villa and the courtyard sparkled with lights. But the
gardens were lit only by reflection from the inner rooms. As one drew
farther away, one could bury oneself in a soft, mysterious darkness and
rest from the movement and noise in the depths of these shadows. The
orchestra would sound  sweetly and faintly here, interrupted often by
gusts of a breeze scented with perfumes. Green velvet carpets had been
thrown as if forgotten on the grass, so that one could sit there without
crumpling one's clothing. And in some places bells of a clear, feeble
timbre were suspended in the trees and, at the least movement of air,
they strewed the leaves with uncertain notes or disconnected harmonies. One could have taken these notes for the frail voices of sylphs
awakened by the swaying of the flowers in which they were hidden.

Bambuccj knew how important it is to avoid everything that can
fatigue the senses when one wishes to arouse voluptuousness in enervated souls. Consequently, inside the rooms the light was not too bright
for delicate eyes. The harmony was sweet and without bursts of brass
instruments. The dances were slow and occasional. Young people were
not permitted to form numerous quadrilles. Because, in the conviction
that man knows neither what he wants nor what suits him, the philosophic Bambuccj had stationed chamberlains everywhere who regu-

lated each guest's dose of activity and repose. These men, skillful observers and profound skeptics, put a rein on the passion of some so that they would not exhaust themselves too quickly, rebuked the lethargy of others in order to arouse their activity. They could read in your expression the approach of satiety, and they found means to prevent this by making you change place and amusement. They could divine, too, in the nervousness of your walk, in the rapidity of your movements, the invasion or development of a passion. And if they foresaw some immediately scandalous result, they knew how to prevent it, either by intoxicating you with wine or by improvising some unofficial fable that disgusted you with your pursuits. But if they saw themselves in the presence of two actors experienced in intrigue, they spared no effort to engage and protect the relationships that could render pleasurable hours to well-matched couples.

And furthermore, nothing was more noble and candid than the affairs of the heart, which flourished there. As a man of refinement, Bambuccj had banished politics, gambling, and diplomacy from his parties. He found that to argue affairs of state, weave plots, ruin oneself, or conduct business in the midst of the pleasures of the ball was in the worst taste.

The joyous Bambuccj understood life too well for that. No complaints of the people and no murmur of underlings reached his ears when he was amusing himself, the good prince. All aggressive counsel, all thinkers who augured ill were banished from his entertainments. He wanted there only charming people, men of art, as they say today, stylish women, complaisant ones, many young people, a few ugly women to make the beautiful ones stand out, and just enough ridiculous guests to amuse the others.

Most of the guests were at the age where they still have illusions, and most belonged to those middle classes which have enough taste to applaud and not enough wealth to disdain. They were the chorus in the opera, a part of the spectacle as necessary as the decor and dinner. These good citizens did not suspect it, but in Bambuccj's salons they played the role of walk-ons. They had in their capacity as actors the profits of the ball, that is to say, pleasure; but they did not have honor. Honor was reserved for a small group of chosen epicureans whom the prince wanted to dazzle and charm. These were his true guests, judges, and friends. But the noisy, dressed-up crowd which passed beneath their eyes excited themselves to the utmost, believing that they were acting only for their own amusement. Admirable discernment of the Prince of Bambuccj!

These people of distinction were, for the most part, fitted to rival *il padron della casa* in wealth and taste. Bambuccj was well aware that he was not dealing with children. He held it a supreme honor to surpass them in inventions and delicacies of all kinds. If he had been served with dishes of vermilion by the Marquis della Pamocchie, Bambuccj displayed plates of pure gold on his tables. If the Jew Zacchario Pandolfi had exhibited his wife crowned with diamonds, Bambuccj adorned his mistress with diamonds down to her evening slippers. If Duke Almari's pages wore clothing embroidered with gold, Bambuccj's footservants wore clothing embroidered with fine pearls. Worthy and touching emulation among enlightened sovereigns of intelligent nations!

One must not be mistaken. The task undertaken by the prince was not easy. It was a grave matter which he had reflected upon more than one night before attempting. First he needed to surpass all those rivals worthy of him in expenditure of money and spirit. Then he needed to succeed in intoxicating them so much with pleasure that, forgetting their pride wounded in defeat, they would have the good faith to admit it. Such an enterprise was no obstacle to Bambuccj's immense imagination, and he threw himself into it sure of victory. He was full of confidence in his resources and in the assistance of heaven, from whom he had asked nine days in advance, through the voice of his clergy, that rain not fall during this memorable night.

Among these eminences to whom the entire province was served as a repast, Lélia, the stranger, occupied first rank. As she had a great deal of money, she always had a few distant "cousins" and a great deal of consideration wherever she found herself. Known for her beauty, her lavish spending, and the singularity of her character, she was the object of the most ingenious attentions of the prince and his favorites.

First she was introduced into one of those dazzling salons which was only the beginning of the progressive display reserved for her eyes. Bambuccj's agents were charged with adroitly stopping the newly arrived here and holding their interest for a suitable time. Now it happened that the young Greek prince Paolaggi entered at the same time Lélia did. The chamberlains could imagine nothing better than to put into each other's presence these social personages, surrounded by people of lesser wealth and nobility who were meant to fill up the spaces between the columns and the emptiness of the mosaic paving.

This Greek prince had the most handsome profile that antique sculpture had ever reproduced. He was as bronze as Othello, for there was Moorish blood in his family, and his black eyes burned with a savage sparkle; he was as tall and slim as the Oriental palm. There was in him something of the cedar tree, of the Arabian horse, of the Bedouin, and of the gazelle. All the women were mad about him.

He graciously drew near Lélia and kissed her hand, although he was seeing her for the first time. This was a man who had manners peculiar to himself. The women pardoned his many originalities, in consideration for the heat of the Asiatic blood that ran in his veins.

He said little to her, but in a voice so harmonious, in such a poetic style, with such penetrating looks, and with such an inspired expression that Lélia paused for five minutes to observe him as a prodigy. Then she thought of something else.

When Count Ascanio entered, the chamberlains went to seek out Bambuccj. Ascanio was the happiest of men. Nothing shocked him, all the world loved him, he loved all the world. Lélia, who knew the secret of his philanthropy, saw him only with horror. As soon as she perceived his presence, her face was filled with such a somber cloud that the terror-stricken chamberlains sought help from the patron himself to dissipate it.

"Is that what's troubling you?" Bambuccj asked the chamberlains in a low voice, throwing his eagle-eyed glance on Lélia. "Don't you see that the most agreeable of men is unbearable to the most melancholy of women? What would be Lélia's merit, genius, and grandeur if Ascanio succeeded in being right? If he could prove that everything is going well in the world, how would she pass her time? Clumsy men, you should know how fortunate it is for certain natures that the world is full of faults and vices. And hurry to rid Lélia of that charming Epicurean because he doesn't understand that it's better to kill Lélia than console her."

The chamberlains went to beg Ascanio to chase the melancholy that was spreading over Paolaggi's handsome brow. Ascanio, convinced that he was going to be useful, began to triumph. He was a good, ferocious man who lived only on the torture of others. He spent his life proving to them that they were happy so as not to give their lives significance. And when he had taken away from them the sweetness of believing themselves interesting, they hated him more than if he had beheaded them.

Bambuccj offered his arm to Lélia and led her to the Egyptian salon. She admired its décor, politely criticized a few stylistic details, and ended by overwhelming the savant Bambuccj with joy when she declared that she had never seen anything better. At this moment Paolaggi, who had rid himself of Ascanio, the happy man, reappeared close to Lélia. He had put on a costume of ancient times. Leaning against a jasper sphinx, he was the most remarkable feature of the tableau, and Lélia could not observe him without feeling the same admiration that a beautiful statue or a beautiful place would have inspired in her.

As she naively divulged her impressions to Bambuccj, the latter swelled up like a father whose son has been praised. It was not that he had the slightest affection for the Greek prince, but the young prince was handsome, costumed as he was, to great effect in the Egyptian room. Bambuccj considered him as he would a precious piece of furniture he had rented for the evening.

Then he began to make the most of his Greek prince. However, in spite of the best established superiority, it is very difficult to preserve oneself from inadvertence in the tumult of festivities of which one has complete charge. He involuntarily looked at the statue of Osiris. Then two analogous ideas unhappily crossed in his mind. It was impossible for him to separate them.

"Yes," he said, "he is a handsome statue . . . I mean to say that he is a distinguished man. He speaks Chinese as well as he does French, and French as well as Arabic. The cornelians in his ears are of inestimable worth, as well as the malachites incrusted on his feet . . . and then he has a head of fire, a head on which the sun has let its devouring influence fall . . . It is a head no one has copied and for which I paid a thousand crowns to one of those English thieves who explore Egypt. . . . Have you read his poem to Délia and his sonnets to Zamora in the manner of Petrarch? . . . I can't be sure that the body is absolutely identical, but the basalt is so similar, and the proportions match so well. . . ."

When Bambuccj perceived his imbroglio, he stopped short. But when he turned his head fearfully to Lélia, he gathered courage again as he saw that she wasn't listening and that she was moving rapidly off.

## XXXIII PULCHÉRIE

Everyone was hurrying in the direction of the Moorish salon, and the masters of ceremony could not control the disorder. A young seigneur claimed to have recognized Zinzolina in a sky-blue masked domino costume.* She was the most celebrated courtesan of the region, and she had mysteriously disappeared a year ago. Each wished to assure himself of the event. Those who had not known Zinzolina were bent on the honor of seeing that woman who was so praised. Those who had already seen her wanted to again. But the blue domino, a supple and elusive phantom, disappeared adroitly in the midst of the crowd to reappear in another salon, where the crowd again pursued her. Whoever wore a sky-blue domino costume was assiduously followed and questioned. When the true fugitive was recognized, a cry of emotion resounded throughout the palace. But she escaped before they could affirm that it was truly Zinzolina beneath that floating satin hood and velvet mask. Finally the masked woman reached the gardens. Then the crowd threw itself out through the doors. The tumult was immense. People scattered through the groves. Lovers profited from this to escape jealous eyes. The orchestra played to empty rooms. Ugly or jealous women put on sky-blue dominoes to find lovers or test their own. There was a great deal of noise, jeering, anxiety.

"Let them be," said Bambuccj to his breathless chamberlains. "They're amusing themselves. So much the better for you. Now you can rest."

This moment of madness and curiosity had given something harsh, unyielding, and uncivilized to the faces in the crowd. Lélia, who believed that she watched the least oscillations of life so attentively, noticed something strange in the mood of the people that night. Lost, forgotten in the crowd, she too began running through the gardens to observe closely the physiological phenomena of this corpse of society which wheezes and sings and, like an old coquette, rouges herself on her deathbed.

---

*A kind of loose cloak, apparently of Venetian origin, with a small mask covering the upper part of the face, chiefly worn at masquerades by persons not impersonating a character.

After walking a long time, passing through many disheveled groups, and finding herself in the midst of a feverish joy that had no charm for her, she sat down, tired, in an isolated spot sheltered by evergreens. Lélia felt oppressed. She looked at the sky. The stars shone above her head, but toward the horizon they were hidden under a thick band of clouds. Lélia was suffering. Finally she saw a pale light glide over the trees; it was a streak of lightning. And she understood the malaise she was feeling because storms always upset her physically, causing a nervous anxiety that all women if not all men have felt.

Then one of those sudden despairs which often seize us with no apparent motive, but which are always the effect of an inner pain engendered during a long time within the silence of the spirit, took hold of her. A horrible sadness seized her by the throat. She felt so discouraged, so out of place in life that she let herself fall to the ground and abandoned herself to those childish tears that express a complete abandon of strength and pride. Lélia appeared stronger than any creature of her sex. No one, since she was Lélia, had ever surprised the secrets of her soul on her impassive face. No one had ever seen a tear of suffering or tenderness run down her colorless, unlined cheeks.

She had a horror of others' pity, and in the midst of her greatest griefs she maintained the instinct to conceal herself. So now she hid her head in her velvet cloak. Far from the world, far from the light, hidden in the tall grass of an abandoned corner of the garden, she spilled out her suffering in vain, cowardly tears. There was something frightening about the suffering of this beautiful, elegant woman who lay there, curled up, terrible in her suffering, like a wounded lioness who sees her wound bleed and licks it while she howls.

Suddenly she felt a hand on her naked arm, a hand as hot and humid as the breath of that stormy night. She shivered. Ashamed, annoyed at being surprised in this moment of weakness which no one had ever seen, she leapt up with a sudden reaction of courage and rose to her full height before the reckless person. It was the blue domino of the ball, Zinzolina, the courtesan.

Lélia gave a loud cry. Then, trying to make her voice as severe as possible, she said, "I recognized you. You are my sister. . . . "

"And if I take my mask off, Lélia," said the courtesan, "won't you cry out that you're ashamed of me?"

"Ah, I recognize your voice too," said Lélia. "You are Pulchérie. . . . "

"I am your sister," said the courtesan, unmasking herself. "Your father's and mother's daughter. Don't you have a word of affection for me?"

"Oh, Pulchérie, you are still beautiful," said Lélia. "Save me, save me from life, save me from despair. Bring me tenderness. Tell me you love me. Tell me you remember our beautiful days, that you are my family, my blood, my only happiness on earth."

They embraced while both wept. Pulchérie was passionate in her joy. Lélia was sad in hers. They looked at each other with moist eyes and touched each other with astonished hands. They couldn't get over finding each other still so beautiful, admiring and loving each other, and, different as they were, recognizing themselves in each other.

Lélia suddenly remembered that her sister was defiled. What she would have excused in any other human creature made her blush in her sister's person. It was an involuntary trace of the strength of social vanity that is called honor.

She let her hands fall from Pulchérie's and stood motionless, overwhelmed by new discouragement, pale, her body bent in two and her eyes fixed on the dark greenery where reflections of the lightning streaks disappeared.

Pulchérie was frightened by this dejected attitude and by the bitter, glacial smile that wandered senselessly over her lips. Forgetting the degradation to which the world had condemned her, she pitied Lélia, so much does suffering establish equality between lives.

"So this is how you are," she said to her with sweetness, as a mother would console her afflicted child. "I have lived for many years away from my sister. When I find her again, she's on the ground, like a worn-out piece of clothing no one wants any more. She's suffocating her cries with the tresses of her hair and tearing at her bosom with her nails. Lélia, this is how you were when I found you. And now you're even worse, because you were crying and now you seem lifeless. You were living through suffering, and now you are no longer living through anything. Lélia, you are reduced to this! Oh, my God, how have all those brilliant gifts served you which made you so proud? Where has the path led you which you took with so much hope and confidence? Into what abyss of unhappiness have you fallen, you who claimed to put your feet on our heads? Jerusalem, Jerusalem, I told you that pride would ruin you!"

"Pride," said Lélia, who felt wounded in the most sensitive part of her soul. "You have nerve to talk about that, poor woman. Which of us was lost sooner in this wilderness, you or me?"

"I don't know, Lélia," said Pulchérie sadly. "I have gone through many experiences. I am still young and beautiful. I have suffered, but I am not weary. I haven't yet said, 'My God, this is enough!' while you, Lélia. . . . "

"You are right," said Lélia dejectedly. "As for me, I have exhausted everything. . . . "

"Everything but pleasure," said the courtesan, laughing a bacchantic laugh which suddenly changed her from head to foot.

Lélia trembled and involuntarily drew back. Then, approaching suddenly, she took her sister's arm.

"And you, my sister," she cried. "Have you really tasted pleasure? Have you exhausted it? Are you still alive as a woman? Give me your secret, give me something of your happiness, since you possess it. . . . "

"I don't have happiness," said Pulchérie. "I haven't looked for it. Unlike you, I haven't lived with deceptions. I haven't demanded more of life than it could give me. I have reduced all my ambitions to knowing how to enjoy what exists. I have put my virtue into not despising, my wisdom into not desiring beyond certain limits. Anacreon has written my liturgy. I have taken antiquity for a model and the naked Greek goddesses for my divinities. I endure the evils of our exaggerated civilization. But to keep me from despair I have the religion of pleasure. . . . Oh, Lélia, you're looking at me and listening so eagerly. Then I don't horrify you any more. I'm no longer the stupid, vile woman you moved away from before with such disgust."

"I never despised you, my sister. I pitied you. Now I am astonished because I don't have to. Do I dare say that I rejoice about this?"

"You hypocritical spiritualists are always afraid to sanction the joys you don't share," said Pulchérie. "Oh, you're crying now. You lower your head, my poor sister. You are bent and broken beneath the weight of this existence you have chosen, but whose fault is it? This lesson can be useful to you. Do you remember our quarrels and our separation? We mutually predicted each other's ruin."

"Alas, I predicted that men would despise you, Pulchérie, that you would be abandoned and live out a horrible old age. . . . I can't be right yet. Thank heavens, you're young and beautiful still. But haven't you felt shame burn you with its red-hot iron? That insatiable, idle crowd is seeking you out now to appease its insolent curiosity. Can't you hear it growling like a foul beast? Can't you feel its hot breath infect you? Listen, it's calling you, claiming you again as its prey. Courtesan, you belong to that crowd. If it comes here, don't say you are my sister. If it were to confuse us, if it dared put its muddy hands on me! Poor Pulchérie, this is your master, your god, your lover. These people, all these people who make noise and who stink in that crowd! You have found pleasure in their embraces. My poor sister, you see very well that you are viler than the dust beneath their feet."

"I know this," said the courtesan, passing her hand over her shameless brow as if to chase away a cloud. "But to face shame is my virtue, as it is yours to avoid it. This is my wisdom, and it leads me to my goal, it survives the anguishes that are always being recreated, and at the cost of this struggle I have pleasure. This is my ray of sun after the storm, the enchanted isle on which the tempest casts me, and if I am degraded, at least I am not ridiculous. Lélia, it is ridiculous to be useless. And to be ridiculous is worse than to be infamous. To serve for nothing in the universe is more contemptible than to serve for the most degrading uses."

"That is true," said Lélia with a somber air.

"Furthermore," continued the courtesan, "what does shame matter to a truly strong soul? Lélia, do you know the power of public opinion? People who submit to it are called worthy, when they are merely servile. One must be strong to resist this. Do you consider an egotistical calculation, which is so easy to make and so encouraged and rewarded by the world, to be virtue? Can you compare the labors, the sufferings, the heroisms of the mother of a family with those of a prostitute? When both are at grips with life, do you think the one who has had less affliction merits more glory?

"But what is this, Lélia? My words don't make you shudder as they used to. Won't you say anything? This silence is terrible. Lélia, you seem to be effaced like a wrinkle in a wave or a name written in sand. Does your noble blood no longer rise to the effrontery of matter? Wake up, Lélia! Defend virtue if you want me to believe something by that name exists."

"Continue," said Lélia in an ominous tone. "I am listening."

"What does God impose on us?" continued Pulchérie. "It is to live, isn't it? What does society impose on us? Not to steal. But society is so constructed that many individuals are forced, for survival, to practice an occupation authorized by society but given the odious name of vice. Do you know with what steel a poor creature must be tempered in order to live with that? Do you know how many affronts people give this creature to make her pay for the weaknesses she has surprised and the brutalities she has appeased? Under what mountains of injustices she must accustom herself to sleep, to walk, to be lover, courtesan, and mother! These are three conditions of woman's fate that no woman escapes whether she sells herself in a market of prostitution or by a marriage contract. Oh, my sister, so many unjustly dishonored creatures have the right to despise the crowd that afflicts them with its curse after sullying them with its love! Do you see, if there is a heaven and hell, heaven will be for those who have suffered most and who have found a few joyous smiles, a few benedictions for God, even on their bed of suffering. Hell will be for those who have monopolized the most beautiful part of existence and failed to appreciate its value. The courtesan Zinzolina, in the midst of the horrors of social degradation, has confessed her faith by remaining faithful to voluptuousness. The ascetic Lélia, in the depths of an austere, respected life, has denied God every moment as she closed her eyes and her soul to the blessings of existence."

"Alas, you accuse me, Pulchérie. But you don't know if it has been up to me to make a choice and follow a plan in life. Do you know what my life has been since we separated from each other?"

"I knew what the world said about you," responded the courtesan. "I saw only that you had a questionable existence as a woman. I knew that you were surrounded with mystery and poetic affectation, and I smiled with pity as I reflected on that hypocritical virtue which consists of deriving vanity from impotence or fear."

"Humiliate me," said Lélia. "I have so little confidence in myself today that I find nothing to justify myself. Do you want to hear about this moral life, so arid and pale but so bitter? Then you can tell me if there is a remedy for sufferings which have lasted so long and for such profound discouragement."

"I am listening," said Pulchérie. She was leaning her round, white arm on the foot of a marble nymph which smiled affectedly, half-hidden in the dark branches. "Speak, my sister. Tell me the miseries of your life. First, let me say that I already know what they are. You used to walk in the depths of our woods, leaning on my arm, pale and thin as a sylph, attentive to the flight of the birds, the hues of the flowers, the changing aspect of the clouds, but unaware of the young hunters who followed us with their eyes through the trees as they passed. Lélia, then I already knew that your youth would be consumed in the pursuit of vain dreams and with contempt for the only advantages of life. Do you remember those endless walks we took on our paternal fields and those long evening reveries when we sat by the gilded rail of the terrace? You would look at the white stars above the hills, while I would watch the dusty horsemen who rode down the path."

"I remember all that very well," said Lélia. "You attentively followed all those travelers who were already effaced by the fog of sunset. You could scarcely make them out, but you took a liking or a disdain for each according to whether he descended the hill boldly or cautiously. You laughed pitilessly at the prudent horseman who dismounted to lead his uncertain, lazy horse by the bridle. You applauded the one who affronted the dangers of the steep slope with a firm, steady trot. Once I remember that I reproached you severely for waving your handkerchief in a transport of admiration to encourage a young madman who was galloping. Two or three times he reined in his horse barely in time to avoid rolling into the ravine."

"But he couldn't see or hear me," said Pulchérie. "My fierce sister, you were indignant at the interest I gave to a man. You were sensitive only to the elusive beauties of nature, to sound, to color, never to a distinct, material form. A distant song would make you shed tears. But as soon as the shepherd with his naked legs appeared at the top of the hill, you turned your eyes away with disgust. You stopped listening to his voice or finding pleasure in it. Reality wounded your overly sharp perceptions and destroyed your overly demanding hope. Isn't that true, Lélia?"

"That is true, my sister. We did not resemble each other. Wiser and happier than I, you lived only to enjoy. More ambitious and less submissive to God perhaps, I lived only to desire. Do you remember that heavy, hot summer day we stopped beside a stream beneath the cedars of the valley in that mysterious, dark retreat where the noise of the water falling from rock to rock mingled with the singing of cicadas? We stretched out on the grass, and while we were looking at the hot sky over our heads through the trees, a heavy sleep, a profound freedom from care came over us. We awakened in each other's arms without being aware that we had fallen asleep."

At these words Pulchérie trembled and pressed her sister's hand. "Yes, I remember that better than you, Lélia. The memory burns me. I've thought of it often with an emotion full of charm and perhaps shame."

"Shame?" questioned Lélia, withdrawing her hand.

"Haven't you guessed that?" asked Pulchérie. "I would never have dared confess it to you then. But now I can say everything to you, and you can learn. Listen, my sister . . . in your innocent arms, on your virginal bosom, God revealed the power of life to me for the first time. Don't move away like that. Listen to me without prejudice."

"What prejudice do I have?" said Lélia, drawing near. "At least that would be a belief. Speak. Tell me everything, sister."

"Very well," said Pulchérie. "We were sleeping peacefully on the moist, hot grass. The cedars exhaled their exquisite odor of balsam, and the midday wind passed its burning wing over our damp brows. Until then, carefree and laughing, I had welcomed each day of my life as a new blessing. Sometimes brusque, penetrating sensations made my blood churn. An unknown fervor seized my imagination. Nature appeared to me under the most dazzling colors. If I looked at myself in the mirror at those moments, I found myself rosier and more beautiful. Then I wanted to embrace that reflection in the glass which inspired me with a senseless love. Then I would begin to laugh, and I would run more lightly amid the grass and flowers. Because for me nothing revealed itself through suffering. I didn't tire myself out as you did with useless questions. I found because I didn't seek.

"That day, happy and calm as I was, a strange, delirious, unheard of dream revealed the mystery which until then had been impenetrable and tranquilly respected. Oh, my sister, deny the influence of heaven if you will. Deny the sanctity of pleasure. You would have said, if you had experienced this ecstasy, that an angel sent from the bosom of God had taken it upon himself to initiate you into the sacred trials of human life. But as for me, I simply dreamed of a man with black hair who leaned over me to brush my lips with his hot, rosy ones. I awakened oppressed, throbbing, happier than I had ever imagined I could be. I looked around. The sun cast its reflections over the depths of the woods. The air was soft. The cedars raised their long, finger-shaped branches, like immense arms and hands, toward the sky. Then I looked at you. Oh, my sister, how beautiful you were. I had never found you so before that day. In my complaisant young girl's vanity, I had preferred myself to you. I had felt that my brilliant cheeks, my rounded shoulders, and my golden hair made me more beautiful than you. But at that instant I awakened to the beauty of another creature. I no longer loved only myself. Now I needed to find an object of admiration and love outside myself. I rose softly and looked at you with singular curiosity and a strange pleasure. Your thick, black hair clung to your face, and the close curls tightened as if a feeling of life had clenched them next to your neck, which was velvet with shadow and sweat. I passed my fingers through your hair. It seemed to squeeze and draw me toward you. Your fine, white blouse pressed against your breasts made your skin, tanned by the sun, still darker than usual. And your long eyelashes, weighted with sleep, stood out against your cheeks, which were animated then with a more solid color than they are today. Oh, Lélia, you were so beautiful! But your beauty was different from mine, and that troubled me strangely. Your arms, thinner than mine, were covered with an imperceptible black down that has long since disappeared because of cosmetic care. Your feet, so perfectly beautiful, bathed in the brook, and long, blue veins were outlined against the skin. Your breathing raised your chest with a regularity that seemed to express calm and strength. In all your features, in your position, in your appearance, which was more rigid than mine, in the deeper tint of your complexion, and especially in that fierce, cold expression on your face as you slept, there was something masculine and strong which nearly prevented me from recognizing you. I found that you resembled the handsome young man with the black hair of whom I had just dreamed. Trembling, I kissed your arm. Then you opened your eyes, and your gaze penetrated me with shame. I turned away as if I had committed a guilty action. But, Lélia, no impure thought had even presented itself to me. How had it happened? I knew nothing. I received from nature and from God my first lesson in love, my first sensation of desire. . . . Your expression was mocking and severe, as it always was. But it had never intimidated me as it did at that moment. . . . Don't you remember my confusion and my blushing?"

"I even remember something you said, which I couldn't explain to myself," replied Lélia. "You made me lean over the water, and you said, 'Look at yourself. See how beautiful you are.' I replied that I was less so than you. 'Oh, but you are much more beautiful,' you said. 'You look like a man.' "

"And that made you shrug your shoulders scornfully," said Pulchérie.

"I did not realize," said Lélia, "that a destiny had just been traced out for you, while for me none would ever be."

"Begin your story," said Pulchérie. "The sounds of the festivities have grown distant. I hear the orchestra taking up the music again. They have forgotten you, and they have given up looking for me. We can be free for some time, so talk."

# PART THREE

# XXXIV

"I won't tell you detailed, precise facts," said Lélia. "All that has made up my life would take days to recount. But I will tell you the story of an unhappy heart, led astray by a useless wealth of intelligence and feeling, withered before having lived, worn out by hope, and rendered impotent perhaps by too much strength."

"And that makes you deplorably vulgar, Lélia," said the courtesan, pitiless in her good sense. "You are like all the poets I have read. Because I do read the poets. I read them to reconcile myself with life, which they paint so falsely. Life is too good for them. I read them to find out what pretentious and scandalously erroneous ideas I must protect myself from to be wise. I take only what is useful—that is, I appropriate their luxuriant manner of expression, which has become the ordinary language of our time, and I read them to protect myself from adopting their foolish ideas. You should have confined yourself to that. My dear Lélia, with your fertile mind you should have been able to embellish reality in order to appreciate it more. You should have applied your superior intellect to enjoy, not to deny, because if you don't what good is intelligence?

"And you are right, cruel one," said Lélia bitterly. "Don't I know all that? You have pointed out my failing, and you scoff at me when I complain to you. I am afflicted by having a personality that typifies the sufferings of an entire sickly, feeble generation, and you respond with contempt. Is this how you console me?"

"Forgive me, *meschina*," said Pulchérie smiling, "and continue."

Lélia said, "I don't know whether God created me out of anger or apathy, out of indifference or hatred. Sometimes I hate myself so much that I think I must be the wisest but the most terrible synthesis of an infernal will. At other times I despise myself as an inert product engendered by chance and matter. I don't know whom to blame for my misery, and my greatest suffering has always been to fear the absence of a God to curse. I seek Him on earth, in heaven, and in hell—that is to say in my own heart. I seek Him out to crush Him. What upsets me is that He has given me the enormous power of attacking Him through myself, but He hides Himself, seated in all His glory and deafness, somewhere above all the efforts of my thought.

"However, I was born under apparently happy auspices. My head was well-formed. My eyes were black and inpenetrable, as the eyes of a free, proud woman should be. My blood circulated well. No withering, unjust infirmity afflicted me. My childhood is rich in memories and in sensations of an inexpressible poetry. It seems the angels rocked me in their arms, and magic illusions spoiled nature for me before I realized the meaning of what I saw.

"As my sense of beauty developed, all the world seemed to smile on me. Each day the power of love and admiration blossomed in my heart.

"This power was so precious that I felt it emanate from me like a sweet perfume. Far from distrusting it and regulating its flow in order to enjoy the fruits longer, I stimulated this power. How imprudent and unhappy I was!

"I exhaled this power of love through all my pores. I gave my love to everything as if it were an inexhaustible source of life. The least object of esteem or amusement inspired me. A poet was a god for me, the earth my mother, and the stars my sisters. I would bless heaven on my knees for a flower blooming in my window box or for a bird's song sent to awaken me. My feeling of well-being bordered on delirium.

"Day by day this power of love increased, exciting my sensitivity and spreading itself unrestrainedly all around me. I threw all my thought, all my strength into the void of an elusive universe which sent me back all my sensations blunted. My vision was dazzled by the sun; my desire was fatigued by the sight of the ocean and the blurred horizon. My belief was shaken by the mysterious algebra of the stars and the muteness of all things. I reached adolescence in a fullness of sensitivity that could go no further without breaking its mortal envelope.

"When I entered active life, I was naive in the ways of the world, but I had no new emotion to feel. This is the story of an entire generation.

"Then a man came, and I loved him as passionately as I had loved God, the sky, the sun, and the ocean. Only I stopped loving these things and spent all my emotion on him.

"Alas, this man had not lived with the same ideas. He was familiar with other pleasures, other ecstasies. He wanted to share them with me. But my body had grown impoverished as a result of austere mystical contemplations. My blood had grown fatigued through the immobility of study. I scarcely felt youth stick its goads into my flesh. My dreams had been too sublime. I could no longer descend to gross material appetites. Although I was unaware of what had happened, a complete divorce had been effected between my body and spirit. When the time came to live, it was too late: I had lived.

"But if the youth of the body lasts only a day, which must be grasped because it never returns, the youth of the soul is long and the life of the spirit immortal. My heart was outliving my senses. I dedicated myself to spirit.

"You are right to say that poetry has led men astray. She has desolated the real world, cold, poor, and wretched as it is compared with the dreams she creates. Drunk with her promises, lulled by her sweet mockeries, I could never resign myself to reality. Poetry had created other sensitivities in me that nothing on earth could satisfy. Each day marked the ruin of my destiny in the face of my pride, the ruin of my pride in the face of its own triumphs. Because I despised everything, I began to despise myself as a foolish, vain creature.

"While poetry intoxicates, she does not let us know that she betrays. She makes herself as beautiful, simple, and austere as the truth. She takes a thousand different faces. She makes herself man, angel, and God. One becomes attached to this phantom. One prostrates oneself before her, believing one has found God and conquered the Promised Land. But alas, her bright raiment dissolves into shreds under the eyes of analysis, and human misery no longer has even a rag to cover itself with. Then man weeps and curses God. He demands reparation for his disappointments. He feels cheated and wants to die.

"And why does God deceive him? What glory can the strong find in deluding the weak? Because all poetry comes from heaven and is only the instinct of a divinity present in our lives. Materialism destroys poetry and reduces everything to the simple proportions of reality. It limits the universe, while religious faith peoples it with phantoms. Does the Divinity behind these impenetrable veils laugh at our worship and at the angelic creations with which our morbid minds surround it? Alas, all this is profoundly discouraging."

"You must neither dream nor pray," said Pulchérie. "You must be content to live and simply accept the belief in a good God. This would be enough for man if he had less vanity. But man wants to examine this God and evaluate His works. He wants to know Him, question Him, make Him responsive to his needs, responsible for his sufferings. He wants to deal with God as an equal. Man's pride has invented poetry and placed all these deceptive dreams between earth and heaven. God is not the author of your miseries. . . ."

"Pride and confidence," replied Lélia, "are two different words to express the same idea, two different ways of looking at the same passion. No matter what you call it, this feeling completes us and is the keystone of our intellectual architecture. God has crowned His work with this vague thought, painful, but infinite and sublime. He imposed this restlessness and anxiety on us when He raised us above other living creatures. 'You surpass the strength of the camel, the skillfulness of the beaver,' He told us, 'but you will never be satisfied with your creations. Beyond your terrestrial Eden you will always seek the elusive promise of a better abode. Go. You will divide the earth among yourselves, but you will desire heaven. You will be powerful, but you will suffer.' "

"So it is," said Pulchérie. "Suffer in silence, pray on your knees, wait for heaven, but resign yourself to the evils of life. To resent the sufferings imposed by God is not man's task. He must accept them. You have only one chance for greatness on earth, and you despise it. You know very well that it is not enough to find the chalice bitter; one must drink it to the dregs. You must submit, but you never do. Don't you fear that by knocking so imperiously you will render the abode of the angels inaccessible?"

"You are right, my sister. You talk like Trenmor. Amorous of life as you are, you submit just as he does, and he is so detached. You have the same calm in disorder that he has in virtue. But I have neither virtues nor vices. I don't know how to endure the boredom of existing. Alas, it is easy for you to prescribe patience. If, like me, you were placed between those who still live and those who no longer do, you too would be stirred with deep rage and tormented by an insatiable desire to be something, either to begin life or to finish it."

"But didn't you tell me that you had loved? To love is to live for two."

"For you, certainly it is. You sought a well-known termination in love, which you could realize. But I could not be anyone's equal in love. The coldness of my senses placed me beneath the most abject women. The exaltation of my thoughts elevated me above the most passionate men. I loved out of need. But not tasting the joys I gave, I could not attach myself to the object of my sacrifices by any real emotion of deep-founded gratitude. This frantic desire for happiness, which I pursued through him and which no human pleasure could satisfy, was torture. If my spiritual ardor had not destroyed my salutary egotistical calculations, I would never have been able to love. But, not knowing where to expend my intellectual vigor, I threw it, groveling and tenacious as I was, at the feet of an idol created by my homage because he was a man like the others, And when I was weary of prostrating myself, I broke the pedestal. Then I saw him reduced to his true height. But I had placed him so high, in my ceremonious worship, that he had seemed to me as great as God.

"This was my most deplorable error! I was reduced to regret the illusion as soon as I had lost it. Alas, I had nothing more to put in its place. Everything seemed small to me next to that imaginary colossus. Friendship seemed cold, religion false, and poetry had died along with love.

"With my illusion I had been as happy as characters of my temperament can be. I enjoyed the expansion of my mind and feelings. I felt intoxicated with truly divine ecstasies. I plunged myself as far as I could into that burning, terrible destiny which after breaking me was to devour me. I experienced an inexpressible state of sadness and joy, of despair and energy. My afflicted soul took pleasure in this ill-starred tossing that consumed me fruitlessly. Calm only made me fearful. Repose only annoyed me. I demanded obstacles, fatigues, devouring jealousies to repress, cruel ingratitudes to pardon, great works to pursue, great misfortunes to endure. This was a glorious career. Had I been a man I would have loved combat, the odor of blood, the pressures of danger. Perhaps in my youth I might have sought to reign by intelligence and to dominate others by powerful speeches. As a woman I had only one noble destiny on earth, which was to love. I loved *valiantly*. I submitted to all the evils of blind, fierce passion at grips with social life and with the real selfishness of the human heart. For long years I resisted anything that could dampen or extinguish it. Now I endure people's reproaches without bitterness, and I listen smilingly to their accusations of insensitivity. God knows that I have accomplished my task. I have furnished my share of weariness and anguish for the great abyss of anger into which men's tears fall endlessly. I know that I have used my strength in devotion, that I have abjured my pride, effaced my existence behind another's. Yes, my God, You know this. You have broken me beneath Your scepter, and I have fallen into the dust. I have stripped my pride at the altar of the man You offered to my doomed homage."

"You boast, Lélia. Your work has been a pure loss, and I am not surprised. You wanted to be noble, but you weren't even praiseworthy. That comes of wanting to isolate yourself from vulgar joys and carve yourself a choice, exceptional destiny. You felt yourself too superior to share happiness with another human being. You wanted to give without receiving. You wanted to be generous. You have only been prodigal. If you had been truly great, you would have put his happiness in the place of your own. In your lover's arms you would have tasted a greater pleasure than his—that of giving him everything. I have often desired this supreme pleasure. I have often regretted that I couldn't extinguish the heat of my blood and moderate my impetuous desire so that I could contemplate a man lying happy on my bosom. I would have liked to mingle the purified joys of the spirit with the feverish joys of the body. Why do they seem to exclude or suffocate each other?"

"Because we know how to differentiate between them," said Lélia.

"I have known the generous pleasures of the soul separated from matter. But this wasn't enough for me, because human selfishness is ferocious. It is indomitable, it constantly renews itself, it dully consumes us, or it awakens in us all of a sudden with a tearing sensation. You are right to mock the enormous ambition of platonic love. The spirit vainly seeks to raise itself. Suffering always brings it back to earth. Oh, I remember the burning nights I passed pressed against a man's flanks in close embrace with him. During those nights I thoroughly studied the revolts of pride against the vanity of abnegation. I sensed one could simultaneously love a man to the point of submitting to him and love oneself to the point of hating him because he subjugates us."

"And then," said Pulchérie, softening the tone of sarcasm with which she had been speaking and taking her sister's hand in a movement of sympathy, "men are coarse. You see, Lélia, in our lives of love affairs and change, similar things happen to us. We are heaped with riches by one man, and we share them with another. Usually we hate the man who loves us enough to pay. We share our wealth with the one who is indifferent enough to be at our service. But man is brutal, and he does not know the limits of a woman's devotion. He does not know that he is mad to accept the gifts of a loving heart and an unfettered spirit. She offers with abandon, she gives joyously, then, astonished, she stops herself and despises the man who has not blushed to receive her gifts although he is stronger and more powerful. Man is stupid and woman is unstable. These two beings, so alike and yet so different, are made so that there is always hate between them even in the love they feel for each other. The first emotion that follows their embraces is disgust or sadness. This is a supreme law against which it is useless to revolt. Providence must have designed the union of man and woman to be fleeting. Everything opposes their continued association, and change is a necessity of their nature."

"What was cruelest for me," said Lélia, "is that he failed to appreciate the extent of my sacrifices. He always brushed aside the idea of my resignation, as if gratitude would have embarrassed him. He pretended to believe me abused by a sentiment of hypocritical modesty. He affected to take for signs of rapture the moanings torn from me by suffering and impatience. He laughed harshly at my tears. At times his infamous selfishness was fed by his pride. When he had broken me in ferocious embraces, he slept brusque and uncaring at my side, while

I devoured my tears so as not to awaken him. Oh, misery and enslavement of woman! You are such a part of her nature that society ought to strive at least to soften you!

"However, I loved him with passion, this master I had chosen. I accepted him as a fatal necessity. I venerated him with a secret complaisance. I loved him madly. The more he made me feel his domination, the more I cherished it, the greater pride I took in wearing my shackles. But I also began to curse my slavery at the first moment of freedom he left me either through forgetfulness or indifference. I made my love a religion, a virtue. But I wished he had been grateful, while he obeyed only his instinctive preference. I was wrong. He could only despise my heroic frailty, while I cherished his lax rule over me. . . .

"What caused me to love him a long time (long enough to weary my entire soul) was without doubt the feverish irritation produced in me by the absence of personal satisfaction. When I was near him I felt a sort of strange and delirious greed which, taking its source from the keenest powers of my intelligence, could not be satisfied by any carnal embrace. I felt my bosom devoured by an inextinguishable fire, and his kisses shed no relief. I pressed him in my arms with a superhuman force, and I fell next to him exhausted, discouraged at having no possible way to convey to him my passion. With me desire was an ardor of the soul that paralyzed the power of the senses before it awakened them. It was a savage fury that seized my brain and concentrated itself there exclusively. My blood froze, impotent and poor, before the immense soaring of my will. Then I wanted to die. But the egotist never consented to strangle me while he pressed me against his chest. However, this was my only hope for sensual pleasure. I hoped at last to know the languors and delights of love while sleeping in the arms of death.

"When he was drowsy, satisfied, and at rest, I would lie motionless beside him. I passed many hours watching him sleep. He seemed so handsome to me! There was so much force and grandeur on his peaceful brow. Next to him my heart palpitated violently. Waves of blood mounted to my face. Then unbearable tremblings passed through my limbs. I seemed to experience again the excitation of physical love and the increasing turmoil of desire. I was violently tempted to awaken him, to hold him in my arms, and to ask for his caresses from which I hadn't yet known how to profit. But I resisted these deceiving entreaties of my suffering because I well knew it wasn't in his power to calm me.

God alone could do this, if He had deigned to muffle the morbid vigor of my soul. Then I fought the demon of hope that stayed awake with me. I fled that voluptuous and miserable couch, that sanctuary of love which was the coffin in which all my illusions and strength were buried. I paced the cold marble of my rooms. My head was on fire in the night air. I threw myself on my knees and prayed God to regenerate me. If someone had promised to renew the impoverished blood in my veins, I would have let myself be stabbed like Eson and, like him, cut into pieces.

"Sometimes in sleep, prey to those rich ecstasies that devour ascetic minds, I felt myself carried away with him on clouds by balmy breezes. Then I swam on waves of pleasure, and, passing my arms languidly around his neck, I would fall on his breast murmuring vague words. But he awoke. In place of that angel who had rocked me in the wind with his wings, I found this man as brutal as a wild beast, and I would flee with horror. But he would pursue me. He didn't want to have been awakened from his sleep for no reason, and he savored his pleasure on the bosom of a woman who was fainting and half dead.

"One day I felt so worn-out with loving that I stopped suddenly. When I saw how easily this bond was broken, I was astonished at having believed in its eternal duration for so long.

"I wanted to let myself fall into a state of sweet, indifferent exhaustion. So I retired into solitude. A large, abandoned monastery, half-destroyed by the battles of the revolution, offered itself as a retreat. It was situated on one of my estates. I took a cell for myself in the least devastated portion. The prior had formerly lived there. You could still see the marks of the nails on the wall where his crucifix had hung, and his knees had hollowed out their imprint on the paving-stone beneath. I took pleasure in restoring that cell with the austere insignia of the Catholic faith: a bed in the form of a coffin, an hourglass, a human skull, and images of saints and martyrs raising their bloody hands toward the Lord. With these objects, which reminded me that I was dead from now on to human passions, I mixed the happier attributes of the life of a poet and naturalist: books, musical instruments, and vases filled with flowers.

"At first I had loved the surrounding country for its uniform sadness and for the silence of its vast plains. There I had hoped to entirely detach myself from quick sensations, from exalted admiration. Eager for rest, I believed I could, without fatigue or danger, look out over the flat horizon with its ocean of heath. An occasional tough oak, a bluish marshland, and colorless sand did little to relieve its barrenness.

"I had hoped that in this absolute isolation, with the Spartan habits I was creating for myself, I would find forgetfulness of the past and freedom from care about the future. Little strength remained in me for regret, still less for desire. I wanted to consider myself as one dead and bury myself in these ruins so that I could freeze myself completely and return to the world invulnerable.

"I resolved to begin by physical stoicism in order to reach a stoicism of the spirit. I had lived in luxury. Through habit I wanted to become absolutely insensitive to the material rigors of a hermit's life. I dismissed all useless servants. I received only my nourishment and the objects absolutely necessary for my existence from the hands of an invisible person who glided each morning through the abandoned passages of the cloister as far as a grating outside my cell, and who retired without having any direct communication with me.

"Reduced to the most frugal consumption, forced to work myself at the cleanliness of my dwelling and at the conservation of my life, sur-rounded by objects of great severity, I wanted to impose a still harsher physical test on myself. In society I had been used to the easy, continual activity that wealth procures. I loved rapid exercise, the spirited run-ning of horses, travel, fresh air, hunting. In order to mortify my flesh and destroy the fever in my brain, I decided to submit to a voluntary confinement. In my imagination I restored the crumbled abbey walls. I encircled the courtyard, open to all the winds, with an invisible barrier. I measured the space in which I wanted to enclose myself for an entire year. There were days I felt in such turmoil that I could no longer recog-nize the imaginary line traced around my prison. Then I established it by visible signs. I tore long branches of ivy and clematis off the eroded walls, and I placed them on the ground at the places I had forbidden myself to cross. Then, reassured against the fear of breaking my oath, I felt myself as much enclosed as if I had been in a bastille.

"For a while this life of resignation and regularity rested me from past sufferings. I felt a great calm, and my body became hardened through privations. But my faculties, renewed by repose, reawakened little by little and impetuously demanded exercise. In trying to defeat them, I had revived my strength. By covering the cinders of a dying spark with ashes, I had kept it from going out completely and nursed a fire intense enough to produce a huge blaze. I should have been more frightened at feeling myself reborn. I should have dedicated myself to rendering null all exterior effects on my senses. Instead, solitude created in me new sensitivities and faculties I didn't recognize. I did not try to uproot them but accepted them as a blessing from heaven, when I should have repulsed them as a fresh suggestion from hell.

"Poetry again filled my brain, but it deceptively took on other colors, other forms, embellishing things that until now I had considered without attraction or worth. I had not thought that an indifference for certain aspects of life would inspire me with enthusiasm for things of which I had formerly been unaware. But that is what happened. Regularity, which I had embraced as one wears a hairshirt, became as sweet and alluring as a soft bed. I took pleasure in contemplating this passive obedience of part of me along with this prolonged strength of the other part, this saintly renunciation of matter along with this magnificent reign of calm will.

"In the past I had despised rules in my studies. By imposing them on myself in my retreat, I flattered myself that my thoughts would lose their force. But their force doubled as they became better organized. Because I isolated them from each other, they took on more complete forms. While they had once wandered in a world of vague perceptions, they now developed clarity as I went to the source of each matter. And because of my habit and need of inquiry, they took on a singular energy. This was my greatest misfortune: I reached skepticism through poetry, doubt through enthusiasm. In this way the systematic study of nature led me to praise God while I reviled Him. In the past I had sought only to admire His works. My complacent imagination had either repelled the hideous excesses of creation or forced them to take on a somber, savage grandeur. When I started to examine nature more attentively, to turn its diverse facets inside out with cold, impartial analysis, I found the genius that had presided at creation more skillful, wiser, and more immense. I fell to my knees, penetrated by a sharpened faith, and, while I blessed the creator of this newly discovered universe, I prayed that He reveal Himself still more. I continued to learn and analyze, but science is an abyss that ought to be excavated with prudence.

"When I had intoxicatedly examined the magnificence of colors and forms which make up the universe, I confirmed that each class of beings has something incomplete, impotent, and miserable. I realized that in some creatures beauty was compensated for by weakness, while with others stupidity destroyed the advantages of strength. All had a mission of suffering to accomplish on earth, and a fatal necessity presided over this coincidence of sufferings. Fear seized me. For an instant I felt the need to deny God so that I would not hate Him.

"Then I bound myself to Him through examining my own strength. I again found a divine principle in that wealth of physical energy with which animals endure the rigors of nature, in that power of pride or devotion with which man accepts God's pitiless decrees.

"Torn between faith and atheism, I lost my calm. Several times a day I passed from tenderness to hatred. When you have reached the limits of negation or affirmation and think you have grown wise, you are actually close to madness. Futher advancement is possible only by means of perfection, which is impossible. Otherwise you must be guided by instinctive intelligence which, if uncontrolled by reflection, can drive you to delirium.

"Then I fell into spells of violent turmoil, and as all human suffering loves to pity itself, dangerous poetry came back to place itself between me and the objects I was examining. As the effect of the poetic sense is primarily exaggeration, all evils were magnified and all good things aroused an emotion so intense that it resembled anguish. Anguish itself was more terrible, hollowing out in me deep chasms where my vain dreams of wisdom and repose were engulfed.

"Sometimes I watched the sunset from the height of a half-demolished tower. The part that still stood was encircled by the monstrous sculptures which formerly adorned Catholic places of worship. Beneath me these bizarre allegories stretched out their heads, blackened by time. They seemed to stretch toward the plain and silently to watch the flow of waves, centuries, and generations. These fantastic scaly serpents, these lizards with their hideous bodies, these chimeras full of anguish, all these emblems of sin, illusion, and suffering, lived a life that was inert and indestructible. When the red rays of the setting sun played on their forms, I seemed to see their flanks swell, their spiny fins dilate, their faces contract into new tortures. While I contemplated these bodies engulfed in masses of stone, which the hand of neither man nor time had been able to dislodge, I identified myself with these images of eternal struggle between suffering and necessity, between rage and impotence.

"Far away, beneath the grey, angular masses of the monastery lay the bleak plain. The setting sun would project its gleams after it had slowly disappeared beneath the horizon. Bluish fogs, lightly purpled, would rise, and then the black plain would resemble an immense shroud stretched beneath my feet. The wind would bend the soft heath, making it undulate like a lake. Often there was no noise in this limitless expanse other than a brook among the sandstones, the cawing of birds of prey, and the voices of imprisoned, plaintive breezes beneath the curves of the cloister. Occasionally a stray cow would wander through the ruins, lowing and unquiet, glancing wildly at the uncultivated land. Once a young boy, guided by the sound of the bell, came to look for one of his goats. I hid myself so he could not see me. Night was falling, darker and darker beneath the humid walls. The young goat-herd stopped, struck with terror at the sound of his footsteps that re-sounded under the arches. Then, recovered from his first surprise, he went, chanting all the while, to where his goat devoured the saltpetered vegetation shooting up among the debris. The movement of a person other than myself within this sanctuary was odious. The noise of the sand under his feet, the echoing of his voice seemed an insult and a pro-fanation of the temple in which I had so mysteriously revived worship and where, alone at the feet of God, I had reestablished the commerce of my soul in heaven.

"In the spring, when the wild broom was covered with flowers, when the mallows exhaled their sweet odor around the ponds, and when the swallows filled the air with motion and noise and flew up into the most inaccessible heights of the towers, the country took on an aspect of infinite majesty and the perfume of an enervating voluptuousness. The distant sound of herds and dogs more often reawakened echoes in the ruins, and in the morning the skylark sang songs as sweet and tender as canticles. The viperine and the nettle filled the humid wall crevasses with tufts of sumptuous green. Yellow wallflowers embalmed the naves. In the abandoned garden centenary fruit trees, which had survived the devastation, adorned their angular moss-eaten branches with white and pink buds. Everything up to the massive pillars was covered with this tapestry of rich nuances in which microscopic plants, engendered by the humidity, colored the ruins and the subterranean vaults.

"I had studied the mystery of all these animal and vegetable repro-ductions. And I thought that I had frozen my imagination by analysis. But as nature came to life again and made herself more beautiful, she made me feel her power. She mocked my proud work, and she subju-gated those stubborn faculties which boasted that they belonged ex-clusively to science. It is a mistake to believe that science annihilates imagination and that the eye of the poet is extinguished by the eye of the naturalist, which embraces a vaster horizon. Examination, which destroys so many beliefs, also causes new ones to spring forth because of the light it casts. While study had taken away my illusions, it had revealed treasures to me. My senses, far from being impoverished, were renewed. The splendors and the perfumes of spring, the exciting influences of a warm sun and a pure air, the inexplicable sympathy that seizes a person when the earth in labor seems to exhale life and love through its pores threw me into new anguish. I again felt all the stings of anxiety and of vague, impotent desires. I seemed to become a woman again. I could still feel and love. A second youth, more vigorous and feverish than the first, made my heart pulsate with an unknown vio-lence. I was both frightened and joyful with what was happening inside me, and I abandoned myself to this troubled ecstasy without knowing what would result.

"But with reflection came fear. I remembered the grief of the past. The unhappiness I had experienced made it impossible for me to feel confident about the future. I had everything to fear: people, reality, and above all myself. Reality endlessly wounded me, and people did not understand me because I could neither raise nor lower myself to their levels. Then the tedium of the present seized me with all its force. My retreat, austere, poetic, and beautiful as it was, on certain days seemed frightening. The vow that voluntarily held me there now seemed to be a horrible necessity. In this monastery, without enclosed walls or doors, I suffered the same tortures as a monk, captive behind a moat and iron grating.

"In these alternations of fear and desire, this violent struggle of my will against itself, I consumed my newly found strength. I endured the weariness and discouragement of the experience without trying to do anything about it. When the need to act and live became too in-tense, I let myself be devoured by this emotion until it wore itself out.

Entire nights were spent in the work of resignation. Stretched out on the tombstones, I abandoned myself to the fury of my imagination. I dreamed of the embraces of an unknown demon. I felt his hot breath burn my breasts, and I dug my nails into my shoulders, believing I felt there the imprint of his teeth. I summoned pleasure at the price of eternal damnation, as men did in those days of a naive culture where the devil, more powerful and generous to the living than God Himself, offered himself as a last hope, like a usurer who retards but ensures ruin.

"Often a rainstorm surprised me in the roofless enclosure of the chapel. I made myself endure this, as by doing so I hoped to find relief. Sometimes morning found me broken with fatigue, paler than the dawn, my clothing soiled, and without the strength to raise my disheveled hair from the streaming water.

"At times I tried to find release by crying out my suffering and anger. The birds of the night flew away terrified or answered me with savage wailings. The noise echoed from vault to vault, breaking against those shaky ruins; and the gravel that slid from the rooftops seemed to presage the fall of the edifice on my head. Oh, I would have wished it were so! I redoubled my cries, and those walls echoed my voice with a more terrible and heartrending sound. They seemed inhabited by legions of the damned, eager to respond and unite with me in blasphemy.

"Those terrible nights were followed by days of bleak stupor. After I had managed to sleep for a few hours, when I woke up I would feel a numbness that rendered me incapable all day of expressing any will or interest. At such moments my life resembled those lives of religious men who have been stupefied by habit and submission. I would walk slowly for a short time. I would sing psalms whose harmony lulled my suffering, without any sense passing from my lips to my soul. I enjoyed cultivating flowers on the steep slopes of those rough constructions where there was sand and pulverized cement in which they could take root. I watched the work of the swallow and defended its nest from the invasions of the sparrow and titmouse. At such times all memory of human passions was effaced. Through habit I mechanically stayed within the line of voluntary captivity traced on the sand. I no longer dreamed of crossing, as if a world had not existed on the other side.

"I also had days of calm and reason. The religion of Christ, which I had modified to suit my intelligence and needs, diffused a softness, a true tenderness over the wounds of my soul. In truth I had never been very concerned to ascertain for myself whether or not the degree of divinity dealt out to the human soul authorized men to call themselves prophets, demigods, and saviors. Bacchus, Moses, Confucius, Mohamet, Luther all accomplished great missions on earth and imparted violent shocks to the human spirit in its march through the centuries. Did these men by whose ideas we live and think today resemble us? Did these colossi, whose moral force organized societies, have natures more excellent, purer, and more celestial than our own? If one would not deny God and the divine essence of man, has one the right to deny His most beautiful works? Can't one say that He who, born among men, lived without weakness or sin, He who dictated the Gospel and transformed human morality throughout the centuries is truly the son of God?

"God alternately sends us men who are powerful for evil or good. When it pleases the Supreme Will for the human spirit to take an immense step forward or backward on part of the globe, He can, without waiting out the austere progress of centuries and the slow work of natural causes, effect these brusque transitions through the body or speech of a man created expressly for this purpose.

"Thus it is that Jesus came to put his bare, dusty feet on the crown of the Pharisees, that He broke the ancient law, and that He announced to future centuries the great spiritual law necessary to regenerate an enervated race. He rose up as a giant in the history of man and divided it in two: the reign of the senses and the reign of ideas. All man's animal force was demolished by His powerful hand, and He opened a new path to the human spirit. If you believe in God, doesn't that bring you to your knees, and wouldn't you say, 'He is the Word which was with God at the beginning of time? He has come from God; He returns to Him. He is always with Him, seated at His right, because He has redeemed men.' God sent Jesus from heaven: Jesus was God on earth; and the spirit of God in Jesus filled the space between Him and God. Isn't it a simple, indivisible trinity? Isn't each man who believes and whose faith puts him into communication with God offered a reflection of that mysterious trinity, more or less weakened according to the power of the celestial revelations he receives? The attraction of the soul for an uncreated goal, and the mysterious goal of this sublime impulse, isn't all of this God revealed in three distinct ways: force, struggle, and conquest?

"This triple symbol of the Divinity, traced throughout humanity, was able to produce itself once splendidly and completely between Jesus, the Father of the World, and the Holy Spirit represented by the Catholic faith in the form of a dove, to signify that love is the soul of the universe."

"These mystical allegories make me smile," said Pulchérie. "That is how you are, souls of the elite, pure essences! You must comment on the great book of Revelation. You must submit sacred works to your own philosophical interpretation. And when, through subtleties, you have managed to give a meaning of your choice to the divine mysteries, then you consent to bow down before the faith which has been newly reformed for your use. You deign to prostrate yourself in front of your own work: do you agree, Lélia?"

"I won't try to deny this, my sister. But what does it matter, if this is the only way we can believe and hope? Happy are those who can submit to the letter of the law without the help of spirit! Happy the sensitive, mad reveries that lead the rebel spirit back to submission before the law! As for me, in religious rites and symbols I found a deep source of emotion: the architecture of Catholic churches, the somewhat theatrical decoration of the altars, the magnificence of the priests, the chants, the incense, the intervals of meditation and silence, the antique splendors that reflect the pagan customs among which the Church was born have always inspired me with respect when they surprised me in an impartial mood.

"The abbey was bare and devastated. But, wandering among the debris one day, I had discovered the entrance to a vault which, covered by fallen masonry, had escaped the outrages of a delirious and destructive time. After opening up a passage among the plaster and brambles, I was able to penetrate to a narrow, dark stairway that led to a small underground chapel of exquisite workmanship.

"Its arch was so solid that it had resisted the weight of an enormous pile of debris. The dampness had not damaged the paintings, and in the darkness one could distinguish some somber priest's clothing which seemed to have been forgotten on a prie-dieu of sculpted oak the day before. I approached and leaned forward to see it better. Then I saw a man's form kneeling underneath the pleats of linen and coarse muslin. His head, bent over his clasped hands, was hidden by a black cloak. He seemed plunged into such a deep, imposing meditation that I drew back, struck with terror and superstition. I no longer dared move because the outside air I had let in blew against the powdery garment, and the man seemed to stir as if he were about to stand up.

"Was it possible that a man had survived the massacre of his brothers, that he could have lived on for thirty years, confined by austerity and suffering in these underground vaults of unknown depth and extent? For a moment I believed this, and because I feared to interrupt his meditation, I remained motionless, immobilized by respect, searching for what I was going to say to him, ready to withdraw without daring to speak. But as my eyes grew accustomed to the darkness, I made out the limp folds of the fabric falling flat on his thin, bony limbs. I understood the mystery I was witnessing, and I placed a respectful hand on this relic of a saint. Scarcely had I touched the cloak when it dissolved into dust and my hand encounterd a cold, dried skull. It was both frightening and sublime to see for the first time that monk's head whose tufts of grey hair were still stirred by the wind and whose beard was entwined with the emaciated phalanges of his hands clasped beneath his chin. Certain burial vaults impregnated with a large quantity of saltpeter have the property of drying out the bodies and conserving them for centuries. People have discovered many corpses preserved from decay by natural influences. The skin, as transparent and yellow as parchment, adheres closely to the hardened muscles. The membranes of the lips fold around the solid, brilliant teeth. The eyelashes remain implanted around the enamelless, colorless eyes. The facial features retain a sort of austere calm. And the limbs keep the inflexible attitudes in which death surprised them. This sad debris of man has an undeniable grandeur, and it does not seem, when one looks attentively, that reawakening would be impossible.

"The mortal remains beneath my eyes had something still more sublime because of the situation. This religious man, who had died without agony or convulsion in the calm of prayer, seemed surrounded by an aura of glory. What had happened to him during his last moments? Condemned to an inflexible penitence for some noble fault, had he slept in God, confident and resigned, at the depths of the *in pace,*\* while his pitiless brothers chanted the hymn of the dead above him? This supposition vanished when I assured myself that no part of the underground vault had been walled up and that there was no appearance of a dungeon in this sacred place of worship. Perhaps the storm of the French Revolution had surprised this martyr in his retreat. He would have descended here when he heard the people's fierce cries to escape their profanations or to receive the last blow on the steps of the altar. But there were no traces of wounds. I began to think that the collapse of the upper part of the building under the furious hands of the conquerors had suddenly cut off his retreat and that he had been forced to submit to the punishment of the vestal virgins. He had died without torture, with joy perhaps, in the midst of those terrible days when death was a blessing even to unbelievers. He had rendered his soul to God, on his knees before Christ, while he prayed for his executioners.

"This relic became sacred to me. I often went into this cold vault to obliterate the heat of my blood. I covered the priest's remains with new clothing. Each day I knelt down beside him. He became the companion of my exile and sadness. I confessed to him. I told him of my spiritual anguish. I asked that he place himself as intermediary between heaven and me. And often in my dreams I saw him pass before my pallet like a spirit out of Job's visions, and I heard him murmur words of terror or hope in a voice as feeble as the breeze.

"I also loved a large Christ of white marble placed at the base of a niche in that underground chapel. Formerly it must have been inundated with light from an opening in the ceiling. Now this air hole was obstructed, but a few feeble rays still shone through the chinks of stone jumbled together outside. This bleak, creeping daylight threw a singular sadness over Christ's brow. I took pleasure in this symbol. What is more touching on earth than the image of a human being in physical torture who is crowned by an expression of celestial joy! What is a more profound thought than this martyr God, bathed in blood and tears, stretching out his arms toward heaven! Oh, image of suffering, mounted on a cross and ascending like a prayer, like incense, from earth to the heavens! Often I prayed to you! My soul offered itself on

---

\*Part of the *Requiescat in Pace* given in the Sacrament of Extreme Unction.

that cross and bled beneath those thorns. In the name of *Christ* my soul worshipped human suffering, raised by divine hope. I worshipped resignation, which is acceptance of human life. And I worshipped redemption, which is calm in the midst of agony and hope in the midst of death.

"The second winter was less peaceful than the first. The patient resignation with which I had worked at first to make my existence possible in the midst of isolation and privations abandoned me the following year. The indolence and reveries of the summer had changed my spiritual and physical condition. I felt more robust, but more irritable, more accessible to suffering. All the rigors I had imposed joyously upon myself became bitter. I no longer found that proud, sharp pleasure that had sustained me at the beginning.

"The shortness of the days forbade me the sad pleasure of reveries on the terrace, and inside my cell, where I passed the long hours of the evening, I would hear the north wind weep. Often, weary of the efforts I had made to isolate myself, incapable of attention in study or of logical reflection, I allowed myself to be dominated by the sadness of my exterior impressions. Seated in my window alcove, I would watch the moon rise slowly above the snow-covered roofs and glitter on needles of ice which hung from the lacy sculptures of the cloisters. These cold, brilliant nights had a character of desolation that nothing can express. When the wind quieted down, a silence like death hovered over the abbey. The snow fell in silent flakes from the tops of old yew trees onto the lower branches. One could have shaken all the dried brambles which surrounded the courtyards without awakening a single living creature, without hearing a snake hiss or an insect creep.

"In this bleak isolation my character weakened. Resignation degenerated into apathy, and my thoughts became confused. By turns the most abstract, confused, and frightening ideas besieged my brain. In vain did I seek to retire inside myself and live in the present. A vague phantom of the future floated in my dreams and tormented me. I told myself that my future should have a known form, that it should be traced closely on the present I had created. But soon I perceived that the present no longer existed for me. Although my soul made vain efforts to enclose itself inside this prison, it always wandered beyond. I needed the universe, but I realized that I would exhaust the universe as soon as it was given to me. Finally I felt that the occupation of my life was to turn endlessly toward lost joys or toward ones still possible. Joys I had sought in solitude fled from me. There, as everywhere, at the bottom of the cup I had found the dregs bitter.

"It was near the end of a burning summer that my vow expired. I saw its term approach with a mixture of desire and fear that perceptibly altered my health and reason.

"I felt an incredible need of movement. I summoned life passionately, unaware that I had already lived too much and that I suffered from an excess of life.

"But after all, I told myself, had I not already fathomed the nothingness of life? What pleasures existed whose emptiness I had not discovered? What beliefs would not vanish before my severe examination? Was I going to demand of mankind the calm I had not been able to find in solitude? Would they give me what God had refused? If I exhaust my heart again pursuing a vain dream, if I abandon the retreat to which I have condemned myself in order to disillusion myself again, where will I then find an asylum against despair? What religious or philosophic hope will be able to cradle me when I have penetrated the depths of all my illusions, when I have acquired complete proof of my impotence?

"But I still asked myself, what purpose does retreat serve, and what is the purpose of reflection? Have I suffered less among these ruined tombs than within the bosom of humanity? What is a stoic philosophy if it only creates new sufferings? What is an expiatory religion whose goal is to seek suffering? Isn't all this the height of pride and insanity? Wouldn't men be happier and nobler without all these refinements of thought, if they delivered themselves solely to pleasures of the senses? Perhaps God disapproves of this pretended elevation of the spirit, and perhaps at doomsday He will cover it with contempt.

"In the midst of these irresolutions I sought a direction for my fluctuating will in books. The naive poetry of primitive times, Solomon's voluptuous Song of Songs, the lascivious pastorals of Longus, and the erotic philosophy of Anacreon at times seemed more religious to me in their sublime nakedness than the mystical signs and fanatic hysterics of Saint Theresa. But most of the time I let myself be carried away by a more immediate sympathy for ascetic books. I vainly tried to detach myself from the entirely spiritual impressions of Christianity, but I always returned to them. I had only a transient youth in which to tremble at the songs of *the wife** or smile at the embraces of Daphnis and Chloe. One moment was enough to consume that artificial intensity which a true simplicity of heart could not sustain and which the fires of an Oriental sun did not renew. I loved to read *The Lives of the Saints,*† those beautiful poems, those dangerous fictions, in which humanity seemed so noble that one could no longer lower oneself to look at men as they are on earth. I loved the eternal, profound retreats, the pious sufferings engendered in the cell, the great renunciations, the terrible expiations, all the magnificent mad actions that console one for the vulgar evils of life through a sentiment of flattered pride. I also loved to read about the sweet, tender consolations that the anchorites received secretly in their souls. I loved to read the naive correspondences of François de Sales and Marie de Chantal.‡ But I especially loved those outpourings, full of austere love and dreamy metaphysics, between God and man, between Jesus in the Eucharist and the unknown author of the *Imitation*.§

"These books were full of meditation, tender feeling, and poetry. They promised grandeur through isolation, peace through work, repose of spirit through bodily fatigue. There I found the reflection of such happiness, the imprint of a wisdom so delicious, that in reading them I recovered the hope of reaching the same goal. I told myself that, like me, these saintly men had undergone violent temptations to return to the world, but they had courageously surmounted them. I told myself that if I renounced my work after two years of struggles and triumphs I would lose the fruit of these strong efforts, and I would be acting with more stupidity than cowardice. Instead, by reaffirming my

---

*Source unknown. Possibly this comes from the Song of Solomon.

†A reference to Alban Butler's book, *The Lives of the Fathers, Martyrs, and Other Principal Saints*: first published in London between 1756 and 1759 in four volumes. It was translated into many languages, and it is still considered a classic work.

‡Reboul notes that Marie de Chantal was actually Sainte Jeanne-François Frémiot, Baroness of Chantal (1572–1641), and that Sand had made an error in her name. François de Sales (1567–1622) was a lawyer who became a priest. Together the two founded the religious nuns' Order of the Visitation. By the time of her death Jeanne-François de Chantal had founded eighty-seven convents. She was the grandmother of Madame de Sévigné.

§*The Imitation of Christ*, a famous devotional work written originally in Latin (1417–21) and attributed to Thomas à Kempis or the Abbé Gerson.

resolution, by renewing my vow for a prolonged period, perhaps I would harvest the fruits of my perseverance. I might return to society only to destroy myself, while instead, if I only waited a few more days in the depths of my cloister, I would doubtless enter into the beatitude of the elect.

"After these long struggles which wearied my mind, I became discouraged, and I asked myself, while I laughed contemptuously at myself, if my life was important enough to defend it in this way and to expose its remains to so many storms.

"These irresolutions lasted until the middle of spring. When my vow expired, in order to cut short my anguish I took a middle course: I took refuge in the inertia that always follows great emotions. I let the days pass without fixing on my future, waiting for the awakening of my faculties either to push me into life or imprison me in forgetfulness.

"Indeed, I was not slow to feel the new goads of this desirous, sharp disquiet which had already made me submit to so many evils. I perceived one day that my liberty had been given back to me. No oath consecrated me any longer to God. I belonged to humanity, and perhaps it was time to return to the world if I did not want to lose entirely the use of my intelligence and my senses. The days of despondency that so often filled my life left me with a great fear, and I struggled alternately against the apprehension of imbecility and of madness.

"One evening I felt profoundly shaken in my religious faith, and I passed from doubt to atheism. I lived for several hours under the charm of a feeling of inconceivable pride, and then I fell from that height into the depths of terror and desolation. I felt that vice and crime were ready to enter my life, and I lost the celestial hope that alone up until now had enabled me to endure mankind.

"Thunder sounded over my head. It was the first storm of spring, one of those premature storms that sometimes upset the still cold days of April. I have never heard thunder and seen lightning streak the clouds without a feeling of admiration and enthusiasm bringing me back to the instinct of faith. Involuntarily I shivered, and through habit I cried out, seized with terror, 'Oh, God, You are great! Thunder is beneath Your feet, and Your brow emanates light. . . .'

"The storm increased in intensity. I returned to my cell, the only truly sheltered place in the abbey. Night came early, the rain fell in torrents, the wind howled uninterruptedly through the long passages, and pale flashes of lightning were extinguished beneath the storm clouds, which burst everywhere. Then I found in my isolation, in the security of my shelter, in the austere but real calm that surrounded me amid the confusion of the elements an indescribable feeling of well-being and a passionate gratitude toward heaven. The hurricane carried whirlwinds of dust and chalk away from the ruins, strewing them over the uncultivated shrubs and debris. It tore branches of creeping plants from the walls. From the swallow it snatched the frail shelter of the half-built nest beneath the dusty arches. There wasn't one poor flower, not one new leaf that wasn't blighted and carried away. Thistles filled the air with their dispersed down. The birds folded their wet wings and took refuge in the brushwood. Everything seemed saddened, broken. I alone sat peacefully among my books, occupied from time to time by carelessly glancing at the struggle of the huge yew trees against the tempest and the ravages of hail on the young buds of wild elder trees. I cried out, 'This is the image of my destiny: calm in the depths of my cell, hurricane and destruction outside. My God, if I don't cling to You, the wind of fatality will carry me away like these leaves and break me like these young trees. Oh, take me back, God. Take back my love, my submission, and my vows. Don't let my soul continue to waver between hope and distrust. Bring me back to noble, solid thoughts through an absolute rupture between me and the world.'

"I knelt before the image of Christ, and in an impulse of hope and enthusiasm, I wrote on the white wall a vow which I read aloud in the silence of the night.

'Here a being still full of youth and life consecrates herself to prayer and meditation.

'She swears by heaven, by death, and by her conscience never to quit the abbey of—— and to live there the rest of her allotted days on earth.'

"After this violent resolution I felt a great calm, and I slept in spite of the storm, which increased from hour to hour. Toward day I was awakened by a terrifying noise. I got up and ran to my window. One of the upper galleries that was still standing the night before, its frail pillars and elegant sculptures surrounding the courtyard, had just yielded to the force of the storm and was collapsing. A fresh gust of wind made other parts of the structure crack, and they collapsed too in less than a quarter of an hour. The destruction seemed to progress under the influence of a supernatural will. It was approaching me. The roof sheltering me began to shake. The mossgrown roof tiles flew into pieces, and the framework seemed to move back and forth, pushing back the walls with each new gust of wind.

"Fear seized me because I let myself be governed by superstitious and puerile ideas. I thought that God was tearing down my hermitage to chase me from it, that He was repulsing a bold oath and forcing me to return to people.

"Then I threw myself toward the door, less to flee danger than to obey a supreme will. But I stopped as I was about to cross the threshold, struck by an idea much more in accord with the morbid excitation and exalted disposition of my spirit. I imagined that God, to shorten my exile and recompense my courageous resolution, was sending me a death worthy of heroes and saints. Had I not vowed to die in this abbey? Had I the right to flee because death approached? And what more noble end than to bury myself beneath these ruins which had been charged with saving me from myself? I would render myself to God, purified by repentance and prayer. 'I salute You, sublime guest,' I cried. 'Since heaven sends You, You are welcome. I await You within this cell, which has already been my tomb in life.'

"Then I fell down on the floor and, plunged into ecstasy, awaited my fate.

"The last remains of the abbey were not destined to remain standing that morning. Before sunrise the roof was carried away. A section of wall collapsed. I lost consciousness.

"A priest, whom the storm had led astray in these deserted plains, happened to pass at that moment by the foot of the collapsing walls. At first he moved away fearfully; then he thought he heard a human voice among the furious sounds of the tempest. He risked going into the new ruins covering the old ones, and he found me unconscious underneath the remains, which were burying me alive. Pity, the zeal that faith gives even to those who lack humanity, gave him the cruel strength to save me. He carried me off on his horse, across the plains, through woods and valleys. This priest was named Magnus. Through him I was torn away from death and given back to suffering.

"Ever since I have returned to society my existence has been even more miserable than before. At first I felt that God was talking to my heart through the thousand voices of nature and that there was still time to share my life with a human being who resembled me. I had forgotten, alas, that I was a cursed exception and that this human being did not exist. Because natural, complete love was not possible for me, I hoped to save myself by realizing the myth of Platonism. But, as I knew very well that it would be difficult to find a soul formed for the same destiny as mine, I surrounded myself with subtleties and ruses that no human vision could penetrate.

"I isolated myself with selfish, secret enjoyment. I refused to let the object of my strange love participate in the delicacies and pleasures of my thought. He did not know how I loved him. He believed himself my friend and nothing more. He consoled himself for his suffering by believing me incapable of passion for any man. I was miserly with my happiness. I promised myself to savor it with extreme delight, having only God for confidant. I surrendered to all the violence of inward passion and carefully maintained its flame, hidden beneath the innocent exterior of friendship.

"At first I had some happiness in seeing him happy and tranquil when I knew that one word would be enough to inflame him. When he sat peacefully at my side, holding my hand between his and talking to me of heaven and angels, I would look long and penetratingly at his pure brow and his calm chest. I told myself that if I let my eyes sparkle, if I applied a stronger pressure to my fingers entwined in his, I could instantly set his mind aflame and make his heart pound. It was sweet to feel that feminine temptation and to resist it. I loved the voluptuous suffering that resulted for me from this secret struggle. It rejuvenated me. It likened me to people affected by whole passions and realizable desires.

"Sometimes, close to letting my secret escape, I would feel a flush mount to my face, and I would lean my head on his shoulder to rest from these hidden but violent agitations. Then, troubled to see me this way, he would escape from my arms with terror.

" 'Oh, Lélia,' he said to me. 'Who are you? Are you made of fire or ice? Must I repulse you or do violence to you? You always speak of moral force and triumphant reason. Yet, how is it that when I am near you my moral force succumbs and my reason is bewildered? Alas, you petrify me with your cold, bitter smile which condemns or jeers at everything I say, which repulses all my desires. Why just now were you leaning on me with a burning glance, with half-open lips, with an exciting, cruel indolence? Do you despise me to the point of playing with me like a child? Do you permit yourself this abandon because you forget I am a man? Are you so little of a woman that you cannot understand the confusion and the suffering you cause?'

"When I saw him close to perceiving the truth, I closed myself up into an indifference and lightness that awakened all his doubts. I immobilized his sensual impulses by a glacial irony. Then again I would put on the veil of friendship to console him for my disdain. I malignly aroused him with chaste, sweet caresses. I played with him as a vulture does its prey. Sometimes I made him suffer, and I played with his misery. Sometimes I made him happy with slight concessions. He was always under my domination. He never knew really what caused the sang-froid and the calculation that made me stronger and more clever than he.

"He doubted and hoped for a long time because he desired strongly. When he was convinced of my invulnerability, he grew cold. He showed me the Platonic affection I merely pretended that I wanted. Then sadness and anger awakened in me. Jealousy dug its iron nails into my brain. I was more jealous of my friend than I had formerly been of my lover. In the past I had blushed for suffering too much over sensual infidelity. Now I felt that I could allow myself to weep only over an infidelity of the heart.

"But I could not express my suffering without betraying my secret. I had learned to conquer myself. After having succeeded a hundred times in imposing my will on myself, it was easy for me to deceive others. I became resigned to loving without being loved in return. And I found, in the burning suffering this repressed, bruised love caused me, moments of purer enthusiasm and sweeter resignation than when I had been the object of a love that was passionate but brutal and antipathetic to my nature.

"But man struggles vainly against celestial laws. When he refuses to submit his proud countenance to the yoke that binds his fellow men, he enters into a dangerous freedom. When he goes far from the paths traced by God's will, he becomes lost.

"My contempt for natural duties and my burning aspiration for an impossible life led to a sort of intellectual deprivation. Because I did not feel myself bound to any man through a voluntary consecration of physical love, I let my turbulent imagination traverse the universe, seizing hold of all it found. To find happiness became my only thought, and so far had I descended beneath myself that this became my only rule of conduct and my only desire. After having imperceptibly allowed my desires to float toward the shadows that passed around me, I found myself pursuing these desires in dreams, seizing them in flight, demanding imperiously of them, if not happiness, at least the emotion of a few days. And because the invisible libertinage of my thought could not shock the austerity of my morals, I surrendered without remorse. Not only was I unfaithful in imagination to the man I loved, but each day saw me unfaithful to the one I had loved the night before. Soon a single love of this kind was scarcely enough to fill my soul, which was never satisfied. I embraced several phantoms at once. In the same day and in the same hour I loved the enthusiastic musician who made all my nerves vibrate beneath his bow and the dreamer–philosopher who associated me with his meditations. I simultaneously loved the actor who made my tears flow and the poet who had dictated to the actor the words that reached my heart. I even loved the painter and sculptor whose works I had seen and whose features I hadn't. I was enamored by the sound of a voice, a head of hair, an article of clothing, and then by the mere portrait of a man who had been dead for several centuries. The more I abandoned myself to these excessive admirations, the more frequent they became, but they were passing and empty. God knows, no exterior sign ever betrayed them. But I avow with shame, with terror that I wearied my soul with this frivolous use of energy. And I no longer remember the names of those who, without knowing it, squandered the treasure of my affections.

"As a result of this prodigality my heart slackened. I was no longer capable of anything but enthusiasm, and even that was destroyed by any light cast upon the object of my illusion. I had to change the idol each time a new one presented itself.

"This is how I live now. I am always possessed by the latest caprice that wanders through my sick brain. And even these caprices have become rare and tepid. My enthusiasm has also grown cold. At times, after long days of drowsiness and disgust, I again find brief hours of vitality. Emptiness desolates my life, Pulchérie. Emptiness is killing me. Everything is exhausted for me. I have seen life in nearly all its aspects. When I have succeeded in filling up the chasm of one day, I fearfully ask myself how I will fill up the next. It seems to me at times that there are people worthy of esteem and things capable of arousing interest. But because I am discouraged and fatigued, I renounce them even before I examine them. I sense that there doesn't remain enough feeling in me to appreciate people or enough intelligence to understand things. I turn in on myself with calm despair, and no one knows what I suffer. The brutes who make up society ask themselves what I lack. My wealth has been able to buy all pleasures. My beauty and extravagance have been able to realize all ambitions. No one's intelligence is comprehensive enough to understand that it is a great misfortune to be able to attach oneself to nothing and to desire nothing more on earth."

# PART FOUR

# XXXV

Pulchérie remained for a long time in the pensive attitude she had taken from the beginning of Lélia's narration. Both were silent. Finally the courtesan took her sister's hand and said, "I think one thing alone can save you: return to solitude and God. You see that I have listened to you seriously."

"Pulchérie, there is no longer time to do what you advise. My faith wavers, and my heart is exhausted. To burn with divine love one needs youth and purity more than for any other passion. I no longer have the strength to raise my soul to a perpetual feeling of adoration. Usually I think of God only to accuse Him for what I'm suffering and to reproach His severity. If at times I bless Him, it's when I pass a cemetery and think of the brevity of life."

"You have lived too fast," said Pulchérie. "Lélia, you must change the way you exercise your faculties. Either return to solitude or seek pleasure: choose."

"I come from the mountains of Monteverdor. I tried there to find my former ecstasies and the charm of my pious reveries. But I found only tedium there as everywhere else."

"You would have to be part of a society that protects you from yourself and saves you from your own reflections. You would have to be subject to an alien will, and you would need forced labors to divert you from the continual, gnawing work of your imagination. Become a nun."

"One needs a virginal soul for that. I have only a chaste body. I would be an adulterous wife of Christ, and then you forget that I'm not devout. I don't believe, as do such women, in the regenerative virtue of rosaries and the power of scapulars.* Their piety calms them, refreshes them, and puts them to sleep. I have too sublime an idea of God and of the worship owed Him to serve Him mechanically, to pray with words arranged in advance and learned by heart. My overly passionate religion would be a heresy, and if they took away my exaltation, there would remain nothing for me."

"Very well," said Pulchérie, "since you cannot become a nun, become a courtesan."

"With what?" asked Lélia, with a bewildered air. "I have no senses."

"They will come to you," said Pulchérie, smiling. "The body is less rebellious than the spirit. As it is destined to profit from physical well-being, the body can also be governed by physical means. My poor dreamer, reconcile yourself to this humble portion of your being. Don't continue to despise your beauty, which all men adore. It can bloom again as it once did. Don't blush to demand of matter the joys that intelligence has refused you. You know very well the origin of your suffering: it comes from having wanted to separate two powers God had closely bound together. . . . "

"But, Pulchérie, haven't you done the same?"

"Not at all. I have given preference to one without excluding the other. Do you believe that the heart remains a stranger to sensual aspirations? Isn't the lover you embrace a brother and a child of God who shares God's blessings with his sister? Lélia, with your rich imagination I am surprised that you haven't found a hundred ways to exalt reality. I believe contempt alone stops you, and if you would renounce that unjust and insane state of mind, you would live the same life I do. Who knows? With more energy perhaps you will arouse more

*Short cloaks worn by certain religious orders.

intense passions. Come, let's run together on the tree-lined paths. Over there you can see the gold of the costumes faintly sparkle and the white hat feathers flutter. So many young, handsome men, full of love and strength, wander beneath those trees seeking out pleasure. Come, Lélia, let's excite them so that they pursue us. Let's run past them, brushing against them with our clothing, and then escape like the moths you see in light beams who seek each other, join, separate, and join again, to fall dead, mad with love, in the devouring flame. Come, I'll guide your trembling steps. I know all these men. I'll summon the most charming and elegant to surround you. You can be as haughty and cruel as you like, Lélia. But you'll hear their voices. You'll feel their breath on your shoulders. Perhaps you'll shudder when the evening breeze carries the perfume of their hair to your dilated nostrils. And perhaps this evening you'll feel a faint curiosity to know life in its entirety."

"Alas, Pulchérie, haven't I known it agonizingly? Don't you remember all I told you?"

"You loved that man with your soul. You couldn't imagine tasting real pleasure with him. That's simple. One faculty that has reached its greatest development must stifle and paralyze the others. But here it would be different.

.    .    .    .    .    .    .

The courtesan swept Lélia along with her, talking in a lowered voice.

"But first," Pulchérie continued, "we must dream up a disguise for you. Certainly you don't wish to surrender the noble name of Lélia to the crowd, although, to tell the truth, the continence in which you live provokes graver accusations in people's minds than my love affairs. But perhaps you don't find it beneath you to be suspected of mysterious, terrible passions, while you scorn the vulgar renown of a bacchante. So come along now and put on a domino costume like mine. You will be able, thanks to certain resemblances between us and, especially, between our voices, to descend without danger from the majestic, deplorable role you have chosen. Come, Lélia.

.    .    .    .    .    .    .

The crowd, which thronged around the courtyard columns to admire the large flashes of lightning in the sky, separated the two sisters as soon as they left the dressing room enveloped in their blue satin cloaks. Lélia was swept up by the wave of masked figures. Among them were so many costumes like hers that she scarcely dared try to recognize her sister, Pulchérie. Timid, frightened, already disgusted with the role she was about to attempt, she plunged into the garden. She was resolved to abandon to the caprices of chance what remained of a continually frustrated existence.

This time she penetrated, without knowing it, into part of the groves which the prudent Prince of Bambuccj had reserved for his elect. The entrance to this green labyrinth was guarded by a group of the prince's most expert subalterns. They were aware of all the intrigues of the court, and from hour to hour messengers dispatched hurriedly from the palace came to modify the instructions and to signal the new initiates who could be admitted into the sanctuary. All clumsy, jealous lovers, all touchy protectors were repulsed without appeal. Only women could enter without unmasking themselves: all for love of propriety.

It was a place of refuge for intimate friends who were separated by annoying obstacles elsewhere. Here one was safe, and everything happened with a miraculous regularity. People walked about in groups; they sat down in circles. The paths and greenery were full of light and people. But secret lovers knew very well what path, what door led to the pavilion of Aphrodite, whose immense terraces stretched out beside the sea.

Lélia had only walked a few steps in these dangerous shadows when a voice murmured close to her, "Here is Zinzolina, the celebrated Zinzolina!"

Soon a group of gilded men adorned with plumes pressed at her heels.

"Eh what, Zinzolina! Don't you recognize us? Is this how you treat your faithful friends? Let's go, take my arm, beautiful solitary one, and let's celebrate the ancient divinities."

"No, no," said another, trying to seize Lélia's arm. "Don't listen to that bastard Piedmontese. Come with me. I'm a pure Neapolitan and one of the first who initiated you into the sweet secrets of love. Don't you remember me any more, turtle dove of the voluptuous sighs, serpent of the hot embraces?"

A tall Spanish cavalier took Lélia's arm by force under his.

"The good Zinzolina has chosen me," he said. "Like me, she is of the noble Andalusian race, and nothing in the world would persuade her to make a compatriot and a hidalgo unhappy."

"Zinzolina is of all countries," said a German. "She told me so in her boudoir in Vienna."

"Tedesco!" cried a Sicilian, "if Zinzolina affronts us by preferring you, here is a dagger that will avenge us for her."

"Come, come, let's draw lots," cried a young page. "Zinzolina will mix our names in my cap."

"My name," replied the hidalgo, "is engraved on the blade of my sword."

And he drew it from its sheath with a menacing air.

The prince's men intervened, and Lélia fled.

But she was not alone long. At the turn of a path a Russian prince said to her, "Zinzolina, what are you looking for here? And why are you alone? Do you want to love me for an hour? I'll give you this diamond necklace, which is a gift of the czars."

Lélia made a gesture of contempt. A great French seigneur perceived this.

"What vulgarity!" he said. "How rude and insolent these *foreigners* are! Since when does one talk like that to a woman? Who does that boor take you for, Zinzolina? Listen to me."

And the latter offered his palace, his servants, his wine, and his horses.

"Do you believe so little in the pleasure you offer," asked Lélia, "since you add to it so many enticements to my greed? Are your embraces very hideous, since you pay for them so dearly? Where is love in all this? Where is ardor of the senses? Here is only brutality and corruption. You have no other lures than strength, vanity, or gain. Is pleasure dead, suffocated beneath civilization? Has the love of ancient times abandoned the earth and taken flight toward other skies?"

Then she threw her hood down onto her shoulders. At the sight of that haughty, grave face the crowd dispersed, and Pulchérie's bold admirers bowed respectfully before Lélia.

"Have you renounced your enterprise already?" Pulchérie asked, seizing her by her wide sleeve. "No, no, not yet, Lélia. Everything isn't hopeless. Your hour hasn't yet come."

"My hour won't come," said Lélia. "All this displeases me. Their breath is cold, their hair is rough, their embraces bruise, and their amber garments badly conceal their bitter, gross emanations. In their midst my blood grows calm, my ideas grow clear, my will is revived, and I no longer have any desire but to sit down and watch them pass by while I despise them."

"Very well, then, come with me, Lélia. Listen to a young man whom I've just met and whom I've vainly tried to arouse. Perhaps compassion will be more effective with you than anything else."

Lélia followed her sister to the depths of an artificial grotto, feebly lit by a small lantern.

"Stop here," Pulchérie said to her, hiding her in a dark corner, "and look at that handsome adolescent with the dark hair. Do you know him?"

"Do I know him!" Lélia replied. "That's Sténio. But what is he doing in the special gardens and in this grotto which is, if I'm not mistaken, one of the subterranean entrances to the famous pavilion? Sténio the poet, Sténio the mystic, Sténio the amorous?"

"Oh, listen to him," said Pulchérie. "You'll see that he is insane with love, and he must be pitied."

Pulchérie left Lélia where she was hidden and, approaching Sténio on tiptoe, she tried to embrace him.

"Leave me, Madame," said the young man proudly. "I don't need your caresses. I have told you it isn't you I sought when, deceived by the sound of your voice, I followed you into these gardens. But since I have torn off your mask, I realize very well that you're only a courtesan. Go away, Madame. I can't be yours. I'm poor; and, furthermore, I don't desire pleasures that must be bought. There is only one woman in the world for me: Lélia. Is she here? Do you know her?"

"I know Lélia because she's my sister," replied Pulchérie. "If you want to follow me through these dark vaults, I'll lead you to her."

"Oh, you are lying," said the young man. "Lélia isn't your sister, and you can't show her to me. I've followed you this far like a credulous child, always hoping you would. But you've deceived me. So now you will have to return alone."

"Child, I can lead you to her if I want to. But first, be aware that Lélia doesn't love you. Lélia will never return your love. Believe me, look elsewhere for the joys you were hoping to obtain from her. And if you can't chase this phantom from your spirit, at least intoxicate yourself as you pass the fountains of pleasure. Tomorrow you'll awaken to run again after your phantom. But at least during this breathless, mad journey your life won't be entirely consumed in waiting and dreams. You can have sweet interludes beneath the palms with the daughters of men, and you'll follow the demon of the fiery wings who calls you from the depths of the clouds when you've been refreshed by our caresses. Come, rest your head on my breast, young madman. You'll see that I don't want to keep you long. I only want to comfort you in your painful journey so that you can continue with a more courageous flight toward poetry and Lélia."

"Leave me, leave me," said Sténio forcefully. "I despise and hate you. You aren't Lélia. You aren't her sister. You aren't even her ghost. It is Lélia alone from whom I want joy. If she repulses me, I'll live alone and I'll die a virgin. I won't defile myself with a courtesan."

"Come, Lélia," said Pulchérie, drawing her sister toward Sténio. "Come, reward a fidelity worthy of chivalrous times."

Seeing Lélia, Sténio cried out with surprise, and his joy was so profound that it resembled suffering. He was forced to sit down again, his handsome face paled, and he involuntarily leaned his head against the courtesan's breast.

Lélia talked in low tones with her sister and the latter disappeared. Sténio did not bother to observe by what exit she withdrew.

Then Lélia took the young poet's hand and led him through those somber, cold vaults that were lit at intervals by suspended lanterns. Sténio trembled and believed he was dreaming. He was too troubled to ask himself where Lélia was leading him. He felt her hand in his and feared to awaken.

When they were at the end of the subterranean passage, Lélia put on her mask again and pulled on the silken cord of a bell. A door opened by itself, as if by magic. Lélia and Sténio ascended the steps that led to the pavilion of Aphrodite.

As they were making their way along a silent corridor, where the noise of their steps was deadened by carpeting, Sténio believed he saw a woman run rapidly past him. She was dressed like Lélia or Pulchérie. This didn't upset him because Lelia kept holding his hand, and they entered a delicious boudoir. She removed her mask and threw it into a nearby dressing-room. Then she returned to sit by Sténio on a silk divan embroidered with gold. A bolt was drawn outside by a malicious or discreet hand.

"Sténio, you have disobeyed me," said Lélia. "I'd forbidden you to seek me out again for a month, and already you were running after me."

"Having you brought me here to scold me?" he asked. "After a separation that seemed so long, must I find you again annoyed with me? Isn't it a year since I left you? How do you expect me to know the count of days, which drag when I'm far away from you?"

"Can't you live without me, Sténio?"

"I can't, or I must go mad. See how gaunt my cheeks already are, how my lips are withered with the fire of fever, how my eyes and my eyelids have been ravaged by insomnia. Do you still say that only my imagination is sick? Don't you see that the soul can kill the body?"

"I don't reproach you, my child. Your pallor touches me and makes you handsome. Just now the way you resisted my sister's seductions made me proud. I understand how beautiful it is to be loved like this and, Sténio, I want to try to find my happiness in you. Yes, I have decided. I will search no longer. Only an affection like yours can sweeten life. I don't deserve it, but I accept it gratefully. Don't keep on saying that Lélia is insensitive. I love you, Sténio, and you know this very well. I only struggled against this feeling because I feared to understand and share it badly. But you have often told me that you would accept the love I gave you, even if it were beneath yours. So I will no longer resist. I surrender to God's goodness and the strength of your heart. Look, I feel that I love you. Are you content, are you happy, Sténio?"

"Oh, very happy!" said Sténio bewildered, falling to her feet and covering them with his tears. "Is it true that I'm not dreaming? Is it really Lélia who speaks like this? My happiness is so great that I don't yet believe it."

"Believe, Sténio, and hope. Perhaps God will pity us. Perhaps He will make my heart young again and render it worthy of yours. God certainly owes you this recompense. You are so pure and so pious. Call down a ray of His divine fire on me."

"Oh, don't speak like this, Lélia. Aren't you a hundred times greater than me before God? Haven't you loved and suffered much longer than me? Oh, be happy and rest at last in my arms. Don't wear yourself out loving me, don't torment your poor heart with the fear of not doing enough for me. Oh, I say it again, just love me as much as you can."

Lélia wound her arms around Sténio's neck. She placed a long mother's and lover's kiss on his lips. Then, with an ineffable smile, she showed him the sky, which had just received their vows.

Sténio lay drunk with love and joy at her feet. A long silence followed this embrace.

"Well, Sténio," said Lélia, coming out of a long, sweet reverie. "What do you have to say to me? Are you already less happy?"

"Oh no, my angel!" cried Sténio.

But his expression said the contrary. His hands were trembling convulsively. A cloud had passed over his face.

"Shall we take a ride in a gondola on the bay?" asked Lélia, rising.

"What, leave each other already?" asked Sténio sadly.

"We won't leave each other," she said.

"Isn't it leaving each other to return to that crowd? We were so happy here! You are cruel. You continually need movement and distraction. Confess this, Lélia. Now that you are close to me, ennui already pursues you."

"My love, you are lying," said Lélia as she sat down again.

Her face was so beautiful and radiant that Sténio took courage.

"Very well," he said, "embrace me again."

Lélia embraced him as she had the first time. But when she wanted to remove her lips from his, Sténio moaned with suffering and let himself fall to the carpet.

"Oh, my God, what's the matter with you?" cried Lélia, raising him and drawing his head onto her knees.

"I have a fever," he said. "I feel sick."

"Doesn't my love do you any good, child? How unhappy I am if I still wound you!"

"Lélia, won't you pity me?"

"Pity you! What more can I do? I have surrendered all the rebellious powers of my soul to you. I have given up all my fantastic projects for the future to take refuge in your love. I have devoted to you the purest, most exquisite emotion I am capable of feeling . . . what more do you want?"

"What do I want? What do I want? . . . Lélia, you're cold. Oh, you're as cold as marble. I feel sick. I'm burning. I need air. These perfumes irritate my brain. Take away those flowers, they're killing me!"

Sténio paled. Lélia looked at him soberly.

"You arouse my pity," she said in an almost contemptuous tone. "It's scarcely a soul you want: it's a woman, isn't it?"

"It's both," replied Sténio, "because I am not God and my youth torments me. You know very well, Lélia, that I don't want merely a woman. But you who are God and soul, can't you be a woman for a single day in my arms? How can I believe in your love if you won't depart from any of your pretensions for me? Oh, Lélia, don't you feel that this is the wish of nature? Don't you feel that there must be unspeakable joys in the fusion of two beings who love each other? Isn't it man's essence to want to possess all he admires? When you see a beautiful flower, don't you want to breathe it, tear it from its stem, hide it in your bosom, so that it belongs to you alone? Lélia, you are so beautiful . . . don't you want me to be happier than all those others who look at you and admire you?"

Lélia's brow darkened more and more.

"Always," she said finally with spite, "always gross pleasure mingles with the most sublime impulses of intelligence! Man's sullied breath is always cast over the purest creations of thought! There, is that all you wanted of me? Is that what miraculous, Divine end proposed itself for your poetic passion?"

Sténio, despairing, threw his face against the cushions and bit the embroidery of the divan.

"Oh, you will kill me!" he cried weeping. "You will kill me with your contempt. . . . "

It seemed to him that Lélia left, and he raised his head with fear. He found himself in darkness, and he rose to try to find her in the shadows. A moist hand took his.

"Come," said Lélia in a softened voice. "I pity you, child. Come, lie by me and forget your pain."

# XXXVI

When Sténio raised his heavy head the songs of far-off birds announced the approach of day. The horizon whitened, and the fresh morning air reached the young man in perfumed gusts. His first movement was to embrace Lélia. But she had fastened on her mask again, and she softly repulsed him, signaling him to keep silent. Sténio rose with effort, and, broken with fatigue, emotion, and pleasure, drew near the half-opened window. The storm had entirely dissipated the heavy haze that had filled the sky some hours earlier. Long black bands of clouds were pushed by the wind, one by one, toward the horizon. The sea broke its foamy billows with a light noise on the sand of the beach and on the white marble steps of the villa. Orange and myrtle trees, tossed by the morning breeze, shook their flowering branches over the salty waves. The lights paled in a thousand windows of the Bambuccj palace, and only a few masked figures wandered beneath the columns, which were bordered by pale statues.

"Oh, how delicious!" cried Sténio, opening his nostrils and his chest to this vivifying air. "Oh, my Lélia, I'm saved. I feel myself a new man. I'm living a sweeter and fuller life. Lélia, I want to thank you on my knees. I was dying and you wanted to heal me. You have made me know the delights of heaven."

"Dear angel!" said Lélia, enveloping him in her arms. "Are you happy now?"

"I have been the happiest of men," he said. "But I want to keep on being happy. Lélia, take off your mask. Why are you hiding your face from me? Give me your lips. Embrace me as you did before."

"No, no, listen," said Lélia. "Listen to that music. It seems to come from the sea."

Indeed, the sounds of an admirable orchestra rose on the waves, and soon several gondolas filled with musicians and masked figures successively appeared from a small arch formed by the wood of orange and catalpa trees. They glided softly, like beautiful swans on the calm water of the bay, and they would soon pass in front of the pavilion terraces.

Then the orchestra was silent, and a launch of Asiatic shape cut lightly in front of the little fleet. This boat, frailer and more elegant than the others, was filled with musicians who were playing brass instruments. They sounded a brilliant flourish, and their metallic voices, so sonorous and penetrating, came from the depths of the waves to bound off the pavilion walls. Immediately all the windows opened, and happy lovers, sheltered by the boudoirs of the pavilion of Aphrodite, emerged in couples to lounge on the terraces and balconies. But in vain did the jealous and the scandal-mongers aboard the gondolas try to identify them. They had put on different costumes inside the pavilion and, hidden by their masks, they gaily saluted the fleet.

Lélia wanted to draw Sténio out among them. But she couldn't make him leave the delicious languor into which he was plunged.

"What do their joys and singing matter to me?" he asked. "Can I feel any admiration or pleasure when I have just been introduced to the delights of heaven? At least let me savor the memory. . . . "

But suddenly Sténio stood up and frowned. "Whose voice is singing over the waves?" he asked with an involuntary shudder.

"A woman's voice," said Lélia. "Truly a beautiful voice. See how they are crowding around in the gondolas and on the shore to listen to her."

"But," said Sténio, whose face was visibly changing as the full, low-pitched sounds of that voice ascended, "if you weren't here next to me with your hand in mine, I would believe that voice is yours, Lélia."

"Some voices sound alike," she said. "Weren't you completely deceived last night by my sister Pulchérie's voice?"

Sténio only listened to the voice, which was coming from the sea, and he seemed agitated with a superstitious fear.

"Lélia!" he cried. "That voice hurts me. It terrifies me. It will drive me insane if it continues."

The brass instruments played the phrase of a song. The human voice stopped. Then it continued again when the instruments had finished. And this time it was so near and so distinct that Sténio threw himself forward and flung open the gilded window frame.

"Lélia, surely this is all a dream. But that woman singing down there. . . . Yes, that woman standing alone at the prow of the launch. Lélia, it's you, or else it's your double."

"You are mad!" said Lélia, shrugging her shoulders. "How could that be?"

"Yes, I am mad, but I am seeing your double. I see and hear you in this room beside me, and yet I see and hear you down there. Yes, that's you. That's my Lélia. That's Lélia, whose voice is so powerful and beautiful. It's Lélia, whose black hair floats with the wind of the sea. It's Lélia who advances, carried on by her surging gondola. Oh, Lélia, are you dead? Am I seeing your ghost pass by? Are you a fairy, a demon, or a sylphid? Didn't Magnus tell me that you were two. . . . "

Sténio leaned completely out of the window and forgot the masked woman close to him. He was no longer looking at anything except the woman who resembled Lélia in her voice, posture, height, and costume, and whom he saw approaching on the waves.

When the launch carrying her had reached the foot of the pavilion, daylight shone pure and brilliant on the waves. Lélia suddenly turned toward Sténio and showed him her face as she made a sign of friendly mockery.

There was so much malice and cruel thoughtlessness in her smile that Sténio finally suspected the truth.

"That woman is certainly Lélia!" he cried out. "Oh, yes, that woman who passes before me like a dream, and who moves off while she throws me a look of irony and contempt! But this woman who intoxicated me with her caresses, this one I pressed in my arms while I called her my soul and my life, who is she? Now, Madame," he said, approaching the blue domino-clad woman menacingly, "tell me your name and show me your face."

"With all my heart," replied the courtesan as she unmasked herself. "I am Zinzolina, *la cortigiana*, Pulchérie, Lélia's sister. I am Lélia herself, since I have possessed Sténio's heart and his senses for an entire hour. Come now, ingrate, don't look at me with such confusion. Come, kiss my lips and remember the happiness for which you thanked me on your knees."

"Go away!" cried Sténio furiously, drawing his stiletto. "Don't remain before me a moment more, because I don't know what I'm capable of."

Zinzolina fled. But as she crossed the terrace underneath the windows of the pavilion, she cried out mockingly, "Adieu, Sténio the poet! We are betrothed now. We shall see each other again."

## XXXVII [STÉNIO TO LÉLIA]

Lélia, you have deceived me cruelly! You have played with me cold-bloodedly in a way that I cannot understand. You lit a devouring fire in my senses which you didn't want to extinguish. You summoned my soul to my lips, and you rejected it. I know very well that I am not worthy of you, but can't you love me out of generosity? If God has made you like Him, isn't it so that you would follow His example on earth? If you are an angel sent from heaven, instead of waiting for us to climb to your heights, isn't it your duty to stretch out your hand and show us the way?

You counted on shame to cure me. You believed that when I awakened in the arms of a courtesan, I would suddenly be enlightened. You hoped, in your inexorable wisdom, that my eyes would finally open and that I would no longer have anything but contempt for the joys you had promised me and which you replaced by your sister's lascivious caresses. So be it, Lélia! Your hope is deceived. My love has emerged from this test pure and victorious. I won't blush, because my brow has not retained the imprint of Pulchérie's kisses. I fell asleep murmuring your name. Your image was in all my dreams. In spite of your contempt, you belonged entirely to me. I have possessed you. I have profaned you. My convulsive embraces and the voluptuous trembling of my lips were all for you. Your sister is not unaware of this, because several times before I had repulsed her.

Forgive my sadness, oh, my well-beloved! Forgive my sacrilegious anger. Thankless as I am, have I any right to reproach you? Since my kisses have never warmed your marble lips, did I deserve such a miracle? But I beg you on my knees, at least tell me what fears or suspicions estrange you from me. Do you fear obeying me if you surrender to me? Do you think that happiness will make me an imperious master? Oh, my Lélia, if you doubt my eternal gratitude, then I can only weep and pray that God move you, because my tongue refuses new vows.

You have often told me, and I didn't need your revelations because I had already divined them: men have severely tested your trust and your credulity. Your heart has been furrowed with deep wounds. It has bled for a long time, and it is not surprising that as your wounds closed over, they concealed barely perceptible scars. But don't you know, my love, that I love you for the sufferings of your past? Don't you know that I adore your invincible soul, which has submitted without bending to the storms of life? Don't accuse me of viciousness. If you had always lived in calmness and joy, I sense I would love you less. If anyone is responsible for my love, it must be God because it is He who put the admiration and worship of strength, the devotion to courage into my consciousness. Your memories explain your distrust. In loving me, you fear abandoning your freedom. You are afraid of losing a treasure that has cost you so many tears. But tell me, Lélia, what are you doing with this treasure of which you are so proud? Since you have managed to concentrate all your devouring energy on yourself, are you happier?

Since humanity is no longer anything in your eyes but dust which God permits to be stirred beneath your feet for a brief period, do you find nature a richer and more magnificent spectacle? Since you have retired from civilization, have you discovered in the grass of the fields, in the voice of the waters, in the majestic flow of rivers a surer and more powerful charm? Is the mysterious voice of the forest sweeter to your ears? Since you have forgotten the passions that trouble us, have you penetrated the secret of the starry night? Do you converse with invisible messengers who console you by their confidences for our weakness and our unworthiness? Confess this, you are not happy. You adorn yourself with your freedom as if it were a priceless jewel, but you have only the astonishment and envy of the uncomprehending crowd for amusement. You have no role to play among us, but you are weary of idleness. You have not found a destiny proportionate to your genius, and you have exhausted all the joys of solitary reflection. Without trembling, you have crossed the desolate plains where the vulgar masses can't follow you. You have touched the peaks of mountains that our eyes scarcely dare measure. And there dizziness seizes you, your arteries dilate and hum, and you feel your temples swell. You have only God to shelter you. You have only His throne upon which to sit. You must either be impious or return to us.

God is punishing you, Lélia, for having coveted His strength and majesty. He inflicts isolation on you to punish the boldness of your ambitions. From day to day He enlarges the circle of your solitude to make you recall your origin and your mission. He had sent you to bless and love. He had spread your perfumed tresses of hair over your white shoulders to wipe away our tears. With jealous eyes he had surveyed the fresh velvetiness of your lips, which are meant to smile, and the moist sparkle of your eyes, which are meant to reflect heaven and show it to us. Now He demands an accounting of all these precious gifts, which you have perverted from their proper use. What have you done with your beauty? Do you truly believe that the Creator has chosen you among all women to practice mockery and disdain, to jeer at sincere love, to deny vows, refuse promises, and drive credulous youth to despair?

Lélia, you are proud that your senses sleep. You rashly say, "I can defy men. I no longer fear pressures of the hand or amorous glances. I can feel their burning kisses on my lips while my mind remains calm and untroubled. Without anxiety I can allow myself to watch their torments without sharing them." But don't you fear the awakening of your senses? Don't you fear that, in order to dominate the proud revolt of His slave, one day your master may send you unbridled desire and command the marble to catch fire? If this terrible prophecy were accomplished, the victims you have immobilized on the altar to your pride would be well avenged! You would be reduced to imploring pity from those you disdain. Your lips would defile themselves by begging for the glances that today you scarcely perceive. What humiliation! You would never descend so low.

Ah, rather return to us! Open your arms to me and don't despair about yourself. Let me test the power of my caresses on your numbed senses. Let me embrace you and tear cries of passion from you. Lélia, come to me. I will be patient. Without anger I will wait for your blood to warm and your heart to swell. I won't demand that you experience joy as swiftly as I do. I will devote myself to your happiness, and I am sure a moment will come when our tears mingle. Our souls, merged in a common felicity, will thank God. I will live in you. You will rediscover the intoxication of your younger years, perhaps more intense and less fleeting.

You laugh at my hopes. You pity my confidence. But, my poor Lélia, as long as the wind hasn't swept away the cinders, it is not madness to seek some hidden blaze there which only needs air to be revived. Oh, my Lélia, perhaps in your heart there is a part unknown to you that has not yet bled and that love can reach. Who knows what strength a sincere passion may contain? And who can boast of having exhausted your heaven-sent powers?

If you entrusted your fate to me, no sooner would you understand the happiness that I await from you than you would take on life again to make my days better. You would feel inflamed with a generous emulation. Eager to surpass me in devotion, you would forget the misfortunes of your youth as you strove, like a skillful pilot, to point out the reefs upon which you were shipwrecked. This rapid, continual exchange of maternal protection and filial adoration would have regenerated you while it fortified me against the dangers of the future.

You have often told me, and I believe you, that in your soul there are mysteries I cannot penetrate, obscure recesses that my eyes cannot fathom. But from the day you love me, Lélia, I shall know you entirely.

You are not unaware, and young as I am I have the right to affirm it, that love, like religion, clearly illumines the hidden pathways which reason does not suspect. From the day our souls united in a holy communion, God would reveal us to each other. I would read your consciousness as clearly as my own. I would take you by the hand and redescend with you into your vanished past. I would count the thorns that have wounded you. I would perceive the blood that has flowed beneath your scars, and I would press your scars to my lips as if the blood still ran.

Keep your friendship for Trenmor. Your friendship is enough for him because he is strong. He is purified by expiation. He walks with a firm step and knows the goal of his pilgrimage. But as for me, I don't have the will that underlies the energy and grandeur of a manly role. I don't have the invulnerable egotism that subdues all obstructing passions, interests, and jealous destinies. In the depths of my heart I have nourished only exalted but unrealizable desires. I took pleasure in the contemplation of noble actions, and I hoped that their intimate, familiar presence would fill my reveries. I have always admired superior characters, and I felt within myself the imperious, trembling need to imitate them. But as I wandered without rest from desire to desire, my solitary meditations and my fervent prayers never obtained from God the strength to accomplish what I had desired and brooded over in my dreams.

Lélia, this is why I love you. You have taken on my role, which men refused you. Far from repudiating your role, I beg that you play it out. I am sure in advance that you will desire everything to which I have aspired. And my desires will never cross the august limits of your will.

If I had been given an ordinary nature, I would have found many docile affections on which to plant my hope and ambition. I would have rested my head on the first shoulder I encountered. My brow would have been refreshed by all lips. I would have molded my happiness from a common clay. But God has placed me either higher or lower than all those people. My feet would bleed if I walked the path they have beaten out. However, with the first steps I try to take, I find brambles that I must tear away from me, and the solitude of my journey does not save me from painful wounds.

It is you, Lélia, who ought to be and I hope will be my guide and support. It is you whose severe, constant hand will show me each day the goal to which my heart aspires but which my spirit does not know how to single out. It is you, oh, my well-beloved, in whom I confide and rest. It is your low, calm voice that should impose silence on the discordant noise of my thoughts and on the tumultuous struggles of my mad fantasies. You must be aware that another woman, beautiful and young but weak and wavering, would not find the happiness and security she deserves in my ignorant love. She would vainly demand wisdom I don't have, firmness I still seek. Her naive caresses would torture rather than console me. Her kisses would be indictments and her joyous tears reproaches I could not answer. Each time she said to me, "Go and I will follow you!" I would be ready to ask her forgiveness.

Lélia, this is why I cannot doubt without impiety that God has created you to light my way. He has chosen you among His favorite angels to lead me to the goal, marked in advance by His eternal decrees.

I don't put the entire care of my destiny in your hands because you have your own to fulfill, and that is a heavy enough burden for you. But what I ask, Lélia, is to let me obey you. Let my life model itself upon yours. Let my days be filled with work or rest, movement or study, according to your desires, which I know will never be frivolous.

You have responded by mockery and deception to these humble prayers which you had divined a hundred times in my looks. I have put my last hope in you. It is you in whom I have taken refuge. Oh, Lélia, if I am without you, what will become of me?

## XXXVIII [LÉLIA TO STÉNIO]

Sténio, perhaps I have hurt you. But I am not guilty of the wrong with which you reproach me. I have not deceived you. I did not want to play with you. Perhaps I experienced a few moments of scorn, a few outbursts of anger because of you. But it was against human nature, not against you, pure child, that I was irritated.

It is not to humiliate you, still less to discourage you with life that I threw you into Pulchérie's arms. I was not even trying to teach you a lesson. What triumph could I taste in prevailing over your naivete with my cold reason? I wanted to deliver you from the torment of indefinite waiting and anxiety. Is it my fault if your soul, like mine, like all men's, possesses immense faculties for desire and if your senses are limited in joy? Am I responsible for the miserable impotence of physical love to calm and heal the painful ardor of your senses?

I can neither hate nor despise you for having suffered from a delirium of the senses at my feet. It did not rest with your soul to despoil the coarse frame in which God has exiled it. You were too young, too ignorant to separate the true needs of your poetic and saintly soul from the deceptive aspirations of matter. You took what was only a fever of the mind for a need of the heart. You have confused pleasure with happiness. We all do the same before we know that it is not given to man to realize one through the other.

Destiny, not I, has given you this lesson. While my maternal heart was gloriously filled with your love, I had to refuse myself the humiliating compliance of giving you this lesson. If you were meant to encounter your first deception in a woman's arms, I had the right to put you in the arms of a woman whose profession is to consent and undeceive.

You are right to say that pleasure has not defiled you. I was not trying to embarrass you. I love and esteem you as much now as I did yesterday. I see nothing changed about you except that you have learned and suffered. I pity you, and my tenderness increases. I would have been humiliated and debased if I had served, like Pulchérie, as a torch to light your descent into the abysses of nothingness and solitude. Such a role is repugnant, I confess, to my pride. But that is your fault. It was not necessary to worship me like a divinity and then ask me to be your slave and Sulamite.

I did not want to age and transform you. I hadn't resolved, as you believe, to inspire you with contempt for sensual pleasures. I wish, on the contrary, that you had found them more binding so that for a few days they could have intoxicated your senses and rested your spirit. Then you would have returned to me calmer and more capable of appreciating the pure charm of a chaste affection. Instead, you persistently sought me in another's arms. You tried, imprudent, guilty child, to profane by your thought what ought to be sacred for you. Happily, God has refused you the power of consummation without nourishment. He has placed the objects of your worship beyond reach, for fear that after handling them you would then reject them with scorn. Christ's blood is enclosed in sacred cups and hidden behind the golden walls of the Tabernacle. If the crowd's gaze could enter there, the crowd would quickly learn to doubt and deny. Thus God has placed invisible but insurmountable obstacles between the soul and the vague objects of its anticipations so that the fire of sacred desires will not be extinguished by examination and possession.

This was my mission for you, and I have fulfilled it. More experienced, more proven than you, closer to heaven because I am more detached from earth, I should have shone before you like the star that led the Magi to the feet of the King of nations. The star wasn't God or even an angel. It was a torch lit by the breath of the Omnipotent to light the pilgrims' route. If the pilgrims had been able to command the star, to slow or hurry its flight, to attract it to them and replace it according to their liking in the ether, the star would have paled in their atmosphere. It would have gone out in the wind of their breath, and they would have been abandoned in the darkness, in the bosom of unknown valleys, on the banks of rivers whose names they did not know.

You say I annoy you when I talk like this because I am treating you like a child. Of what do you complain, Sténio, and why does it humiliate you to be younger and happier than me? Have I ever reproached you for not going beyond the course of time and being hardened when up until now you have slept in the flowers of childhood? Alas, child, do you think I am proud of my sufferings? Do you think I have emerged from them without defilement? Does the victim who is torn half-broken from the horrors of torture throw a bold, vain look over the crowd? Has he escaped moaning and blasphemy beneath the iron of the executioners? If he has not betrayed his faith, isn't it because they left him some respite, seeing that he was losing physical strength and the sensation of pain? Oh, so many times, in the agony of my heart, I have let myself fall to the ground, inert, exhausted, and crying out as a last malediction: "God, avenger, slacken your blows. Your efforts are wasted because I no longer feel them!"

Submissive child, God has not yet punished you, and He accepts your prayers like pure incense. Don't envy the fervor and tears of the penitent who beats the temple steps with his brow. Perhaps God will shed mercy on him, but before mounting a throne amid the powers of heaven, he must still creep about for a long time on earth in expiation. Perhaps eternal death will surprise him in a day of weariness and doubt.

Inflexible justice, spare young courages from work, spare delicate plants from the wind! Make life sweet and calm for Sténio. He has no crime to expiate.

Oh, my young poet. I used to talk to you in another language! I have tried to make your rigid wisdom more flexible. I have shown you Trenmor's merits. I taught you to respect the great unfortunates and the great wills. But I never told you to win my love by throwing yourself upon the same reefs. Stay pure, stay calm, I told you. I will love you differently than Trenmor, but perhaps I will love you more. Trenmor will be my brother and you my son. He will be my support, as I will be yours. And all three of us, helped by each other, united in a sacred love will perhaps reach truth, wisdom, repose.

Have I failed to keep my promises? Haven't I kept my respect for Trenmor and my tenderness for you? Have I withdrawn the hand that upheld you? Why is it that at each step, frightened and exhausted, you remain behind, murmuring against the guide you have chosen? Why do shock and fear cause you to lose your grip, while if you would only join with us you could pass through the danger without harm. Now you are annoyed because, in yielding to a child's wishes, I misled them in order to appease them. What profanation did I commit when I delivered you up to the caresses of a beautiful young woman? Pulchérie gave herself to you without degradation and without money. She is no vulgar courtesan. Her passions are not feigned, her soul is not sordid. She does not upset herself with imaginary promises of a durable love. She worships only one God—Pleasure. But she knows how to adorn it with poetry and with a cynical, courageous chastity! Your senses summoned the pleasure she gave you and which my senses refused you. Why despise Pulchérie because she has satisfied you? Why curse Lélia because she searched outside herself for what you asked of her, but what she didn't possess?

As I continue to live, I cannot help realizing that youthful ideas about the exclusive passion of love and its eternal rights are false, even fatal. All theories ought to be allowed. I would give that of conjugal fidelity to exceptional souls. The majority have other needs, other strengths. To those others I would grant reciprocal freedom, tolerance, and renunciation of all jealous egotism. To others I would concede mystical ardors, fires brooded over in silence, a long and voluptuous reserve. Finally, to others I would admit the calm of angels, fraternal chastity, and an eternal virginity. —Are all souls alike? Do all men have the same abilities? Are not some born for the austerity of religious faith, others for voluptuousness, others for work and passionate struggle, and others, finally, for the vague reveries of imagination? Nothing is more arbitrary than the understanding of *true love*. All loves are true, whether they be fiery or peaceful, sensual or ascetic, lasting or transient, whether they lead men to suicide or pleasure. The loves *of the mind* lead to actions just as noble as the loves *of the heart*. They have as much violence and power, if not as much duration. Sensual love can be ennobled by struggle and sacrifice. How many veiled virgins have, unaware, obeyed an impulse of nature as they kissed Christ's feet and spilled hot tears on the marble hands of their celestial spouse! Sténio, believe me, this deification of egotism which maintains the law of moral marriage in love is as insane, impotent, and laughable to God as social marriage is now in men's eyes.

You have confused two very distinct things: sensual and spiritual love. One I can inspire and share. But the other isn't made for me, or rather I'm not made to feel it. Far from despising sensual love, I have only disdainful compassion for the impoverished natures and the warped attitudes that multiply profusely in these times, and of which I'm a sad example. But with whatever discontent I accept my fate, I must submit to what I am, and I must make the best of my infirm condition. I must stop struggling against my impotence. I must reduce my ambitions in order to harmonize them with my own strength.

It's very true that I suffer. I would feel a terrible despair if I did not draw back and give ground day by day to necessity. Isolation of the heart pursues me in the midst of the most pure intimacies. I can never experience those complete outpourings, that embracing of souls, that happiness of which I used to dream but of which I have seized only the shadow! Now I realize that I can only save myself through resignation. New attempts, new errors would embitter me and render me incurable.

Sténio, do you know that it isn't given to many of us to be able to feel strongly both the joys of the soul and those of the senses? If you have this rich nature, it is no reason to become angered if you don't meet your equal in this world. I declare humbly that I am not. The suffering bound up with my sad existence should free me from reproaches of irony and scorn.

Perhaps I shouldn't complain of my lot. Many people tell me that

God endowed me magnificently when He gave me intelligence. But I have often sensed that thought is a dangerous power, a weapon which wounds the hand that raises it, a glaring but deceptive beacon which makes us wander, confused, from abyss to abyss. I have often cursed this source of bitterness. I have often asked God to make me like the animals of the woods. But in the bewilderment of my suffering I formed a wish that I would not have wanted to see fulfilled. I would have consented to dress in the skin of panthers and bury myself in solitudes unknown to man, to possess gulls' wings and cross the seas carried by the tempests, but on condition that human thought survive within me to contemplate the beauties of the desert, the clouds, and the waves. I could not understand the advantages of muscular strength, physical agility, and the extraordinary development of certain senses like the vision of birds, like the voluptuousness of tigers, without the exercise of thought to appreciate their value and without the power of the soul to thank God for them. Even today, wearied as I am by the abuse of my strength and tormented by aimless anxieties, I don't aspire to the isolated possession of physical abilities. Perhaps I would still refuse the careless, mad life of my sister because thought has its ecstasies too, its celestial sensuality, of which an hour is worth an entire youth, an entire life.

And what if your threat were realized, Sténio, if the fire of heaven were extinguished within me and I were delivered to the confusion of the senses. What if, transformed by Divine wrath to the point of losing my will power, I were to throw myself, throbbing and pale with shame, into the arms of men whom I desired but did not love. . . . Oh, if that were so, be reassured that you would not need to blush long for having loved Lélia. When moral strength leaves us, when brutal need dominates, when self-respect ceases to speak within us, and when we are close to plunging into the abysses of infamy, it is because God abandons us. Then we, too, can abandon God. We are freed from the laws of love and gratitude which connect each of us with the infinite, eternal order. We are no longer part of creation. We trouble universal harmony, because a brutalized man no longer belongs to any species and ought to be cut off or at least cast aside. If society is forced to endure him, it insults and crushes him. Men's contempt is horrible when deserved, when behind its implacable justice there is no retreat into the shelter of God's paternal indulgence. Then, Sténio, there are no longer two choices to make. If the macerations of mysticism cannot dominate us, if the counsels of wisdom can no longer contain our gross passions, we must die. There is a refuge from men: suicide. There is a refuge from God: nothingness.

Don't try to change me. That isn't within my power, and you would fail miserably. If I am the only woman you can love, stay near me, my child. I consent. I will be your friend. I won't fail you unless you force me to move off from fear of harming you. You see, Sténio, your fate is in your hands. Content yourself with my purified tenderness and my platonic embraces. I have tried to love you as a lover, as a woman. ... But does a woman's role really confine itself to the transports of passion? Are men just when they accuse a woman of departing from the attributes of their sex if she responds badly to their raptures? Do they count for nothing the intelligent solicitude of sisters, the sublime devotion of mothers? Oh, if I had a younger brother, I would have guided him through life. I would have tried to spare him its sufferings and its dangers. If I had children, I would have nourished them at my breast, I would have carried them in my arms and in my soul. For them I would have effortlessly submitted myself to all the evils of life. I feel clearly that I would have been a courageous, passionate, tireless mother. So be my brother and son, and let the thought of any marriage what-soever seem incestuous and bizarre. Chase away this idea as one chases monstrous dreams at night. If your youth is greedy for permitted plea-sures, let me enlighten you as to the perils you must flee. Let Trenmor guide you in these difficult paths. One can travel them if one has a strong soul and a noble heart. We were born to serve you with support and counsel because we were born before you. Your life is beginning, and ours is ending. We cannot share your passions, but we can direct them. Take responsibility for your life, but come to us when you suffer so that we can heal the bruises the chains of life inflict on you.

In this way all three of us can be happy. Accept this contract of love and chastity. Put your hand confidently between ours. Lean calmly on our shoulders, which are ready to sustain you. But don't keep on deluding yourself. Don't keep on hoping to rejuvenate me so much as to make me lose my discernment and reason. Don't break the link of which your strength consists. Don't overthrow the support you invoke.

If you want to call our affection for each other by the name of love, let it be the love that angels know, where souls burn with the fire of saintly desires.

## XXXIX [STÉNIO TO LÉLIA]

A curse on you! Because I am cursed, and it is you whose cold breath has blighted my youth in its flower. You are right, and I understand you very well, Madame. You assert that I need you, but you don't need me. Of what can I complain? Don't I know that is unanswerable? You prefer to remain in the calmness you claim to possess without descending to share my passions and torments. Truly you have a great deal of wisdom and logic. Far from arguing with you, I keep silence and admire you.

But I can hate you, Lélia. You have given me that right. You have hurt me so much that I consecrate an eternal, profound enmity to you because, without having wronged me in any tangible way, you have succeeded in harming me and taken away my right to complain. Your coldness has placed you in an unassailable position, while my youth and exaltation delivered me up to you defenselessly. You didn't deign to pity me; that's simple. Why would it be otherwise? What sympathy could exist between us? By what works, noble actions, or superiority have I deserved you? You owed me nothing, and you gave me that facile compassion which enables a person to turn away his head when he passes near a bleeding, wounded man. Wasn't that at least enough to give proof of your sensitivity?

Yes, yes, Lélia, you are a good sister and a tender mother. You throw me into the arms of courtesans with an admirable disinterest. You destroy my hope and illusion with a truly majestic severity. You declare that there is no pure happiness, no chaste pleasure on earth, and to prove it you repulse me from your bosom, which seemed to welcome me and promise me heavenly joys. You send me to sleep on one still warm from the kisses of an entire town. Lélia, God was wise in not giving you a child. But He has been unjust toward me in giving me a mother like you!

I thank you, Lélia. But the lesson is strong enough. I don't need another to attain wisdom. Now I am enlightened and disillusioned about everything. I am old now and full of experience. All joys, all loves are in heaven. Fine! But while we're waiting, let's accept life with all its necessities, feverish youth, desire, brutal need, brazen, peaceful, philosophic vice. Let's make two parts out of our being: one for religion, friendship, poetry, wisdom, and the other for debauchery and impurity. Let's leave the temple and forget God on Messalina's bed. Let's perfume our brows and wallow in the mire. On the same day let's aspire to the immaculateness of angels and resign ourselves to the carnality of animals. But as for me, Madame, I understand better than you. I go even further. I adopt all the consequences of your precept. As I am incapable of dividing my life in this way between heaven and hell, and as I am too mediocre, too incomplete to pass from prayer to orgy, from light to darkness, I renounce pure joys and divine ecstasies. I abandon myself to the ardor of my fiery blood. Long live Zinzolina and those like her! Long live the facile pleasures and raptures which there is no need to conquer by study, meditation, or prayer! Yes, truly it would be madness to scorn the faculties of matter. Didn't I taste a happiness as real in your sister's arms as if I had been in yours? Nothing held me back at the beginning of my fall. No secret presentiment warned me of the perfidious exchange you were making, laughingly, beneath my blinded eyes. Pulchérie's carnal emanations of joy thrilled me as much as Lélia's subtle perfumes. I smelled a woman's odor, and in my brutal excitation I did not distinguish Pulchérie from Lélia! I was confused, I was drunk. I believed I pressed the dream of my ardent nights against my heart, and far from being frozen by contact with an unknown woman, I was flooded with love. I blessed heaven. I accepted the most contemptible substitution with tearful delight. I possessed Lélia in my soul, while my mouth devoured Pulchérie, without distrust, disgust, or suspicion.

Bravo, Madame! You have succeeded. You have convinced me. Sensual pleasure can exist, isolated from all emotional or spiritual satisfactions. For you the soul can live without the help of the senses. You are a sublime and ethereal nature. But I am a vile mortal. When I am near a beloved woman, and I touch her hand, inhale her breath, and receive her kisses on my brow, my chest swells and my vision grows blurred. My spirit is bewildered and succumbs. So I must escape these dangers. I must spare myself the contempt of the woman I love with an unworthy, revolting passion. Adieu, Madame. I am fleeing from you forever. You will no longer blush to inspire the passions with which I have been consumed.

But as my soul is not depraved, and as I cannot carry a heart filled with ethereal love while I am in the arms of the infamous debauchees you give me as lovers, I want from now on to annihilate my imagination and close my heart to noble desires. I want to descend to the level of reality that you have made me know, because until now I have lived with fictions. I am a man now, am I not? I know good and evil. I can walk alone. I have nothing more to learn. Retain your serenity; I have lost mine.

Alas, I must have been a childish, miserable fool to believe in the promises of heaven and to imagine that man was as well constructed as the grass of the fields. I believed that his existence could double, complete itself, in merging with another's. I believed it could be absorbed in the embraces of a pure passion. I believed this! I knew these mysteries were fulfilled in the heat of the sun, under God's eyes, in the calyxes of flowers. I told myself, "A pure man's love for a pure woman is as legitimate as these." I no longer remembered the laws and customs that pervert the use of human faculties and destroy the order of the universe. Insensitive to the ambitions that torment men, I took refuge in love, without realizing that society had perverted love, too, and that there remained no other resource for ardent souls than wearing themselves out, destroying themselves with self-contempt in the midst of artificial joys and arid pleasures.

But whose fault is it? Isn't it God's? I have never accused God before. It is you, Lélia, who taught me to be terrified of His decrees and to reproach His harshness. Today the confident superstition that once dazzled me has dissipated. That golden cloud which hid the Divinity from me has vanished. Having descended into my own depths, I realize my frailty and I blush for my stupidity. I have wept with rage at seeing the power of matter and the impotence of my own soul, of which I was so proud. I believed it reigned so assuredly. That is how I know who I am, and I ask my Master why He has made me this way. Why is this grasping intelligence and this proud, delicate imagination at the mercy of the most bestial desires? Why can the senses impose silence on thought, suffocate the instinct of the heart and the discernment of the spirit?

Oh, shame and sadness! I believed that Pulchérie's kisses would find me as cold as marble. I believed my heart would rise up in disgust if I approached her. But I was happy with her, and my soul expanded as it possessed that soulless body!

I am contemptible. I hate God, and I hate you, too. You are the beacon who made me know the horror of these depths, not to save me from them but to precipitate my fall. Lélia, you could have closed my eyes, spared me these hideous truths, given me pleasure for which I would not have blushed and a happiness I would not have detested. Yes, I hate you as my enemy and as the instrument of my ruin. You could have at least prolonged my illusion and kept me a few days at the doors of eternal suffering, but you didn't want to. And you have pushed me into vice, without warning me. You should have written at the entrance: "Abandon hope at the doors of this hell if you wish to cross the threshold and confront the terrors!" I have seen everything and braved everything. I am as wise and unhappy as you. I no longer need a guide. I know what assets I can use, what ambitions I must renounce. I know what resources can repulse the tedium that devours your life, and I will use them, since I must. Adieu! I owe my knowledge to you. A curse on you, Lélia!

# PART FIVE

## XL  THE  WINE

One morning people saw a stranger stop at the gates of the town.
He had come on foot across the grassy valleys, and his shoes were still
wet with dew. He walked alone, with no other weapon than a white
walking stick, and to see his austere costume, his serious face, and his
peaceful gait, one would have taken him for an apostle of ancient times.
Although he had neither clerical bands nor a shaven head, the first
bourgeois whom he spoke to thought he was a priest because of his
black clothing and his long hair. But the worthy man drew back with
surprise when the stranger, in a calm and modest tone, asked in what
quarter of the town Signora Zinzolina's palace was situated.

"Your apostolic seigneur wants to mock his very devoted servant,"
replied the citizen, repressing an exclamation of malicious joy. Your
*eccellenza canonica* must have mistaken the name assuredly . . . la Zinzolina . . . la Signora Courtes. . . . "

The tone in which the stranger repeated his demand was so absolute, so firm, so glacial that all the jokers already grouped around him looked at each other as if to ask who this man was whose voice and gestures commanded fear.

A guide was given to the stranger, who, without taking any rest, immediately went with him to the courtesan's dwelling.

Seeing his worn footwear, his staff, and his broad traveling hat, the lackeys turned their backs and did not condescend to listen to his questions.

Then he sent away his guide and made his way into the palace, raising his staff impassively on all those who tried to stop him. A small page, completely frightened, entered the room where Zinzolina was entertaining her guests.

"An *abbatone*, an *abbataccio*," he said, "has just forced his way into the house, beating his steel-pointed staff against the signora's servants, the Japanese porcelains, the alabaster statues, the mosaic flooring, causing frightful damage and shouting terrible curses."

All the guests immediately rose (except one who was sleeping) and wanted to run to the *abbate* and chase him away. But Zinzolina, instead of sharing their indignation, fell back on her chair and burst out laughing. Then she rose in turn, but to impose silence and request them to sit down.

"Make room, make room for the priest!" she cried. "I love intolerant, angry priests: they are the most damnable. Let the *signor abbate* enter, fling the door wide open, and bring Cyprean wine."

The page obeyed, and when the door was opened they saw Trenmor's solemn, majestic figure come from the depths of the passageway. But the only guest who could have recognized and introduced him was sleeping so soundly that these explosions of surprise, anger, and gaiety did not make him even stir.

As they saw the pretended ecclesiastic draw nearer, Zinzolina's joyous companions realized that this strange clothing was not a priest's. But the courtesan persisted in her error, saying as she went to meet him and making herself as beautiful and sweet as a madonna: "*Viene, signor vescovo, o arcivescovo, o cardinale, ossia papa*; be welcome and give me a kiss."

Trenmor kissed her, but with such an indifferent air and with such cold lips that she drew back three steps, crying out, half angry, half frightened, "By the Virgin's golden hair! This is the kiss of a ghost."

But she soon became impudent again, and, seeing that Trenmor was looking over the guests with somber anxiety, she drew him to a seat placed next to hers.

"Come, my handsome priest," she said, giving him a silver cup engraved by Benvenuto Cellini and crowned with roses in the manner of the voluptuous Greek orgies, "warm your numb lips with this Lachryma Christi."

And she crossed herself hypocritically as she pronounced the name of the Redeemer.

"Tell me what brings you to us, or rather don't tell me, let me guess. Do you want to be given a silken robe and have your hair perfumed? You are the handsomest priest I have ever seen. But why does Your Mercy frown without responding?"

"I beg your pardon, Madame," said Trenmor, "if I respond badly to your hospitality. Although I have come here on foot like a peddler, you receive me like a prince. I like logical, complete natures like yours, and I esteem you as much, courtesan amorous of all men, as an abbess amorous of all saints. But I don't have the time to occupy myself with you, Pulchérie. My visit has another object. . . . "

"Pulchérie!" said Zinzolina, trembling. "How do you know the name my mother gave me? Where do you come from?"

"I come from the place Lélia is now," replied Trenmor.

"Blessed be my sister's name," said the courtesan gravely and reflectively. Then she added in a light tone, "Although she has bequeathed me her lover's mortal remains."

"What are you saying, woman?" asked Trenmor, horrified. "Have you already exhausted so much youth and vitality? Have you already given this child death when he hasn't yet lived?"

"If you're speaking about Sténio," she said, "be reassured. He's still alive."

"He still has a month or two to live," added one of the guests, glancing carelessly at the sofa where a man slept whose face was buried in the cushions.

Trenmor's eyes followed in the same direction. He saw a man of Sténio's height but much thinner. His frail limbs reposed in a despondency that announced drunkenness less than fever. His fine hair fell in loose curls on a neck as smooth and white as a woman's. But the gaunt contours of his face betrayed a sickly and forced virility.

"Is this Sténio?" asked Trenmor in a low voice, looking at the courtesan so fixedly that she involuntarily paled and trembled. "Pulchérie, perhaps a day will come when God demands an accounting of you about the purest and handsomest of His works. Don't you fear this when you think of it?"

"Is it my fault if Sténio is already exhausted when the rest of us here who lead the same life remain young and vigorous? Do you think I am his only mistress? Do you think he gets drunk only at my table? And Trenmor, I recognize you from your speech and I know who you are. Haven't you known delirium and debauchery? And haven't you emerged from the arms of pleasure rich with strength? Furthermore, if any woman is guilty of his ruin, it is Lélia, who should have kept this young poet beside her. God had destined Sténio to love a single woman religiously, to compose sonnets for her, and to dream about the storms of more active destinies from the depths of a solitary, peaceful existence. He should have seen our orgies, our sensuality, and our noisy wakes from afar, in the mirage of his genius. He would have told about them in his poems but not participated. When I invited him to pleasure, did I advise him to quit the rest? Did I tell Lélia to banish and abandon him? Didn't I know very well that with men like him intoxication of the senses ought to be a relaxation and cannot be an occupation?"

"You are right, Madame," said Trenmor, pressing her hand sadly. "Lélia has ruined this young man."

"Have you come here to take him away from our festivities and to lead him back to a reflective life?" asked Pulchérie. "None of us will oppose this. I, who still love him, will be grateful if you save him from himself. Bring him back to Lélia and to God."

"She's right!" cried Pulchérie's companions. "Take him away, take him away! His presence saddens us. He has always been alone among us, and, while he shared our joys, he seemed to despise them. Come on, Sténio, wake up, straighten your clothing, and leave!"

But Sténio, deaf to their clamor, remained motionless beneath the weight of these insulting voices, and the stupefaction of his sleep made Trenmor feel ashamed for him.

"Please, young noblemen," he said gravely, "don't abuse that child. If his reason is asleep, his soul is still awake."

Then he approached to awaken him.

"Be careful," someone said. "Sténio has tragic awakenings. No one touches him with impunity when he sleeps. The other day he killed a dog he loved because, when it leapt on his knees, the poor animal interrupted a dream in which Sténio was taking pleasure. Yesterday, as he was dozing off with his elbows on the table, Emerenciana tried to give him a kiss. He broke his glass across her face and made a wound which, I believe, will leave a permanent scar. When his valets don't awaken him at the hour he has ordered, he fires them. But when they do awaken him, he beats them. Truly, take care. He carries his table knife, and he is capable of plunging it into your chest."

Oh, my God, thought Trenmor, he is so changed! His sleep was as pure as a child's, and when he was awakened by a friend's hand, his first expression would be a smile, his first word a blessing. Poor Sténio! What sufferings have embittered your soul, and what fatigues have ruined your body! You sleep like a gambler or a convict.

Standing motionless behind the sofa, plunged in gloomy reflections, Trenmor gazed at Sténio, whose rapid breathing and convulsive movements betrayed his inner turmoil. Suddenly the young man awakened by himself and bounded up, crying out in a raucous, wild voice. But when he saw the guests, who looked at him with surprise and contempt, he settled down again on the sofa and, crossing his arms, surveyed them with dazed eyes that wine and insomnia had altered.

"Eh there, Jacob!" cried out young Marino ironically. "Have you crushed God's spirit?"

"I was struggling with Him," replied Sténio, whose expression at once took on a hateful, caustic quality, which was even stranger when compared to the Sténio that Trenmor had known. "But now I'm engaged with a harsher champion since I'm struggling with Marino's spirit."

"The better spirit," said Marino, "is the one that holds a man to the level of his situation. We have assembled here to compete, glass in hand, for equanimity of character. The roses crowning Zinzolina's cup have been renewed three times since we've been here, and our beautiful hostess's face still has no frown of discontent or ennui because her guests' good humor has not slowed for a moment. Only one thing could have troubled the festivities if it hadn't been agreed that sad or gay, sick or in good health, sleeping or standing, among the friends of pleasure Sténio doesn't count, because Sténio's star had set from the first hour."

"Why do you reproach the child?" asked Pulchérie. "He is frail and sickly. He slept the entire night in a corner. . . . "

"The entire night?" said Sténio, yawning. "Is it still morning? I hoped, seeing the lit torches, that we had buried the day. Have you been together only six hours, and you're surprised at not yet being bored with each other? That is truly marvelous, seeing the assortment of you gentlemen. As for me, I would keep the festivities going for a week, but only on condition that I could sleep the entire time."

"And why don't you sleep somewhere else?" asked Zamarelli. "The late Prince of Bambuccj, who died last year, full of glory and at a ripe age and who was certainly the most celebrated drinker of his century, would have condemned the ingrate who slept at his table to drink water forever, or at least would have sent him to the galleys. He upheld reasonably enough that a true Epicurean ought to maintain his strength by a well-regulated life and that there was as much impiety in sleeping before the flasks as in drinking alone. What contempt that man would have had for you, Sténio, if he had seen you seeking pleasure in fatigue, doing everything contrary, staying awake and composing poems when others sleep, falling exhausted beside full cups and barefoot women!"

Be it affectation or exhaustion, Sténio did not seem to have heard a word of Zamarelli's speech. Only at the last words did he raise his heavy head a little, saying, "And where are the women?"

"They went to change their costumes so as to appear beautiful and refreshed before us," replied Antonio. "Do you want me to cede my place in a few minutes next to Torquata? She came here on your demand, but since instead of talking to her, you slept all night. . . . "

"It doesn't matter. You did right!" said Sténio, apparently unaware of all these sarcasms. "Furthermore, I no longer care about anyone except Marino's mistress. Zinzolina, have her brought to me."

"If you had made such a demand before midnight," said Marino, "I would have forced you to swallow the shards of your glass. But it's six o'clock, and my mistress has spent all this time with me. Take her now if she is willing."

Zinzolina leaned over and murmured into Sténio's ear. "Sténio, in half an hour Princess Claudia, who is sick with love for you, will be here. She will enter a garden pavilion without being seen. Yesterday I heard you praise her modesty and beauty. I knew her secret. I wanted her to be happy, and I wanted Sténio to be the rival of kings."

"Good Zinzolina!" said Sténio affectionately. Then, becoming indifferent again, "It is true I found her beautiful, but that was yesterday . . . and then one doesn't need to possess what one admires because one would defile it and have nothing left to desire."

"You can love Claudia as you understand love," said Zinzolina. "Go down on your knees, kiss her hand, compare her to angels, and then withdraw. Fill your soul with that ideal love which used to go with the melancholy of your thoughts."

"No, don't say anymore about her," said Sténio impatiently. "Tell her I'm sick or dead. In my present mood I feel she'll displease me and I'll tell her that she is shameless to forget her rank and honor and give herself up in this way to a libertine. Page, take my purse and go fetch me the gypsy who was singing last night beneath my window."

"She sings very well," said the page with a respectful calm, "but Your Lordship hasn't seen her. . . . "

"And what does that matter to you!" cried Sténio, enraged.

"Your Excellency, she looks a fright," said the page.

"So much the better," said Sténio.

"Black as night," said the page.

"In that case I want her immediately. Obey, or I'll throw you out the window!"

The page started to obey. But hardly was he at the door when Sténio called him back.

"No, I don't want women," he said. "I want air. I want daylight. Why are we shut up like this in darkness when the sun is climbing in the sky? This is like a curse."

"Are you still asleep? Don't you see the glow of candles?" asked Antonio.

"Take them away and open the blinds," said Sténio, whose face was growing pale. "Why deprive us of pure air, of bird songs, and the perfume of flowers opening? What crime have we committed to lose sight of the sky in full daylight?"

"Here speaks the poet," said Marino, shrugging his shoulders. "Don't you know that you can't drink in daylight unless you are a German or a boor? A meal without candles is like a ball without women. And furthermore, a guest who knows how to live ought to ignore the hours and not concern himself about whether it's day or night outside, whether the bourgeoisie are sleeping, or whether the cardinals are awake."

"Zinzolina," said Sténio in an insulting, contemptuous tone, "this air is foul. This wine, these viands, these steaming liquors, all this resembles a Flemish tavern. Give me air, or I'll overturn your torches, and I'll break your windows."

"It's you who will leave and take the air outside," cried the guests, rising with indignation.

"Eh, don't you see that he is incapable!" said Zinzolina, running to Sténio, who was falling in a faint onto the sofa.

Trenmor aided her in helping him. The others settled down again.

"What a pity," they said, "to see Zinzolina, the maddest of women, infatuated with that consumptive poet and taking all his affectations seriously."

"Come back to yourself, my child," said Pulchérie. "Breathe these smelling salts. Lean against the window. Don't you feel the air reaching your face and ruffling your hair?"

"I feel your hands warming and irritating me," said Sténio. "Take them away from my face. Go away, you smell of musk. You smell too much the whore. Give me some rum, because I feel like getting drunk."

"Sténio, you are insane and cruel," said Zinzolina with great softness. "Here is one of your best friends. He has been with you for an hour. Don't you recognize him?"

"My excellent friend," said Sténio, "deign to lower yourself, because you seem so tall to me that I would need to rise to see you, and I'm not sure your face is worth the trouble."

"What have you lost," said Trenmor, without bending, "vision or memory?"

Sténio made a gesture of surprise as he recognized that voice. He turned away brusquely. "So it's not a dream this time?" he asked. "How can I distinguish reality from illusion when my life is spent sleeping or in delirium? Just now I dreamed that you were here singing the most buffoonish and smuttiest songs.... This amazed me. But after all, haven't I amazed those who used to know me? And then I seemed to wake up, to be quarreling, and you seemed to be here still. At least I thought I saw your shadow floating on the wall, and I no longer knew if I were awake or asleep. Now tell me, are you really Trenmor, or are you merely a shadow, an effaced dream, the ghost, and the name of someone who used to be a man?"

"I am certainly not the ghost of a friend," said Trenmor. "If I don't hesitate to recognize you, I don't deserve to be unrecognized by you."

Sténio tried to press his hand and smile. But his features had lost their naive mobility, and even in the expression of his recognition there was now something haughty and preoccupied. His eyes, stripped of lashes, no longer had that veiled slowness which suited his youth so well. He gazed at you directly in the face, with something brusque, fixed, and almost arrogant about him. Then the young man, fearing to abandon himself to memories of former days, rose. He drew Trenmor to a table and, with a singular mixture of inner shame and audacious vanity, he challenged him to a drinking contest.

"Eh what, are you still intending to hasten the end of your life?" cried Zinzolina reproachfully. "A little while ago you were dying. And now you are going to devour what remains of your youth and strength with these burning drinks. Oh, Sténio, go away! Go away with Trenmor! Don't make your recovery impossible. . . . "

"Go away with Trenmor!" said Sténio. "And where would I go with him? Can we inhabit the same places? Am I not banished from Mount Horeb, where God reveals Himself? Don't I have forty years to wander in the desert so that one day my descendants may see the land of Canaan?"

Sténio gripped his glass convulsively. A black veil seemed to lower itself over his face. Then it was suddenly animated with that feverish flush which spreads in patches over faces altered by debauchery and which differs essentially from the fine, well-blended coloring of youth.

"No, no," he said. "I won't leave until Trenmor has gotten to know his friend again. If that young, confident, credulous man no longer exists, at least he must see the intrepid drinker, the voluptuous dandy who has emerged from Sténio's ashes. Zinzolina, have all the cups refilled. I drink to the shades of my patron, Don Juan. I drink to Trenmor's youth. —But no, that isn't enough. Refill my cup with devouring spices; pour in pepper, which creates thirst, clove, which arouses love, ginger, which gnaws the entrails, and cinnamon, which quickens the circulation of the blood. Come, brazen page, prepare me that detestable mixture so that it can burn my tongue and exalt my brain. I will drink it, if they have to hold me by force to make me swallow it, because I want to become insane and feel young, be it only for an hour, and die afterward. Trenmor, you will see how beautiful I am when I'm drunk, how Divine poetry descends through me. The fire of heaven ignites my thought, while the fire of fever courses through my veins. Come, the fuming cup is on the table. I challenge all you sickly drinkers and pale debauchees. You have mocked me. Now let us see which one of you dares hold your own against me."

"Who will deliver us from this beardless braggart?" Antonio asked Zamarelli. "Haven't we endured his insolent ways long enough?"

"Let him do this," Zamarelli replied. "He is working himself up to rid us of his person soon."

A moment after having swallowed the spiced wine, Sténio was seized with atrocious suffering. Fiery red mottlings appeared on his withered skin. Sweat ran down his face, and his eyes took on an almost fierce gleam.

"Sténio, you are suffering!" cried Marino with an expression of triumph.

"No," said Sténio.

"In that case, sing us some of your drunken rimes."

"Sténio, you can't sing," said Pulchérie. "Don't try."

"I shall sing," said Sténio. "Have I lost my voice? Am I no longer the one you used to applaud enthusiastically and whose accents threw you into an intoxication sweeter than that produced by wine?"

"That is true," said the drinkers. "Sing, Sténio, sing!"

And they crowded around the table. None of them could contest Sténio's gift of inspiration. They all felt enthralled and dominated by him when they came upon a flicker of poetry at the core of the nervous irritability into which his disorder had thrown him.

He sang in an impaired voice. But it was vibrant and accentuated in the sweetest language of the universe.

### Inno Ebbrioso (Hymn to Drunkenness)

> Let the burning cyprus circulate in my veins!
> Let's efface in my heart hopes that are vain
> And even the memory
> Of vanished days whose disturbing image,

Like a dark cloud at the depths of a pure lake,
  Would trouble the future.

Let's forget, let's forget! The supreme wisdom
Is to ignore those days spared by drunkenness
  And not to know
If the night was sober, or if the most beautiful
Of our years have already disappeared, blighted
  Before the hour of evening.

"Sténio, your voice is growing weak!" cried Marino from the other end of the table. "You seem to be seeking out your verses and drawing them with difficulty from the depths of your brain. I remember when you could improvise a dozen stanzas without keeping us in suspense. But you are deteriorating, Sténio. Your mistress and muse are equally weary of you."

Sténio responded only by a contemptuous stare. Then, beating on the table, he continued in a more assured voice:

Let them bring me a flask, that my cup, refilled,
Overflow, and let my lips plunge into the dregs
  Of this radiant flood,
Thirst, dry out, and again demand
New heat from this devouring wine
  Which equals me to the Gods!

Over my dazzled eyes let a thick veil descend.
Let the blurred torch pale! And let me hear
  At midnight
The resounding shock of your knocking cups
Like waves agitated on the ocean
  By fleeing winds!

If I look up in the midst of the orgy,
If my trembling lips reddened with wine
  Seek kisses
That my ardent desires, on the naked shoulders
Of these women of love, here for my pleasures,
  Cannot appease,

Then let their lascivious caresses rekindle

> The convulsive ardors of a twenty-year-old priest
>> In my impoverished blood.
> Let the flowers on their brows be strewn by my hands,
> Let me entwine my fingers in the perfumed tresses
>> Of their floating hair.

> Let my furious teeth tear from their trembling flesh
> A cry of fear. Let their faltering voices
>> Demand mercy.
> Let our sighs mingle in a last effort.
> Let us answer each other's cries in a last challenge
>> And let me die this way!

"Sténio, you are growing pale!" cried Marino. "That's enough singing, or you'll give us your last breath on the last stanza."

"That's enough interruption," cried Sténio angrily, "or I'll plunge my glass into your throat!"

Then he wiped away the sweat running down his brow, and in a full, manly voice that contrasted with his emaciated features and the bluish pallor spreading over his inflamed face, he rose and continued:

> Or if God refuses me a fortunate death,
> Crowned both with glory and happiness,
>> If I sense my desires,
> Through an impotent rage of immortal agony,
> Like the pale reflection of a dim flame
>> Survive my pleasures,

> Oh, my jealous Master, insulting caprice,
> Let this generous wine cut short the torture
>> Which makes the body numb.
> Let our lips grip each other in a farewell kiss.
> Let a frozen sleep annihilate all my desires,
>> And let God be cursed.

As he finished this last phrase, Sténio turned ashen. His hands trembled, and he let the cup he was carrying to his lips fall. He tried to look triumphantly at his companions, who were amazed at his courage and enchanted with the manly harmonies he had even now been able to draw from his exhausted lungs. But the body could no longer resist this frenzied struggle with the will. It collapsed, and Sténio fell to the floor in a dead faint. His head hit Pulchérie's chair, and her dress was reddened with his blood. Hearing Zinzolina's cries, the other courtesans came running. When they saw them return, dazzling in their dress and beauty, the other guests no longer thought of Sténio. Pulchérie, aided by her page and by Trenmor, carried Sténio to the shade of the garden, near a jetting fountain carved out of the most beautiful Carrara marble.

"Leave me alone with him," said Trenmor to the courtesan. "Henceforth he belongs to me."

Zinzolina, good and careless creature that she was, bestowed a kiss on Sténio's cold lips, recommended him to God and Trenmor, sighed deeply as she moved off, and returned to the banquet, where an even livelier and noisier joy now reigned.

"Next time," Marino said to Zinzolina as he returned her cup to her, "I hope you won't lend this beautiful cup to your drunkard, Sténio. It's Cellini's work, and it was nearly ruined when it fell."

## XLI  CLAUDIA

When Sténio regained consciousness he received his friend's zealous attentions with contempt.

"Why are we alone here?" he asked. "Why have they put us outside like lepers?"

"You must not return to your companions of the orgy," Trenmor said, "because they despise you. You have lost and ruined everything. You have abandoned God. You have exhausted human passions. Nothing but friendship remains. And there a refuge is always open to you."

"What will friendship do for me?" asked Sténio bitterly. "Didn't friendship first weary of me and declare itself impotent for my happiness?"

"You repulsed it. You did not recognize it, and you denied its benefits. Unhappy child! Return to us, return to yourself. Lélia is calling you back. If you renounce your mistakes, Lélia will forget them. . . . "

"Go away," said Stenio angrily. "Don't utter that woman's name in my hearing ever again. It is her influence that corrupted me. It is her irony that opened my eyes and showed me life in its naked ugliness. Don't talk to me about Lélia. I no longer know her. I've forgotten her face. I don't even know if I ever loved her. A hundred years have passed since I left her. If I saw her now, I would laugh with pity as I reflected that I have possessed a hundred women who were more beautiful, younger, more naive, more passionate, and who overwhelmed me with pleasure. Why shoud I go on my knees now before that idol with marble thighs? I'd need the fire of Pygmalion and the good will of the gods to bring her to life. What would I do with her? Would she give me more than the others have?

"I once believed in infinite joys and celestial ecstasies. I dreamed of supreme beatitude, angelic ecstasy at the feet of the Very Holy while in her arms. But today I no longer believe in heaven, angels, God, or Lélia. I know human joys. I no longer exaggerate their value. It is Lélia herself who carefully enlightened me. I know enough of her! Don't let her call me back, because I would render her all the harm she has done me, and I would be too much avenged."

"Your bitterness and anger reassure me," said Trenmor. "I was afraid I would find you insensitive to the memory of the past. I see that it deeply upsets you and that Lélia's resistance has remained in your memory like an incurable wound. God be blessed! Sténio has lost only physical health, but his soul is still full of energy and potential."

"Superb philosopher," cried Sténio furiously. "Did you come here to insult me or do you take some sort of idiotic pleasure in displaying your impassive calm before my torment? Return where you come from, and let me die here. Don't despise the last efforts of a soul, blighted perhaps by its confusion, but not degraded by the compassion of others."

Trenmor silently lowered his head. He tried to find words that could sweeten the bitterness of that savage pride, and he was overwhelmed with sadness. His face lost its habitual serenity, and tears glistened in his eyes.

Sténio perceived this, and in spite of himself he was moved. Their eyes met. Trenmor expressed such sadness that Sténio, overcome, abandoned himself to a wave of self-pity. The jeering and indifference in which he had lived for so long had accustomed him to feel embarrassed about his sufferings. When he felt his heart softened by tenderness, he was surprised and subjugated for an instant, and he threw himself into Trenmor's arms. But he was almost immediately ashamed of this gesture, and, suddenly moving away, he perceived a woman enveloped in a long Venetian cloak who was plunging into the shade of the arbors. It was Princess Claudia, followed by her loyal governess. She was making her way toward one of the garden pavilions.

"Decidedly," said Sténio, as he readjusted his batiste shirt collar and fastened its diamond clasp, "I cannot let that poor child languish for me. Zinzolina probably forgot that she was supposed to come. It is to my honor to be the first at the rendezvous."

Sténio turned his head to the side where Claudia was walking. For an instant his nostrils dilated like those of a stag when he seizes the soft scents of the doe in the mountain air. A ray of youth gleamed on his devastated face. He withdrew his hand from his friend's and began running lightly toward the pavilion to get there before Claudia. But after a few steps he slowed down and gained his goal with effort and nonchalance.

He arrived at the casino entrance at the same time she did, and out of breath he leaned against the balustrade. The young duchess, red with shame and trembling with joy, believed that the poet, the object of her love, was seized with emotion and confusion just as she was. But Sténio, who had been a little revived by the sparkle of her black eyes, offered her his hand to climb the stairs with the assurance of a military officer and the obsequious grace of a chamberlain.

When they were alone and she was seated, trembling, with her face on fire, Sténio silently contemplated her for a long time. Princess Claudia was barely more than a child. Her figure had not yet acquired its full development. The excessive length of her black eyelashes, the sickly tone of her prematurely smooth, satiny skin, the light blue shadows around her greedy, languishing eyes, her morbidly humble attitude, all announced a precocious puberty and a devouring imagination. In spite of these signs of a fiery constitution, Claudia, owing to her extreme youth, was still clothed in all the charm of modesty. Her agitation betrayed itself beneath her chaste demeanor. Her trembling mouth seemed to call out to be kissed, while her eyes were wet with tears. Her unsure voice seemed to demand grace and protection. Desire and fear overwhelmed this fragile being.

Seized with admiration, Sténio was at first surprised to have such a rich treasure at his disposal. It was the first time that he had seen the princess so close and that he had given her so much attention. She was much younger and more desirable than he had imagined. But his blasé senses could no longer deceive his spirit, which was now skeptical and cold. In a single glance he examined and possessed Claudia entirely, from her elaborate hairdo, enclosed in a net of pearls, to her tiny feet, encased in satin. With one thought he foresaw her entire future, from this first folly that was leading her into a poet's arms to the hideous love affairs of a princely, debauched old age. Saddened, frightened, and above all disgusted by his vision, Sténio looked at her strangely and did not speak to her. When he perceived the ridiculous situation in which his preoccupation placed him, he tried to make conversation. But he could never pretend love he did not feel, and he said, with almost severe curiosity as he took her hand in an entirely paternal fashion, "How old are you?"

"Fourteen," replied the young princess, bewildered and almost out of her mind with surprise, grief, rage, and fear.

"Very well, child," said Sténio, "go tell your confessor to absolve you for coming here, and thank God that He sent you here a year, that is to say a century, too late in Sténio's life."

At these words the princess's governess, who had remained in the window alcove to observe the two lovers' conduct, threw herself at them and received poor, tearful Claudia in her arms.

"Insolent man!" she shouted at Sténio. "Is this how you receive the grace that your illustrious sovereign grants you when she has descended so far as to honor you with her gaze? On your knees, vassal, on your knees! If your brutal soul is left untouched by the most excellent beauty of the universe, at least your audacity can bow before the respect you owe to the daughter of the Bambuccj."

"If the daughter of the Bambuccj has deigned to descend to me," said Sténio, "she should have resigned herself in advance to being treated as my equal. If at this hour she repents, so much the better for her. It is the only punishment she will receive for her imprudence. She can boast of being protected by the Holy Virgin, who led her here the morning after and not on the eve of an orgy. Listen, you two women, listen to the voice of a man whom the approach of death renders wise and disinterested. Listen, you old *dueña* with the sordid soul and infamous ways. And you, young girl with the precocious passions and a fatal, dangerous beauty, listen. First of all, you, titled courtesan, marquise whose heart conceals as many vices as your face shows wrinkles, you can thank the forgetfulness that will efface the recollection of this incident from Sténio's memory before an hour has elapsed. Otherwise, you would be unmasked in the eyes of this court and chased, as you deserve, from a family whose frail scion you wish to defile. Leave her, vice and greed, whorishness, servility, treason, leprosy of nations, scum and shame of the human race.

"And you, my poor child," he added, tearing Claudia from her governess's arms and drawing her into the daylight, blushing and distressed as she was. "Listen carefully. If one day, carried by destiny and by your passions, you cast a fearful glance behind you at your beautiful lost years and at your tarnished purity, remember Sténio. Then stop yourself at the edge of the abyss. . . . Look at me, Claudia, look directly into my eyes, without fear or uneasiness. Look at this man with whom you believe yourself infatuated and at whom you have probably never looked. At your age the heart is agitated and impatient. It summons a heart which responds, it risks itself, it gives itself, it trusts. But misfortune to those who abuse ignorance or guilelessness! Claudia, you have heard the songs of a man you believed to be young, handsome, and passionate. Look at him now, poor Claudia, and see the illusion you loved. See his bald head, his emaciated hands, his dull eyes, and his withered lips. Put your hand on this exhausted heart. Count the slow, moribund pulsations of this old man twenty years of age. Look at these grey hairs around a face where the beard has not yet grown. Tell me, is this the Sténio you had dreamed of? Is this the religious poet, the glowing sylph you believed you saw pass through your celestial visions when you sang his hymns on your harp at sunset? If you had glanced at your palace steps you would have been able to see the pale specter you are now talking to seated on one of the marble lions that guard the entrance. You would have seen him as you do today, degenerate, exhausted, indifferent to your angelic beauty and melodious voice, curious only to hear how a fifteen-year-old princess was phrasing the melodies inspired by drunkenness and written in debauchery. But Claudia, you didn't see him. Fortunately for you, your eyes sought him in the sky, and he wasn't there. Your faith lent him wings while he crept beneath your feet among the riff-raff who sleep at the gates of your villa. . . . Young girl, it will be like this with all your loves and illusions. Remember this deception if you want to conserve your youth, beauty, and spiritual strength. But if you can still hope and believe after this experience, don't be impatient. Rein in the desire of your ardent soul. Prolong this blind hope and this childishness of the heart with all your strength. These qualities live only for a day and never return. Govern wisely, guard vigilantly, and spend frugally the treasure of your illusions. The day will come when you want to obey your fiery thoughts and eager senses, but you will see your idol of gold and diamonds change into gross clay. You will hold in your arms only a phantom without warmth or life. You will vainly pursue the dream of your youth. In your breathless, fatal career you will only overtake a shadow, and you will soon fall exhausted, alone amid a swarm of regrets, starving in the bosom of satiety, degenerate, and dying, like Sténio, without having lived an entire day."

After speaking in this way, he left the casino and prepared to rejoin Trenmor. But the latter tapped him on the shoulder as he was descending the bottom steps. He had seen and heard everything through the open window.

"Sténio," he said to him, "the tears I shed just now were an insult, and my suffering was a blasphemy. You are unhappy; but, my son, you are greater than Lélia, more experienced than Trenmor, and purer than the saints."

"Trenmor," said Sténio with deep contempt, "I see that you are mad. Don't you realize that all this morality I have just displayed is only the miserable comedy of an old soldier fallen into childhood who constructs fortresses with grains of sand and believes himself entrenched against imaginary enemies? Don't you understand that I love virtue the way old libertines love young virgins? I praise charms of which I have lost the enjoyment. Do you believe, foolish, virtuous dreamer, that I would have respected that girl if the abuse of pleasure had not rendered me impotent?"

Ending these words in a bitter, cynical tone, Sténio fell into a deep reverie as Trenmor drew him along, far from the villa. Sténio did not seem to be at all concerned about where he was being led.

## XLII THE CAMALDULES

Trenmor, who liked to travel on foot, nevertheless procured a carriage, because Sténio would not have had the strength to walk. They went in easy stages, contemplating at leisure the magnificent countryside they were traveling through. Sténio was taciturn and peaceful. He did not once ask about the duration and goal of this journey. He let himself be led with the apathy of a prisoner of war, and his indifference about the future seemed to give him joy in the present. He would look admiringly at the beautiful views of this enchanted countryside and would often beg Trenmor to stop the horses so that he could climb a mountain or sit beside a river. Then he would rediscover glimmers of enthusiasm and poetic impulses to understand nature and celebrate it.

But in spite of these moments of awakening and rebirth, Trenmor could observe the irreparable ravages of debauch in his young friend. Formerly, his active thought had seized on all things and given color, form, and life to all exterior objects. Now Sténio ordinarily vegetated in a sensual, distressing stupefaction. He seemed to scorn making use of his intelligence. But the reality was that he was no longer master of it. Often he summoned it in vain, because it no longer obeyed. Then he would affect contempt for the faculties he had lost. But the bitterness of his gaiety betrayed his anger. He secretly rebuked his rebellious memory. He thrashed his lazy imagination. He dug spurs into the flanks of his insensible, wearied genius, but all in vain. He would fall exhausted again into a chaos of dreams. His ideas passed through his brain, incoherent, weird, ungraspable, like imaginary sparkles that seem to dance in the darkness. They follow each other, multiply, and finally efface themselves forever in the eternal night of nothingness.

One evening at sunset they entered a valley covered with thick forests. The most beautiful waters ran silently in the shadow of myrtle and fig trees. Vast clearings, where half-wild herds grazed, were cut by borders of a tender green. This region was rich and wild. Only scattered cottages were visible, nearly hidden in the greenery. One could enjoy there both the graces and blessings of fertile nature and the great beauty of uncultivated nature.

Halfway down the hill the travelers were descending in order to enter that beautiful valley, Trenmor set his companion on foot. The carriage and horses followed them at a walking pace, with precaution, over a steep, dangerous road. While they walked, they reached the fertile, softly undulating ground of the valley.

For a moment Sténio felt refreshed and consoled by the view of that beautiful countryside.

"Happy," he cried, "are the carefree, rough shepherds who sleep in the darkness of these silent woods with no other worry than the care of their herd and no other study than the rising and setting of the stars! Happier still are the wild foals that bound lightly through this brush and the goats that effortlessly climb the steep rocks! Happy are all the creatures that enjoy life without fatigue or excess!"

As they were turning a curve of the road, Sténio perceived through the evening mist, eating imperceptibly at all the contours of the countryside, a large white line on the mountain slope. It encompassed the valley in a vast, majestic circle.

"What's that?" he asked Trenmor. "A splendid architectural foundation, or a chalk wall? An immense waterfall, a road, or a palace?"

"It's a monastery," said Trenmor. "It's the monastery of the Camaldules."

Sténio did not hear the response. He continued walking as he whistled.

Night came. The road became so dark that the postilion could advance no further without knocking into all the trees. They found lodging for the night at a cottage. But because the two travelers found it too early to sleep, they continued to wander haphazardly through the woods.

Trenmor knew the countryside perfectly, but he pretended to be lost. Fearing to awaken Sténio's revulsion and arouse his sense of independence if he told him his plan, he affected not to know where they would spend the night.

Little by little they approached the mountains. Seeing that Sténio was fatigued, Trenmor proposed that they go back to the place where they had left their baggage.

"I would rather die on the spot than go back over the road I've traveled," replied Sténio. "I'm exhausted. I won't go any farther."

"You can't," said Trenmor, "sleep without danger on this wet grass and in the mist of these cold, stagnant waters. Make an effort to climb the base of the mountain. We are on a soft, easy road. When we have attained a certain elevation, we can find a healthier refuge in some grotto."

Sténio let himself be carried along. When they had crossed through a thicket of small trees that fringed the foot of the mountain, they saw the elegant, rich walls of the Camaldule monastery rise before them in the first glimmers of the moon. Trenmor proposed that they ask for lodging there. A lay-brother received them, and, without speaking a single word in answer to their request, he conducted them to the room reserved for pilgrims.

Sténio, overwhelmed with weariness, slept so deeply that he lost all awareness of his surroundings. The next day he found himself standing and dressed without being able to remember the night before and to recognize where he was. He did not even think of calling Trenmor. He had forgotten Trenmor, his own departure from Villa Bambuccj, and his journey through regions whose names he did not know. He felt as if he had just gone abruptly from a noisy, populous abode to a deserted, silent dwelling. He left his room and looked with lazy astonishment and heedless indecision over the objects that presented themselves to his vision.

First there was a long gallery with a white marble arch upheld by Corinthian columns of pink marble veined with blue. These columns were separated from each other by a malachite vase where aloes raised their large, spiny edges. And then immense courtyards succeeded each other in a depth truly *Piranesian*. They were filled, like spread-out carpets, with flowerbeds variegated with the most beautiful flowers. The dew with which all the plants were freshly bathed seemed to clothe them in a silver veil. In the center of the symmetrical patterns these flowerbeds formed on the earth, fountains flowing into jasper basins raised their transparent jets of water into the blue morning air. The first beams of sunlight were beginning to pass over the top of the building, and as they fell on that fine, bounding rain, they crowned each jet with a crest of diamonds. Proud Chinese pheasants, which scarcely stirred beneath Sténio's feet, displayed their filigreed plumes and velvet thighs among the flowers. The peacock spread out its dress of jewels over the grass. The musky duck, with its emerald breast, pursued golden flies that formed disappearing circles on the surface of the water within the basins.

To the mocking or plaintive cries of these captive birds, with their melancholy, proud bearing, were mixed the thousand joyful, noisy voices and curious familiarities of the free birds. The mischievous, confident goldfinch settled upon the motionless faces of statues. The insolent sparrow came to steal birdseed from the domestic birds, but flew away terrified at the least clucking of the hens. The goldfinch fought with the wind for the flower crests. The insects also awakened and began to hum beneath the grass, warmed and steaming from the first heat of day. The most beautiful butterflies of the valley arrived in droves to take their fill of the nectar from the exotic plants. They were so intoxicated by the taste that they would let themselves be taken in one's hand. All these voices of the air and all these morning perfumes ascended to the sky like a pure incense, like an artless canticle, to thank God for the blessings of creation and for man's labor.

But among all these animal and vegetable existences, all these works of art and these splendors of wealth, man alone was lacking. The sand paths had been recently raked, as if to efface the memory of human steps. Sténio felt a sort of superstitious fear about imprinting his own. He felt as if he were going to destroy the harmony of this magical scene and make the enchanted walls of his dream fall upon him.

Because, in the confusion of his poetic ideas and sick aberrations, he did not want to believe in the reality of what he was seeing. When he perceived from afar, behind the transparent colonnades of the monastery, the wild valley depths, he willingly imagined that he had fallen asleep in the bosom of the woods beneath a fairy's favorite tree. And he imagined that, upon his awakening, the coquettish queen had surrounded him with the impalpable wonders of her palace, to drive him amorous or mad.

As he let himself go softly into that fantasy, intoxicated by the sweet odors of jasmine and datura, content to be alone in this beautiful place, and believing himself almost a king or a god, he approached a long, high casement window. The stained glass, sparkling in the sun, resembled a curtain of shadowed harem silk. He seated himself on the side of a pool filled with fish and amused himself in following through the limpid water the trout, which wears a supple silver armor strewn with rubies, and the carp, dressed in pale gold shadowed with green. He admired their indolent games, the sparkle of their metallic eyes, and the inconceivable agility of their fearful flight when they perceived his moving shadow on the water. Suddenly, chants such as the saints must sing at the feet of Jehovah's throne issued from the depths of the mysterious edifice. These voices, mingling with the vibrations of the organ and the metallic sound of the buccin,* filled the entire monastery. Everything seemed to become silent to listen. Sténio, struck with

---

*A crooked trumpet.

admiration, instinctively kneeled as he had in his childhood.

Deep, full men's voices ascended to God like a fervent prayer full of hope. And the penetrating, silvery voices of children responded like far-off heavenly promises expressed through the pure voices of angels.

The monks were singing:

"Angel of the Lord, stretch your protective wings over us. Shelter us with your vigilant goodness and your consoling pity. God made you indulgent and compassionate among all the Powers of heaven. He destined you to aid and console men, to gather the tears shed at Christ's feet into an undefiled vase and present them in expiation before Your eternal justice, Oh, Very Holy!"

And the children responded, from the height of the nave:

"Place hope in the Lord, oh, you who labor amidst tears, because the guardian angel spreads his great golden wings between man's weakness and the Lord's anger. *Praise the Lord.*"

Then the monks took up again:

"Oh, youngest and purest of angels, God created you last. He created you after man and placed you in Paradise as His companion. But woman came and was more powerful than you over man's spirit. The angel of anger descended to punish them. You followed them into exile, and you cared for Eve's children, oh, Very Holy!"

The children responded again:

"Thank him on your knees, all you who love God. Thank the guardian angel because he ascends and descends constantly between earth and heaven with his powerful wings. He carries prayers from below and brings back blessings from on high. *Praise the Lord.*"

A young monk's manly voice chanted this verse:

"With your hot breath you heat the plants numbed with cold in the morning. You cover man's crops, menaced by hail, with your virginal robe. With a protective hand you support the fisherman's hut shattered by the winds of the sea. You awaken sleeping mothers and, calling them softly in the middle of their dreams at night, you tell them to give the breast to newborn babes. You guard the purity of virgins and place the orange branch above their beds, invisible talisman which turns away evil thoughts and impure dreams. In the midday sun you seat yourself in the furrow where the harvester's child sleeps. And you turn the snake and the scorpion ready to creep over its cradle away from their path. You open the pages of the missal when we seek in the sacred text a remedy for our evils. You make us find the verse needed for our misery, and you place beneath our eyes the sacred lines which repulse temptation."

"Invoke the guardian angel," chanted the children's voices, "because he is the most powerful among God's angels. When the Lord sent him on earth, He promised that each time he reascended to Him, He would bestow grace on a sinner. *Praise the Lord.*"

"Let us invoke the guardian angel," took up a voice more trembling than the others which Sténio believed he had heard before. "Let us ask him to efface the memory of the past from our hearts. Let us implore him to spread out a crêpe mourning cloth, an impenetrable veil over the seductions of a deceptive world, over the attractions of false idols. Let us beg him to illumine the fire of saintly desires within us and extinguish the painful intensity of guilty ones. Let him give our madonnas' brows a more severe aspect, their marble feet a more perceptible cold, so that when we look at those august features and kiss those undefiled feet we have no impure thought. Let us pray to him, too, when he appears in our dreams, not to take on the delicate lineaments, the tender expression, the floating garments, and long hair of a woman."

The monk stopped abruptly. A long silence, produced perhaps by surprise and confusion, ensued in the choir after this unfinished verse. Finally, the children's voices completed the canticle as they repeated:

"Invoke the guardian angel. *Praise the Lord.*"

At this moment Sténio saw a monk, still young, leave the chapel and agitatedly plunge himself beneath the arches of the cloister. He seemed to recognize in the man's gait, as in the sound of the voice that had struck him, the Irish priest whom he had seen insane, Magnus.

## XLIII   THE SEPULCHERS

When the group had filed slowly before Sténio and when the last monk's robe had disappeared behind the arcades of the courtyard, Trenmor rejoined his friend. As he sat beside him, he tried to read upon Sténio's face what impressions he was receiving. But because the moment of exaltation that inspired Sténio's romantic fantasy had vanished, Sténio had fallen back into his habitual state of apathetic coldness. Then he remembered the incidents which had brought him to this place, and he said in a tone of indifference, "Is it true that you told me last night these religious men are of the Camaldule order?"

"Yes," said Trenmor. "This is one of the wealthiest, most peaceful, and most lenient communities of the Roman Church. The beauty of their buildings, the extent of their lands, and the freedom they enjoy permits them to devote themselves to the arts and sciences. Among them can be counted a great number of excellent musicians and learned astronomers. Some are poets and painters. Others are so dedicated to chemistry and physics that in the eyes of the masses they seem to perpetuate the ancient traditions of alchemist and astrologer monks. Finally, if sacred poetry, enlightened faith, and patient, conscientious study have found a refuge somewhere on earth, it is in this monastery. Aren't you struck by the magnificence displayed here, by the austere knowledge and patriarchal simplicity presiding over the cultivation of these gardens and over the construction of these aviaries? Don't you see here the realization of all legitimate desires, the satisfaction of all worthy needs, noble ambitions, and innocent fantasies? I feel that an agitated soul must grow calm as it approaches this sanctuary and that a fatigued mind will find rest among these peaceful, wise habits. What do you think, Sténio?"

"I think," replied Sténio, "that the insatiable desire of the soul survives all these satisfactions. I think that man's indefatigable restlessness renders useless all his efforts to content himself with the possible."

Trenmor, seeing that the moment had not come to dominate and lull that bitter, obstinate reason, took him to dine in the prior's chamber. Then he proposed that they visit the cemetery.

It was situated on the slope of the mountain. On one side it extended to the monastery through a passageway of twisted columns. The other side was bordered by a bare, sandy ravine, at the bottom of which a small lake slept in bleak repose. There was no possible way to descend over its borders because of the motion of the steep sands that surrounded it and the total absence of any support. No rock had been able to arrest itself on that precipitous slope. No tree had been able to bury its roots in that crumbling earth. While waiting for the avalanches which had hollowed it out to fill it up, the crater lake nourished a rich vegetation within the bosom of its motionless waves. Gigantic lotus plants and sweet water corals twenty arm-spans long brought their large leaves and their varied flowers to the surface of that water, which was never rippled by a fisherman's rod. On their entwined stalks, beneath the shelter of numerous cradles, emerald-skinned serpents and smooth-skinned salamanders with yellow eyes slept gaping in the sun, sure of not being tormented by man's nets and traps. The lake's surface was so thick and green that one might have taken it from on high for a meadow. Reed forests reflected their springing stalks and velvet tufts, which the wind bent like a field of wheat. Sténio, charmed by the wildness of this ravine, wanted to descend and place his feet on the perfidious network of leafage.

"Stop, my son," said a monk who was accompanying them, his hood lowered over his face. "This flower-covered lake is the image of worldly pleasures. It is surrounded with seductions, but it conceals bottomless abysses."

"And what do you know of them, Father?" asked Sténio with a smile. "Have you sounded this abyss? Have you walked over the stormy waves of passions?"

"When Peter tried to follow Jesus over the waves of Genezareth," replied the Camaldule, "after several steps he felt that his faith was lacking and that he had risked too much in wishing, like the Son of Man, to walk upon the tempest. He cried out, 'Lord, we are perishing!' And the Lord, drawing him toward Himself, saved him."

"Peter was a bad friend and a cowardly disciple," said Sténio. "Did he not deny his master through fear of sharing his fate? Those who fear danger and withdraw from it are like Peter. They are neither men nor Christians."

The Camaldule lowered his head and said nothing.

Trenmor, inviting Sténio to return, made him admire the view of the cemetery. Monstrous yew trees whose growth had never been directed by man covered the tombs with a curtain so dark that one could hardly make out in full daylight the marble figures stretched out over the coffins with the mournful pallor of kneeling monks. A terrible silence hovered over this asylum. The wind could not penetrate the mysterious thickness of the trees. Not a single sunbeam could penetrate. Light and life seemed to be arrested at the doors of this chaos. If one tried to cross, it was to reenter the cloister or go to the edge of the ravine, which was even more silent and desolate.

"Well done!" said Sténio as he seated himself upon a tomb. "This cemetery suits me better than the paneled, perfumed interior of the monastery. I like each thing in its place: luxury and softness with courtesans, austerity and mortification with the religious. But tell me, Father, why do you insist on hiding your face from me? I know the sound of your voice very well. We have met before in better times."

"Better!" said Magnus, slowly letting his hood fall and leaning his already bald head on his withered hand in an attitude of doubt.

"Yes, better for both you and me," said Sténio, "because at that time the roses of youth were spread over my face, and even though you were confused and feverish the last time I met you on the mountain, your beard was black, Father, and your hair thick."

"Do you truly attach great value to the youth of the body, to that devouring energy of the blood which burns the brain?" asked the troubled monk.

"And what is more precious?" replied the young man. "What other real wealth do we possess?"

"Youth is the age of sufferings and danger," said the priest. "Happy are those who have passed beyond it without perishing!"

Sténio fixed his eyes for an instant upon Magnus's pale wrinkled face. Then he turned to Trenmor with a mixture of sadness and irony. "Why did you bring me here?" he asked. "Why have you put this living specter and these verdant tombs before my eyes? Is it to prove that death is happier and more fertile than life? Is it to give me a foretaste of the sweetness of the void? Do you think you have chosen your place and your subject well? Don't you know that I apparently have more desire to die than to live? As for this man, perhaps you don't know that I talked with him on Mount Rosa one day when he was mad. What courage do you want me to draw from these tombs where I wish I were already sleeping? What confidence do you hope to give me through this priest's words when I have seen him led astray through his passions?"

"Sténio, I wanted to show you," the sage said, "that life can be as calm as death and that man can regain his confused reason and submit it to his all-powerful will. I wanted to show you the immense resources God has given us and the treasures within our reach. You see, one can without confusion, weariness, or excess enjoy what is noblest on earth: poetry, science, and the arts. If you stay here even a little while you will see that the most powerful and the most elect natures have come to find repose and new strength in the heart of this retreat while they await the mysterious destinies of the other life. You will see that here they have found the slow but certain healing of their poisoned wounds and the extension of their most precious faculties."

"You will see above all," added the Camaldule, "that God is merciful and His love immense. His pity is tireless and His grace all-powerful. You will weep at the feet of sacred altars, and these pious tears will soothe the wounds in your heart. Day by day you will feel the salutary effects of this blessed captivity. Your tempestuous desires will break beneath the yoke of captivity. Your noble desires will once again dominate. The joys of resignation and of gratitude will efface within you even the memory of those delirious errors and accursed passions of your youth."

"You are angry with youth, my brother," said Sténio. "But you are only a few years older than me. This morning you added a verse that was not in the liturgy to the canticle of the guardian angel. It betrayed more youth in your imagination than there is now in my entire being."

The priest paled. Then he placed his yellow, calloused hand on Sténio's pale, bluish one. "My child," he said, "have you truly been unhappy too, since you are so cruel?"

"Suffering that one has endured," said Trenmor in a sad, severe voice, "should make one compassionate and good. Feeble souls are corrupted by adversity. Strong souls are purified by it."

"Don't I know this very well?" said Sténio, moved finally and shedding all his irony to take the priest's arm in one hand and Trenmor's arm in the other. "Don't I know that I am a soul without grandeur and without energy, an infirm, miserable nature? Would I be where I am now if I were Trenmor or Magnus? But alas," he added, letting go of their arms and sitting down again with a somber, angry motion on a tombstone, "why tempt me to vain efforts? Why give me advice from which I cannot profit and examples which are beyond my strength? What pleasure do you find in displaying your wealth before me, showing me with what strength you are gifted, of what efforts you are capable? Strong men, heroic men! Elected vessels. Saints who have emerged from a galley-slave and a priest. You, convict, have assumed all the punishments of social life on your head. You, monk, have concentrated all the tortures of the soul in a few years of your inner life. You two have suffered all that men can suffer of satiety and privation. One of you has been broken by blows and the other by fasting. However, you stand here with your faces raised to heaven while I creep about like the prodigal child in the midst of foul animals, that is to say, gross appetites and impure vices. Let me die in my filth and don't torment me with the spectacle of your glorious ascension toward the heavens. This is how Job's friends vaunted their prosperity to the victim stretched out on the dung heap. Let me be! Let wisdom and humility watch over your conquests. Avoid the childish desire to show them to those who have nothing, because in his anger someone who is poor, jealous, and full of hate could spit on these riches and tarnish them. Trenmor, is your glory as real and brilliant as you think? Could my bitter intelligence find a trivial explanation in the triumph of will over deadened passions and over effaced or satiated desires? Magnus, take care. Is your faith so solid that I could not break it with mockery or doubt? Is the victory of the spirit over fleshly temptations so complete that I could not still make you blush and pale by pronouncing a woman's name...? Go on and pray. Burn incense before the Virgin's altar. Beat your head against your church paving-stones. Compose your treatises on mortification and resignation. But let me enjoy my last days. God did not favor me, as He did you, with a superior nature. He put within my grasp only common realities and vulgar pleasures. I want to use them to the end. Haven't I too taken an immense step on the path of reason since we left each other? Seeing that I couldn't attain heaven, haven't I begun to walk on earth without bitterness or disdain? Haven't I accepted life such as it was destined for me? And when I felt within myself anxious, rebellious passions, vague, eccentric ambitions, and unrealizable desires, did I not do everything I could to crush them? I took another path from you, my brothers, that is all. I made myself calm through abuse, while you healed yourselves with the hairshirt and abstinence. Great souls like yours need these violent means and these austere expiations. The usage of human things would not have sufficed to break your rocklike characters or exhaust your supernatural strength. But all these human things were made to Sténio's measure. He delivered himself up to them without blushing. He satiated himself without ingratitude. Now, if his body is too weak for his appetites and if consumption has seized this puny child of pleasure, it is because God did not destine him to live many years on earth. He was not suited to be either a soldier, priest, gambler, savant, or poet. There are plants meant to die as soon as they have flowered. There are men who are not condemned by God to a long exile on earth. See, Father, you are bald like me. Your hands are withered, your chest sunken, your knees weak, and your breath short, your beard is greying, and you are less than thirty. Perhaps your agony will be a little slower than mine. You may survive me an entire year. But all the same, haven't we both managed to vanquish our passions and freeze our senses? We have both emerged from the crucible purified and reduced, haven't we, Father? I am even more diminished than you. My trial was stronger and surer. I am near the goal. I have overcome the enemy. Perhaps you would have done better to take the same path I did; it was the shortest. But this does not matter, and you will reach suffering and death just as surely. Give me your hand. We are brothers. You were great, I was miserable. You had a vigorous nature, I a poor one. But the tombs will soon open for us and will inherit no less from each than the same bit of dust.

Magnus had grown agitated while Sténio talked and had raised his eyes to the sky with an expression of fear and distress. Now he appeared calmer and more assured. "Young man," he said, "we won't finish with these frail envelopes, and our souls won't be given as nourishment to the worms of the tomb. Do you believe God judges us equally? At Doomsday won't there be greater mercy for the one who has mortified his flesh and prayed in tears, a more severe justice for the one who has prayed before idols and drunk at the poisoned sources of sin?"

"Father, what do you know of it?" asked Sténio. "Whatever is contrary to the laws of nature may be abominable to God. Some have dared to say this, in this century of philosophic examination, and I am among them. But I will spare you these popular ideas, against which you are on guard, assuming that I had the bad taste to use them, and I will limit myself to asking you one question: Suppose that tomorrow at dawn, after falling asleep amid tears and prayer, you were to awaken in the arms of a woman who had been carried to your bed by malicious, dark spirits. After the surprise, terror, struggle, victory, and exorcism, which I don't doubt that you would carry out, tell me, would you be able to say mass immediately afterward and touch Christ's body without the slightest apprehension?"

"With God's grace," replied Magnus, "perhaps my hands would be pure enough to touch the sacred host. But I would not dare go through such a temptation without purifying myself first through penitence."

"Father, it is clear that you are less purified than I. At this time I could sleep an entire night beside the most beautiful woman without feeling anything for her but disgust. You have wasted your time fasting and praying. You have accomplished nothing, since the flesh can still overwhelm the spirit. You have managed to hollow out your stomach, irritate your brain, and derange the harmonious working of your organs. But you have not reduced your body to passivity as I have. You would not be able to undergo the test I mentioned and go immediately to communion without confession. You have obtained only a slow physical suicide, that is to say, a deed which your religion condemns as a frightful crime, and you are as much under the dominion of evil desires as you were in the first days of your penitence. God has not supported you very well, Father!"

The monk rose and, drawing himself up to the full height of his tall, feeble figure, he looked at the sky once more. Then he put his two hands on his forehead and cried out with terrible anxiety, "Is it true, oh, my God? Have You refused me help and forgiveness? Have You abandoned me to the spirit of evil? Have You drawn away from me without consenting to listen to my cries? Have I suffered in vain, and is all this life of struggle and torture lost? No!" he cried with intensity, raising his long, frail arms out of their homespun sleeves, "I will not believe it! I won't let myself be discouraged by this contemporary child's impious words! I will go on to the very end. And if the Church has lied, if the prophets have been inspired by the spirit of darkness, if the Divine word has been diverted from its true meaning, if my zeal has exceeded Your demands, at least You will consider me because of my stubborn desire and because of the ferocious will that has separated me from earth to make me conquer heaven. You will read in the bottom of my heart that burning passion which devoured me for You, God, and which speaks so loudly in a soul devoured by other terrible passions. You will pardon me for having lacked wisdom. You will weigh only my sacrifices and intentions. And if I have carried that cross until my death, You will give me my share in the sweetness of Your eternal repose."

"Is repose part of the universal plan?" asked Sténio. "Do you hope to be great enough to deserve a new universe created for you alone? Do you believe that idle angels and inert virtues exist? Don't you know that all forces are active and that unless you are God you will never reach that immutable existence? Yes, God will bless you, Magnus, and the saints will sing your praises on their golden harps. But when you have carried that elite soul, virgin and intact, to the feet of the Master, when you say, 'Lord, You gave me strength, I conserved it, I render it to You, Give me eternal peace as a reward,' God will reply to that prostrate soul, 'That is well, My child. Enter into My glory and take your place among My glittering hosts. Now you will accomplish noble works. You will drive the moon's chariot into ether plains. You will roll the thunder in the clouds. You will harness the courses of rivers. You will make the tempest bound beneath you like a neighing mare. You will command the stars. Divine Substance, you will be in the elements, you will have commerce with men's souls. You will carry out sublime missions between Me and My former brothers. You will fill up the earth and heavens. You will see My face, and you will converse with Me.'

"All this is beautiful, Magnus. Poetry finds its substance in these sublime aberrations. But I would not want it to be that way, even if it were. I am not great enough to be ambitious, nor strong enough to wish for such a role. It suits your gigantic pride to sigh after the glories of another life. As for me, if I doubted Divine goodness so much as to hope for something other than nothingness, for which I am made, I would ask to be grass, which feels no shame when it is crushed by human feet, or marble, which doesn't bleed beneath the chisel, or a tree, which doesn't feel the wind. I would ask for the most inert, obscure, and easiest of existences. I would even find it too demanding to be reborn in the gelatinous substance of a mollusk. This is why I don't work to gain heaven. I don't want it. I fear its joys, harmonies, ecstasies, and triumphs. How could I desire anything but to finish with it all? So I am more content than you, Father. I go without anxiety or fear into eternal night, while confused, trembling, you approach the supreme tribunal where the lease of your suffering and weariness will be renewed for eternity. I am not jealous. I admire your destiny, but I prefer mine."

Magnus, frightened by what he was hearing, and feeling scarcely any strength within himself to respond, leaned over to Trenmor. He squeezed the wise man's hand in both of his. His anxious eyes seemed to demand the support of his strength.

"Don't upset yourself, my brother," said Trenmor. "Don't let the sufferings of this wounded soul alter in any way the confidence of yours.

Don't tire of working. Let the temptation of nothingness grow dulled
like a deceptive caress. It would be more difficult for you to become
a skeptic than to maintain the treasure of faith. Don't listen to him.
He is lying to himself, and far from desiring the things he affirms, he
fears them. As for you, Sténio, your efforts to extinguish the sacred
torch of intelligence within you are useless. Its flame revives, stronger
and more beautiful, with each of your attempts to suffocate it. You
aspire to heaven in spite of yourself, and your poet's soul cannot chase
away the grievous memory of its fatherland. When God, recalling it
from exile, has purified and healed it, your soul will look behind and see
that frightening, dark dream of human life effaced like a cloud. It will
be astonished at having crossed through these darknesses without hoping to awaken. 'God, where were You then?' it will say, 'And what has
become of me in this whirlpool which momentarily carried me away?'
But God will console your soul and perhaps submit it to other trials,
because your soul will earnestly demand them. Happy and proud at
having regained its strength, it will want to use it. Your soul will demand its place among the Celestial Dominions and will perform brilliantly; because God is good, and perhaps He sends the worst tests of
despair to His elect in order to render the use of their strength more
precious. Desire is the divinest faculty of the soul. It is only sleeping
within you, Sténio. Let your body recover strength, give yourself a few
days rest, and you will feel this saintly ardor reawaken. Desire is the
infinite aspiration of intelligence that makes a man a man and makes
him worthy to command things here below, elements on high."

    "A man is a man," said Sténio, "as long as he can control his horse
and resist his mistress. What better use of strength has heaven given
such puny creatures? Man is capable of a certain moral greatness, which
consists of believing nothing and fearing nothing. The man who kneels
at all hours before the rage of a vengeful God is only a servile slave who
fears the punishments of another life. The man who makes an idol
out of some illusion of will, before which all his appetites are crushed
and all his caprices broken, is only a coward who fears being carried
away by his fantasies and finding suffering in his pleasures. The strong
man fears neither God, men, nor himself. He accepts the consequences
of his inclinations, good or bad. The scorn of the masses, the distrust
of fools, the blame of rigid moralists, fatigue, misery have no more
power over his soul than fever and debts. Wine exalts but does not

inebriate him. Women amuse but don't control him. Although glory sometimes spurs him on, he treats it like other prostitutes and shows it the door after he has possessed it, because he despises everything that others fear or respect. He can go through the flame without leaving his wings there like the blind moth and without falling into ashes before the torch of reason. Ephemeral and frail as the moth, he lets himself be carried by all the breezes, attracted to all flowers, gladdened with all light. But skepticism preserves him from everything. The wind of inconstancy carries him along and saves him. Today empty meteors, deceptive illusions of night; tomorrow the bursting sun, sad spy on all miseries and on all human uglinesses. The strong man has no assurance as to his future and withdraws before no danger of the present. He knows that all his hopes are registered in a book whose leaves are turned by the wind, and that all projects of wisdom are written in sand. He knows that there is only one virtue, wisdom, and strength in the world: to wait for the wave and remain firm when it inundates you, to swim when it carries you along, to cross your arms and die heedlessly when it submerges you. The strong man is also the wise man because he simplifies his joys. He limits them. He divests them of their entourage of errors, vanities, and prejudices. His enjoyment is completely positive, real, personal. It is his divinity. He strips his enjoyment naked and crushes the useless ornaments beneath his feet, which have been concealing it. More faithful and sincere than the hypocritical professors of its temple, at all times in his life he bows down before it with contempt for the useless anathemas of a stupid world. He is martyr to his faith. He lives and suffers for it. He dies through it and for it, while denying or braving that other absurd, evil God you worship. The man who draws his sword to struggle against tempests, impious and rash though he be, is more courageous and greater than the God which stirs up thunder. As for me, I would dare this and you, Magnus, would not. Trenmor, who is listening to us, is more philosophic than Christian, Father, don't deceive yourself. He is more stoic than religious. He esteems strength more than faith, perseverance more than repentance. In a word, let Trenmor judge between us and see who has better conserved and defended the highest of his faculties: energy."

"I won't judge between you," said Trenmor. "Heaven has given you diverse qualities, but you each received a beautiful portion. Magnus was gifted with a greater persistence in ideas. And if, Sténio, you will disregard your ideas for a moment to contemplate the spectacle of a victorious will, you will be struck with admiration for this monk, who was once impious, amorous and mad and who is now calm, fervent, and submissive to the regularity of monastic habits. Where has he found the strength to resist these terrifying struggles for so long and to raise himself after having been cursed and broken? Is this the same man you heard deny God at dying Lélia's bedside? Is this the same man you saw run confused on the mountain? This is a new man, but he still has the same stormy, passionate soul, the same fiery senses, terrible, always new and always virgin. He always returns to God through an inconceivable strength and through a focus of sublime hope. Oh, Father, even if it is true that we don't have the same form of worship and that we invoke God with different rites, you are still three times saintly, three times great in my eyes! You have fought, you have raised yourself up from beneath the feet of your enemy, and you continue to fight valiantly, furrowed with wounds, spent in sweat and blood, but determined to die sword in hand. Continue in the name of Jesus, in the name of Socrates. The martyrs of all religions and heroes of all ages watch you and applaud your efforts from the heavens. . . . But you, Sténio, child born with a star on the brow. Your beauty made one imagine the form of angels. Your voice was more melodious than the voices of the night which sigh on Scottish harps. Your genius promised the world a new youth full of love and poetry, because singers and poets are prophets sent to revive men's enervated spirits. Sténio, in your youth you walked in grace and purity that clothed you like a stainless garment and with a luminous aura. I cannot despair of your future. Like Magnus, you submitted to the great test, the terrible agony reserved for the powerful. And from this life you will rise up again like him. You are still struggling and all bloody with the torture. You don't recognize the hand that tries you. But soon we will see you, obscured star, burn whiter and more beautiful in the arch of the heavens."

"And what is needed for that, Trenmor?" asked Sténio.

"You need only to rest," said Trenmor, "because nature is good to those like you. Your nerves need time to calm themselves; your mind needs the leisure to receive new impressions. Perhaps it is a good thing to crush desires through weariness, but to excite these desires, to treat them roughly like broken-down horses, to impose unnecessary suffering upon oneself, to go beyond one's strength into joys more intense and pleasures sharper than reality permits, to stir up within an hour the sensations of an entire lifetime is a way to lose both the past and the future. You lose the past by contempt for its timid pleasures. You lose the other by the impossibility of surpassing the present. Today you are not disposed to receive more advice. But in time, I flatter myself, my son, you will be ready to give me a proof of affection."

"Always," said Sténio, pressing his hand.

"Very well," said Trenmor, "promise me, swear to me that you will stay here until my return. If at the end of thirty days I have not returned, you will be released from your oath."

They rose and went back to the monastery. The next day Trenmor left, after having obtained, not without difficulty, Sténio's word.

## XLIV DON JUAN

One evening Sténio took Magnus's arm and led him to the edge of the lake. He loved this wild place, these grand cedars leaning over the precipice, these sands silvered by the moon, and this motionless water in which the stars were reflected calmly as if in another ether. He loved the tender, melancholic hissing of snakes, the murmuring of the water amid the rushes, and the silent flight of bats among the tombs. Here he sought hope. Because he was calm and silent for a long time, Magnus believed that God had pitied him and opened up the treasure of divine hopes. But suddenly Sténio spoke, breaking the silence and stopping him beneath the pure, white moonlight while he penetrated him with his cynical gaze.

"Monk, tell me about your love for Lélia and how, after she made you an atheist and renegade, she finally drove you insane."

"My God," cried out the pale Camaldule with confusion, "remove this bitter cup from me!"

"I will let you be, Magnus," said Sténio, "if you tell me the whole truth. Yes, if you answer me without false shame or hypocrisy, I swear that I will no longer throw disorder into your thoughts with my irony."

"Ask, cruel child," replied the monk, "and if I can do so without sin, I will answer you honestly."

"Honesty can never be a sin," said Sténio. "But pride and pretense are crimes before God. Speak. Tell me if your macerations, your retreat, your prayers, your will, and all your efforts have truly crushed the enemy of your repose. If you swear in the name of Christ that they have, I will believe you."

"Your question is very hard, Sténio. What satisfaction can your vanity expect from my response?"

"Magnus, my vanity has been broken like a straw. It is not my vanity that arouses this burning curiosity. I need a certainty, a hope. If your faith has saved you, if through tears and prayer you have obtained this ennobling confidence, I too will prostrate myself and pray. Perhaps God will save me, too."

"Pray, Sténio, and hope . . . " said the monk. "The realm of heaven. . . . "

"Be quiet!" Sténio interrupted violently. "This monk's cowl gives you all the same language just as it gives you the same walk. Do you really want to help me? Swear!"

"I swear to answer you," replied the trembling monk.

"By Christ?" asked Sténio.

"By Christ," said Magnus, "since it concerns your salvation."

"Very well, tell me. Has grace saved you, or your own strength? Has faith clothed you in an armor of diamonds, or has your prudence entrenched you behind these protective walls? Is it because you are wise, and you feel weak, that you have fled here to escape women's burning glances? Or is it that, having broken Satan's pride, you came here to rest and sleep peacefully beneath the arches of this cloister while waiting for death to open its doors of eternal glory?"

"I am a weak man," said Magnus. "I have not crushed the demon. Without grace, I would have lacked even the strength to flee danger."

"Then you are no more advanced than you were on the first day of your flight."

"Don't say that, Sténio. Does the firm desire to resist count for nothing?"

"It counts for nothing, Father," said Sténio harshly. "Ambition without power is the most despicable thing in the world. You believe yourself noble because you fast to dull your passions, because you erect stone walls between yourself and the world. And when you have buried yourself alive in this tomb, you gnash your teeth in silence, you bite the earth, you curse in a low voice, and you believe yourself a saint because in a day of enthusiasm or cowardice you descended here. If your worship had purified you, your zeal had hardened you, and your courage had made you greater, you would be able to return to the world and spread your blessings, in which you are rich. You would be able to heal and console men without fear of contagion or despair at the sight of their anguish. Magnus, you would be able to find the woman whose eyes used to devour you and talk calmly with her about heaven and God. But this is not so. You are a martyr, not a saint. You would have the strength to feel boiling oil and melted lead penetrate your veins without renouncing Christ, but you would not have the strength to pass a night alone with a woman without being carried away by evil desires. Oh, nature is stronger than your feeble brain. Nature is God. Your faith is only a gilded dream, a mad ambition. But for the man who has reflected, who has felt, and who has experienced at their greatest depth all the realities of life there is no salvation, no hope in your books and traditions."

"Oh, my son, don't speak like this," cried the suffering priest.

"And you, Father," said Sténio, "give me an affirmation that can convince me. Tell me that you would not commit the sin of adultery in your heart if Lélia slept with you in your cell. Answer, and don't forget that you have sworn by Christ."

The monk lowered his head and leaned against the trunk of an enormous yew tree in a state of deep sorrow.

Sténio sat down on the ground against a rock at the edge of the ravine. Between the rock and the lake was only the steep slope of white sand, upon which the clouds traced great moving shadows as they passed over the moon.

"Oh, I knew it so well," Sténio cried in a strong, deep voice that moaned into the depths of the lake. "I knew it so well, I knew it, my God!"

He suddenly rose, as if he were going to throw himself over the edge. Magnus trembled and plunged forward to restrain him. But Sténio then sat down again and the priest, fearing to awaken the thought of suicide in him, did not dare beg him to leave the place.

"I knew so well," said Sténio in the same frightening, depressed tone, "that nothing of men's dreams was true, and that once truth was unveiled there remained nothing more than the patience of boredom or the resolution of despair. When I said man could find pleasure in his individual strength, I was lying to myself and others. He who has attained power which has no value and no end is only an energetic madman to be distrusted.

"In my youthful dreams, in the ecstasies of my poetry, an illusion of love constantly hovered over me and showed me heaven. Lélia, my ideal, my Elysium, what have you become? Where has your ghost fled? Into what ungraspable ether has your immaterial substance vanished? When I learned that you were impossible, my eyes opened, and life appeared to me completely naked in its beauties and horrors, always subject to laws that cannot be annulled. As my former fantasy became obliterated (this fantasy of the unrealizable, which alone beautifies man's days and binds him for a few years to his frivolous pleasures), as my soul grew weary of seeking in the arms of a flock of women the ecstatic kiss that Lélia alone could give, weary of seeking in wine, poetry, and praise what a word of love from Lélia could have concentrated, I became enlightened. . . . Listen, Magnus, and let my words profit you. I became enlightened to the point of knowing that Lélia herself is a woman like any other. I realize that her lips have no softer kiss and her words have no more powerful virtue than the kisses and words of other lips. Today I know Lélia entirely, as if I had possessed her. I know what made her so beautiful, pure, and divine: my youth. But in the measure that my soul has withered, the image of Lélia has too. Today I see her as she is: pale, with dull lips, her hair strewn with those first silver threads which invade us the way grass invades the tomb. Her face shows those ineffacable lines old age imprints upon us, at first with indulgent lightness, then with deep, cruel nails. Poor Lélia. You are indeed changed! When you appear in my dreams with your diamonds and the costly garments you used to wear, I can't help laughing bitterly and saying, 'It is well that you act the queen, Lélia, and display a great deal of wit, because you are no longer beautiful. If you were to invite me today to the celestial banquet of your love, I would prefer the young dancer, Torquata, or the joyous courtesan, Elvira.'

"And after all, Torquata, Elvira, Pulchérie, Lélia, who are you all to arouse and bind me with this iron yoke which bloodies my brow, to hand me from the gallows where my limbs are broken? Swarms of blond- and ebony-haired women with ivory feet, with dark shoulders, modest girls, laughing debauchees, timid sighing virgins, brazen-faced Messalinas, all you women that I have possessed or dreamed of, what

I wanted to equal. I found myself feeble, puny in mind and body. I mistook imagination for intelligence, desire for need, will for strength, and I destroyed myself trying to struggle against the weakness of my body and spirit. Trenmor, you condemned me when you said that unhappiness only tries great souls. Lélia, you condemned me when you wrote to me that a fallen man ought to die.

"What can your tepid, banal friendship do for me now? Lélia, Trenmor, have you each reached that point of foolish charity where a man's life like mine seems as precious to save as a horse's, a cow's or a useful servant's? Go care for your grooms and dogs. They will be of use to you. But as for me, I would only be a burden to you. Pity is akin to contempt. The hand that upholds a tottering friend soon grows numb. Furthermore, you don't believe in friendship. You uselessly offered me your friendship to support and guide me into the future. But you must realize that you were lying to yourselves, because you have both abandoned me. Where were you when I was destroying myself? You were in the calm of your sublime repose and renunciation. You knew that Sténio was struggling against the agony of his entire being. You merely said: 'Too bad for Sténio.' Sheltered from the storm, you were aware that down below a skiff was breaking apart on the reefs. But you said: 'God loves him. God will save him. Fate is watching over him. The trial will be salutary for him. He will come back, so let him struggle a little.' And during this time I was perishing! You didn't tell yourselves that friendship is the only fate men should invoke, and that if friends truly existed they would play the role of God with each other. No, it's just the same with friendship as with everything else. Our soul has the feeling for it but lacks the power. It conceives of affections and virtues, just as it dreams of ladders mounting from the earth to the stars. The imagination scales the sky endlessly, while man remains numb in his mud. The brain conceives; actions abort. The heart promises; the hand refuses.

"Oh, contempt and pity on all those paralytics who think they support each other but who drift about stumbling, falling on their infirm knees, unable to lift up a reed to help themselves! Poor one-armed people who speak of the strength of their arms. Poor cripples who believe they are always ready to run. Poor liars who shamelessly repeat the same vows they always betray.

"What is this mysterious, incomprehensible, perhaps sublime impulse in these souls of clay? What is this need we have for outpouring, for affection that devours us? Toward what shadows of tenderness and goodness spring these aspirations of the suffering heart and these cries of weakness demanding help? The fatal lessons of experience have vainly taught us that this moving sand ought to yield beneath our steps. Our imprudent feet still risk themselves there. What is this power, rather this obstinate fever which pushes us toward disappointment and grief? Why doesn't this thirst for love calm itself? Why do we always grow credulous at a friendly word or a tender-hearted look? Why do we feel the need to help someone who is perishing and to thank someone who saves us? Why do we feel ourselves the involuntary, necessary friend of the man we see suffering? Why do we let ourselves fall on the shoulder of anyone who invites us? And why does this prostituted phrase 'I *will comfort you*,' whether it come from a woman's lips, a dog's eyes, a friend's letter, or a priest's pulpit, still have an irresistible power? Why does this flash of trust and joy spurt up from our exhausted spirit, the last convulsion of a dying person who tries to grasp life again, the last effort of a shipwrecked man who, believing that he is grasping a plank, embraces the corpse of one of his companions and sinks with him?

"Weakness and misery of man, Don Juan has vainly tried to establish greatness within you. He has vainly tried to make precious virtues out of your suggestions and fears, but Don Juan realizes only deception and vanity!

"Lélia, Trenmor, my friends, a curse on you for the good you have failed to do me! You deceived me with a mad hope. You disgusted me with real life. You led me to expect joys you have not given me. You opened the doors of happiness to me, only to shut them again. Without you, I would have accepted the poor life and sober pleasures of reality. I would have lived alone, without tedium or anxiety. You told me there were sublime joys in the exchange and association of souls. I believed this. And here I am now alone and desolate, uselessly enlightened as to the emptiness of your promises. You have let my ruin be consummated. Today you come too late. . . !

"And You, Unknown Power which I naively adored in former days, mysterious Master of our frail destinies whom I still recognize but before whom I no longer prostrate myself. If my duty is to bow down and bless You for this bitter life, manifest Your presence so that I may at least hope to be heard by You. . . ! But what have I to hope or fear? Who am I to excite Your anger or deserve Your love? What have I done on earth which was either good or evil? I obeyed the nature that I had been given. I exhausted reality and aspired to the impossible. I accomplished my task as a man. If I have hastened the end of my life by a few days, what does that matter to You? If I have obliterated my intelligence by the abuse of pleasures, what does it matter to the universe if Sténio leaves a few hundred verses more or less in men's memories? If You are vindictive, whatever I do I shall not escape the expiations of the other life. If You are just and good, You will welcome me into Your heart and heal me of the evils I have suffered. If You are not . . . oh, then I am my own god and master and I can destroy the temple and the idol. . . .

"Father, approach me," he added. "Give me one grace: go pray for me before the Christ of your chapel."

"I would not dare leave you in the state of mind you are in," said Magnus. "Come with me."

"What do you fear?" asked Sténio coldly. "Didn't I swear to Trenmor that he would find me here? The term does not expire until tomorrow, and I won't be free until then to leave you if Trenmor hasn't returned yet. What thought is rolling about in your frightened eyes?"

I was mistaken, thought the credulous monk. His designs are not evil. Trenmor will return tomorrow, and tonight I am going to pray.

The monk knelt on the marble where the moon strewed reflections of amethyst and pale rubies from the stained glass window. After an hour he returned to the edge of the lake. Sténio was no longer there. The monk had a feeling of dread. He leaned over the lake. The moon had set, and one could distinguish at the depths of the abyss only a bleak mist stretched over the reeds like a shroud. A profound silence reigned everywhere. The scent of irises mounted feebly on the listless breeze. The air was so soft, the night so blue and peaceful that the monk's sinister thoughts were involuntarily dulled. A nightingale began to sing so sweetly that Magnus dreamily stopped to listen to it.

"Is it possible that a horrible tragedy has been played out just now in such a calm place, on such a beautiful summer night?" This black idea became effaced. Magnus slowly and silently continued along the path to his cell. He crossed through the cemetery, enveloped in darkness, through the trees and tombs, directed by instinct and habit. However, he sometimes stumbled against a marble cenotaph and found himself gripped by the hanging branches of old yew trees. But no plaintive voice and no hand still warm stopped him. He stretched out on the rushes of his pallet, and the hours of the night sounded in the silence.

But he vainly tried to sleep. Scarcely had he closed his eyes when he saw uncertain, menacing images rise up before him. Soon a more distinct, terrible image awakened him. Sténio with his blasphemies and impious doubts, Sténio whom he had left alone by the lake. Magnus seemed to see him wandering around his pallet, and he seemed to hear him begin again his cruel, abusive questions in order to torment the poor priest's soul. Magnus got up, and, as he leaned on his bed with his face bent against his trembling knees, he asked himself, as if it were for the first time, about Sténio's designs. Why had the poet sent away the witness of his anguish? After tearing into shreds all the beliefs taught by the Church, after digging into all the shameful wounds of the priest's heart with bloody, pitiless fingers, why had he sent the priest off to pray? Oh no, Sténio no longer knew how to pray! Was he waiting for Trenmor? But the sage was not due to return until tomorrow. Was he waiting for Lélia? At this thought the priest leapt from his bed; for an instant he hoped for Sténio's death.

But soon this ungodly desire gave place to more generous anxieties. He feared that, weary of struggling against an inexorable God, Sténio had accomplished a sinister project. He fearfully remembered some speeches the young man had made on nothingness which absolved suicide, on eternity which did not forbid it, on Divine anger which could not prevent it, and on the merciful indulgence which ought to permit it. Magnus had not forgotten that Sténio's present life was a punishment that defied all the coming sorrows with which the Church threatened him.

The anxious priest crossed his cell with hurried steps. There was only one way to ascertain Sténio's fate: to make sure that he had returned to the monastery. But in order to do that, Magnus would have had to penetrate the rooms reserved for the secular, and the Camaldule rule strictly forbade this. Two or three times he asked himself whether, to save a man's life and a Christian soul, he was not permitted to violate the laws of ordinary discipline. But the monastic spirit, which in feeble brains shrinks the intelligence and withers sensibility, rendered it more terrifying for him to imagine the prior's anger than the remorse of his conscience. He preferred to incur the reproaches of God rather than the punishments of his order. And so he resolved to wait for day.

In his memory he reviewed all the years of his youth. He compared his sufferings with Sténio's. He glorified himself in his resignation. He tried to despise the anger of the unhappy man whom he had just left. He stuttered a few haughty, disdainful words. Broken by fasting and insomnia, he murmured a few confused syllables between his teeth, as if he wished to congratulate himself on a decisive victory over his passions. Then he hurriedly recited a few mutilated verses, which consoled his pride without sweetening the bitterness in his heart.

Each time the chapel clock sounded the hours Magnus trembled. He counted the passage of the hours. He stared at the sky. He counted the obstinate stars. Then, when the sound vanished and everything returned to silence, when he found himself alone again with God and his thoughts, he mechanically took up again his monotonous, plaintive prayer.

Finally day appeared as a white line on the horizon, and Magnus returned to the edge of the lake. The wind had not lifted its veils of fog, and the monk could make out only nearby objects. He sat down on the stone where Sténio had been the evening before. Day came slowly, and his anxiety increased. As the light grew brighter, he believed he could distinguish letters traced on the sand at his feet. He bent down and read: "Magnus, tell Trenmor that I have kept my word. He will find me here. . . ."

After this inscription a footprint, a light cave-in of sand, then nothing more but the steep slope whose dust no longer kept the imprint, the lake with its water lilies, and a few black teal in the white mist.

Stirred with more intense terror, Magnus tried to descend the ravine. He went to look for a spade in the cemetery. Then cautiously opening up a stairway for himself in the sand as he buried his uncertain feet, after a thousand dangers he reached the edge of the tranquil water. On a carpet of tender, velvety green watercress slept the blue-eyed young man, pale and peaceful. The azure of the sky was reflected in the immobile crystal of Sténio's eyes, as in water whose spring has run dry but whose pool is still full and limpid. Sténio's feet were buried in sand. His head rested among flowers with cold calyxes, bent over him by a feeble breeze. The long insects that flutter over reeds had come by the hundreds to surround him. Some drank deeply of the trace of perfume impregnating his wet hair. Others stirred their blue gossamer garments over his face, as if to curiously admire its beauty, or as if to skim it with the fresh breeze of their wings. This spectacle of tender, coquettish nature around a corpse was so beautiful that Magnus could not believe what his reason told him was true. He addressed Sténio in a strident voice and seized his icy hand as if he hoped to awaken him. But, seeing that the child had been drowned for several hours, a superstitious fear captured his timorous soul. He believed himself guilty of this crime and, prepared to fall down next to Sténio, he uttered dull, inarticulate cries.

Some herdsmen from the valley who were passing on the other side of the lake saw this desolate monk as he was making vain efforts to drag his friend's corpse out of the water. They descended by a less precipitous slope, and with ropes and branches they carried both the dead and the living men back onto the opposite slope.

The herdsmen did not know the secret of Sténio's death. They carried the monk and poet religiously on their shoulders, questioning each other with curious, unquiet glances. Sometimes they would break the silence of their walk to try out some timid conjecture, but not one had a suspicion of the truth.

Magnus's fainting seemed to these rude, gross intelligences a spectacle worthy of pity rather than sympathy. They asked themselves why a priest, who had sworn to console the living and bless the dead, was losing courage like a woman rather than praying over someone God had just recalled. They did not understand why the Camaldule, who had followed so many funerals since he entered the monastery and who had gathered in the last breaths of so many agonizing souls, conducted himself with such cowardice in the presence of a corpse no different from all those he had seen.

With the awakening of nature, the awakening of active life soon followed. Work that had been interrupted began again with the new day. When the inhabitants of the plain saw the herdsmen approaching, they crowded around them. But at the sight of the branches on which Magnus and Sténio rested, the question they were about to ask died on their lips. Their naive curiosity gave way to a mournful, mute silence. Death passes unperceived only in populous towns. In the silence of the fields, amid austere country life, it is always acknowledged as the voice of God. Only those who pass their days forgetting to live turn away from death as an importunate spectacle. Those who kneel both morning and evening to give thanks never pass indifferently before a coffin.

About a hundred feet from the shores of the lake the herdsmen stopped and deposited their pious burden on the wet grass. The rising sun had colored the horizon with purple and orange tones. Abundant, warm dew floated above the hillsides, ascending to the sky like the ardor of a grateful soul returning to God, Who has set him on fire with His love. Each mountain narcissus was a diamond. The cloudy summits were crowned with a diadem of gold. All was joy, love, and beauty around the rustic catafalque.

A group of young girls were crossing the valley, leading heifers with spotted flanks to the edge of the lake. They were singing rude ballads, more simple than prudent, whose refrain sometimes reached even the monks in prayer. These dark mountain children stopped before the funeral ceremony without terror. But beneath their large men's chests, simple nature had let their upright, compassionate women's hearts live on. They were moved to pity, without weeping, by the fate of these unfortunate men. And they charged themselves with explaining it to the herdsmen. "This one," they said, pointing out the monk, "must be the drowned man's brother. They probably wanted to fish for lake trout. The bolder of the two went out too far and cried for help, while the other was afraid but lacked the strength to save him. We must gather herbs to heal him. We will put these red sage leaves on his tongue and tansy on his temples. We will burn resin around him and fan him with these fern leaves."

While the oldest girls searched in the wet grass for the aromatics to help Magnus, some matrons recited the prayer for the dead in low voices, and the youngest mountain women knelt around Sténio, half meditative, half curious. They touched his clothing with a mixture of fear and admiration. "He was a rich man," said the old women. "How unfortunate that he is dead." A small girl passed her fingers through Sténio's blond hair and wiped them on her apron with a care in which veneration and the serious pleasure of playing with an unusual object were mixed.

At the sound of their confused voices, the priest awakened and looked around with frightened eyes. The matrons came to kiss his gaunt hands, and they demanded his blessing. He trembled as he felt their lips press against his fingers.

"Go away, go away," he said, repulsing them. "I am a sinner. God has withdrawn from me. Pray for me, because it is I who am in danger of perishing."

He rose and stared at the corpse. Assured then that he was not dreaming, he shuddered with a mute, inner convulsion and sat down again on the ground, overwhelmed by his shock.

The herdsmen, seeing that he was in no condition to give them orders, offered to carry the corpse to the monastery. This proposal reawakened all the monk's anguish.

"No, no," he said, "that cannot be. Only help me drag myself to the monastery gate."

Later Magnus knelt before the prior.

"Bless me, Father," he said, "because I come to you sullied with a great crime. I have caused a soul to be damned. I have badly counseled Sténio, the traveler, the sage Trenmor's friend, that child of the century whom you permitted me to converse with often in an attempt to lead him back to the truth. I lacked the strength and religious fervor to convert him. My prayers were not passionate enough. My intercession was not agreeable to the Lord. I failed.... Oh, Father, will I be forgiven? Won't I be cursed for my weakness and impotence?"

"My son," said the prior, "God's designs are impenetrable and His mercy is immense. What do you know of the future? The sinner can become a great saint. He has left us, but God has not abandoned him. God will save him. Grace can reach him everywhere and draw him out of the most profound abysses."

"God did not wish it," said Magnus, whose glassy eyes were fixed on the ground with fear. "God let him fall into the lake...."

"What are you saying?" cried the priest, rising. "Is your mind confused? Is the sinner dead?"

"Dead," said Magnus, "drowned, lost, damned...!"

"How did this misfortune happen?" asked the prior. "Did you see it? Didn't you try to prevent it?"

"I should have foreseen and prevented it. I lacked perseverance. I was afraid. For an hour he talked in a loud, lamenting voice. He accused fate, men, and God. He invoked a justice other than the one to which we confide ourselves. He crushed our most sacred beliefs beneath his feet. He summoned nothingness. He jeered at our prayers, sacrifices, and hopes. As I listened to him blaspheme like this, oh, Father, forgive me, instead of being inflamed with sacred indignation, I wept. Standing several feet from him, I half heard his fatal words. Sometimes the wind would seize them and carry them off to heaven, which alone had the power to absolve them. When the wind quieted down, this gloomy voice with its terrifying curses came back to strike my ears and freeze my blood. I was a coward. I was beaten. I vainly tried to raise a wall between his envenomed words and my trembling soul, but discouragement and despair insinuated themselves into me like a poison. I wanted to stop him. The idea of his frightful smile chained my tongue. I wanted to lead him away. The boldness of his contemptuous stare paralyzed me. I had only one thought, one need, one insurmountable temptation: to flee, pray in the chapel, escape this danger I could not avert from him that was invading me. —Then he begged me to leave him. I did so mechanically, happy to withdraw from my suffering and take refuge at Christ's feet. I was too much occupied with myself. I forgot the safekeeping of the sinner which God had entrusted to me. Instead of taking the lost sheep on my shoulders, I feared the solitude, the night, and the devouring wolves. A bad pastor, I returned alone to the sheepfold. I had abandoned the lost sheep, and when I returned I could no longer find him. Satan had carried off his prey. The spirit of evil had dragged that victim down into the pit of eternal damnation."

"Where is the sinner?" cried the prior, quickly uncovering his white head. "What do you know of his death?"

"This morning I found the body in which the soul no longer resides amid the vegetation of the lake. I have nothing more to do or hope for Sténio. Give me a harsh penitence, Father, so that I can fulfill it and cleanse my soul."

"Speak to me of Sténio!" the prior cried out severely. "Forget yourself a little. Is your soul more precious than his, that we abandon him like this? Let us begin by praying for the sinner whom God has punished. Then we will see about purifying you. Where is the body? Have you recited the psalms over his mortal remains? Have you sprinkled holy water? Have you had him carried to the chapel door? Have you told the Chapter to assemble? The sun is already high in the sky. What have you done since dawn?"

"Nothing," said the dismayed monk. "I fainted. And when I regained consciousness I told myself that I was lost."

"And Sténio, Sténio!" cried the old man.

"Sténio," said the monk. "Isn't he irremediably lost? Have we the right to pray for him? Will God revoke His immutable decrees? Didn't he have the same death as Judas Iscariot?"

"What death?" asked the shocked priest. "Suicide?"

"Suicide," said Magnus in a hollow voice.

The old prior fell back onto his oaken chair and clasped his yellow, wrinkled hands together in horror and inexpressible dismay. Then, turning to Magnus, he reprimanded him heatedly.

"Such a catastrophe took place nearly beneath your eyes. Such a scandal was accomplished within confines consecrated to worship, and you did not prevent it! You prayed like Mary when you needed to act like Martha. You raised up your head in the temple like the Pharisee. You said, 'Look at me and bless me, God, because I am a holy priest, and this impious man dying below can do without You and me.' You slept and dreamt, imbecilic, selfish, cowardly monk, when you should have attached yourself to the steps of that unfortunate sufferer, thrown yourself at his feet, dragged yourself in the dust, used tears, threats, prayers, and even force to prevent him from consummating his terrible sacrifice. Instead of fleeing from the sinner as an object of horror, shouldn't you have gone on your knees and called him your brother, to soften his heart and give him courage, if only for a day? Wouldn't one more day have been enough perhaps to save him? Does the doctor desert the bedside of the sick from fear of contagion? Did the Samaritan turn away with disgust when he saw the Jew's hideous wound? No, he approached fearlessly and applied balm. He carried him on his mount and saved him. But to save your own soul, you wasted the opportunity of bringing back the prodigal son to his Father's arms. It is you, with your narrow, hard soul, who will shudder with terror when God cries out during your sleepless nights, 'Cain, what have you done with your brother?' "

"Enough, enough, Father!" cried the monk, falling to the stone floor and dragging his beard in the dust. "Spare my breaking head and confused reason. Come," he cried, grasping the prior's robe, "come with me to pray over his remains. Pronounce the words that unbind, touch the hyssop that cleanses, say the exorcisms that break Satan's pride, pour the holy oil that removes all defilements of life. . . . "

The priest, touched by his suffering, rose sadly and irresolutely.

"Are you very sure he inflicted his own death?" he asked. "Is it not the effect of chance, or rather a celestial severity which we are not permitted to interpret, and at the end of which his soul will have found forgiveness? What do we know? He might have made a mistake . . . in the darkness of night . . . an accident can happen. . . . Speak, my son, do you have sure proof of suicide?"

Magnus hestitated. He wanted to say no. He hoped to deceive Divine clairvoyance and send this condemned soul to heaven by means of the Church sacraments. But he did not dare. Shuddering, he avowed the entire truth. He told about the words written in the sand, "Magnus, tell Trenmor he will find me here."

"Then it is too true!" said the prior, letting tears roll down his white beard. "There is no way of escaping this fatal evidence, my poor child. Oh, my God, Your justice is severe and Your anger is terrible. . . !"

"Go, Magnus," added the old man after a moment of silence. "Close the doors of the monastery and beg some woodcutter or herdsman to bury this corpse. The Church forbids us to open the temple doors to it and bury it on sacred ground. . . ."

This decree frightened Magnus more than anything else. He beat his head against the paving stone, unaware that blood ran along his pale cheeks.

"Go, my son," said the prior as he rose, "take courage. Let us obey the holy Church, but let us hope. God is great. No one has penetrated to the depths of His mercy. Furthermore, we are weak, limited men. Let us obey the letter and not question the spirit of the sacred laws. No man, even if he is pope, has the right to condemn another man irrevocably. Perhaps the sinner's agony was long. As he struggled against the approach of death, he may have been suddenly enlightened. He may have repented and prayed so fervently and with such purity that he has been reconciled with the Lord. You know that it is contrition, not the sacrament, which absolves. An instant of sincere, profound contrition can be worth an entire life of penitence. Let us pray and be humble. Perhaps Sténio's virtues were sublime enough in his youth to cleanse all the iniquities of his subsequent life, and in our past there may be such stains that all present and future abstinences can hardly absolve them. Go, my son. If the rule forbids me to admit this corpse into the monastery and accompany it to the cemetery with religious ceremonies, at least the Church empowers me to give you a special authorization. This is to watch over the corpse and accompany it to its last abode, praying in such a way as charity dictates to you, provided that this does not conform to the rite reserved for Christian burials. Go, it is your duty. It is the only way you can repair, as much as is in you, the evil you did not know how to prevent. You must try to obtain grace for him and for yourself. I too will pray. We will all pray, not in chorus and not in the sanctuary, but each of us in our own cell and in the fervor of our souls."

The unfortunate monk returned to Sténio. The herdsmen had lain him in a place sheltered from the sun at the entrance to a grotto where women were burning cedar resin and juniper branches. These pious mountain folk were waiting for Magnus to return and give orders to carry him to the monastery. They had placed Sténio on a stretcher made with more art and care than the first. Intertwined pine and cypress branches formed a bed of dark greenery for the corpse. The children had strewn aromatic herbs over him, and the women had placed a crown of white star-shaped flowers on his brow. White morning glory and clematis were suspended at the arch in gracious, wild festoons. This fresh, rustic, uncultivated funeral bier, surmounted with a dais of flowers and bathed in the softest perfumes, was worthy to protect the last sleep of a young, handsome poet who slept in the Lord.

The mountain people knelt when they saw the priest kneel. The women, whose number had increased considerably since morning, began to say their rosaries. Everyone prepared to follow the monk and the corpse as far as the entrance to the Camaldules and then return to the edge of the lake and watch the funeral rites from the opposite shore. But, after a long wait, they saw the sun descend toward the horizon, and Magnus still had not told them to carry off the corpse, nor had the monks, dressed in their black capes covered with bones, come to meet them. Then they began to wonder and risked questioning all this. Magnus looked at them fearfully, tried to answer them, and stammered uncertain words. When they saw how much his suffering had upset him, they feared to afflict him still more if they pressed him with questions. Then one of the oldest woodcutters from the valley decided to go to the monastery with his sons and ask orders of the prior.

After an hour the woodcutter returned. He was silent, sad, and reflective. He did not dare speak in front of Magnus. As everyone was questioning him with their looks, he signaled his companions to follow him aside. Drawn by curiosity, all those surrounding the corpse noiselessly removed themselves and joined him at some distance. There they learned with surprise and terror of Sténio's suicide and of the prior's refusal to bury him in sacred earth.

If the prior needed all the firmness of a generous spirit and all the warmth of an indulgent soul not to despair of Sténio's salvation, this was all the more reason why these simple, limited men were terror-stricken by a crime so severely condemned by Catholic beliefs. The old women were the first to anathemize him. "He has killed himself!" they cried out. "He must have committed some crime. He does not deserve our prayers. The prior refuses him a tomb in consecrated ground. He must have done something terrible, because the prior is so indulgent and saintly! He must have had a shameful wound of the heart to despair of forgiveness and create his own justice. Let us not mourn for him. Anyway, it is forbidden to pray for the damned. Let us go away. The monk is doing what he is supposed to. It is up to him to keep watch over the corpse during the night. He has the power to renounce exorcism. If the devil comes here to claim his prey, the priest will conjure him away. Let's leave."

The terrified young girls did not have to be persuaded to follow their mothers. And more than one, as she returned home, believed she saw a white figure pass in the depths of the brushwood and believed she heard on the grass wet with evening dew the wandering steps of a plaintive shadow which was murmuring sadly, "Turn, young girl, and see my pale face. I am the sinner's soul, and I am going to the judgment." They hurried their steps and arrived breathless and pale at the doors of their huts. But while they slept that night, a feeble mysterious voice seemed to repeat at their bedside, "Pray for me."

The herdsmen, accustomed to night watches and forest solitudes, were less vulnerable to these superstitious terrors. Some rejoined Magnus and resolved to guard the dead with him. At the four corners of the stretcher they planted large resinous pine torches, and they spread their goatskin cloaks to shield themselves from the night cold. But when the torches were lit, they began to project ghastly red gleams on the corpse. The wind which agitated them made sinister gleams pass over this face that was on the threshold of decay, and there were instants when the flames' movements seemed to communicate themselves to Sténio's features and limbs. He seemed to be opening his eyes,

shaking his hands convulsively, about to get up. Terror seized the herdsmen, and without daring to confess their fears to each other, they
tacitly decided to retire. The monk, whose presence had reassured
them, began to terrify them more than the corpse itself. His immobility,
silence, pallor, and something somber and terrible in the wrinkles of
his bald, gleaming brow gave him the aspect of a spirit of darkness.
They thought that the devil had taken this form to damn the young
man and throw him into the lake, and that he was here now, watching
over his prey and awaiting the hour of midnight, when the mysteries
of the Satanic sabbath would be accomplished.

The most courageous offered to return at dawn to dig the ditch and
lower the corpse into it. "That won't be necessary," replied one of the
most disheartened, and this response was understood. They looked at
each other silently. Their pallor mutually frightened them. They descended toward the valley and separated with trembling steps, ready
to take each other for ghosts.

## XLV LÉLIA

Lélia and Trenmor were approaching the valley. The day was ending, and they pressed on the horses and guides because they wanted
to arrive before dark. The rapid team of horses flew through the dust,
and the plains disappeared behind them like clouds carried off by the
wind. Suddenly a horse fell. The carriage rolled over it and overturned
violently. Trenmor was severely injured. Lélia was spared all harm.
Perhaps God had His designs.

They carried Trenmor to a nearby house on the road and gave him
unsparing attention. As soon as he had regained consciousness and they
had dressed his wound, he took Lélia's hand.

"Leave, my sister," he told her. "Do not lose an hour, not even a
moment. The last day of his appointed time is approaching. If one of
us is not at the Camaldule monastery this evening, who knows Sténio's
thoughts? Go to our child. Leave me here. I can do without you. You
can come back to get me tomorrow, later, whenever you can. Don't
concern yourself with me. Leave."

Lélia did not hesitate. Because the carriage was broken, she ordered a horse brought to her, hurriedly mounted it, and soon disappeared into the dust of the horizon.

The sun had set when she reached the level ground of the valley of the Camaldules. Her retinue was far behind her. Her steaming horse stumbled from time to time in the brambles of the brushwood as it gasped for breath. With her hair in disarray, she pitilessly pressed her mount on. She did not stop before any obstacle. She haphazardly forded rivers, crossed through thickets instead of going around them, and did not even look behind at the dangers she had just affronted. She had the madness of sublime confidence.

Unsure at the entrance of a clearing cut by two parallel paths, she was forced to stop and ask a woodcutter the way to the monastery.

"This way," said the woodcutter, showing her the right, "but if you count on entering the monastery tonight, I advise you to have an order from the pope. The gates are closed. The bells have not sounded. The prior is shut up in his cell, and all the monks are in retreat. They are not speaking to anyone, because the angel of death has marked a cross over the door."

Lélia, terrified, questioned the woodcutter. She learned of Sténio's death. She tried to doubt it and to hope.

A group of mountain folk came along to confirm the words of the first. Lélia fell rigidly into their arms. They carried her into their hut.

Magnus, who had remained alone by the corpse, had not perceived the herdsmen's desertion. He stayed on his knees, but he was neither praying nor thinking. His strength was broken. He was aware of his existence only through the acute suffering in his head, which he had nearly smashed on the stone paving of the prior's cell. This physical disturbance, combined with the frightful emotions he was experiencing, had plunged him into a depression that resembled imbecility.

Little by little the pain in his head became so violent that he put his hand there. Pale blood was sticking to his hair. He looked at his red hand without understanding that it was bloody. Only the sensation of wet heat and the odor of blood produced a sort of contraction in his finger muscles and dilated his nostrils as alcoholic or sensual intoxication would have. The soul was numbed, dead perhaps. The ferocious animal grief that hid beneath the monk's hairshirt reawakened with its carnivorous instinct and its fierce appetite for pleasure. He opened his eyes, as glassy as a corpse's, and leapt up as if an electric shock had struck him.

But when he saw Sténio's pale form sleeping the sleep of angels, he stopped, smiled hideously at Sténio's white winding sheet and his crown of flowers, and murmured in a voice filled with emotion, "Oh, woman, oh, beauty. . .! "

Then he took the corpse's hand, and its coldness calmed his delirium and chased away his feverish illusions. He realized it was not a woman sleeping but a man stretched out on the coffin, a man with whose death he reproached himself.

He looked around, and seeing nothing but the black sides of the rock against which the torch flames wavered, hearing nothing but the wind moaning in the larch trees, he felt all the fear of solitude, all the terrors of night fall on his head like a mountain of ice.

He believed he saw something move and creep on the rock near him. He closed his eyes so as not to see, then he opened them again and involuntarily looked. He saw a frightening black, motionless figure at his side. He looked at it for nearly an hour, not daring to move, holding his breath for fear of arousing this phantom's attention, ready to stand up and walk over to him. The resin torch, which was throwing Magnus's profile against the grotto wall, went out, and the phantom disappeared. The monk did not realize that he had been looking at his own shadow.

Light steps skimmed the thicket on the hill. It might have been a chamois curiously approaching the torches that still burned. Magnus crossed himself and threw a trembling glance at the path leading to the valley. He believed he saw a white-robed woman wandering and alone in the night. Restless desire made his heart surge. He rose, ready to run to her, but imbecilic fear held him back. A ghost was coming to summon Sténio, a specter come out of the sepulcher to howl in the darkness. He buried his face in his hands, covered his head in his cloak, and rolled himself into a corner, determined to see and hear nothing.

When no noise any longer reached his ears, he felt a little reassured and raised his head. He saw Lélia kneeling next to Sténio.

The monk tried to cry out, but his tongue cleaved to his palate. He tried to flee, but his legs became colder and more motionless than the granite of the rock. His eyes remained haggard, his hand open, his face hidden by his cloak.

Lélia was bending over the funeral bier. Her long hair, uncurled by the humidity, fell along her pale cheeks, and she seemed as dead as Sténio. She was the worthy fiancée of a corpse.

She had listened to the herdsmen speaking. She had escaped from their care, their consolations. She wanted to embrace Sténio's dust. Guided by the sinister beacon lit in front of the grotto, she had come alone, without fear or remorse, perhaps without suffering.

However, at the sight of this beautiful face covered with the shadows of death, she felt her soul soften. Tender pity sweetened the harshness of this soul, somber and calm in despair.

"Yes, Sténio," she said, without being apprehensive or perceiving the monk's presence, "I pity you because you have cursed me. I pity you because you did not understand that when God created us He had not resolved the union of our destinies. I know you believed that I took pleasure in multiplying your tortures. You believed I wish to avenge on you the suffering and disappointments of my earlier years. You believed that I accepted your vows through contempt and indifference, to compensate my vanity for all the betrayals that men had inflicted on me. You were mistaken, Sténio, and I forgive you the curse that you pronounced against me. He who judges our thoughts even before we can foresee them, He who leafs through the book of our conscience at all hours and who reads unambiguously the mysterious plans that are not yet written has not received your threats, Sténio, and He will not realize them. He will not punish you, because you were blind. He will not chastise your weakness, because you refused to trust a wisdom that was not yours. You have paid too dearly for the light which illumined your last days for Him to reproach you for having wandered in ignorance for a long time. The grievous, terrible knowledge that you carry off with you has no need of expiation, because your lips have already been withered in tasting the fruit you plucked.

"Sténio, I loved you without being able to console you. Without being able to respond, I admired that undefined need of expansion and devotion that devoured you. I regretted the implacable proofs which convinced me of my impotence. But would it not have been a cowardly deception to deny them? If I had told you, 'The wounds I showed you are not incurable. Let us hope that trust and mutual abnegation will warm my tepid heart. Let us hope that if I lean on you I will again find the sense and worth of my sufferings, which I accept now without understanding,' I would have lied, Sténio. I would have deserved your contempt, and your anger could not have descended low enough to decry my hypocrisy.

"Is it for my honesty that you have called down on me the punishments God reserves for the wicked? Is it because I confessed to you the infirmities of my nature, without embarrassment or confusion, that you demanded lightning to strike me, as if I had abused my power?

"On my path I met many faithless souls who deceived me. My ears were wearied with listening to impotent promises. More generous and courageous than they had been, I refused your affection because I could not repay it. I sacrificed the perfidious, transient joys of a few days to the security of your future. I did not wish to pledge a treasure I no longer possessed. My heart had exhausted all its credulities. Beneath the earth that you trampled with rapid, confident steps I saw the lava of the volcano boiling up that was to demolish the edifice of your ambitions and to disperse it far and wide.

"To retain your love, I would have needed to degrade myself. My frozen senses could do nothing for your pleasures. If I had tried to tremble beneath your embraces, poor Sténio! Lélia, grimacing voluptuously, commanding her eyes to smile and pretend ecstasy. Then Lélia would have been only a hideous monster, the ridiculous simulacrum of a courtesan.

"But I have the firm confidence that God will reunite us in eternity. Seated beside each other at His feet, we will listen to His counsels. Then we will know why He separated us on earth. As you read on His radiant brow the secret of His will, impenetrable to mortal eyes, it will be as if your shock and anger had never existed.

"Sténio, then you will no longer try to hate me. You will no longer accuse me of injustice and cruelty. God, giving each of us the portion He merits, will distribute our work according to our strength. Then you will understand, my beloved, that we could not follow the same path or walk toward the same goal here below. The sufferings He sent us were not alike. The Severe Master we have both served will then explain the mystery of our sufferings to us. As He opens the exploding perspective of an eternal outpouring before us, He will tell us why it pleased Him to prepare the reunion of our two souls by obscure means which our eyes did not suspect.

"Sténio, He will show you my heart, to which you imputed contempt and hardness, in all its bleeding nakedness. The terror that you felt when you listened to me, the humiliation that obscured your vision when I confessed that I could not love you, and the trembling confusion of your thoughts will change into deep compassion. Lélia, whom you despaired of reaching, will lower herself before you. We will both forget the admiration and respect with which men surrounded my steps. You will know why I went alone and without ever demanding help.

"Merged beneath God's eyes, in permanent felicity, each of us will courageously accomplish the task we have received. As our glances meet, our confidence and strength will double: the memory of our past miseries will vanish like a dream, and we will ask if we were truly alive.

"Console yourself, Sténio. Your trial is finished, but mine continues. You no longer hear the imbecilic crowd hum in your ears. You no longer have before you the spectacle of deceptive joys which are stunned with the noise of their own lies. Now I implore your strength and wisdom in my prayers, because you know the emptiness of the pleasures for which you longed. You regard pityingly the glories that used to dazzle you. You no longer desire, but you enjoy. The presence of God is enough for your ecstasies. Aren't the smiles you begged from me on your knees and the caresses you would have paid for with your blood now, with your luminous clairvoyance, objects of mockery for you?

"But no, I am sure of this, since you *know*, since the Divine hand has opened your eyes as It passed Its fingers over your lids, that your soul, which was once angry in its ignorance and weakness, today is indulgent and serene. The tumult of our hopes and the ambitious visions of our dreams are incomplete but sincere expressions of our present humility before you, as before God. If we aspire so high, it is because our soul remembers its origin, it suffers in its terrestrial envelope, and it feels that to recover its flight and power it needs to strip away the swaddling clothes in which it is pinioned.

"So, Sténio, you have gone before me. God prefers you to Lélia, since He called you first. The anguish and exhaustion of your precocious decay merited a more prompt recompense than Lélia's isolation and patience. I don't accuse Him of indifference. I don't pity myself. Certainly He must have measured the pilgrimage according to the pilgrim's strength. He brought the celestial city closer to your tottering feet. He bent the branch to your faltering hands. Blissful Sténio! Now you can shake the dust from your shoes and rest. It is for you to intercede for me to the Master so that I can go and sit by your side.

"Disinterested now, you defy the passions that devoured you. You judge and applaud your deliverance. To whom would your regrets address themselves? To me? But the future belongs to the two of us. To Trenmor? But Trenmor would have saved you, had your salvation on earth been possible. Since his soul, purified by expiation, could not find words eloquent enough to convince you, and since his arms, tried by tortures, lacked sufficient energy to divert you from the fatal path you had entered, it is because God did not wish it. When he let you go, Trenmor realized that your flight held the mysterious trace of a decree which it was not his part to interpret. He followed you with his eyes and cried out persistently, 'Come back, Sténio, come back. We will support you.' But when your rapid flight had put an unbridgeable distance between you and Trenmor, then he was silent.

"You have thrown yourself into death's arms. From that jealous, inexorable mistress you have demanded a refuge from the deceptive seductions of life. May her caresses be sweet, Sténio. Sleep in peace on the cold bed where you wanted to espouse oblivion!

"Still, you are so young and handsome! Why didn't you hope? Why am I, who have seen everything exhausted and blighted around me, still standing? Why am I, who can no longer give or feel love, here contemplating you? Why am I not stretched out in this coffin?"

Lélia grew silent and crossed her arms over her chest as she silently contemplated the beauty of the man whose outbursts of feeling she had refused. She loved his ashen pallor, his lips which were like a damp blue flower, the hair which was sparse on top of his head, long and thick on his shoulders. His blond hair had been uncurled in the water, dried by the wind, and then taken on again the natural undulation of its graceful curls. This last richness had resisted the ravages of sickness. This last beauty would survive the immediate dissolution of the corpse. It floated, silky and alive, on that glacial brow, as in the days when the poet child had run in the morning sun on flowered mountain paths.

Lélia remembered when she had loved him most. It was when he was poet rather than lover. In those first days of their affection, Sténio's passion had a romantic, angelic quality. He did not think of anything but singing to Lélia, praying for her, dreaming of her, or contemplating her in mute ecstasy. Later his eyes would grow animated with a more virile fire. His greedy lips would seek and demand kisses. His poetry would express more savage outbursts of feeling. Then the impotent Lélia had felt frightened, fatigued, and nearly disgusted with this love she did not share. Now she had found the old Sténio again, calm and reflective as she had once known him, as she had loved him.

"There you are, my poet," she said, "as I often contemplated you when you were unaware of it. You were weaker than Trenmor and me, and often during our dreamy outings you would give in to tiredness and fall asleep at my feet under a hot midday breeze, among the forest flowers. Bent over you, I would protect your sleep. I would remove harmful insects from you. I would cover you with my shadow when the sun pierced the branches to plant a burning kiss on your beautiful, girlish brow. I placed myself between you and the sun. My despotic, jealous soul enveloped you in its love. My tranquil lips sometimes skimmed the hot, perfumed air that trembled around you. I was happy then, and I loved you! I loved you as much as I could love. I imbibed you like a beautiful lily. I smiled on you as I would on a child full of genius. I would have liked to be your mother and be able to press you in my arms without awakening in you a man's senses.

"At other times I would surprise the secret of your solitary walks. Sometimes you would bend over a limpid pool formed by a spring or support yourself on the century-old rock moss to look at the sky reflected in the water. Usually your eyes were half-closed, and you seemed dead to all exterior impressions. As now, you seemed to gather in and look inside yourself at God and the angels reflected within the mysterious mirror of your soul. Here you are, as you were then, a frail adolescent, still without vigor and without desires, a stranger to the delirium and suffering of physical life. Fiancé of some golden-winged virgin, you had not yet tossed your ring into the stormy waves of our passions. Have so many days, so many evils been endured since that serene morning when I found you like a young bird opening its trembling wings to the first morning breezes? Have we lived and suffered since that hour when you asked me to explain love, happiness, glory, and wisdom to you? Child, who believed in all those things and sought those imaginary treasures in me, have so many tears, terrors, and disappointments separated us from this melodious pastoral? Have your steps, which had only bent flowers, since walked in the mire and gravel? Has your voice, which used to sing such sweet harmonies, become hoarse crying out drunkenly? Has your chest, which expanded in the pure mountain air, withered and burned in the fire of orgies? Have your lips, which angels came to kiss in your sleep, been defiled by infamous lips? Have you suffered and struggled so much, oh, Sténio, beloved son of heaven?

"But you are still as handsome and calm as in the days when you leaned your head on my lap to sleep in the wind of maritime nights. Your hands are white and pure. Your knees are not broken by so many falls. But, poor poet, you have crept amid thorns and been scraped by sharp rocks. You have grown bloody, stained, and exhausted as you gripped hideous reality. You fought against this rough-furred lion. You inebriated yourself with the stench of its foul thighs. Seized with horror and disgust, you fell beneath it. To avenge itself, it devoured your entrails. But God was protecting you. No orgy, amorous woman, or deceptive friendship could possess you. You remained virgin in a body prostituted to all debaucheries. You were a diamond whose fire had been stolen from the purest sunbeams. The lewd did not suspect the treasure you were hiding, which you wished to render to God as sparkling and pure as you had received it. You did well to die, Sténio. Your great soul was suffocating in this delicate, frail body and in this sunless world. We were unworthy of you. You finally refused us your love. You withdrew your desires and caresses from us. Return to God, angel led astray amid our impure paths. Protect us, and forgive us for having given you nothing of what you asked. It is that we were human, and you were worth more than us.

"Go, Sténio, we will find each other again. And then we will be worthy of each other. My soul is the sister of yours. It is weary, angry with everything. Like yours, my soul has desired without attaining and worked without harvesting. God condemns me to longer expiations because, more prudent and more fearful than you, I drew back before the trials you endured. I avoided the dangers into which you plunged yourself. A slower evil must devour me, that eternal justice be satisfied. But what worth have these long days on earth in the eternity you have already entered? What will they be when I have rejoined you?

"Perhaps we will be equals, lovers, and brothers. Today I hardly dare regard myself as your fiancée. And my respect, which death has rendered you, is not enough to open this sanctuary of love and hope. Oh, Sténio, let me implore you as you used to implore me! Let me fear and venerate you as a power above me. Let me pray and moan. God permits you this vengeance. I love you. I go on my knees to tell you that I love you now that you seem deaf to my avowals and insensitive to my caresses. Receive my vows and kisses. Oh, Sténio, I loved you more than you could understand. I felt myself unworthy of you. I did not want to defile the sanctity of your soul. If God had deigned to give me back my passionate youth and my virgin heart, if my imagination had not been depraved in the pursuit of twenty phantoms, if my love had not been given and withdrawn, if error, despair, and weakness had not blighted me, I would have been yours. In your youth you believed you saw in me all the virtues, all the greatness I no longer had. You would have given yourself to me unreservedly, and I would have impoverished you. No, I did not want to profit from your error, and now that is my only claim upon you. Adieu, Sténio, adieu. I have loved you alone with a noble, strong love. Pity me, I am going to live."

She planted a last kiss on Sténio's violet lips, detached a withered flower from his crown which she put next to her heart, and she continued on the valley path, unaware of the monk who stood in the shadows with his back stiffly against the grotto wall and who darted his glittering eyes on her.

Magnus's reason had abandoned him. He understood nothing of Lélia's speech. He saw only her, and he found her beautiful. His passion reawakened violently, and he no longer remembered anything but the desires he had repressed for so long. They devoured him now more than ever.

When he saw her embrace Sténio, a terrible jealousy, which he had never known before because he had never had occasion to feel it, burst out in him. He would have struck Sténio if he had dared, but this corpse made him fearful, and desire was aroused in him even more intensely than vengeance.

He sprung behind Lélia and seized her arm as she was turning the path.

Lélia turned, without crying out or trembling, and looked at this gaunt figure, the bloody eyes and trembling mouth, without fear and almost without surprise.

"Woman," said the monk, "you have made me suffer enough. Console me. Love me."

Lélia did not recognize in this bald, stooped monk the young, proud priest of only a few years before. She stopped, astonished.

"Father," she said, "address yourself to God. Only His love can console you."

"Don't you remember, Lélia," replied the monk without listening to her, "that it is I who saved your life? Without me you would have perished in the ruins of the monastery where you spent two years. Do you remember, woman? I threw myself into the midst of the falling debris, which nearly crushed me. I carried you away. I put you on my horse, I traveled the entire day holding you in my arms, and I did not even dare to kiss your garment. But since that day a devouring fire has been burning in my heart. In vain have I fasted and prayed. God does not want to heal me. You must be mine. When I have been appeased, I will be healed. Then I will do penitence and be saved. Otherwise I will go mad again and be damned."

"Magnus, I clearly recognize you," she replied. "Alas, this then is the fruit of your expiations and struggles!"

"Don't jeer at me, woman," he said with a somber expression, "because I am as close to hate as to love, and if you repulse me . . . I don't know what anger can push me into. . . . "

"Magnus, let go of my arm," said Lélia with calm disdain. "Sit down on that rock, and I am going to talk to you."

There was so much authority in her voice that the monk, habituated to submission, obeyed as if by instinct and seated himself two paces from her. His heart was beating so strongly that he could not speak. He took his bloody, painful head in his two hands and reassembled what remained of his strength to listen.

"Magnus," said Lélia, "if you had consulted me about your future when you were still young and capable of realizing a social existence, I would not have advised you to become a priest. Your nature was to render impossible for you those rigid duties, which you only accomplish in deed. You have been a bad priest, but God will forgive you because you have suffered much. Now it is too late to reenter ordinary life. You have lost the strength to attain any virtue. You must hold to abstinence. Although I have little faith in the effectiveness of your mortifications and in the practices of your monastic life, I think that you ought to await the end of your sufferings in retreat. The end will not be long in coming. Look at your hands and grey hair. So much the better for you, Magnus! Were I also near the tomb! Unfortunate man, we can do nothing for each other. You were mistaken. You cut yourself off from life, and then you felt the need to live. And now you are frightened of yourself, and you believe it will be possible for you to calm your desires by enjoyment. Senseless child! It is too late to dream of this. A few years ago you would have been able to find happiness in liberty. Your reason could have been enlightened and your soul hardened against vain remorse. But today horror, disgust, and fear pursue you everywhere. You would not be able to recognize love. You would always take it for sin, and the habit of casting aspersions upon legitimate joys in the name of sin would make you criminal and vicious in the eyes of your conscience and in the arms of the purest woman. Resign yourself, poor monk. Abase your pride. You believed yourself great enough for this terrible virtue of the cloister, but I tell you that you were mistaken. What does it matter? You are reaching the end of your hardships. Apply yourself so as not to lose their fruit. You are not great enough for God to forgive your despair—You are not Sténio."

Magnus had listened vainly. His brain refused to understand what she was saying. He was suffering. He believed Lélia was jeering at him. The woman's proud tranquillity deeply humiliated him. There were instants he detested her and wanted to flee, but he believed he had been seized and fascinated by the eyes of the devil.

Finally his feeble reason succumbed in this last struggle. He rose and took her arm again.

"Now," he said, "I see what you are. I often believed I recognized the devil in you, but this was hidden beneath such beautiful features that, in spite of myself, I took you for a woman. Now my eyes are open and I feel myself strong enough to combat and overwhelm you. Return into the earth, Satan. In the name of Christ, I curse you!"

Lélia, seeing the fury and confusion in his eyes, struggled forcefully to extricate herself from the iron hand that was bruising her arm. But he was pronouncing formulas of exorcism, and, astonished that she did not disappear, he became entirely insane and no longer thought of anything but killing her, as he had often thought of doing.

"Yes, yes," he cried out, "when you are dead, I will no longer be afraid of you! I will forget you, and then I will be able to pray."

He choked her until there was only a faint breath of life left within her.

One hour before day the inhabitants of the valley heard frightful howls near their dwellings, as if a man devoured by wolves were fleeing, dragging his entrails on the way. The superstitious terrors, which had made them abandon the grotto, prevented them from going out. These men were brave before real danger and compassionate, ready to help all unfortunates who could be helped. However, they did not dare confront what they took for a diabolic mystery.

It was the monk who was fleeing the site of his crime and who howled with terror, believing himself pursued by the specters of Lélia and Sténio. They did not see him any more in the region.

Lélia dragged herself on her hands and knees as far as the funeral bier where Sténio reposed. She still had the strength to embrace him and say to him in a broken voice, "Blessed be God, who already reunites us...!"

Then she turned her last look toward the sky, which was lightening at the horizon.

"The morning will be beautiful," thought Lélia. "Earth, rejoice. Everything passes, everything dies... everything returns to God...."

She fell. They found her dead at Sténio's feet. Magnus's rosary was so tightly wound around her neck that the silken cord had to be cut to take it off.

Lélia was buried on sacred ground, but not in the enclosure reserved for the burial of the religious. In the part of the cemetery that bordered on the ravine they raised a tomb to her similar to the one on the opposite shore where Sténio's remains were deposited.

One evening Trenmor, having recovered from the effects of his fall and having attended to the funerals of his two friends, descended slowly along the lake shore. As the moon rose, it threw an oblique ray on these two white tombs that the lake separated. Lights rose up, as usual, on the misty surface of the water. Trenmor sadly contemplated their pale sparkle and their melancholy dance. He noticed two which, coming from the opposite shores, joined, mutually pursued each other, and remained together the entire night, whether they played amid the reeds, whether they let themselves glide over the tranquil waves, or whether they embraced tremblingly in the fog like two lanterns ready to go out. Trenmor let himself be dominated by a sweet and superstitious idea. He spent the entire night following the inseparable lights with his eyes. They sought each other out and followed each other like two amorous souls. Two or three times they came close to him, and he called them by two cherished names, shedding tears like a child. When day appeared, all the lights had gone out. The two mysterious flames held each other for some time in the middle of the lake, as if it caused them pain to separate. Then they were each driven in contrary directions, as if they were each going to return to the tombs they inhabited. When they had vanished, Trenmor passed his hand over his brow as if to chase away the enfeebling dream of a night of sadness and tenderness. He climbed toward Sténio's tomb, and for one moment he stopped, uncertain.

"What will I do without you both?" he cried out. "For what will I be useful? In whom will I interest myself? Whom will my wisdom and my strength serve if I no longer have friends to console and support? Wouldn't it be better to have a tomb by this beautiful shore, near those two silent tombs? —But no, the expiation is not yet finished. Perhaps Magnus is still alive. Perhaps I can heal him. Furthermore, everywhere men struggle and suffer. Everywhere there are duties to fulfill, strength to use, a fate to fulfill."

He saluted from afar the marble that enclosed Lélia. He kissed the tomb where Sténio slept. Then he looked at the sun, that torch which was to light up his days of work, that eternal beacon which showed him the land of exile where he needed to act and walk, the immensity of the heavens always accessible to men's hope.

He picked up his white walking stick and continued on his way.

# SELECTED BIBLIOGRAPHY

## BIOGRAPHICAL WORKS

Barry, Joseph Amber. *Infamous Woman, The Life of George Sand*. Garden City, N. Y.: Doubleday, 1976.

Cate, Curtis. *George Sand*. Boston: Houghton Mifflin, 1975.

Dostoevsky, Feodor. *The Diary of a Writer*, 2 vols., trans. Boris Brasol. New York: Scribner's, 1949. Reprinted by Octagon, 1973.

Edwards, Samuel. *George Sand, A Biography of the First Liberated Woman*. New York: McKay, 1972.

Howe, Marie Jenney. *George Sand: The Search for Love*. New York: John Day, 1927. Reprinted by R. West, 1973.

James, Henry. *French Poets and Novelists*. London: Macmillan, 1908. Reprinted by Folcroft, 1973.

_____. *Literary Reviews and Essays on American, English, and French Literature*, ed. Albert Mordell. New York: Vista House Publishers, 1957.

_____. *Selected Literary Criticism*, ed. Morris Shapira. New York: Horizon Press, 1964.

Maurois, André. *Lélia, The Life of George Sand*, trans. Gerard Hopkins. New York: Harper, 1953. Reprinted by Penguin, 1977.

Moers, Ellen. *Literary Women*. Garden City, N. Y.: Doubleday, 1976.

## WORKS BY GEORGE SAND

### In French

*Correspondance*, 9 vols., ed. Georges Lubin. Paris: Garnier, 1964-77.

*Correspondance inédite: George Sand–Marie Dorval*, introd. and notes by Simon André-Maurois, preface by André Maurois. Paris: Gallimard, 1953.

*George Sand et Sa Fille d'après leur correspondance inédite*, ed. Samuel Rocheblave. Paris: Calmann-Lévy, 1905.

*Histoire de ma vie*, 4 vols. Paris: Calmann-Lévy, 1926.

*Journal Intime* (Posthume), published by Aurore Sand. Paris: Calmann-Lévy, 1926. Reprints of this work in translation have been published under the title *Intimate Journal of George Sand*. New York: Gordon, 1976, and Haskell, 1974.

*Les Lettres de George Sand à Alfred de Musset et à Sainte-Beuve*, introd. Samuel Rocheblave. Paris: Calmann-Lévy, 1876.

*Lettres inédites de George Sand et de Pauline Viardot*, introd. Thérèse Marix Spire. Paris: Nouvelles Éditions Latine, 1959.

*Oeuvres Autobiographiques*, 2 vols., ed. Georges Lubin. Paris: Gallimard, 1970.

*Oeuvres Completes*, 110 vols. Paris: Michel Lévy, 1886.

*Souvenirs et Idées*. Paris: Calmann-Lévy, 1904.

*In English Translation*

*The Masterpieces of George Sand, Amandine Lucille Aurore Dupin, Baroness Dudevant*, 20 vols., trans. G. Burnham Ives with Mary W. Artois. New York: AMS Press, Gordon Press, 1976. Reprint of 1902 edition.

*The Companion of the Tour of France (Le Compagnon du Tour de France)*, trans. F.G. Shaw. New York: Fertig, 1976. Reprint of 1847 edition.

*The Country Waif (François le Champi)*, trans. Eirene Collis. Lincoln, Neb.: University of Nebraska Press, 1976.

*The George Sand–Gustave Flaubert Letters*, trans. Aimée McKensie. New York: Liveright, 1921, 1970.

*The Haunted Pool (La Mare au diable)*, trans. Frank H. Potter. San Lorenzo, Ca.: Shameless Hussy Press, 1976.

*Indiana*, trans. G. Burnham Ives. New York: Fertig, 1975. Reprint of 1902 edition.

*Lavinia*, trans. G. Burnham Ives. San Lorenzo, Ca.: Shameless Hussy Press, 1977.

*Little Fadette*, trans. Eva Figues. London & Glasgow: Blackie and Sons, Ltd., 1967.

*Mauprat*, introd. by Diane Johnson, no translator's name given. New York: Da Capo, 1977. Reprint of 1899 edition.